Y0-BQS-495

A Plague of Sinners

JUL 2 6 2011

HAYNER PUBLIC LIBRARY DISTRICT
ALTON, ILLINOIS

OVERDUES 10 PER DAY, MAXIMUM FINE
COST OF ITEM
ADDITIONAL $5.00 SERVICE CHARGE
APPLIED TO
LOST OR DAMAGED ITEMS

HAYNER PLD/DOWNTOWN

Also by Paul Lawrence

The Sweet Smell of Decay

HAYNER PUBLIC LIBRARY DISTRICT
ALTON, ILLINOIS

OVERDUES 10 PER DAY, MAXIMUM FINE
COST OF ITEM
ADDITIONAL $5.00 SERVICE CHARGE
APPLIED TO

A Plague of Sinners

being the second chronicle of Harry Lytle

by

PAUL LAWRENCE

Beautiful
Books

First published 2010

Beautiful Books Limited
36–38 Glasshouse Street
London W1B 5DL

ISBN 9781905636914

9 8 7 6 5 4 3 2 1

Copyright © Paul Lawrence 2010.

The right of Paul Lawrence to be identified as the author
of this work has been asserted by him in accordance with the
Copyright, Designs and Patents Act 1988.

All rights reserved. No part of this publication may be reproduced,
stored in or introduced into a retrieval system, or transmitted, in any form,
or by any means (electronic, mechanical, photocopying, recording or
otherwise) without the prior written permission of the publisher.
Any person who does any unauthorised act in relation to this publication
may be liable to criminal prosecution and civil claims for damages.

A catalogue reference for this book is available
from the British Library.

Cover design by Head Design.
Typesetting by Misa Watanabe.
Printed in and bound in the UK by CPI MacKays, Chatham ME5 8TD.

MYS
F
LAW

b196663286

For Ruth, Charlotte, Callum, Cameron and Ashleigh.

CHAPTER 1

HERMES TRISMEGISTUS
Upon the first decumbiture of the sick
To him therefore that would either cure the sick or heal the lame, the position of heaven ought to be well considered and known.

When Hedges fell face first into his dinner after giving birth to an almighty sneeze, the rest of us just sat and stared at the gravy dripping down the backs of his ears. We watched in silence, gaping at the back of his large unmoving head and the pieces of lamb and fish stuck in his hair. His mouth gaped open and a thin stream of sauce dribbled from the side of his mouth. Still we waited, willing him to blink, sit up again and wipe the food from his forehead.

I dined at the house of Oliver Willis and his glorious daughter Elizabeth. Why Willis invited Nathaniel Hedges to dinner was a mystery, for Hedges was not a popular man despite his virtue. He was a member of London's

College of Physicians, a prestigious body of wise men who admired themselves very much. Most medics had left London weeks before; only he remained behind, an act of bravery for which he needed regular watering.

The four of us sat together at one end of a table that could take eight. The table heaved beneath the weight of a plethora of steaming dishes; carp, lobster, salmon, rabbit, chicken and lamb. Long candles lit up bright new tapestries hung from the walls, country scenes full of yellows, reds and greens.

Elizabeth Willis sat straight-backed in a luminous dark blue dress with fine silver braiding, bodice pulled tight, breasts perked up like little puddings. Her nose was small and straight, ears perfectly formed that a man might want to tickle them gently. She tended to Hedges' thirst by asking if he did not fear contracting the disease himself. Shallow lines of concern writ clear upon her forehead and I desired to smooth them out with my manly fingers.

Hedges smiled toothily out of the left side of his face. 'I take great care, madam. I place a nutmeg in my mouth as soon as I wake up and suck upon lozenges all day. I have a lozenge in my mouth right now.' Which explained why the right side of his mouth did not move.

'That is sufficient to protect you?' asked Liz.

'Also I take about with me a scuttle of coals onto which I throw quicklime, herbs and spices when I visit sick houses.

This disperses the miasma.' He nodded brightly, keen to dispense further wisdoms. 'And in the evening I have a glass of sack to defeat any infection that may have penetrated my defences, and a plate of boiled meat and pickles to fortify my system for the next day.'

Liz opened her innocent eyes wider and sucked in her lower lip. 'So, if every man in London were to suck nutmegs and lozenges, drink sack and eat boiled meat and pickles, then the plague would be thwarted?'

Hedges shook his fleshy head regretfully. 'Coal is expensive these days. Not every man can afford it, nor nutmeg, sack nor boiled meat. The wealthy can, but the wealthy have gone. The poor cannot, but the poor remain.'

Liz's speckled green eyes stayed wide. I took a slow, deep breath, for this was the mask behind which she cultivated private and mischievous thoughts, before releasing them upon unsuspecting recipient with brutal savagery.

Oliver Willis studied her closely from above his jutting chin. He changed the subject before his daughter could speak again. 'Are you not contemplating leaving London, Harry?'

Not I. The plague raged rampant outside the city walls, not inside, and I wished to get to know Liz better. I pulled a sad face and attended to my plate. 'The city's finances are in a perilous state following the hard winter. The parishes have insufficient funds to support the sick and all depend on the guilds.'

Hedges scowled so hard I could barely see his eyes beneath his hirsute brow. I had unwittingly deprived him of his eminence. 'You work for Sir Thomas Player?' he growled.

'I work for the King,' I replied carefully, 'and for Lord Arlington, and for the moment for Sir Thomas, aye, at Lord Arlington's request.'

Hedges placed his hands flat on the table and pushed down hard. 'Might you then remind Sir Thomas I have not been paid since I was appointed?'

'He has a fine eye for detail,' I said, 'and juggles the city finances with sensitivity and wise judgement. What funds he collects he dispenses to those cases most needy.'

'Aye, so,' Hedges blustered, torn now between the role of munificent saviour of London's poorest, and that of harshly treated creditor. He sat back and shrugged his shoulders like it was no matter.

Liz turned her sharp senses upon me, the clearing of her throat a sure sign her curiosity was pricked. 'And what role, Harry, do you play in executing such important affairs?'

I met her gaze for a moment before allowing my attention to wander to those wicked sweet lips. How to answer her question? I had not made the best impression upon Thomas Player, since he was very punctual and I arrived thirty minutes late for our first appointment. Since then he entrusted me only with the auditing of the churchwardens' account books, a tedious task indeed. Yet I did my best, for this plague represented an opportunity to advance my cause, a chance to secure a position of real importance at long last. I turned up every morning on time and kept my eyes open until day's end.

'I do as I must.' I waved a nonchalant hand. 'But now is not the time to talk of rank nor status.' I looked to Hedges for help.

'Aye.' He seized upon my olive branch and proceeded to wax lyrical about his own humble function. Meanwhile Liz bestowed upon me her melting gaze, a faint smile about the ends of her rose-crayoned lips. It was like bathing in warm honey. Oliver watched us, sharp eyed.

Hedges coughed loudly, for no one listened. 'Should you have the misfortune to become infected, or any of your household, then I hope you will consider calling upon me for help, Mr Lytle.' He leaned over and placed his hand uncomfortably close to mine.

'What about you, Oliver?' I asked, denying Hedges once more the attention he craved. The hand withdrew. 'Will you stay?'

'I still have the house at St Albans,' he muttered.

'We will stay too, Harry,' Liz said, watching her father. 'May God keep us from the plague.' Two hot little circles burned newly bright upon her cheeks and the muscles about her jaw tightened. Oliver Willis looked away. Strange.

'I will visit often.' Hedges leaned toward Liz with lopsided smile. 'To ensure your health.'

Liz glared as if she would slap his face.

Oliver Willis contemplated a bottle of sack stood upon the dresser. 'Thank you, Nathaniel. You are a good friend. I hope you can stay awhile betimes. I would talk to you of business.'

Hedges smiled wide, grease glistening upon his thick lips. 'I should be delighted.' He clapped his hands together in a show of unconvincing bonhomie. 'How wonderful that we are all committed to remain. The pest is the judgement of God, as all men know. If your soul be clean and your conscience clear—then fear not!' He laughed loud and a piece of salmon shot out of his nose. He snorted and rubbed his nostrils vigorously.

I wanted to lean over and poke him in the eye. John Foster, a friend of mine, died the week before at Newgate Market. He was not a bad man; he visited church regularly, which was more than I did. Now his wife and three children were left to survive without him. How dare this preening pillicock imply it was deserved?

'An interesting perspective, Mr Hedges,' Liz said quiet, her temple pumping as it always did when she was angry. 'If you be so godly, then why the elaborate precautions?

Why not trust in him to protect you?' I demanded to know.

Hedges arched his hairy brows, placed his hands on his inflated belly and stared at me like I was an evil sinner.

'Aye, Mr Hedges,' Liz echoed, 'why does a man need lozenges and nutmeg if he has God's blessing?'

Hedges gathered his shirt about his neck with stubby fingers. 'God fearing people need not fear the pestilential streams.' His brow shone with a wet film of sweat. 'The miasmatic air affects only those engaged in sluttish behaviour. Those that flee it invite God's close inspection, for He will wonder why.'

I leaned over and pointed my fork at him. 'Outside the walls many good men have died who lived their lives meticulously.'

Hedges wrinkled his nose as if he detested the smell of his own top lip. 'Because thou hast made the Lord, which is my refuge, even the most high, thy habitation; there shall no evil befall thee, neither shall any plague come nigh thy dwelling.' He licked his chops and rubbed his gushing brow, looking most uncomfortable. The price of wearing too many clothes on a hot summer evening, I supposed.

'Mr Hedges!' Liz said, stern. 'If the godly are protected then why have all the godly men fled?'

'Enough!' Oliver Willis held up a weary hand. 'I have not asked Nathaniel to dine with us that we might question his faith.'

Hedges watched us from above his pile of chins. Water poured from his head as though he were dissolving. It was then, as I searched for words that might restore his humour, that he sneezed and fell into his dinner.

'Nathaniel?' Oliver Willis broke the silence.

'I fear he is dead, sir.' The servant Edward's face stretched taut, eyes wide like little bowls.

Oliver stared with open jaw. All mischief vanished from Liz's fair face, leaving only bare shock. For the sneeze was the sound of plague.

I craned over to see his neck, looking for a bubo. Most of his neck hid beneath three layers of clothes.

'What will we do?' exclaimed Oliver Willis, arms held out sideways like a little crab. Edward stood immovably stiff, eyes transfixed upon the dead medic.

I approached Hedges closer and attempted to see beneath his shirt with a knife from the table. Would I could see the plague and stab it.

'You must inform the Examiner of Health,' Liz finally replied in shocked whisper. 'The master of the house must report it within two hours.'

Willis looked at his daughter, pleading. 'Then they will lock us up here for forty days.'

'What else is there?' she demanded, face contorting in terrified spasm. 'Else we will be punished by the alderman and be disgraced.'

Though the prospect of being locked up in the same house as Liz for forty days was enticing, I could not tarry here. 'I have a notion,' I said.

Everyone except Hedges turned to look at me.

'Hedges lives at Fenchurch Street,' I thought aloud.

Oliver Willis nodded.

'Might he not have died while on his way home?'

Oliver and Liz regarded me as if *I* were the plague.

'He has not been here long,' I argued. 'It is unlikely others of us are infected. In any case, we may take what precautions we may while we have the choice.'

'If he died on his way home, Harry, then they shall lock us up in any case.' Liz spoke slow and carefully, still watching her agitated father.

'Then we found him dead outside the door before he arrived.'

Oliver Willis looked hopefully at his daughter. More silent communication.

Tears welled in Liz's eyes. 'What of his wife, Harry?'

'His wife has lost her husband,' I answered. 'Someone must tell her it kindly and allow her to bury him where she would see him buried.'

'Who will tell her?'

'The churchwardens will tell her so long as they have the opportunity,' I replied.

Oliver Willis' mouth hung open and his eyes glistened

with hope, like a dog that has not eaten for a week. At that moment I perceived his reluctance to leave London. He had laboured hard this last five years, ambitious to succeed. I suspected he had borrowed more than he could afford. With London emptying, so his trade would fast disappear. By the time forty days passed he would be destitute.

'We take him out respectfully, and lay him down upon the road. Then I visit the churchwardens and say I saw him there as I arrived,' I offered.

Liz put her hands to her mouth as if she prayed. Oliver appeared as though a great weight fell from his shoulders, and the two servants in the room looked like they would die of fright.

'All we need do is move him,' I pointed out. 'If Edward can help me then we will do the job now.'

'Edward's back is weak,' Liz objected.

'Then James can help,' Oliver Willis countered impatiently. 'Let's to it.'

I turned back to Hedges, this foolish man who ventured beyond the city wall with his nutmegs and his lozenges. 'He no longer breathes, so he is not contagious. If a man had gloves we could move him without exposure to the sticky atoms that may sit upon his clothing.'

'I have gloves,' Oliver Willis exclaimed eagerly. 'Go fetch them, Liz.'

Liz hesitated a moment before doing as he bid. When she returned she hovered, uncertain to whom she should give them. Since it was my grand scheme, I took them. I bid my face look happier than my soul, put on the gloves and turned back to Hedges. I did not want to touch him, even with the gloves.

His face had slowly slid sideways in the buttery garlic sauce. I considered closing his eyes, but his eyelids were too greasy.

'Put this in your mouth.' Oliver Willis handed me a sprig of mint.

Though Hedges was but a short man, his top half burgeoned formidably large. I stood behind him, placed my hands above his shoulders and pulled hard. His plate travelled with him a short distance before it clattered back upon the table. His mouth sneered like he had not yet finished the sneeze. Rich currant sauce coated his face.

Liz looked angrily at her father. 'We must clean him up if it is to be believed he has not dined here.'

'Aye,' Willis nodded eagerly, 'and clear away the table as if we have not eaten.'

The searchers would arrive quick once news of his death became public. Outside the wall, searchers were forced to live with the gravediggers, away from the general population, and many took to drink. Here the plague was still new and the searchers more alert.

As I grabbed him beneath the armpits I could not help but wonder whether buboes lay beneath my fingers, ready to explode, so I attempted to lift him only by the tops of his arms. As a consequence he slid from my grasp. His head bounced on the floor and gravy from his hair splashed over the wall. Liz gasped and clasped her hands before her nose like he was a fragile piece of porcelain.

'We will have to wash his hair,' I realised. 'Else his wife will wonder why he smells of fruit.' His face and mouth besides, for Hedges' manner at the table had been quite slovenly.

We wiped him clean as we could, then dragged him. The servant called James took him by the ankles, carelessly, as though he had no thought of the pest. We carried him to the front door. Oliver Willis opened it slowly, as if afraid there waited an army of outraged citizens. Outside was peaceful though, dark and warm. The day had been hotter than any could remember, and still the sun's heat lingered, dissipating only slowly from the ground and the buildings. It was a strange feeling to step out into this night air, scuttling and alive, like there was no longer any time for sleep.

'I can see no one,' Willis whispered hoarsely.

I hesitated, feeling someone watched. 'Are you sure?'

'Aye, sure!' he answered through gritted teeth. 'Now let's be done with it!'

James and I shuffled out with Hedges between us, and

deposited him just a few yards away on the road upon his back. There he lay, gazing up at the night sky as if it was the first time he had seen it. His mouth hung open in miserable wonderment, as if, now taken unawares by the Lord his God, he waited to discover the consequence of it. I wished him well.

'It is done.' Willis scanned the street once more before hurrying us all back inside.

Liz held her hands together and stared at the door still, like she feared she committed a grievous sin.

I leaned over and kissed her upon the cheek. 'I must go.'

'Be careful, Harry,' she whispered.

As I turned to leave the last face I saw was James', lit up bright, still thrilled by the excitement of it all.

Then the door closed and I was alone, street deserted as the hour neared curfew. Hedges still lay on his back staring at the stars. If he was not collected soon then the rats would be at him.

The sense of being watched clung stronger now. I walked fast up the road, unnerved by the emptiness and silence. Pitch and tar slowly sizzled in the burning braziers that lined the lane, and scented smoke drifted about the jetties of the houses, laced with pungent substances intended to cleanse the air. I had not thought it to be dirty afore now.

No birds tonight. Some said they scented the plague

months before its arrival. The swallows left London six months since, a desertion that raised heckles even before the flight of the comet across our skies. How then could I have thought myself to be so safe? I cursed myself, my blind pig-headedness.

Truth was I had nowhere to go. To Cocksmouth, to stay with my mother and her disgusting brother, Robert? They lived in the middle of a field somewhere, surrounded by simpletons and whoballs. Robert kept a pig in the house. Otherwise a boarding house somewhere—to do *what* all day?

I recalled how excited I had been upon being accepted into the intelligence service only eighteen months ago. I had anticipated a life of political intrigue and advancement. Instead, I spent my days at a desk reading papers and sorting them into piles. Much as I had done before escaping my mundane existence as clerk at the Tower. I stayed here, I realised, because others left. I was desperate for some opportunity to demonstrate my sharp wit, meantime pretending the plague would not penetrate our walls. The events of this evening had revealed my vainglorious stupidity for what it was. We would have to leave.

As I walked toward St Olaves', I wondered again what inspired Oliver Willis to invite Hedges into his house. The medics were supposed to keep to themselves, obliged to carry a red rod wherever they travelled. Why invite a medic into your house when he likely carried pestilence with him?

I heard a noise behind me, a heel catching on the cobbles. I stopped and peered back into the gloom, yet all I saw were shadows, flickering shifting shapes dancing in the light of the candles that lit the windows. I chastised my lily liver, cursed myself again for my stubborn intransigence, and hurried to find the churchwarden.

CHAPTER 2

Of the signs and conjectures of the disease
The moon in Libra by Saturn afflicted, the disease has its origin from some surfeit of wine, gluttony, or meat not fully digested.

Davy Dowling was a butcher. He stood tall and broad, arms thick as hams and big knotted hands the size of dinner plates. His wide leathery face gazed serene from beneath a bed of white bristled hair. His clothes were never clean. Pieces of old meat clung to his shirt and trousers, and flakes of dried blood fell like old scabs. I shuddered whenever he came close, for he loved to take a man to his chest and squeeze him.

Dowling was my partner. We had not chosen to be allies, rather we were thrust upon each other. Me for my wit and intelligence, I like to think, and he for other reasons which were still not apparent. We had worked together three times in the service of Lord Arlington, with whom Dowling had the closer relationship, much to my frustration.

He had worked as an investigator longer than I.

'I am sent to fetch you,' he announced in his soft Scot's burr, walking into my kitchen uninvited.

I struggled with a tough piece of cold goose. Jane, my maidservant, bought it as a special delicacy after I announced our imminent departure, and now stood as witness to my enjoyment, making sure I finished it. 'I am busy all day,' I told him. 'We have decided to leave.'

'Leave?' Dowling looked to Jane, broad smile across her pale face, arms folded across her chest. 'You who have spent the last month bemoaning the faint heart of those that left already?'

'God spoke to me,' I replied.

Dowling growled, for he well understood my lack of faith. 'Last afternoon you scorned the idea of leaving, today you make preparations.' His eyes narrowed. 'Where did you go last night?'

'I dined at the house of Oliver Willis.'

Jane fetched Dowling some goose, which served him right. 'Where does Oliver Willis live?' he asked.

'Seething Lane.'

'You walked all the way from Seething Lane at night?'

'It was barely past curfew. I cannot think I was infected if that be your concern.' Which words sounded false as soon as they left my mouth.

'What journey did you take?'

'Fenchurch Street and Cheapgate,' I confessed.

'Fenchurch Street?' Dowling snapped. 'Why did you not avoid it?' Fenchurch Street was one of the few areas affected by plague inside the wall.

'I could have,' I replied warily, 'but I had an errand to run for Oliver Willis.'

He scowled. 'So you walked Fenchurch Street in the middle of the night, the same night you decide to leave London?'

'Why do you care so much?' I demanded.

He sighed, bowed his head and poked at the goose with his finger. A thick smear of red streaked his silver hair. Cow's blood, I reckoned. 'Lucy left this morning. She is gone north.'

I couldn't imagine the butcher living without Lucy. She was a strong woman with a quiet wisdom and unfailing sense of humour. As was required, living with him. 'Why did you not go with her?'

'I have duties in the parish,' he muttered.

'What duties?'

'I am appointed one of the churchwardens.'

'You would stay here and manage the gravediggers rather than be with your wife?' I snorted. 'Go be a churchwarden up north.'

'I have responsibilities to God, Harry, which you would not understand.' He pushed his chair back and stood straight.

'And I did not ask you for advice.'

'Aye, well there is more than enough advice to be had these days,' I ceded. 'So I will content myself with calling you a great pudding-head.'

'Aye, well, pudding-head or not, Lord Arlington is waiting for us at the Vintners' Hall.'

I choked on a piece of meat. 'Arlington?' Lord Arlington, head of the intelligence service. My lord and master, who had never deigned to meet me once in more than a year. 'What does he want?'

'Sooner we get there, sooner we'll know.' Dowling headed toward the door. 'We shouldn't keep him waiting.'

A low hissing sound emanated from betwixt Jane's lips. She glided toward me, dress swishing, green eyes fixed upon mine, like a terrible serpent. 'We must be ready to leave before tomorrow morning and you have much to do.'

'Aye,' I agreed, 'but would you have me keep a lord waiting?'

'No, but I would have you return in good haste.'

A man might ask why a King's man, such as I, allows himself to be managed by his maidservant. Certainly a question I asked myself, for though she was permanently enraged and frightening to behold, she was but a woman and quite a small one besides. Moreover she was indebted to me since I supported most of her odd assortment of ill-fated relatives through various charitable donations of food, clothing and money. Yet how quiet my little house would be without her; my life besides.

'I will return as soon as I am able,' I said, clutching about me what vestiges of dignity I could muster. 'Which will be when I am able.' With which magnificent rejoinder, I hurried out the house in the sanctuary of Dowling's shadow.

The Vintners' Hall towered afront of us like an ancient Greek temple, four tall columns supporting an ornate roof upon which was carved their coat of arms. A ship, three barrels and two swans, with grapes hung about their necks. The vintners were the only legal owners of swans upon the Thames, together with the dyers and the King himself.

Wide arched windows stood in a line, each holding a dozen small panes besmirched with thick layers of city grime. The wrought-iron gates hung loose upon their hinges, propped open with stacks of bricks for fear they would fall if pushed.

The vintners were once a powerful guild, presiding over an entire trade, but their importance fell away during the Interregnum. An ungrateful Charles II now took every opportunity to bleed their finances further.

Dowling and I walked across the courtyard. The painted sundial, faded and chipped. The squat stone well, broken and full of rotting vegetation. Grass grown long, unburdened by the passage of men. The heavy oak door hung rough, polish worn away. A thick crack ran diagonal, so wide you could see right through it.

A bedraggled fellow appeared from within, lean and poorly dressed, dark hair matted and tangled like an abandoned nest. He held a thick baton in his right hand, reluctant to show it. 'You can't come in here. It's closed.'

Dowling pushed past. 'Lord Arlington sent for us.'

'Lord Arlington?' the man exclaimed. 'Then you may pass, for he is here already.' He scuttled after us like a strange crab. 'It was me that found him, you know. He will tell you, me that found him hanging from his neck.'

I followed Dowling through a dingy corridor, straw upon the floor. 'Found who?'

'Thomas Wharton, the Earl of St Albans.' He danced upon his tiptoes, stopping still when he saw a tall fellow walking toward us from the end of the passage.

'My name is Newcourt,' the new man announced. He was better dressed than I and tall like a heron. His silk doublet and ornate petticoat breeches were of the latest fashion, his velvet jacket impossibly soft. 'You must be Dowling and Lytle?'

The dishevelled man bowed his head and edged back away toward the main door. He scratched under his armpit and grimaced. I immediately thought of buboes; the sinister black swellings that signalled plague, growing unobserved, heralding death.

I skipped forwards. 'I am Lytle.'

'Indeed.' Newcourt peered down his nose with such contempt I felt like tweaking it. 'Follow me.'

Sunlight poured into the great hall through tall windows onto the carnage about us. Plaster peeled from the walls, exposing naked brickwork. Planks of wood lay in great piles about the dirt floor. Ornate frescoes of vine and grape decorated the ceiling, broken and crumbling, beneath which hung two bare feet, black-soled, twisting gently in mid-air.

It was a naked man, the tip of his yard peering down at us. The body dripped, wet, tinged with scarlet stain. I nearly slipped in a foul puddle of piss, wine and shit as I stepped back to avoid a drop falling from his toes. The rope led upwards to the balustrade of the gallery above and disappeared over the rail.

Against the far wall stood a substantial figure, hands behind his back, chest inflated like an old soldier. Without doubt it was Lord Arlington, for no other noble walked about London with a black plaster across the bridge of his nose. He gazed out stern from beneath heavy lids, eyes dark and steady. A strand of brown hair poked out from beneath a magnificent black wig. He dressed conservative, doublet buttoned to his neck, breeches hooked to the bottom of it. The black plaster bestowed upon him a sinister effect.

'Lytle and Dowling?' he called, a powerful deep voice brimming with conviction. 'You work for me, I believe?'

We approached like small children. 'Yes, your lordship.'

He nodded at the corpse. 'What do you make of that?'

'It is a man hanging by his neck, your lordship, whose head has been set alight.' Dowling squinted. 'His eyes glint strangely.'

'His eyes always did glint strangely.' Arlington watched us intently. 'Though not as bright as they do today.'

The corpse's head was as black as soot and the eyes gleamed metallic when they caught the sun. Something protruded from his mouth, round and green.

'That is the Earl of St Albans?' I ventured, watching the small scrawny buttocks spiral slow.

'So it would seem,' Arlington replied. 'You'll find his clothes upon the balcony and a wine bottle pushed down his throat.'

'He drank a lot of wine?' I asked.

Arlington stared like I was a great fool. 'The Earl was a shirker and a shammer,' he declared. 'He recently cheated a merchant of the city out of a considerable fortune, which everyone does know.'

'Henry Burke,' Dowling guessed.

Who the boggins was Henry Burke?

Arlington nodded. 'Burke complained to me three times, each time the same complaint. He claimed Wharton asked him to procure the most expensive wines in Europe for a great event at which the King would attend. Burke pledged to supply the finest wines to be found anywhere in Europe, and so he did. Then Wharton's men seized his wines without paying a crown.'

'Burke was a fool then,' I concluded.

'He says the transaction was guaranteed by a lord.' Arlington stared into space. 'Though he would not tell me which.'

'Why would he not tell you?'

'*I* don't know, Lytle!' Arlington barked, cheeks reddening. 'Stop asking me so many damned questions.' He glanced sideways at Newcourt. 'You two will discover who killed the Earl. Is that clear?'

Dowling raised his eyebrows. 'Us?'

He waved a hand. 'There is no one else able. Most of my agents fled the city weeks ago.'

A real assignment, I realised; the murder of an earl. The opportunity I waited for these last two years. I wanted to roar out in triumph. At the same time I felt a small knot of terror in my stomach, a fear we might fail, a fear of remaining in London.

Arlington rocked on his heels and placed his hands on his hips. 'I must leave for Hampton Court today to attend

His Highness, but Newcourt here will stay in the city and be available to you if required. Won't you, Newcourt?'

Newcourt nodded, sullen.

'Here is a letter of authority bearing my seal, and certificates of health for you and Dowling, should you so need them.' He snapped his fingers and Newcourt retrieved a satchel, which he then gave to me. 'Do of your best and I trust it will be a short investigation. I will present your conclusions to the King.' Arlington strode toward the door. 'Your first job is to cut Wharton down and carry the body to St Albans for burial. That you must do today, for if he is not buried quick he will rot in the heat. Good day!' He waved a hand and left, footsteps echoing down the corridor.

'Come on,' Dowling beckoned, marching toward the staircase in the corner of the hall. I followed, watching the dead man sway.

The stairs were loose and broken. I trod with care up to the gallery, praying it was sturdier than the rest of the building. The rope stretched taut across the top of the balustrade to a stanchion by the wall.

'Godamercy!' Dowling breathed, leaning over the balcony.

The corpse's head stared so close I could reach out and touch it. The face was charred and flaking, hair burned away from angry red scalp, raw and ridged. In place of its eyes were two gold coins, buried deep within swollen eye sockets, and out of its broken jaws projected the bottom of a wine bottle. The rope dug deep into its neck and white shoulders glistened like bone beneath a thin sheen of red wine.

'Godamercy!' Dowling exclaimed again, while I crouched upon the floor, gulping deep breaths in slow steady rhythm. The air tasted dirty and clung to the inside of my nostrils. I struggled to quell the nausea that washed my stomach.

'Come on, Harry.' Dowling tugged at my shoulder. 'We'll pull him up rather than cut him down, else he'll fall twelve feet.'

I breathed deep again, yet the air was too warm. I needed cold air. My stomach cramped and knew I would vomit. I ran as far as I could down the gallery afore emptying the contents of last night's splendid dinner upon the boards.

'You feel better now?' Dowling called, pointing at the rope. 'You pull from the back, I'll pull from the front.'

I wiped at my brow with the sleeve of my jacket, sweating, feeling much improved. Returning to the scene, I stepped as far from the balustrade as I could, out of sight of the body, and gripped the rope with both hands. Dowling grunted, satisfied, and braced his knees against the railing. I hoped it would hold. I had visions of his fat arse disappearing into the space below.

'Pull hard and I'll drag him over the rail!' Dowling called

over his shoulder.

I hauled as hard as I could, too hard, for the corpse's head hit the balustrade with a sharp crack. Dowling stuck up his hand and muttered to himself. He leaned over, seized the body beneath the arms and drove backwards with his legs. Then he staggered, tripped, and lost his balance, crashing against the gallery floor. The body slithered against his chest like a strange fish, bright red buttocks pointed in the air. Dowling groaned, pushed the corpse away in disgust and pitched to his feet, wiping at his sodden shirt. A thick red globule of whatever foul liquid soaked Wharton slid down his cheek. My nausea returned.

Dowling wiped at his lips and spat over the railing afore kneeling down next to the corpse, oblivious to what rotten substance covered the floor. He tried to roll the body over onto its back, struggling to hold it firm as it slipped between his fingers. 'And it shall come to pass, that instead of sweet smell there shall be stink. Isaiah, Chapter Three.' A thick stain seeped slowly up Dowling's trouser legs toward his thighs. He prodded at the coins in the man's eyes, but couldn't get a grip. I did my best not to retch.

'The coins were pushed hard into his eyes before he died,' he declared. 'Which is why the flesh has swollen about them. I reckon his wrists were tied to stop him pulling them out.' He took a short knife from his trousers and slipped the blade behind one coin. He prised it out then tossed it toward me. 'The eye is pushed flat into his head,' he said, face contorted with disgust.

I picked the coin up gingerly, holding it between my fingertips. Four heraldic shields on one side and Charles II's big nose on the other. A gold guinea. 'Aye, well.' I put the coin in my pocket. 'It's definitely Thomas Wharton.'

Dowling looked up. 'How can you tell?'

I pointed. 'His clothes are over there in a pile, as Lord Arlington said.' Blue silk breeches and a shirt cut of fine linen. Beneath them a long woollen jacket and a distinctive purple hat with a long black feather. 'His hat.'

'Aye,' Dowling grunted. 'His silly hat. Whoever killed him did so with a fury. Pushed the bottom of that bottle right up to his teeth.' He rubbed his wet hands across his scalp. 'O Lord my God, in thee do I put my trust: save me from all them that persecute me, and deliver me.'

The same Lord God who sent plague to kill us all? 'There are no other marks upon the body, nothing to tell us who may have killed him?'

Dowling held out a bloody hand, seeking assistance in climbing to his feet. I declined. 'You don't think the bottle and the coins are clue enough, Harry?' He grimaced as his back straightened.

Quick steps sounded across the hall below, then up the stairs; heavy and confident, not the stride of the poor fellow who admitted us. I wondered if it was Newcourt returned, or even Arlington himself. Instead a great black shadow, a giant, wide chest draped in flowing cloak.

'Who are you and what are you doing?' the man challenged, eyes glittering perspicacity and cunning. He swept off his hat, revealing a huge bony face, long wide nose and big lips. A scar ran from the corner of his mouth to the top of his ear.

'We are King's men.' I stepped forwards. 'Who are you? No one is supposed to be here.'

'I know him. You do not.' He advanced upon the corpse and crouched next to its head, cupping the back of it in one giant hand. Then he gripped the base of the bottle with his right hand and ripped it loose, holding it aloft against the sunlight. 'Brandevin,' he declared. 'With Burke's mark upon it. Which of you forced it down his throat?'

'Us?' I exclaimed. 'We only just got here.'

Dowling wiped his hands on his knees and crouched next to the stranger. 'We are here to find out who killed him, good fellow. Who are you and what are you doing here?'

The big man stood slowly, eyeing the stains upon Dowling's skin and clothes. 'Never mind.' He tossed the bottle in the air and caught it by the neck. 'You may go now.'

'*We* may go?' I repeated, indignant. 'We are taking the

body back to St Albans at Lord Arlington's request.'

The man smiled without humour, mouth stretched wider than a man's hand. 'Arlington, you say.'

'Lord Arlington.'

He threw the bottle at my chest and I caught it, too late to consider where it had been. 'Come to cover his tracks, have you?'

'We have asked you twice already, sir.' Dowling took the bottle from me. 'Who are you?'

'Find out for yourself.' He surveyed the disfigured face once more, then inspected the rest of the body, paying special attention to the penis. Then he grunted and turned his attention to the pile of clothes. He took the hat in one hand, the silken shirt with the other. 'His clothes.' He tossed them back to the floor. 'What will you do now?'

'Find out who killed him,' I replied.

'And who will that be?' he sneered.

'Who do you think?'

The man stepped toward me like he would pick me up and throw me from the gallery, then placed a thick forefinger upon my forehead. 'Rest assured,' he said, hoarse. 'Rest assured.' He tapped me hard, then smiled again, turned and marched back the way he came.

I leaned over the balcony and watched the top of his huge head disappear, black hair with streaks of white. 'Who in God's name was that?'

Dowling shook his head. 'A friend of Wharton's is what he said.' He lifted the bottle to his nose and sniffed. 'Brandevin.' He passed it to me. 'You agree?'

I held the tall cylindrical neck between thumb and forefinger, imagining that some of Wharton's flesh must still reside within it. The bulbous base was mottled and cracked. I held it to my nose, but not too close. The smell was sharp and fruity. 'Aye, brandevin, and he said it had Burke's mark upon it.' I turned it upside down. 'It has no mark that I can see.'

'Methinks the smell is the mark and Burke is the supplier,' Dowling said.

'Then it must be part of the shipment that Henry Burke supplied Wharton.' I recalled Arlington's testimony. 'So why did he ask if it was *us* that forced it down his throat?'

Dowling shrugged, wiped his palms upon his wide rump and sighed. 'We had better get him clean and boxed,' he said. 'If we are to take him to St Albans today we must set off soon. We cannot fetch him in this state. They will think themselves cursed.'

We should close his eyes, I supposed, if he had eyelids remaining. 'How will you hide a burned head?'

'Ceruse,' Dowling answered. 'Undiluted. And cochineal upon his cheeks.'

'He will look like a grinning harlequin.' I stared at the blackened corrugated head. 'His wife will die of shock.'

Dowling scowled. 'We must take him to an embalmer if we can find one, and do the best that is possible.'

'At least we might put his hat back on,' I said.

'I will go and see if our friend has ordered a coffin.' Dowling headed off.

'I will come with you.' I hurried after him, for I had no desire to be left alone with the monstrosity that used to be Thomas Wharton.

CHAPTER 3

If one shall find the party at home he would speak with
If the Lord of the seventh house be in any of the four angles, you may conclude the party is at home with whom you would speak with.

Dowling secured us a butcher's cart, stained a deep enduring red, testament to a regular procession of bloody carcasses. Now the Earl lay there, wrapped in sheets and blankets, lain straight inside his coffin. I tried to ignore the sound of his body bouncing in the box as we negotiated the uneven track.

The road north to St Albans led through the parish of St Giles, one of the worst affected by plague. These church bells pealed all day long, a ceaseless reminder to a parish already on its knees. The sky was a perfect blue, as it had been all summer, no clouds to blunt the rays of a fierce yellow sun. It was said the sun conspired with the pestilence, heating up the ground to release the poisonous miasma.

I sat, nervous, up on the wagon next to Dowling, shirt

burning against my back, praying no one would set upon us, no infected destitutes hungry for food. The best outcome would be that we solved this mystery early and convincingly. Then I might withdraw from London for the few weeks it would take for the plague to tire of itself, and return soon to more responsibility, a grander title and some money.

Frightened faces peered from the windows of poor mean houses, speaking of misery and bewilderment. Here the sound of cartwheels was as common at night as it was during day, for the death-carts emerged from the graveyards at dusk, to rattle about the streets in search of the newly deceased. Bearers loaded bodies onto the back of their wagons and fetched them to the plague pits, where they threw the bodies down in piles and attempted to spread them out tidy.

'What did you not tell me this morning?' Dowling mused, staring ahead.

The cart lurched as we ran across a deep rut dried into the road. I thought of deceiving him, but had not the will. 'There may be illness in the Willis household.'

Dowling glanced sideways. 'What illness?'

'Dr Hedges was dining with us when he dropped dead of the pest,' I said. 'I dragged him to the street and told the churchwarden he died afore he reached us.'

Dowling's eyes stretched wide as dinner plates.

'You are my confessor, Dowling, so ye may not tell anyone I told you it.'

'How do you know you are not diseased, Harry?' Dowling exclaimed. 'They lock people behind closed doors for a reason.'

'Aye,' I agreed, 'but not a very good reason. Hedges had walked to all parts afore he came to dinner. Any man might have been infected. For my part I kept as far from him as I could while we ate, for he was not a pleasant fellow.'

He shook the reins, angry. 'You sat at the same table!'

'It was a long table.'

He cast me a furious gaze and clamped his jaw closed.

We left houses behind for open fields. The further north we rode, the more families we encountered camped by the roadside, belongings spread out beneath the bushes. Others set up residence in the fields. These were those without credentials to pass the turnpikes. They would wait for nightfall before seeking covert passage through fields and forest.

Just before Whetstone the sharp crack of a musket shot rang out, crisp against the still morning air. Around the corner a crowd gathered, their passage blocked by a long turnpike manned by a dozen men with guns held up. One musket smoked, its owner a young fellow holding his weapon to his chest, body trembling.

We stopped as close to the turnpike as we could reach,

our progress blocked by a wall of thirty or forty angry men leaning forwards into the barrier.

Dowling jumped from his seat and marched into the mob. 'What happens here?'

A short strong fellow shoved him in the chest. 'Who do you think you are?'

Dowling shoved harder and sent him sprawling. 'King's man.' The crowd parted, yielding reluctantly to the hard authority they heard in his voice. I followed close behind.

As we emerged from the steaming rabble three muskets rose to point at Dowling and one at me. Dowling brandished his credentials. 'King's men heading north up the King's road at King's request.'

A sentry stepped forwards, thick linen shirt hanging down above rough loose trousers. His nose was packed with herbs, sage it appeared, which enjoyed no protective qualities I knew of. His cheeks were stuffed with something else besides. He frowned, cheeks swollen like an angry mouse.

'Turn about and go back to London,' he mumbled.

'We have business in these parts,' Dowling replied.

He raised his rusty weapon. 'Not today you don't.'

'We are King's agents and you cannot deny us access to the King's highway.'

He scratched his head and looked back at his three

colleagues. Then he glared at us. 'Show us evidence you are King's agents.'

Dowling held out both our certificates of health and Arlington's seal.

The sentry pointed at Dowling with the tip of his stick. 'You read it.'

Dowling read the flowery text out loud and showed our man the seals up close.

The man squinted through keen brown eyes. 'How do we know you don't carry the plague with you?'

'Sir, we have the King's authority and are protected from the plague by his holy influence,' Dowling answered in all seriousness.

The man surveyed the crowd behind us. 'You have horses?'

'We have a cart.'

'What is in your cart?'

'The body of Thomas Wharton, Earl of St Albans.'

The sentry leapt back as though he stood on a snake. 'He died of plague?'

'No,' Dowling assured him. 'He died of a broken neck. There are no tokens nor buboes upon him, nor any sign of the plague. You may look for yourself.'

'Fetch your cart,' the sentry directed.

Dowling nodded obediently and returned to the wagon while I waited at the turnpike. Our horse was large and steadfast, not averse to treading on a few feet if required. Rather like Dowling.

The sentry licked his lips, eyeing the throng. He pulled the gate open and stood waving his arms frantically until we were through. The crowd surged behind us and another shot rang out. Three sentries leapt up onto our cart and fired into the middle of the mêlée while their comrades succeeded in closing the gate.

'Show me this body,' our sentry demanded, lips tight, body taut.

'Have you seen the body of a man hanged by the neck?' Dowling climbed over to the back of the cart. 'It is a sight that stays with most men longer then they would wish.'

'Show me,' the man commanded.

Dowling prised open the box, carefully loosened the wrappings about the corpse, then slid back the coverings from Wharton's face. It seemed grey now. It had been white before we set off, but the ceruse and cochineal had rubbed off during the ride. The puffiness about the eyes had subsided, leaving big black patches about empty holes. The mouth hung open again, jaw bouncing loose about the body's chest.

The sentry put his hand over his eyes. 'I did not ask to see the head,' he groaned. 'I would see the armpits and the groin for buboes, the chest for tokens.'

Dowling obliged without further commentary. The sentry

nodded weakly, easily convinced the body was clean.

We enjoyed easier passage at the turnpikes further north, since most without credentials were turned back at Whetstone. By early afternoon we were through St Albans. I was astounded to see two doors with red crosses on Sopwell Lane, for I didn't realise the plague penetrated so far so fast.

We kept riding, conscious of the stares of those about us, angry and suspicious. How things changed. London was the life-blood of this town, the destination for those who stopped to rest here. Not now.

The Earl's Old Palace was located but a mile in the direction of Harpenden. In truth it was but a quarter of a palace, for three-quarters of it was demolished by the previous owner who planned to build something more splendid. The Restoration thwarted his grand ambitions however, and now he languished, a pauper, somewhere out east. The Earl, on the other hand, enjoyed elevation to loftier heights, through some mysterious services to the King. Not great services, I supposed, else he would have got a whole palace.

Narrow latticed windows speckled the front of the house, a ready vantage from which to spy unseen. We rode slowly to the coach house, across the front of the silent building. One man laboured easily to clean the stables, where stood just two horses.

A tall figure emerged from a door at the base of a squat little tower attached to the house. He strode toward us, a strong young man, oddly energetic amidst such dormant surroundings. 'May I help you?' he asked in a Scots accent. To my ear he spoke similar to Dowling, yet Dowling tensed.

'We work for the King. We would talk to Lady Wharton,' Dowling said, eyes unmoving.

The young man eyed the rough attire of the butcher, then looked to me. Though my clothes had crumpled and become sticky, I evidently presented a more comforting aspect. The young man's black hair lay cropped close to his scalp, his face swarthy, his eyes brown and inquisitive.

'We have urgent news of the Earl.' I showed him the thick wax seal. 'News that cannot wait.'

He ran a finger over the seal and scowled.

We followed him into the tower, a dark musty passage, walls lined with oak panels, thick and warm. Black and white tiles covered the floor, worn and polished. Noiseless, save for the crashing echo of our own steps reverberating across unseen halls and spaces. Cracked paintings hung on the walls, long forgotten faces peering out in awkward pose, the selfconsciousness of moments gone, buried beneath thick layers of varnish and grime.

We emerged from the gloom into a luminous space,

where tall foggy windows turned bright sunlight into ghostly white effervescence. Then back into the bowels of this sickly place, past a series of open doorways giving view only to faded tapestries, shrouded furniture and emptiness.

We turned a corner into a fresh passage into which light flooded from far ahead, beneath a square stone archway. As we advanced, so the banqueting hall came into view, a magnificent structure towering above us like the inside of a cathedral. The roof was built of oak, an artful lattice of ornate carved beams. Tapestries climbed the walls from floor to the height of three men, patchworks of red and green flowers. Above the tapestries, a row of arched windows allowed the sun to burst through thick walls, bathing all in a bright warm light. Yet none banqueted here in recent times. The several long tables that ran the width of the hall were bare and dusty. Chairs sprawled as if those that dined here last left suddenly, never to return.

'My name is Conroy.' The young fellow bowed. 'Please wait here, gentlemen, and I will see if her ladyship is disposed to see you.' He turned and left.

'This place has about as much life about it as Wharton himself,' I noted, sitting down.

Dowling shook his head. 'The Lord maketh poor, and maketh rich. He bringeth low, and lifteth up.'

'The Earl was brungeth low, it seems.'

'Aye,' Dowling growled.

I watched the sun creep from one window to another. I worried what was happening to the corpse in the afternoon heat.

Finally she arrived, dressed in such formal elegance I understood why time dragged. Mercilessly boned, bedecked in deep scarlet skirt and gold braided pale green underskirt, she radiated a severe strain of beauty. These were not the clothes of a woman in mourning. She wore an intricately arranged wig, a heavy burden in this hot weather. Beads of sweat erupted in small globules about the edges of the paint upon her face.

My eyes didn't linger, for she had with her a child as ugly as any I had seen in all my life. The bones of its head rippled like a wave, and the sockets of its eyes bulged too large. Dry raised sores covered its yellow skin and it scratched itself continuously.

'Why do you stare at him?' Lady Wharton asked with tremor in her voice. She held my gaze, demanding an answer. I could not reply truthfully, for it would be uncivil, yet I could think of no suitable lie. Conroy glowered from where he lingered in the shadows.

Dowling knelt and took the child's hands. 'Who shall ascend into the hill of the Lord? He that hath clean hands, and a pure heart.'

Not something I could have said without sticky sweetness

44

cementing my teeth together in deathly grimace, but it seemed to satisfy Lady Wharton. She stared at Dowling with eyes and lips slightly narrowed, yet all she would see was sincerity shrouded in an unquestioning allegiance to God. Then she turned again at me. I did my best to look noble.

'I understand you have come from London. My husband is not at home.'

'Lady,' Dowling spoke, sombre. 'Hell hath enlarged herself and opened her mouth without measure.'

'Hell and destruction are never full,' she replied in a high faint voice.

Dowling clutched his hands together in strange anxiety. Unusually tongue-tied today, I thought. Was he intimidated by her nobility? 'I can think of no kind way of conveying the news that we bear,' he stuttered.

'Faith cometh by hearing,' she said.

It seemed as if the Scots baboon was about to cry, so I decided to put him out of his misery. 'We found your husband dead last night.'

Dowling's baleful stare and stiff jaw signalled a lack of gratitude.

Lady Wharton bowed her head and clutched her white hands to her mouth. I waited for her to ask how, or when, but she said nothing at all, just stood unmoving. Her eyes stared at the floor, yet without anguish, nor even a tear.

'Would you be alone a while? We can wait until you are ready?' Dowling offered. Good of him, I ceded, but also a nuisance.

'Do I lack composure?' Her voice deepened.

'No, Lady,' I answered on his behalf, for he was about as useful as a bag of wet wool. 'We hoped you might tell us something of his life, something that might help establish the circumstances of his death.'

She raised her chin and cast upon me the same steely gaze I saw before. 'What circumstances?'

'He was killed.' I spoke gentle as I could. 'Slain.'

She looked to the unlucky child, as if her thoughts turned straight to their welfare rather than the demise of her husband. We waited in awkward anticipation of her interest in the nature of the killing. Conroy's brown eyes sparkled like those of a great bear. She stood stiff, chest rising and falling with the steady tides of her breathing. 'How was he slain?'

No need to discuss wine bottles and coins. 'Hanged by the neck at the Vintners' Hall,' I said. 'Dowling and I are charged with finding the murderer.'

She allowed her eyes to wander unbridled from the bottom of Dowling's filthy shapeless trousers to the tip of his spiky hair. Then she stared at me as if I was the killer.

'What enemies did he have?' I asked.

'He has no enemies that I know of,' she replied, lips

46

shrunk tight. 'Though his business is in London.'

'What of family?' I asked.

'His family are all dead.' She breathed deep. 'I trust you will spare me further questions.'

Dowling twitched unhappily. The child stared unseeingly, as if blind.

'We brought his body with us, your ladyship,' I said.

She paled.

I nodded. 'In a plain box.'

She stood stiff, staring out the window. 'Indeed,' she whispered. Conroy stepped silently to her shoulder. 'I cannot bear the thought of sleeping tonight beneath the same roof.' She turned to Dowling. 'You must think me cruel.'

He shook his head. I would not have wished to sleep under the same roof as Wharton's body neither, the state it was in. 'Would you have us take it to the church?' I offered.

'Yes,' she agreed, with strange eagerness. 'I expect we should arrange for his burial quickly.'

'His family are all dead then?' I repeated. Surely someone must still be alive.

Fear and doubt dissolved, leaving only anger. 'Have you come here to interrogate me?'

'No.' I clapped my hands. 'We will take the body to the church immediately.'

She bowed her head silently, still regarding me like I

sought to entrap her.

Dowling bowed stiffly. 'Thank you.'

I hadn't seen him bow before. What he thanked her for, I struggled to comprehend. It was us that fetched her husband all the way from London.

'Conroy will escort you,' she said, and beckoned him with one finger, face frozen once more in a mask of icy disdain. Then she walked away, she and the monstrous child. By the time they reached the door, at the end of the great hall, they stood two tiny figures, close together like little dolls, alone and unloved. An image flashed through my mind, a picture of them still stood there in the same pose in twenty years time, dusty and web covered, in an evening dusk. I shivered.

'What ails you?' Dowling growled.

'I am becoming psychic.'

'Follow me, gentlemen.' Conroy squared his shoulders and set off at sharp pace in the direction we had come.

As we walked I contemplated once more the behaviour of her ladyship. Strung tight as her own bodice. She spoke of her husband as if she hardly knew him and was quick to declare his family dead. I detected not a trace of grief.

Meantime, Conroy shepherded us out the house. 'Wait here,' he ordered, once we reached the wagon. 'I will saddle a horse for myself and we will begone.'

Dowling climbed up onto the wagon and stared into space, sullen sulk pasted upon his sagging chops.

'You spoke as with another man's teeth,' I declared. 'I have never seen you so butter-tongued.'

'Aye, well.' Dowling clamped his mouth closed. The tips of his ears glowed red. 'You wouldn't understand.'

'Speak to me, Dowling, as you usually do, without subtlety or consideration.'

He cleared his throat. 'Ye shall not afflict any widow or fatherless child. If thou afflict them in any wise, and they cry at all unto me, I will surely hear their cry.'

'You think I spoke to her roughly.'

He nodded, regarding me with condescending pity. Then he shook his head and clucked like a chicken.

Let him cluck, for he did not judge the good lady well. She was not about to cry unto God, nor indeed to anyone at all.

'I have seen no other servants but him and the stablehand.' I watched Conroy disappear into the stables. 'The Earl was hard up.'

'Else he was neglectful,' Dowling replied.

True. If Wharton cheated Burke then surely he had monies. I wondered who else might tell us something. 'I want to have a quick look at the gardens round the back.'

'Go quick then,' Dowling snapped.

49

I followed the path beneath a brick archway and saw a man wrestling with a tree and a ball of twine. He was trying to tie it to a stick, but the tree had grown too much already, its trunk all bent and twisted.

'Hoy!' I cried. 'Can I ask you a question?'

He looked up for a moment, but didn't reply.

'Why are there so few servants around the place?' I asked.

'Hah!' he exclaimed with bitterness. 'A good question! By next week there will be two servants fewer besides, for me and my boy have been told we must leave.'

'Why? Have you not done a good job in the garden? Methinks it a fine garden!' Actually it resembled the head of a man long overdue a good haircut.

'I have worked here nigh on thirty years,' he said. 'But this estate is poor, though it is not my place to say so.'

I nodded. 'I can see there is a story to be told.'

'Hah! A simple enough story. The Earl gained tenancy on this estate and the tenancy expires before two more years are up. Those were the terms and don't ask me how I know it.'

'How do ye know it?'

'All in the house know it!'

'So he does not own it?'

He looked at me like I was a fool. 'A tenant does not own the property he resides in.' He shook his head and muttered mournfully.

'Does the Earl not visit?' I asked.

'Aye, he visits.'

'Mr Lytle!' Conroy's strong accent called out from behind. The gardener busied himself with stringing, head down and silent, while Conroy watched me, cold-eyed and grim as his mistress. He turned and headed back toward the front of the house.

The local church appeared bright and happy, cheerful square facade sat on bright green grass framed by a perfect blue sky. We left the cart upon the street, close to the gate. As we arrived the church was emptying after Evensong. The usual mix seen anywhere in England. First to emerge were the poorest and the shabbiest, since they were not assigned pews and so sat at the back. Some avoided my eye, resigned to another miserable day. Others glared, curious or aggressive. I found myself distinguishing between those who might deserve the plague and those not, an uncharitable thought for which I quickly repented.

'We will take the coffin about the side and through the vestry,' Conroy declared. 'One of you help me carry it.'

Indeed it was light enough for two men to carry, since it was made only of thin pine. So thin it might snap in two if they did not carry it carefully. Dowling was closer in size to Conroy, so I was left alone.

A fellow with lively blue eyes and a thick grey beard appeared at my elbow, pipe in hand, shovel in the other. 'Who's in the box?'

'The Earl of St Albans,' I replied.

He took the pipe from his mouth. 'Well, well,' he declared, and stuck the pipe back in. 'What did he die of?'

'He was killed.'

He sucked sharply at the pipe. 'Well, well. Who killed him?'

'I don't know,' I confessed. 'It's our job to find out, but we haven't found out much.'

He nodded and blew out a mouthful of smoke. 'My brother works in the palace gardens, worked there thirty years. Not no more.' He tutted. 'Not right.' He puffed at the pipe again. 'The Earl dead, you say? Will they find another earl you reckon?'

'I don't know.'

'Can't give it to the brother, that's for sure.' He frowned. 'Hope not anyway. Wouldn't want a lunatic as a lord, would ye?'

'His brother is a lunatic?'

'Aye.' He pulled the hat off his head and brushed back thick hair with gnarled old fingers. 'The boy is the son of the brother.'

'What boy?'

He met my eyes with sideways glance. 'Have you not

been to the palace then?'

'You mean Lady Wharton's son?'

The old fellow pointed with the stem of his pipe. 'That's not her son. That's the son of the brother of the Earl, what is now a lunatic and has been for twenty years. They say he went mad when they handed him the boy. Now he is at Bedlam.'

'The boy cannot be older than ten years,' I protested.

The old man took one last long draw before tapping the bowl out upon his heel. 'I don't know about that. But the Earl has a brother, I know that, and the boy is the brother's son. *My* brother told me.' He put the pipe in his pocket and stretched his arms out wide. 'Back to work then,' he declared. 'I hopes they let me dig the hole.' He grinned. 'That'd be something to tell my brother.' He shambled away, back betwixt the gravestones.

Dowling emerged with Conroy. They stopped to exchange brief partings.

'Wait,' I called, running over.

Both stopped.

'Is it true the Earl has a brother who is a lunatic at Bedlam, who is the father of that boy we saw?'

Conroy's ears and neck turned red. He drew his sword and raised it to my chest. He pressed the tip of the blade into my sternum and twisted it. My flesh tore and my blood spilled forth in a warm flow upon my shirt.

Dowling stepped forward and shoved him away. 'Enough!'

I looked down and saw a big red circle.

Conroy lowered his weapon, sheathed it, then pulled hard at the front of his coat. 'Do not come back,' he said, hoarse. 'You are not welcome.' With that he turned on one heel and marched back to the church.

'I suppose I spoke harsh to him too?' I said to Dowling. The cut upon my chest was three inches wide.

Dowling watched Conroy retreat, anxiety scored into his craggy face. 'Who told you Wharton had a lunatic brother?'

Many were afraid of lunatics, believing lunacy to be the mark of the Devil.

'It matters not,' I said as I watched Conroy disappear. 'Since it is evidently true.'

CHAPTER 4

Of marriage

The Lord of the seventh in the ascendant, the party desired loves best: The Lord of the ascendant in the seventh, the querent loves best.

My father (now dead) sent me to Cambridge to learn theology. I took happily to drink instead, also gambling and benevolent women. Time not dedicated to one or other I spent in the company of John Ray, a phytologist with whom I used to walk the morning fields in search of new plants. A pleasant way to clear the head. So it was next morning I treated the wound on my chest with mine own preparation of powdered middle fleabane while studiously avoiding Jane. She bustled about the hallway and my front room, stacking my belongings in small piles ready for transportation.

'I told you to return in good haste,' Jane growled, unable to resist sniffing at the wound as I dressed it. She was a passionate advocate of Sir Kenelm Digby's sympathetic powder, the main ingredient of which purported to be moss harvested from dead men's skulls. She viewed the red flesh with furrowed brow, afore running a finger across my damp forehead. 'You are feverish,' she declared triumphantly.

'It will pass,' I assured her.

She disappeared into the kitchen and returned with a wet towel. 'A pleasant ride through the countryside can but help.' She slapped it across my forehead and stood back with folded arms. 'What time do you wish to leave?'

I placed a piece of linen across the wound and reached for my shirt. 'Not for a little while.'

'This afternoon?'

I edged toward the door, where waited my jacket. 'Perhaps next week.'

She breathed hard through her nose, eyes shining green against the red of her hair and the pink of her face.

I held up my hands afront of my chest. 'Lord Arlington summoned us to the Vintners' Hall. He ordered us to investigate a murder.'

She stamped her foot so hard, the floor shook. 'What nonsense! There are men slain every night. They fall over as they walk! You said we could leave.' She jabbed a finger at my wound. I knocked her hand aside.

'We will,' I assured her. 'It shouldn't take us long to find the man who did it.'

'You and the dunderhead butcher?' she snorted.

'*You* might leave today,' I suggested. 'And I will follow.'

'Hah!' She stabbed again at my chest. 'You would have me travel alone?' She thrust her freckled face in front of mine, so close I could have kissed her, had I wished to have my lips bitten off. 'Do you not care?'

'I do care,' I protested. 'Few take as good care of their servants as I do. Most people who leave, leave their servants behind to manage their property.'

She placed her hands upon her wondrous hips and bared her teeth. I opened the door and ran down the street afore she thought to bar the way, not stopping until I reached Knightrider Street.

I gathered my jacket about my shoulders and bid my heart stop beating, striding slow. The sun shone high already and sweat poured down the ridge of my back. I wondered again how I permitted her such latitude. Perhaps because I trusted her judgement. Part of my own being raged as violent as she, that to stay here was madness. Yet I could not pass up the opportunity to impress Arlington. I thought of this wine merchant he told us of, the man who Wharton cheated. One conversation with him might be all that was required to solve the crime. First, though, I needed to discover how Liz fared.

I approached Seething Lane from the north, past St

Olaves'. I walked slow, ready to turn should I spot a watcher outside their door. But the street was clear save for two women, walking arm in arm, chattering furiously. Surely they would not be so oblivious were there a fresh red cross there to attract their attention.

I knocked, and Edward opened the door, Willis' servant, tall and silver-haired. His mouth smiled but his eyes did not. He took a short step sideways, reluctant it seemed, to let me pass. The hall smelled of vinegar, sign that the house had been scrubbed and scoured.

Liz emerged from the dining room dressed only in an old morning gown. 'Harry,' she greeted me in sober tones. Her face gleamed clean and pale. She placed a hand upon my sleeve. 'You have come back.'

'I came to see what happens.'

'Come in then.'

I allowed her to pull me gently over the threshold and up the stairs to a bright room overhanging the street below. She sat upon the edge of a wide armed chair and turned her green eyes upon me. Today they gleamed like glass, bright and sharp, bereft of warmth.

'I told the churchwarden where to find him,' I told her.

'I know you did,' she whispered.

'Did you hear anything of it?'

She bowed her head. 'Yes. The churchwarden discovered it and told Mrs Hedges and she will have him buried.

Tomorrow, I think.'

'You look tired.'

She nodded. 'We spent all that night cleaning the house. Mrs Allen, the searcher, arrived shortly after dawn.' She dabbed at her eyes and bowed her head. 'She was very good.'

Something was wrong. My chest weighed heavy with dread. 'So all is right?'

'No,' she exclaimed, tears flowing. 'James is gone.'

My mouth dried as I struggled to recall the face of the eager young man who had helped me that night. 'Dead?'

'No!' she cried out. 'At least that's not what I meant.' She sniffled. 'He became feverish soon after you left, so I sent him to his bed. In the morning he was gone.'

'He has relatives?'

'No.' She shook her thick auburn hair about her slender shoulders. 'He has lived with us since he was a boy. He is almost my age.' She attempted to dry her face with a flimsy mouchoir. 'He wouldn't leave without telling us where he went. I am afraid something is wrong.'

I recalled the memory of James wiping sauce from Hedges' face, eager to help, careless how close he put his face to the body. That night had been a grand adventure for him. Liz said he became feverish. Feverish with plague was clearly her fear.

I leaned over and took her hands gently. 'I am sorry, Liz.'

Her hands tensed. I wondered if she blamed me for James' departure. It had, after all, been my idea to deposit Hedges upon the street. My idea that James helped to carry him. On the other hand perhaps Hedges contracted the plague here, while he ate, and James contracted the disease from here also. I thought of letting her hand go.

'I wish I could do something,' I offered, without thinking.

She raised her pretty chin and turned those eyes upon me once more. My soul grew little wings and tried to fly out my throat. 'Perhaps you can,' she murmured.

'Name it.'

She selected her words with great deliberation. 'Will you help us find James?'

'Of course,' I replied, fearful what this might lead to. 'Where have you looked?'

'Father has been walking the streets since yesterday. He is out there now.' She turned to the window. 'I don't know where he looks, but I doubt he will find him.'

I detected some lack of faith in her bitter tone, and wondered what it meant. Had Willis disappointed her some way? I first met Oliver Willis while conducting an investigation on behalf of Lord Arlington. I had been assigned to follow him on the basis he might be complicit in the illegal trade of wool, working with smugglers to sell the luxury goods they received in payment. So I followed him dutifully until he became curious, and apprehended me one day at the Exchange. By that time I was convinced of his innocence, since he spent most of his time arguing with a bellicose merchant whose customers lived mostly in the north of England. When I told him why I followed him he provided me with some intelligence as to the guilty parties. Though I did nothing with it, the men were arrested shortly after, for which Oliver professed his undying gratitude. Through Oliver I met Elizabeth.

'Are you angry with your father?' I asked.

'Yes,' she said. 'For we should have left London long ago. Yet Father will not have it.'

'Why not?' I wondered, thinking guiltily of Jane.

'He does not say,' Liz sighed. 'But it is something to do with his business, some matter unresolved.'

I squeezed her hand. 'Well, I am glad for my sake that you stay.'

She pulled her hands away and placed them on her lap, blinking again like she would cry. 'Harry, I wish with all my heart that we could leave London. It is only because my father has the soul of a donkey that we remain. But for that James might still be with us.' She dabbed at her eyes again. 'Now is not a time for courting and currying favour. Now is a time to withdraw valiantly and weather out God's storm. Once the clouds have parted and peace reigns again, that is the day to consider our lives and not our deaths.'

A morbid speech, and not very romantic. Death and disease were ever present, and a life spent shivering in fearful anticipation was a life wasted.

She lifted her chin and managed a weak smile. 'I do enjoy your company though, Harry, while we remain.'

'And I yours.'

'I know so little about you.' She stared deep into my eyes. 'I know you are peddled about the city as a pleasant prospect, yet in your case I cannot fathom the reason for it.'

I had no idea what to say in response. Though her words cut like a short blade to my belly, I was struck by her candid nature. Courtship, in my experience, was usually a game of tedious riposte. The suitor was obliged to find ever new ways of paying compliments to the lady, who rarely displayed the same ingenuity in accepting them. I chose to interpret her meaning as relating solely to my prospects and not my personal qualities, the thought lightening my spirit. 'I am a King's man,' I replied, hoping I masked my resentment.

'Yes, Harry, I know that, but I don't know what a King's man is. My father is impressed, but I don't know why, nor do I understand whether your role is important. There are hundreds of people, nay thousands I imagine, that perform duties on his behalf. Some of those duties are quite important and others more menial. The man that keeps his closet stool is a King's man. What do you do for the King, Harry?'

'Well.' I sat up. 'As of this moment I am investigating the death of the Earl of St Albans.'

She took a sharp breath. 'Thomas Wharton?'

'Yes,' I answered. 'You know him?'

'No.' She shook her head, sharp. 'Though I have heard of him. He was a scoundrel. Why are you investigating his death?'

'Lord Arlington asked me to.'

'I see.' Her eyes began to well again.

I was confused. 'Why do you weep?'

Her hair fell over her face. I restrained myself from reaching over to brush it off. She started to cry, for James I supposed. It made sense he may be plagued. If he believed himself to be infected, then his motive for leaving was clear. The only place such a man might go would be a pest-house.

'Did James take money with him?' I asked.

'He took some clothes, not many.' She held her fingers to her face. 'And, yes, he took several pounds of his own money.'

To pay his way, I reckoned. He would turn up at one

of the pest-houses and declare himself to be of this household, sent by his master. Then he would pay the fee and lie there. To recover or die.

'You will help us look for him, Harry?' she pleaded. 'Despite what I have said.'

I concentrated on ensuring what I felt did not reach my face. Cripplegate Pest-house would be the first place to look, a ramshackle slum of wooden sheds, the capacity of which was exceeded weeks before. I knew they built new sheds recently, and knew also how quickly the task was achieved. It was full again already, so they said, full of bodies already so diseased they served no purpose other than to propagate the pestilence. To go to the pest-house was to take my good fortune and rub it in the Devil's face so hard he could not help but smite me. It was not feasible. Yet it stood next to Bedlam, where Wharton's lunatic brother resided. 'Yes,' I replied, unable to resist pleasing her.

'Thank you, Harry.' She twisted the little kerchief so it fitted up her nostril.

I allowed myself to stare at her soft lips, whilst my inner rage hopped up and down with a knife, stabbing at my guts. What had I just done? Bedlam and Cripplegate. The itinerary from Hell.

CHAPTER 5

Whether the disease be in the body, mind or both
If that planet who rules the sign wherein the Lord of the ascendant is in, and he who is dispositor of the moon be unfortunate in their fall, detriment or otherwise very much afflicted, the disease reigns more in the mind than in the body.

The Hospital of St Mary Bethlehem was more than four centuries old. Once she stood amongst green fields. Now she slumped, bent and broken, an old lady dragged to her knees by the thick poisonous blanket of slums and hovels that sullied her pristine innocence. St Mary Bethlehem was now Bedlam, and Bedlam was a terrible place.

Until the sickness came, people paid to visit this terrible place. To walk the corridor between the open cells, to pull faces at the comically strange, to throw stones at those that refused to entertain. Not now though, for Bedlam stood outside the city wall, in the middle of a parish now sodden with disease.

I stopped at the Bedlam gate, Purgatory before me. Fingers of panic teased their way about my heart. Dowling stood as solemn as I, his faith sorely tested, I reckoned.

A fat fly landed upon my sleeve, the size of a grape, with large green eyes that stared at me hungrily. I hated to think upon what it had fed. My body shuddered and I struck at it with an unsteady hand. I missed, and it lurched off lazily in search of a quieter place to sit and digest.

'God help me, Davy. I cannot go further.'

Dowling patted me on the shoulder. 'God help us all, Harry. Be strong and of good courage. Fear not, nor be afraid of them; for the Lord thy God, He it is that doth go with thee; He will not fail thee, nor forsake thee.'

'They say it was God sent us the plague in the first place,' I retorted. 'A fickle fellow, by all accounts.'

Dowling withdrew the comforting hand and took a step forwards. 'If you would wait for me here, I will understand.'

'A kind offer,' I replied, angry. I stepped out of the shade into the burning grounds of Hell.

In the middle of the yard rested an old coach with no wheels, just a tattered peeling body. Old clothes and stiff rags, bottles and bones, filth and a mouldering dead dog. I could feel the sticky atoms hanging in the air, waiting to cling and creep upon my skin. Behind the coach was a large hole, for Bedlam hosted a plague pit.

Only the poor ended up in the pits. These bodies were

not buried in coffins but in sheets, one body thrown atop another from dusk until dawn, when a thin layer of dirt would be thrown upon all in anticipation of the next night's visitation. Now the pit was quiet, yet the dirt was piled high, sprinkled with lime.

I shivered. Two men leaned against the main door, one alert, the other bleary eyed, stinking of wine.

Dowling hurried to them. 'Where is Pateson?' he demanded. 'The keeper of this place.'

'He is not here,' answered the long thin man to the left, red hair hanging over his eyes. He appeared young and pale, white skin flecked with raised purple patches. He waved a hand across his face before digging a forefinger into his ear. 'He doesn't come often.'

The short rounder man stirred. He resembled a potato, face covered with round yellow growths. 'He cannot abide his wife. Says she is the most brutal of all the lunatics in the house.'

'What of the plague?' I asked, wary as to what lay before us.

'What of it?' the thin man replied. 'When one has it we place him in his own cell until he is dead, then the bearers take away the body.' He grinned. 'It is not far to travel.'

'How many have died?'

He scrunched up his face in intense concentration.

'Two,' declared the shorter man brightly, 'which is not

so many. They are gone in the pit.'

I wished I were somewhere else. 'Then you must show us about, for we are King's men.'

The short round man licked his lips and seemed reluctant. 'Well, this be a royal abode, so I suppose you have the right.' He walked up the two flat stairs, pushed open a thick wooden door and bid us follow, sniffling unhappily.

Bedlam had not been maintained since first established. Iron gates, thick chains and all manner of harness and restraint hung from damp perspiring walls. Rain fell freely through wide airy holes in winter, and autumn leaves sailed happily to the floor where they slowly rotted until covered by next year's fall. If someone did not demolish it soon then a few more seasons of wind and rain would do the job cheaply.

The wailing and groaning of the frantic and insane filled our ears, an opera of pain and melancholy.

The round man screwed up his face. 'What do you want to see?'

I screwed up mine too, for the lewd ammonic smell streamed through my nose like the filth of Fleet ditch on a wet and rainy night.

Dowling sniffed the air as if discerning its vintage. 'We seek one man in particular, but we don't know his name. Will you show us them all?'

The man nodded without enthusiasm. 'Very well.'

The passage before us loomed dark and shadowy, lit by

a comb of white teeth, shafts of light stabbing through holes in the roof onto the filthy straw below. Thin green moss covered stone walls, thriving in the moist heat. Our guide led us to the end of a long narrow corridor before turning to face us with an attempt at good cheer.

'Where we stand now is the old dairy, which may be why it smells so bad, I always say.' He waited for us to laugh, but showed no visible disappointment when we failed him.

'Beyond this door afront of us is where the rectory and servants' quarters were located. Now they house our guests. Eight cells line the first corridor and fourteen the second, twenty-two in all, and beyond the Abraham Ward, where the less afflicted wander freely. At present time we have fifty-seven lunatics here, including twenty cells with two lunatics in each. An arrangement that encourages garrulity, but I reckon the company is good for them and makes them happier.' The dirgeful sound of torment from behind the door suggested otherwise.

'What is your name?' I asked.

'Robert Morrison, sir.'

Behind the door awful wailings welled loud and piercing, drilling into my ears and bouncing about my skull. Morrison stood to one side, compelling us to pass through. 'Take heed of mad folks in a narrow place,' he muttered.

I led the way, pushing through the noise like it was a

wall of water. Morrison danced between us on his toes before holding up a dainty finger to bid us stop, once more in role of guide.

'Behold!' he cried loud.

He invited us to inspect the first cell upon our left, inside of which were two lunatics. Both were manacled to the wall with thick chain. The first was naked, lain on his back in the straw, feet astride and hands clasped over his stomach. The second had done all he could to remove himself from the splendour of the first man's nudity.

Morrison cleared his throat and spoke to the ceiling. 'The immodest fellow is Thomas Miller. Senseless and beast like. Lieth in the straw and will suffer no clothes. Teareth all things and will piss in the corner.'

Peering about the bare cell, I could see nowhere better he might relieve himself.

'The modest man is Henry Ringe, tormented by guilt after he lay with a woman that was not his wife. Now he says he is possessed by four spirits named Legion, Simon, Argell and Ammelee the tempter. Ammelee doth regular battle with the good angel that resides within him. He saith things loudly.'

'Saith things?' I said.

'Aye, sir.' Morrison disappeared back from whence he came in a great hurry and returned quickly with a stout cane. He held it up. 'My stick.' Then he stuck the cane betwixt the bars and poked Ringe hard in the ribs. A pitifully sad, grey-lined face looked up at us with red-bagged eyes and slack jaw.

'Ho, Ringe!' Morrison bent down and talked to the man as if he was a small child. 'Tell us what the tempter tells ye.'

The man's dull eyes rolled downwards to fix themselves upon Morrison's thick black belt. He licked his lips and began to recite. 'Leave tempting of me, and I will my soul freely unto thee.'

'Now tell us what the good angel says.'

'Christ shall have my body and soul.' Ringe's second voice shrilled high.

'Now the tempter again,' Morrison commanded.

'Then thou must take it out of God's hands. God shall have it from thee!'

Both tempter and angel spoke with a strange intensity, triggering the surrounding crescendo to a higher pitch. If you were not a lunatic upon arriving, likely you would be one afore you left. 'How long have these men been here?' I asked.

Morrison scratched his head. 'Miller has been here for years, Ringe for two years or so.'

'Could either be related to an earl?' Dowling rumbled.

'An earl?' Morrison repeated, eyes wary. 'No, sir, I think not. Nor Richard Pudsey.' He moved on to the next cell.

'They took him from his house, naked, in a great rage, just last March.'

Jane stormed about my house in a great rage most days, though she did not discard her clothes, shame to say. 'Is that enough to call him a lunatic?' I asked.

Morrison pointed at Pudsey's hands, held clutched to his stomach, left hand hid within the grasp of the right. 'He cut off the fingers of his left hand and claimed the spirits of the air told him to do it,' Morrison explained.

I stared at Pudsey's hands. 'Why the left hand?'

'He is right handed.' Morrison wiped an eye and blew his nose upon his sleeve. 'When he is distracted he shouts and screams, and talks to himself very fast, and none can understand. He holds his hands to his ears and strikes himself about the temples.'

Pudsey turned his head and bared his teeth, an anguished grimace speaking of terrible anxieties. The yellow straw stuck to his hair, slimy and damp.

'Now we'll on to the widow Adams.' Morrison stepped smartly to the next cell along. 'You might ask her a question.'

The widow sat on a bench in a cell by herself, without chains, next to the bars. She wore a long grey dress that might once have been black, and a hat tied about her chin, despite the airless heat.

'How are you this day, Mrs Adams?' I called out, not

sure whether she would leap at me or throw a curse.

Her tiny head turned to me. 'The day be fine and I am well, though I be cursed—my soul in Hell,' she addressed me softly. I had to crouch to catch every word.

'She speaks in rhyme?' I wondered how long it took to develop this parlour trick. I decided to test her. 'Tell me what you see in my eyes.'

Her face gaped in melancholic oblivion. 'Feeleth your heart like it shine as the sun? Your eyes tell me not, that you be only one. Thinketh you long of the joy that you bring? Nay, your soul sleeps in winter, where no voices sing.'

I snorted. 'She is a widow and speaks rehearsed rhymes of her own situation.'

'Nay.' Dowling shook his boulderous head from side to side. 'She describes you like she be your mother.'

'My mother?' My mother hadn't spoken a sensible word to me in years.

He regarded me solemnly. 'I have not seen a smile upon your face this last year, and Faith knows you have been enveloped in a cocoon of self regarding misery that renders you senseless of others.'

'I smile when I fancy, Dowling, which is not often when I am in your company,' I snapped. 'And I am not senseless of others.' I stared into his old face, brows arched like he would place a hand on my head and bless me. 'And when did you ever laugh, you miserable great baboon?'

Morrison's eyes lit up with eager curiosity.

Dowling's expression was so saintly I thought he would sing a psalm. 'You are a good man, Harry, yet you wallow in a melancholic mope at the twitch of a mouse's whisker.'

'If you are the mouse, then I concur,' I retorted, to which he waved his paw at me in a manner so assured it made me want to kick his draggy arse. 'You are a great oaf.' I walked away.

The next cell contained a thin man who panted fast and shallow like a dog in pain. Chains about his ankles bound him to the stone wall and he lay sideways in the straw. A physician and assistant stood watching, waiting for something. The physician's large round face resembled a big pudding. Upon it balanced a thick and bushy wig. His assistant stood dutifully, bearing a pair of tongs to open the lunatics' mouths. The man on the floor stared out through bloodshot eyes. He breathed hard in and out of his nose before vomiting violently against the bars. The physician grunted in satisfaction and scrawled an entry into a large black book.

'What did you give him?' I demanded.

The physician turned to regard me. 'Tobacco.'

I eyed the mess with disgust. 'Why do you not just whip them as you used to?'

The physician regarded me with similar abhorrence before moving to the next cell.

Morrison grabbed my sleeve and bid me stop. 'If you want to view the whippings then you must come at three o'clock tomorrow,' he whispered.

I shook my head, appalled. 'So still you beat the sin away like the dust out of a carpet?'

'It is how we help them be rid of the evil within,' Morrison assured me. 'The physician comes in and purges them all once a week, the astrologers make them all amulets they may wear about their necks, and we are told to whip them.'

I walked further on down the corridor, searching for the shine of metal against grey-white skins. 'I don't see amulets about their necks.'

'They are lunatics, sir,' said Morrison. 'If we left the amulets about their necks then they would swallow them, else throttle themselves.'

I lifted a handkerchief to my nose. The whole house stank of bile. 'Morrison,' I said with great deliberation. 'We thank you for the tour thus far, but methinks we might proceed hastier.'

He bowed. 'As you say, sir.'

So we walked down the narrow corridors, Morrison behind us rapping his stick against any body part that strayed beyond the bars. We saw men and women, the frantic, frozen and insensible, but none that might be recognised as the brother of an earl. When we reached the Abraham Ward, Morrison held out an arm inviting us to return from whence we'd come. A thin man approached me from behind and kept tapping me upon the shoulder. He reminded me of Newcourt.

'Which of these might be related to nobility?' I asked.

An iron glint formed a grey sheen upon Morrison's eyes.

'There is one man here that is brother to the Earl of St Albans,' I asserted.

'What makes you think it?'

'Lady Wharton told us it,' I lied.

Morrison rubbed his arm over his head and pulled a face. 'There are two others living here,' he said at last. 'One might be the man you seek.'

'One would be Daniel,' Dowling guessed. Daniel was a giant, once Oliver Cromwell's porter. Like Cromwell before he died, he nurtured an unreasonable obsession with God and all things godly. 'He has his own library,' Dowling told me as if I did not already know it.

'Aye, he does,' said Morrison, 'and it is best to leave him in it, sirs, for he is a most devout prophet, and prophets loudly to all that will hear it. Not in the manner of a lunatic, but in a way that upsets the other lunatics.'

A version of Dowling, I considered.

'Who is the other?' I demanded, impatient.

'Edmund Franklin. Not so famous. Mr Gallagher, the steward here, will not have him with the other lunatics.'

'Why not?'

Morrison clasped his hands in front of his chest. 'He is the most dangerous of all the lunatics. If aroused he makes a noise like the beasts.'

'You keep him together with Daniel?'

'Aye, sir. Mr Gallagher decreed it.' Morrison nodded. 'Daniel will not speak when in the presence of Franklin, and Franklin stares at Daniel, which keeps him quiet besides.'

'And Edmund Franklin is related to nobility?'

Morrison sucked in his breath between his teeth. 'He may be. I have not been here long, so cannot be sure.'

'Might Pateson tell us, or Gallagher?' Dowling demanded.

'Mr Pateson has not been here for a week or so, and Mr Gallagher is not here today.'

'Where is he?'

'Perhaps he is sickly,' said Morrison.

'Well then, let us see Franklin.'

'There is little object in it,' Morrison wrung his hands. 'For he is a lunatic and talks to no man.'

'Still, we would see him,' I insisted.

'I don't take no man into Franklin's cell,' Morrison protested.

'We are King's men, Morrison, and will go where we please,' I said.

'You would see Edmund Franklin then,' Morrison whispered, as if it were a great calamity. He turned and led us into the nave of the church, the windows of which were broken. The roof opened to the blue sky above.

'Ye can discern the face of the sky and of the earth; but how is it that ye do not discern this time?' Dowling shared one of his Bible quotations with us.

Morrison stared at the butcher as he did the inmates. 'It is just before twelve.'

'He refers the ungodliness of the age or some such thing,' I explained. 'He does it a lot.'

Morrison nodded at Dowling, impressed. 'As you say.'

He bustled ahead on little legs. Heavy wooden doors bolted with metal staves barred the way ahead. 'The sacristy is empty these days.' Morrison withdrew his key. 'Not so the chapter house. I am the only steward allowed access.' He opened the door, deliberately slow. 'You must wait here, while I check what humours flow within him. Wait a moment.' He slipped inside the door and pushed it behind him, leaving it ajar.

I heard words within, low and soft. Then Morrison emerged.

'Did the physic purge these two?' I asked.

Morrison shook his meaty head. 'The clerics don't venture in here neither. The last man to beat Franklin left here more distracted than he, and none could make a mark on Daniel.' His face was red and wetter than before. 'You may go in, but only for a short time.'

We ascended into Heaven. From a stinking gloomy dungeon, awash with urine and foul discharge, into this fresh space with clean straw upon the floor and a thick shaft of yellow light cutting through from a small rectangular window high opposite our heads. Everything bathed in holy suffusion.

Inside to the left stretched one wall of iron bars, to the right another. Inside the cell to our left sat a huge man upon a chair so vast it resembled a throne. He sat with his back to the other cell, facing the wall, staring ahead, body rigid. The books upon the shelves on the wall said this was Daniel. Franklin stood watching from behind the bars of his cell, looking like he had just feasted on something rich and bloody. It seemed we interrupted something.

Morrison cleared his throat, nervous, daring to look upon Franklin for only a moment. 'Franklin is to your right. You may stay a few minutes and knock upon the door when you are ready to depart.' The door closed behind.

I approached the cell bars, heart pounding. Dowling trod as graceful as a drunken drayman behind me. Franklin turned his back on us when we reached the cell door.

'Good day, Mr Franklin.' I could think of little else to say.

The lunatic turned his head slowly, framed in a bright shard of the blessed light. I stared into the face of a demon. Big brown eyes stared out beneath a bony brow, no eyelids, eyelashes or eyebrows visible. His mouth hung open as if he waited to be fed. He cocked his head, a giant bird eyeing a worm.

'You are the brother of Thomas Wharton?' I asked.

A line appeared on his brow and he crept closer. Greasy raven hair looped in long slick curves. He drew a long black cloak about his figure, beneath which protruded exceedingly thin white legs, naked, and covered with tiny red sores. He clutched at the bars with his fingers, then leaned forwards and licked one, up and down. His eyes scanned every detail of my body, from my shoes to my hair, then lingered upon the area between my legs. He drew back his lips as if to bite. His teeth were deep yellow, crooked and cracked.

'I don't know if he talks,' I whispered to Dowling.

Franklin jumped, as if startled. His gaze flicked between us. Then he drew back his head, looked to the ceiling and screamed, a long piercing shrill, so loud it hurt my ears. He was immediately echoed by howls from within the asylum, a baying chorus of wails and shrieks.

The door opened, and Morrison bustled in, twitchy and afraid. He watched Franklin as he breathed deep into his chest and drew a finger across the edge of his tongue, before turning and withdrawing into the gloomy depths of his cell.

'Now you must go.' Morrison pulled at my sleeve. 'He will not talk, never has talked. I don't know what you hope to gain by being here.' His brow glistened wet and his lip speckled with beads of sweat. 'You leave when he demands it, and he has demanded it.'

We left the way we came, past the cells, the eyes, the shuffling, the misery and anger. I sensed an edge that was not there before. Morrison seemed keen for us to be gone as quick as he could walk us to the front door.

'Will you be coming back?' he asked as we emerged beneath the blessed sunshine.

'I hope not, Mr Morrison.' I contemplated the filthy yard. 'You spoke lightly of the pest before. Do you truly have no dread of it?'

He laughed quickly, eyes betraying his true fears. 'There is much to be afraid of in the world, would ye not say?'

'Aye.' Dowling wrapped an arm about his shoulders and squeezed him hard. 'Fear not though; for God hath heard the voice of the lad where he is. Get ye to church and God will look after you.'

Morrison wriggled free of Dowling's clutches before bidding us a quick farewell. He pushed the door closed behind, leaving us to contemplate the filth ahead of us. Two rats, black and bristling, scurried about the wheels of the decrepit coach, long scaly tails dragging in the dirt.

So Wharton did indeed have a lunatic brother. How he fathered a child was a mystery to me, but not one I dwelled on for long. From the plague pit and asylum, the only sensible destination was back behind the city walls, protected from the sickness. But I had promised to look for James and the pest-house was the most likely place.

I walked with Dowling to Cripplegate at least and bid him farewell. He was keen to hurry away, with duties to perform for the parish.

It was but a short walk across the stinking expanse of Moorfields, up Moorgate, to the Cripplegate Pest-house and the pit next to it. The pest-house was not a house at all, but a shabby congregation of long wooden sheds that stood here since the last great plague thirty years ago.

A tall man strode out of the nearest shed with shirt sleeves flapping and a rich mane of dark hair bouncing above a long straight head. 'What-ho!' he called without stopping. 'What do you want?'

'You are the physician?' I asked.

'Yes.'

I hurried after him. 'A man called James, a servant in the Willis household at Seething Lane. Did he arrive yesterday or today? I would see how he fares.'

'James?'

'Aye, of the Willis household.'

'Ah, yes,' he grimaced. 'He had a fever when he came. Ye might find him over there.' He stopped and pointed at the third shed back. 'I will attend to him shortly.' He waved a hand dismissively and walked away. I headed to the shed, though my legs did not will it.

Smoke drifted gently out the open door, a thin black smoke forming a protective barrier against the dangers of the air without.

I approached with caution. From outside I heard the sound of men groaning, peppered with occasional sharp shrieks of agony. Through the cloud of smoke I saw cots, ten of them, side by side with a narrow corridor along their feet, each one occupied. The walls and roof were made of planks, light shining through thin cracks in the wall, roof newly pitched. They said few died here, yet it was hard to credit. Fill a room with sick men; what prospect for recovery?

I walked down the corridor as quiet as I could. Some didn't move, most writhed in pain. Once more I felt the terror, that one of these men might sit up straight and stare at me, that the pest itself might pounce upon me and alight upon my breast with talons of thorn.

None resembled James, though I found it difficult to recall what James looked like. 'James?' I called softly. Two men stirred and cast a bleary eye in my direction, provoking me to leave quick.

I moved to the next shed, which was larger. A woman carried a pail of water, tending to all as if they were her own. Another woman lay motionless, black hair fallen in limp strands across her pale face. Her brown eyes were dull and cold, reminding me of a candle at the end of its wick. Upon her neck grew a large yellow growth, the bubo. I had not seen one so close. It lay like a giant leech, buried beneath her skin, blackness about its edges. Once ye had the bubo upon you then your only hope was to have it lanced. Yet mostly they lay too deep. I stepped back quickly, again unable to linger, and moved to the next shed, which is where I found James.

I recognised him instantly. He lay bent, staring at the ceiling. Last time I saw him his face beamed alive and ruddy, hair spiked in all directions, eyes full of young courage and innocent of pain. Now he shivered, white as ice, eyes cloudy as an old man's, hair matted in soaking plaits. Blood flecked his chin. Then he jerked and lay taut.

He was but a boy. Why had I not stopped him when he first went to lay hands upon Hedges' infected body? I cursed myself and willed him to recover.

'James?' I whispered, but he did not stir. As I watched, a fly landed upon his nose and walked up his nostril and out of sight. By the time it walked out again, still James had not moved.

He was dead.

CHAPTER 6

To what part of the world, or of this kingdom, he might best apply himself to live in
Because the moon applied so strongly to the trine aspect of Jupiter, and that he and Venus were in Taurus, and the sign signifies Ireland; I advised him that Ireland would well agree with his constitution.

I ambled back into the city, cursing the twitchy nose that led me into such perilous predicaments. Why could I not be a sensible man? This was not a time to be wandering the streets looking for murderers, not while the sickness lay upon the city like a deathly cloud. I had little fear of pestilence when I was able to choose my passage through the streets, to walk only where the plague had not visited. But in only two days I had already ridden through St Giles, toured Bedlam and searched a pest-house. If the plague was indeed carried by sticky atoms, then my clothes were covered in them. Though this green suit was silk, quite new and very expensive, it would have to go, linen shirt and drawers besides.

I returned home, relieved to find Jane out. I disrobed carefully, using only my fingertips to touch the fabric. Then I threw it all in the fireplace and set fire to it. I imagined the sticky atoms writhing in agony and prayed none escaped. I dressed anew and hurried downstairs to find a pipe and tobacco. Tobacco was supposed to be the best protection against plague. Any remaining atoms I would smoke off.

I sat in my chair, in my front room, where usually I found both relaxation and solace. Not today. It was best this investigation be settled early, and Burke seemed to be prime suspect. We would track him down that afternoon, I resolved. Track him down, confront him, arrest him and leave London.

The front door crashed open.

'You have a visitor,' Jane appeared in the doorway. 'This is Owen Price and he is an astrologer.'

A short man with serious eyes entered the room. He wore the furry robe and thick felt hat that all astrologers wore. His face glowed red and glistened sticky wet, like he had just been born. He held up a large bag. 'I am told you are struggling to make an important decision?'

'I am?' I replied.

'He is,' Jane answered. 'I will talk to you after.' She stepped outside and slammed the door closed.

Price watched the door for a moment as if he feared it

might open again quick. 'Your maidservant tells me you seek guidance as to whether you should leave London or stay.' He pulled the table from the wall and opened his bag. 'Is that true?' he asked, eyes evasive.

I scratched my prickly scalp, annoyed. So Jane wanted the astrologer to persuade me to leave. I would have to play this intelligently. 'I had not thought to seek guidance from the stars,' I answered carefully.

From the bag he extracted a great bound book, a tarnished golden item resembling a skeleton of the earth bound in a woman's girdle, and a pointed stick. He laid them all upon a red velvet cloth, then pulled up a chair and bid me sit opposite. 'You appear to be wealthy,' he waved a hand about the room. 'Why would you stay?'

The hairs prickled on the back of my neck, for I suspected he mocked me. Much though I loved my little room, I would not call it splendid. The wainscotting was ancient and chipped, with little holes in it. I owned but two threadbare tapestries, both handed down to me by my parents. The tapestries had not been washed in my lifetime and their suspiciously idyllic country life scenes were practically invisible. What business was it of his anyway?

'Why would I not stay?' I replied. 'It is the parishes outside the wall that are worst affected. It has spread even as far as St Albans already. Inside the wall we are safer.'

'The plague breached the wall weeks ago,' Price

pointed out.

'Aye, but it hasn't spread,' I argued. 'And if you believe it to be unsafe, then why do *you* linger?' I knew the answer full well. A blazing star passed over London last December, and then again in March, a slow-moving dull object. The astrologers told us it foretold of a terrible judgement, a proclamation that served them well once the plague arrived. Now they all made fast fortunes. He stayed for the same reason I did—his own advancement.

'In these difficult times people are forced to make decisions upon which their lives may depend.' Price lifted his chin and spoke nobly. 'I provide a useful service.'

Just as I had justified my strategy to Liz Willis. It was like looking in a damp mirror. 'Your chart says you will not be touched, I suppose.'

'Indeed.'

At least he believed in this art he peddled. As did many others, the King included. 'Have you not been asked the question many times now? Could you not simply write us all a sign telling us to stay or to leave?'

His eyes widened in sweaty surprise. 'You have not been read to before?'

I shook my head wearily. 'Though now you'll tell me it depends upon the hour at which the question is asked. What I cannot fathom is how your reading depends on the hour when the plague itself is constant.'

'The answer is simple.' Price's nose twitched like a rabbit. 'You may ask only once. You may indeed discover a different answer each time you ask the question, but only the first answer is true.'

'Is now then a good time to ask?'

'Were I to work out my readings aforehand then the readings would have no value,' Price explained. 'That is the rule.'

'Very well, Mr Price,' I consented. 'Tell me what to do.' I sat back and readied to watch him.

He nodded happily, opened his tome to a fresh page and stabbed his quill into an inkpot. 'So will I draw the twelve houses of Heaven.' With great diligence he scratched out a sequence of cross-hatched boxes. 'Now will I write in the day of the year and the time.' Which he proceeded to do with utmost care. 'Now we can assess your fate through the asking of several questions.' He sat back. 'First, I might ask if you are likely to live long, which is a question of the first house. Or I might ask if you shall have children, a question of the fifth house. The sixth house might tell us of disease, though it would be better if you had the disease first.' His smile faded. 'The eighth house shall tell me of your death, the ninth house the wisdom of a long journey, the tenth house whether or not you shall acquire high office and the eleventh house if you shall have the thing you wish for.'

I immediately thought of Liz Willis. I unfolded my arms and leaned forwards. 'All sound interesting to my ears.'

He seemed pleased, and set to penning cramped little symbols all upon the lines, representing the different planets in whatever trajectories they might be today. I recognised the three sticks of Scorpio and the small head and long horns of Taurus. He incised his etchings with great seriousness, tongue stuck between his teeth so hard I feared he might bite off its tip.

I waited in stifling sufferance for longer than I thought possible before he smiled wistfully and coughed into his hand.

'Not good news?' I ventured.

'You are certain you have not asked these questions before?' he asked, brows arched hopefully.

I shook my head.

'Oh dear.' He returned to his book. 'I have rarely seen such a dismal prognosis.' He grimaced. 'The Lord of the Ascendant be under the influence of the Sun, which indicates combustion. Also it is unfortunate by the planet that has dominion in the eighth house.'

'What does that signify?' I asked, dry mouthed.

Price put his hands together and squirmed apologetically. 'That the sickness you are soon to be troubled with shall end your life.'

I felt a sharp pain in my belly. 'Plague, then.'

'The ascendant in the fifth house is Scorpio, which indicates ye shall remain barren.' His brows beetled together to form one thick black line. 'You don't have children now?'

'No,' I confirmed, busy reassuring myself that my belief in astrology was no greater than my belief in God.

'Have ye taken your urine to be inspected by a physician?' he asked.

'No,' I replied again. 'I am not sick.' Not that I knew of. Some men died sudden of the plague though. Like Hedges, one sneeze was all that signalled it.

'Aye, well, if you do contract the plague then rest assured ye will know of it.' Price pointed at the ink upon the page. 'The Lord of the sixth house is an earthly sign, which signifies a long painful fever.'

'Do you have no good news at all?' I demanded, angry.

'No.' Price shook his head regretfully. 'Your significators are extremely afflicted and the Lord of the first house be in conjunction with the Lord of the eighth house.' He leaned back on his chair and adjusted the heavy hat. 'Methinks I have said enough, Mr Lytle.'

'I think so too,' I agreed, 'but I don't see how this will help me decide whether to leave London or not. You are telling me I am bound to die of the plague whatever path I choose.'

'That is so.' Price lay his hands upon his belly. 'Though

it saddens me to say it.'

'Jane will not be happy with you,' I warned. 'She was hoping you would advise me to leave London forthwith.'

His half closed eyes opened wider and his mouth dropped an inch. He no longer looked smug. 'So she was.'

'Aye, and she is the one paying you.' I smiled.

Price stared. 'She is the querent then?'

'What does that signify?'

'It is complicated.' At last he removed the furry hat, revealing a thick mat of black hair, lain wet across his pate. 'I didn't know she was the querent.'

'Does that change the movement of the stars?'

'No indeed.' He wiped his wet palms upon his trousers. 'But now I am not sure if it is your reading I have prepared, or else that of your maidservant.' He bit his lip. 'I will have to take advice.'

A small knot of vengeful satisfaction quivered in the base of my stomach. It laughed. 'Methinks the best advice is not to tell Jane what ye have just told me.'

Price's eyes lit up. 'Perhaps if I were to prepare another reading for you and you were to pay me for it, then it would become clear.'

'I thank you for the offer, Mr Price.' I sat up straight and stretched. 'But I have digested sufficient of your words of wisdom this fine day. Though I will happily sit here while you prepare a reading for yourself. What befalls the man that disappoints a fiery woman.'

The door opened and Jane stood simmering in the doorway. 'What news?' she demanded of the astrologer.

Price fiddled with his pointy stick and replaced the dripping hat upon his round head. 'I was just informing Mr Lytle of the outcome,' he flustered. 'So, Mr Lytle.' His eyes begged for mercy. 'The separation of the Moon from the square of Saturn tells me you have strong conflicts as to what path you might choose to take.'

What was he up to? I decided to humour him. 'And what state is the Moon in?'

'Not good.' He shook his head grimly. 'It is wandering.'

'You imply it usually stands still?'

He sighed sharply. 'The wandering Moon indicates a path that leads nowhere in particular.'

'Which describes his life most eloquently,' Jane interrupted.

Enough. 'This is not what you told me before, Mr Price.'

Price lifted his brows. 'What did I tell you before, Mr Lytle? Perhaps you didn't understand.' He waited for me to say more, like a man who thinks he has won an important wager. He knew I would not tell Jane that either of us was predicted to die soon. Jane stared at me like she contemplated biting off my head.

'A lack of purpose, however, is not the only possible interpretation.' Price bowed his head as if in prayer. 'Your future is unclear. The question to ask yourself is which path leads to greatest certainty.'

He seemed to have finished.

Jane blinked and stared at him. 'You would be paid for such advice?'

'I am not finished,' he startled. 'Mercury is the Lord of the ascendant and Saturn is in conjunction with Taurus, and since Saturn is also the Lord of the sixth house then this tells us the evil influence is strong, and it is time for you to be attentive of what is going on around you, rather than within you. This is sound advice which, if you follow it, will guide you well.' He nodded slowly and returned Jane's gaze. 'And hear this.' He straightened. 'You are faced with a big decision.'

Jane started to growl, a discomfiting sound to those who had not heard it before. I began to enjoy the performance. 'Mars is conjunct with the cusp of the seventh, as is Gemini,' he said.

'What does that signify?' I encouraged him.

He leaned closer, crimson skull smelling of grease and sweat. 'When the choice comes, you must take the road leading north.'

'I took the road leading north yesterday,' I told him. 'No doubt I will have to do it again soon.'

'That is not what he means,' Jane hissed.

The door flew open and Dowling appeared, tired and grumpy.

'All well?' I asked.

'As well as it will be,' he groused. He regarded Owen Price's short round form huddled beneath his great furry coat. 'Are you not hot, sir?' he asked.

'He is an astrologer,' I explained.

'Aye then.' Dowling tore his gaze from Price. 'How fare thee, Jane?'

'What are you doing here?' she replied. She treated Dowling better than she treated me, as she did anyone who went to church on a regular basis.

Dowling eased his gargantuan frame onto one of my old chairs. 'I have come to plan what your master and I shall do next. We have some choices to make.'

'Choices?' Price repeated, eager, casting upon me a meaningful gaze.

'Aye,' Dowling growled. 'Choices.'

Price raised an eyebrow and tapped his nose while Dowling stared at him as though he contemplated kicking him out the front window.

'When the choice comes, you must take the road north.' Price declared, waving a finger in the air.

'Astrologer.' Dowling leaned over and slammed his book closed. 'We are at Bread Street. When I leave here I will go to my house at Newgate, which is north. Will that satisfy you?'

Jane did not protect the astrologer this time. She tossed her head and clicked her tongue, furious at his limp showing.

Price coughed and sought to hide his face, then concentrated on gathering his tools back into his brown bag. 'I will send you my bill,' he said, avoiding Jane's eye. He picked up the bag and hurried out the door.

The butcher watched him depart with great curiosity. 'I think that man took a bath this morning and got dressed before drying himself.'

'I told you,' I reminded him. 'He is an astrologer.'

'Astrology is foolery and those that practise it are cunning, irreligious and self-deluding.' Dowling snorted. 'Now will you sit here all day?'

Jane placed herself afore me. 'What did Owen Price say to you before I came into the room?'

'It was difficult to fathom,' I replied. 'Something about Mercury being in opposition to Saturn, I think. Though it might have been Jupiter. Evidently I did not understand him well. Now I must fetch my jacket.'

She folded her arms and tossed her fiery red hair back off her forehead. 'What did he say to you?'

'He spoke with great prescience,' I assured her. 'He said that everyman should beware the plague, wherever he be and wherever he goes.'

'Good advice,' Dowling muttered.

'What?' Jane exclaimed, furious. 'He told you that? And what did you say to him?'

'I said little,' I answered. 'For I was not paying him, and I did not wish to be rude.'

Jane narrowed her green eyes and peered like she would see inside my head. 'What did he say?'

'Little that made sense.' I tried to squeeze past her delicate frame.

She let me leave, mouth hanging open, still trying to work out how Price had failed her so completely. I would not be wearing Owen Price's shoes. Jane knew where he lived.

Dowling followed me out, sombre. 'She will not rest until you take her north.'

'Aye,' I whispered. 'But I am not sure I want to go just yet.'

'Then you have my deepest sympathy and I pray to God He guides you wisely.' Dowling waved a mighty paw. 'Now let's get to Burke's house. I have the address.'

CHAPTER 7

Whether the goods be in the custody of the thief
Behold the signifier of the thief or thieves; and if he or
they give their power to another planet, the things stolen
are not in the keeping of the thief or thieves.

Henry Burke lived upon Leadenhall Street, not a sniff from
Aldgate. I tried knocking on the door while Dowling hid
inside the graveyard of St Katherine Cree, watching. Yet
the servant wouldn't admit me entry, nor give me any clue
as to Burke's whereabouts. I returned to the graveyard
frustrated.

'Keep walking,' Dowling hissed as I approached. 'I'll swear
he watches you from the house.'

I continued round the perimeter of the church and back
to where Dowling crouched, walking stooped so none
might see me over the wall.

'You saw him?' I whispered.

'Aye,' Dowling growled from beneath the shadow of a
yew tree, peering across the street. 'I saw someone with

nose pressed to the window, someone with a periwig and a bright white collar. Not a servant.'

'So he sits in his house and refuses guests.' I leaned with my back to the wall and plucked a sprig of wormwood. 'We wait for him to leave, follow him, and confront him in some public place where he cannot escape us.'

'He will not linger long,' Dowling predicted. 'He dashes about like a wormy dog.'

He lingered nearly two hours, as afternoon became evening. It wasn't until six that the front door opened and Burke's fleshy head appeared. He looked both ways up the street afore emerging into the humidity, pulling the door closed behind, and hurrying off up the street, short legs pumping hard. He wore a jacket and overcoat over a stiff black waistcoat, a ridiculous outfit for such a warm night. Wet hair stuck like plaster to his sweaty pate. At least he left the periwig behind.

We followed his bouncing buttocks west along Leadenhall before they turned right up King Street toward the south gate of the Guildhall, the very same place I toiled for Thomas Player. It was easy to follow from a distance, for every second house was closed and the streets were almost empty.

Burke marched beneath the south porch, across the marbled hall, and out into the courtyard. He stopped for a moment before heading toward the chapel of St Mary

Magdalen, where these days they held the Court of Requests. Here apprentices sought their release, else otherwise made complaint against their masters. We gave him a few moments afore following him through the entrance and into the old church.

The main proceedings all happened at one end of the hall. A weary looking official stood upon a wooden lectern fielding the complaints of several men at once. Burke stood deep in conversation with another important looking fellow, speaking quick, arms and hands working hard. The official let him talk, nodding unhappily, then beckoned him toward a desk where he took a quill and wrote on a piece of paper. Burke waved the paper in the air, folded it carefully and slipped it into his coat. He drew a breath, scanned the room, then froze, staring in our direction. I looked away, bewildered that he seemed to recognise us, barely noticing the swish of a velvet jacket against my thigh. When I glanced again Burke stood stiff between two tall fellows, one fair, one dark.

The fair man swaggered, tall and strong, beaver fur hat cocked at an angle. A powder blue mouchoir billowed from his breast pocket, draped against the deeper blue of his smooth velvet jacket, same jacket that rubbed against me. He picked at his nose like he cared not who saw him. The older man wore a beautiful red silk suit and strutted, arrogant. His hair was black as coal, eyelashes long as a woman's. A small brown mole nestled beneath his left nostril.

The fair man wrapped an arm about Burke's shoulders and spoke into his ear, toying with the lapels of his coat. Burke slumped, shrank back into his jacket and dropped his gaze to the floor. Then suddenly, too fast for me to anticipate, the man with the hat caught my eye. I looked away quick, pretending a fascination with the proceedings afore us. A twitchy young man, with surly expression upon his spotty face, stood lonely at the bench.

Dowling tugged at my forearm. All three were gone. By the time we reached the courtyard they were out the gate, cutting the corner in front of St Lawrence Jewry. We gave them thirty yards lead before trailing them down the hill at a distance until they stepped into The Mermaid.

Dowling stopped behind the Standard and I poked him in the ribs. 'Ye cannot stop here, Davy, what if they pass through onto Friday Street?'

'There is more than one door?' He looked surprised. 'You go then. I'll run round to Friday Street and watch they don't leave. If they do, I will fetch you.' It was a scheme that appealed, for Dowling would stand out in The Mermaid like a duchess in a brothel. He detested taverns, and disdained those that frequented such establishments, myself included.

I bumped into the hostess afore I finished opening the

door. Though it was evening, most of the tables were empty and quiet; no sweet smell of tobacco, no singing, no laughter, nor any sign of Burke and friends. The hostess clutched her apron to her lap and led me through a thin cloud of acrid smoke toward the fireplace.

I spoke low into her ear. 'Do you know Henry Burke? He came in with two other men.'

Her hand alighted on my arm like a little bird. 'He is in conference, sir, and with men who will not countenance disturbance. You might wait.'

I allowed her to seat me at a small table of my own, next to the slow fire burning in the grate, a heady brew of tar pitch and frankincense. My eyes watered, but I stayed for the protection it offered from the plague.

She fetched a mug of ale, before drifting off, distracted.

No more than a dozen of us sat there in the wide open space and I was the only one to drink alone. I felt like the word 'spy' was writ upon my forehead. Time passed slow. Nerves stretched tight inside my chest, taut and fine-tuned. I stared toward the corridor to my left, the passage that led to the private rooms. The hostess passed in and out two times, both times with a tray of three ales, each time smiling all airy and innocent.

I drank as slow as I could, yet my pot was long empty afore they finally appeared. Burke slouched, trudging slow, anguish painted in thick red strokes upon his ruddy cheeks.

I slumped into my chair, shy of being seen. I thought I watched discreetly until the one with the beaver hat stopped and stared straight at me. My heart tripped a beat. Not a muscle of his hard face moved. I pretended he wasn't there, but my skin burned hotter than the embers in the grate.

He kicked at the leg of my table. 'Who are you?'

I tried feigning injured innocence. 'No one.'

He smiled, a humourless expression of contempt. He rested his hands upon the table and lowered his young hard face into mine. 'You are a spy. Who do you work for?'

I signalled to the hostess and avoided his eye. 'I work at the Guildhall for Sir Thomas Player, and I live close by.'

'What is your name?' He spoke each word with great deliberation.

'What is *your* name?' I replied, indignant.

He breathed long and hard out of his nose then looked around as if he weighed up whether to punch me. I wondered where Dowling was. Was he not curious why we stayed so long? Instead the hostess came to my rescue, pecking at our sleeves and twittering in our ears.

The fair headed brute stood straight and stared down his nose like he would pick me up by the scruff of the neck and throw me out the door. The dark haired man placed a hand upon his shoulder and whispered into his ear, glancing at me long enough to ensure he remembered my face, then the two of them headed to the door. Before he disappeared, the fair haired man tapped his temple and pointed it at me, straight to the pit of my bowels. I breathed steady in an attempt to calm my beating heart.

Burke sat alone, slumped forward onto his elbows, raking at the back of his head with his fingers. I asked the hostess for another ale and watched him dig his nails into his scalp while I waited. He nursed his beer like it was his last.

Time to screw my courage to the sticking place. I sank another half a pot afore dragging myself to his table and falling into a chair at his side. 'Who is that coarse lout, talking to me like I be some common criminal?' I slammed my palm upon the table. 'Have I offended him?'

Though Burke's flesh was soft his eyes were callous. 'How should I know if you have offended him? I don't know who you are.'

'I am Harry Baker,' I lied. 'Who is he then? I saw you with him.'

Burke shook his head. The corners of his mouth sloped downwards and the lines about his eyes wrinkled in abject loneliness. He supped at his ale, saying nothing.

I pressed on. 'I worked as a clerk at the Tower, before the plague. Now the Tower is commandeered and I cannot work there until the sickness is lifted, and how long might that be? Every week the bills show more dead and the pest grows stronger.' All true, though I toiled at the Tower a long time afore the plague started and harboured no intention of ever seeking employment there again, sickness or not.

Burke grunted.

I dangled some bait. 'My maidservant would have me leave because she is afraid to stay, yet I cannot persuade her that to leave would be doubly dangerous.'

Burke scowled at me. 'Your maidservant.'

I waved a hand. 'She is insistent.'

'Hah!' Burke exclaimed. 'You have problems with your maidservant.'

'Every man has his problems.' I did my best to act offended. 'What great problems do you have?'

Burke snorted and sat sullen.

'I have enough money to live a few years, if I live so long,' I taunted him again. 'And I am not sure I want to be a clerk again, for I find little fulfilment in it.'

Burke's lip curled in filthy disdain. 'You lack fulfilment?'

I did my best to appear as miserable and self distracted as he. 'Aye, I am not fulfilled.'

'Sir, I don't know who you are, but look about you.' His small red mouth pouted angrily amidst the abundance of his face. 'Death is in all parts, and you complain you are not fulfilled?'

I waggled a finger as Dowling often did at me. 'Verily I say unto you, this generation shall not pass away, till all be fulfilled.'

'What nonsense!' Burke sneered. 'You have sufficient funds to last a few years? I once had prospect of becoming the wealthiest merchants in London, until cheated by nobility.'

'Nobility?' I laced my words with doubt.

'Aye, nobility.' Burke gripped his pot so tight the veins on the back of his hand stood out like roots from a tree. 'Now I have more debt than cash and will likely lose my business, my house and all else that I own.'

I patted his sleeve. 'Well, let me buy you another ale and a pipe.'

'Aye, well, thanks,' he ceded reluctantly.

We both shuffled upon our chairs and worked out where best to put our elbows. He blinked slowly while staring at the table. The wench appeared quickly with fresh mugs and full pipes.

'You say nobility cheated you.' I sucked at the pipe and blew smoke out upon my own arms. 'That would make the nobility most ignoble.'

Burke glared at me. 'You worked at the Tower, you say?'

'Aye,' I nodded keenly, 'and in my role enjoyed insights into the machinations of the court. The dignity and wisdom of our noble lords never ceased to impress.'

Burke's head bobbed up and down, incredulous. 'How so?'

How so indeed? All I learned was that our noble lords maintained their status and fortune by means of ruthless self interest. So I shrugged and tried to look smug.

'Are you really such a fool?' Burke asked.

I smiled. 'You say I am a fool, yet you are the one cheated by nobility.'

'You say *I* am a fool?'

I puffed again at the pipe. 'It was you said it, not I.'

'You listen to me.' He jabbed a short stubby finger at my chest. 'One lord cheated me, guaranteed by another!' His face turned bright red.

'So you say.'

He growled and shook his wobbly head. 'He said he planned a great party for the King and invited me to supply the wine. Every vintner in the city coveted the contract.'

'Guaranteed by a lord,' I prompted.

'Aye!' Burke crashed his fist upon the table.

'What lord?'

He wiped a sleeve across his mouth. 'It is no business of yours.'

'Then you should reclaim your money,' I said.

'I have tried every avenue to reclaim it,' he snarled.

'Those men you were with,' I realised. 'They represent this lord.'

'Enough!' Burke slammed the palm of his hand upon the table.

'No business of mine,' I remembered. 'Why did you not simply take back the wine once this nobleman didn't pay for it?'

Burke rumbled, a deep guttural noise speaking of wretched pain. 'He is a devil and guards himself with four black dogs. Black beasts no man dare cross, for they will rip you with their teeth and tear you with their claws.'

'Dogs or men? I am confused.'

'Violent men with no fortune to lose, kennelled at Winchester's Palace on the south side of the river.'

'Men are men, and dogs are dogs,' I said. 'Who feeds them anyway?' I laughed heartily and cuffed him about the shoulder.

Burke grabbed my wrist and held it tight. 'Don't mock me!'

'I do not mock you,' I protested, pulling back my hand. 'Yet you must concede it is an unlikely tale.'

He sighed, anger exhausted. 'You are a clerk and live a closeted life. I should not rile at your ignorance.'

I pretended to take offence. 'You call me ignorant? So I tell you I doubt your tale, for it reads like fiction. Four men you call black dogs. Four men are four men, and you let four men stand between you and your prospects.' I clicked my tongue.

Burke beheld me keenly. The dark clouds of ale and anger lifted, revealing sharp clear eyes. 'Who are you?'

'Harry Baker is my name, formerly a clerk at the Records Office, now poor and unfulfilled.' I lifted my pot.

'You came here to find me.'

'I came here to escape my maidservant.'

'No,' he snapped. 'You ask too many questions about Wharton and his colleagues. No idle curiosity, methinks.'

'All curiosity is idle,' I replied. 'I drank alone when you came in and disturbed my peace.'

'Nay, nay.' he shook his head sharply. 'I have lived long enough now to smell deception. God knows I have experienced sufficient of it, and I smell it about your person as strong as old cheese. Methinks I saw you at my house earlier this afternoon. So now I will take your leave.'

I remained seated as he stood. Then he leaned across and spoke low and wet into my ear. 'Beware that coarse lout,' he warned. 'Methinks he will wait for you on the street. When he talks to a man that way he usually means to kill him.'

I finished my ale and left through the other door, hurrying out on to Friday Street where I prayed Dowling awaited. The street was dark and quiet. I placed a hand upon my chest and breathed deliberately slow. I didn't want to leave this place alone. A heavy hand landed upon my shoulder.

'Your breath stinks of ale,' Dowling whispered into my ear.

'Burke insisted,' I replied, hiding my relief. 'Now walk me to Cheapside.' I still had one last errand to run before curfew, a task to be completed without Dowling.

At Seething Lane Liz opened the door before I finished knocking. I reckoned she waited by the door for her father's return. Her lips were blue and the skin about her cheeks stretched dry and tight. I felt guilty I had not come straight from Cripplegate.

'Did Oliver find him?' I asked, praying he got there before me.

Her eyes ranged the cobbled street behind, hair gently rippling in the evening breeze. 'He is not returned.'

The nerves in my gut shrunk upon themselves. 'I'm sorry.' I stepped back into the street.

'Why did you come, Harry?' she asked, distracted.

Trapped. 'I found James.'

She held herself tight about her chest. 'Where?'

In the pit by now. I eased into the house, determined to talk where she might grieve in private. I climbed the same stairs we climbed that morning, she following.

Once she entered the room she slammed the door closed behind and stood afront of me, legs apart, fists clenched. 'I asked you where?'

'I found him at the Cripplegate Pest-house,' I said. 'You said he was fevered. So he was.'

She clasped her hands to her mouth, misunderstanding what I tried to explain. 'God have mercy! We must make sure he is well cared for.'

I caught a breath and felt my face flush. 'I am sorry, Liz, but James died.'

She didn't weep, nor scream, nor indeed react much at all. Her face paled from white to whiter, and the fingers of her clasped hands clawed at each other.

'Well then,' she whispered. She hesitated a moment. 'Thank you for coming, Harry.' She shivered, opened her mouth and closed it again, then walked quickly from the room, taking a piece of my pickled soul with her. I trudged home, exhausted and miserable.

My plans to go straight to bed were thwarted. Jane stood afront of me so I couldn't pass, dress billowing as though fanned by some gust of fury emanating from somewhere betwixt her legs. She held the remnants of my burned clothes up against my nose. 'Where have you been?'

I attempted to squeeze past, but she threw herself against the wall to prevent it. In her rage she forgot to maintain the distance between us and I felt the wetness of her breath against my throat. I stopped trying to escape and moved so she breathed against my mouth. 'Bedlam,' I confessed.

Her arms fell to her sides. 'Bedlam?'

'Aye.'

'And did you see the pit there?' she hissed.

'Aye, I did.'

'Full, was it?'

'Aye, full,' I said. 'You can smell it this side of Cripplegate.'

'You can smell it this side of *Watling Street!*'

I placed a hand on her shoulder. An image of the black bubo upon the dying woman's neck shaped itself unbidden in my mind, swollen and growing still. 'Aye, terrible to behold.'

She threw my hand away. 'You walk into the midst of it and bring it back with ye.'

I stepped quickly past. 'I burned all my clothes and smoked a pipe.'

She pushed me in the back as I headed toward the kitchen. 'Why go there at all?'

'The King,' I answered.

'The King?' she repeated slowly, 'asked you to go to Bedlam?'

'In a manner.'

'What manner? The King left London two weeks ago.'

'Lord Arlington then,' I conceded.

'Lord Arlington told you to go to Bedlam?'

I edged about the kitchen table so it stood between us. 'He told us to find out who killed Thomas Wharton. His wife told us to go to Bedlam,' I lied.

'What is at Bedlam?'

'A lot of lunatics and a pest pit.'

'What is that to do with the death of her husband?'

'That remains to be established.'

'The King is at Hampton Court,' she repeated, fury mounting within her slender frame.

I took a step toward the stairs. 'Aye, Jane, so he is, and we are still here in London where I will likely remain until I find out who killed Thomas Wharton.'

'Harry.' She seized my jacket and gazed into my eyes. 'We must leave *soon*, afore it is too late.'

I pulled away. 'Then I must find out who killed Wharton soon, afore it is too late.' I was tired, too tired to talk. I ignored the hurt I saw in her face and hurried upstairs afore I said something even more loathsome. I crept into bed feeling like the Devil himself.

Just as my eyes closed so Dowling's fist pounded at the door.

CHAPTER 8

Arguments of death

When the five hylegical places at the hour of birth, at time of decumbiture of the sick, as also the Lord of the ascendant, are oppressed, judge death immediately to follow.

We heard the crowd before we saw the light. A hundred men at least. Half the gathering stood back, watching, torches held high. The other half formed a tight heaving mass, surging again and again against the front of The Bull Head tavern. Apprentices mostly, giving vent to their ungratified appetence. I kept my distance, anxious to avoid the mass of sweaty bodies, wet and dripping. Somewhere in the tavern afore us another man was murdered.

'They gathered two hours ago,' Dowling said. 'As soon as the killing was discovered.'

'Why?'

Dowling put his mouth to my ear. 'Every event is a sign these days, Harry. If a man is murdered in a tavern, then God is angry with those who drink.'

Which was ludicrous. It wasn't Satan who turned the water into wine. I stood upon the tips of my toes, yet still couldn't see what happened at the front of the throng.

'How will we get in?' I asked Dowling, for he was taller.

'The only way is through.' Dowling looked east. 'They have blocked the alleyway leading to the back.'

'Hold!' a deep voice cried. The crowd hushed a moment, a pack of dogs scenting new prey. 'Hold!' it cried again, from near the tavern door.

'Is that Benson shouting?' I asked. The landlord.

'No,' Dowling stretched his neck. 'It's Andrew Vincent, standing on a box.' Which explained why Dowling's jaw twitched.

Vincent was a dissenter, forbidden to preach by the Conventicle Act. Yet with so many clergy having fled London, many parishes welcomed any man of God with open arms. Since most of the Church and the Court left London weeks ago, few resisted their reappearance. Just Sir John Robinson and his garrison at the Tower. Dowling bristled like a wounded bear.

We eased our way forwards, Dowling barging aside ill-tempered adolescents. We closed to within ten paces of Vincent, close enough to see the deep lines scored upon his mouldering white head. His voice belied his age, echoing cavernous and rich. He lifted a finger to his lips and created a hush.

'Come forth, all you drunkards,' he exclaimed, 'who have intoxicated your brains with the fumes of excessive drinking.' The apprentices voiced their appreciation, forbidden to drink by their masters, jealous of those that partook. The crowd squeezed in on us, greasy, malodorous and vicious.

'Come forth, you who have drowned your natural wit and ingenuity, which might have rendered you useful in the church where you lived.' Vincent opened his arms as if he would welcome the whole crowd into his house, and paused to observe the effect of his words. A vein pulsed upon his forehead and his skin turned red. 'You would have your strong drink without measure, and now also you shall have a cup to drink the wine of the wrath of the almighty God. By the wine of the wrath of God, we mean especially the dregs and bottom of it; the great *plague* and other eternal punishments of Hell!' He lifted his arms to the heavens and the apprentices howled. 'It will be most fierce, and so powerful that all the powers of men and devils shall be unable to make the least resistance.'

Two apprentices eyed my silk jacket and twitched their noses. I dug a fist into Dowling's ribs. 'We have to keep going,' I whispered.

Vincent sucked in a deep breath. 'The wrath of God

will come upon all the hypocrites. The hypocrites are those full of rottenness. They make it their business to appear religious, but are rotten at heart and cover carnal designs with a cloak of profession. As their sin is most offensive unto God here, so his wrath will certainly come upon them with the greatest severity hereafter.' The crowd roared as one, sensing the possibility of redemption, for now he laid the blame for their sins at the feet of the clergy—those wretched cowards that fled the city.

I pushed harder against Dowling's back.

A long thin face leaned toward me and breathed foulness into my face. 'Where are you going?' it spluttered.

'Into the tavern,' I replied, wiping spittle from my face.

'You dare defy God's word?' he bellowed, ensuring others turned to watch.

'We are King's men,' I assured him, expressionless, 'and the King is God's agent on earth. We are sent here to investigate this murder.'

He leered. 'It is the act of the Lord God himself.'

An interesting theory, though hard to prove. Dowling looked over his shoulder. I caught his eye and jerked a thumb forward. He shoved hard, leaning into the wall of bodies afore us, pulling men aside by the collar. At the tavern door half a dozen apprentices exchanged insults with a gang of burly watchmen, pug-faced and ugly, itching to crack heads.

'John Cummins,' I called, recognising a short man amongst the watchers, flat-headed, with a scar upon his forehead.

'Harry!' He slid through the pack and stuck out his hand, wide grin slapped across his face. 'I haven't seen you for weeks. What you doin' here?'

'We've come to see the body.' I waved a hand at Dowling. 'We work for Lord Arlington.'

Cummins looked Dowling up and down. 'Him? He looks like a butcher.'

'He is a butcher and he works for the King too. We need to pass through, John.' Apprentices surrounded us, listening to our conversation with dull expressions.

Cummins stepped backwards into his colleagues, creating a corridor through which we gratefully passed. His smile vanished when two apprentices attempted to follow. He punched one in the stomach, the other fled.

Behind the front door George Monck watched down upon us with fierce intent from within a thick gold frame, silver armour draped in blue velvet. In the background a naval scene, the return of Charles to England, I supposed. It was Monck who financed Charles' to return to England in 1659, then famously held audience at this very tavern, drinking sack and doing his business.

I knew The Bull Head well, knew what a maze it was for the drunk and disoriented. The door to the left stood ajar. Four men sat about a round table playing at cards, mugs afront of them, legs laid out loose.

'What cheer?' I pronounced.

'All is cheerful,' replied one of them, face screwed up in concentration. 'So long as you don't drink the wine.'

The other three laughed as if it was the funniest joke in London. They all stank like they hadn't washed for a year, the acrid odour tempered by the thick cloud of tobacco smoke.

'Have you not drunk enough?' Dowling declared, disgusted.

'We can't get out,' protested one, laying a card upside down. 'They are all out there shouting of the evils of drink.' He belched.

'Where is Benson?' I asked. The landlord and lessee.

The man jerked a thumb then played a card. 'Back there with the barrel.' He shivered and shook his hands.

We left them to it and made our way deeper into the building through a passage bright with candles. More paintings of Monck, some of Charles II, lots of ships and battle scenes. We emerged into the main room where Monck had held court all those years ago. Long tables stretched the length of the room, mostly empty. Three men stood about a giant cask of wine in the corner.

'Benson,' I called out. 'What's the story?'

A tall fellow with grey hair turned calm brown eyes

upon me. 'Good day to you, Harry Lytle.'

'This is David Dowling.' I pointed at Dowling again. It felt strange dragging the pious butcher round taverns.

Benson stepped forth to shake Dowling's hand before standing back to fold his arms. 'Haven't had the barrel but two days. Tap stopped flowing this morning so I stuck a hook up the tap and poked it against something solid. Took the lid off and found the body.'

The top of the cask had been opened with an axe. A mop of black hair broke the surface and a pair of man's knees. The body was pushed in tight with thighs up against its chest; a big body. Dowling reached down and lifted the head up straight. Large nose, thick brow and heavy square jaw.

Dowling peered into the half open eyes. 'Recognise him?'

'No,' I answered, feeling sick. I looked to Benson.

Benson shrugged. 'None of us know who he is.'

'You hadn't opened the cask before?' I asked.

Benson shook his head. 'Only just delivered. Must have come with him inside it.'

'Time to get him out of it.' Dowling rolled up his sleeves. 'What are your names?' he asked Benson's men.

'Cuttinge,' said one.

'Sadler,' said the other.

'One arm each, gentlemen, and I will take his legs,'

PAUL LAWRENCE

Dowling instructed, eyeing my fine jacket. 'Mr Lytle here is squeamish.'

The three of them took off their poor jackets and shirts.

'Lift him by the arms, fellows.' Dowling pushed them forwards. They stared into the wine, reluctant. 'There is no art to it,' Dowling urged, impatient.

Cuttinge sighed and Sadler stuck out his bottom lip afore both bowed down and touched the corpse upon the shoulders.

'He is slippery,' Cuttinge complained.

'Get a grip on him,' Dowling growled.

They leaned down, grasped the body gingerly, and attempted to lever him up straight.

Dowling peered up from beneath his grey brow, patience waning. 'You need to pull harder.'

'He's big,' Cuttinge gasped, tugging.

Dowling walked about briskly and helped Sadler get a grip upon the man's wet skin. 'Stand him up and I'll lift him by the legs.'

The three of them heaved the body up high, grunting loud. Sadler grappled it about the chest and attempted to drive backwards with his feet, but slipped over and hit the ground hard. The body slid back into the vat of wine until Dowling seized it by the underarms. Sadler beat his fist upon the floor and cursed out loud, then leapt to his feet in foul temper. This time they organised themselves more effectively and succeeded in working the body free and easing it to the floor.

'God save our souls,' Benson said, solemn. The huge figure lay upon its back like a great hairy baby, legs akimbo, belly round and distended, mouth hanging loose. His skin gleamed and the black hair all about his body lay in long bedraggled mats. I could not help but regard his long thin yard, trailing proudly to the floor.

Dowling knelt and rubbed his hands gently upon the man's bulging stomach. 'Hard as a drum,' he pronounced, curious.

'The dead bloat, do they not?' said Benson.

'Not like this.' Dowling prodded hard with one finger. 'His belly is full, stretched unnatural.' He pushed down with both palms. 'I reckon he be full of wine.'

'Oddfish,' I reckoned.

Dowling stuck a finger betwixt the man's wet jaws, then scratched his head and returned to the barrel. 'No man could drink this much. Someone forced him to drink.' He searched for a cup and dipped it in the cask before holding it up to the light. 'Vomit.'

'Best not tell the customers,' said Benson.

Sadler moaned and stuck out his tongue. Cuttinge put a hand upon his own stomach and paled. Beads of sweat erupted from his temples.

'He was alive when they dropped him in the barrel.'

Dowling placed the cup upon a tabletop. 'Yet I don't understand why there be not more vomit in the wine, for with that much fluid in his stomach, he could not help but discharge it.' He rubbed a finger upon the body's lips. 'You can see foam about his mouth, but not much of it.'

He pulled the man's lip down with his fingers. Something caught his eye and he peered deeper into the mouth. 'There is bruising here.' He pushed two fingers down the man's throat and ran his fingers up and down.

'Perhaps he was a fat man,' Benson suggested. 'Most fat men's bellies are hard.'

'No.' Dowling struggled to his feet and scratched his head, perplexed. He stared at the offending gut as though he wished to burst it.

Benson nudged me in the ribs. 'When can you take him away?'

'Stand aside,' Dowling muttered. He stepped up so his feet touched the torso, then turned round so his heels were against the ribcage. He crouched and leaned back with his right hand to hold the body's face flat against the floor, then launched himself upon the swollen stomach with all his weight. He looked over his shoulder to see what effect he had, then bounced again as hard as he could. He kept bouncing, grunting with the exertion.

'Have ye known him long, Harry?' Benson whispered.

'Aye,' I nodded. 'He doesn't frequent taverns. What are

you doing, Davy?'

'Wait.' He turned about, placed one palm upon the other, both upon the corpse's belly, and pushed as hard as he could. 'Ah!' he exclaimed triumphantly, as a flood of wine and gastric juices gushed from the corpse's mouth. He reached down into the vile stream and extracted a long smooth cylinder, a thick cork. 'Whoever killed him filled him with wine, then pushed this down his throat. He died of suffocation.'

Benson watched the contaminated wine flow across his floor and sighed.

'Where did you get this barrel from?' I asked.

'Same as always,' Benson said. 'Henry Burke.'

CHAPTER 9

If a servant shall get free from his master?

If he demand—shall I be freed from the service or slavery of this man my master, in which I now live?—then see if the Lord of the ascendant be cadent from an angle.

We arrived at Burke's house before sunrise. Yet even as we arrived he clambered into a smart blue coach, which quickly departed, trundling across the empty cobbles, too fast for us to follow. 'Boggins!' I cursed.

I ran across the street and knocked upon the door. The servant who answered glowered furiously from beneath perspiring brow. 'I have an appointment with Henry Burke,' I lied.

'He's gone,' snapped the servant.

I feigned puzzlement. 'How peculiar. He was quite specific he wished to meet at six. He sought my advice on financial matters.'

The servant relaxed like I was the King himself, ready to cure all with a touch of his finger. The floor behind was dusty and unswept. A faded tapestry hung choking behind thick layers of dirt. 'Financial matters, you say? Are you his banker?'

'Aye, his banker.' I agreed. 'But he is gone, you say?'

The servant scowled. 'He won't be back for a week or more. Says he'll pay us when he returns.'

'A week or more?' I pursed my lips. 'Very well. Ask him to write upon his return and perhaps we might arrange another meeting. In September, perhaps.'

'Are you sure you are not supposed to meet him at the Guildhall?' The servant nudged me out onto the street. 'He said he is meeting someone there.'

'Ah!' I raised both brows. 'Of course.'

The servant shooed me away. 'Go then. Hurry!'

I walked as fast as I could, conscious the servant stood watching me. Dowling caught me up once we reached the quiet splendour of Cornhill.

'To the Guildhall,' I urged him, breaking into a trot.

Our steps echoed loud upon the empty cobbles, all hawkers and criers now banned by the Plague Orders. A cat disappeared down an alley, a rare sight since the Guildhall ordered them killed. A pale face stared out of a window, then quickly withdrew.

New Kings Street led into the heart of the Guildhall, the wide courtyard surrounded on all sides by the palatial magnificence of the hall itself. The street ploughed straight through the middle of the yard, up to the black mouth of the main entrance. Usually this courtyard was full of people, for the Guildhall stood at the heart of the city, but at this hour and in these times, it was deserted, save for three men stood together in the middle of the vast cobbled square. One was Burke. We stopped on Lothbury to spy from afar.

Burke stood with two big bags at his feet, talking to the same two men he met the night before. The fair haired man took one bag, then led him back toward where we hid. We withdrew into the early morn shadow and watched them pass by. The dark haired man walked behind, strolling slow, and we gave them long leash.

On Cheapside they stopped at the Tun, once a lock-up and now a cistern. Burke's attendants leaned languid against the battlements, facing east, while Burke stood with arms folded, fidgeting and staring south. They waited a while before the fair fellow led Burke away again, leaving the older man behind.

'You think he waits for others?' I whispered.

'No,' Dowling growled. 'Methinks they are cautious.'

He pulled me by the sleeve down the narrowest of filthy alleys, floor awash with thick streams of feculence, onto Iron Monger Lane, and through the grounds of the Mercers' Hall. We emerged onto Cheapside in time to see Burke and the younger man turn down Bucklersbury, a narrow street winding south and east. We scuttled after them, sticking to the shadows of the black eaves.

I cast a glance west to see if the other noticed us, but he had gone. We hurried down Wallbrook, sticking to the shadows. They dashed across the crossroads with Cannon Street, not once looking back. Again I glanced behind as we hastened after them, afraid the other followed us. A wolf ahead and a wolf behind. Not a pleasant prospect. Dowling grabbed me by the coat and dragged me this time into the mouth of Tun Wheel Lane. Burke and partner disappeared out of sight toward Thames Street.

I wrenched at his hand. 'We will lose them!'

'Wait,' he urged. Sure enough, the older man slipped out of the entrance to Elbow Lane, swarthy-faced and watchful. I held my breath as he scanned north and south before heading after the other two.

'How did you know?' I whispered, hoarse.

'I felt it,' Dowling answered. 'They are sly. Now we keep going.' He crept out back onto Dowgate Hill and set off again.

The older man turned right onto Thames Street, back toward the Vintners' Hall, then left to the river.

Three Crane Lane was grim and dark, even in the early morning sunshine. The houses on one side stretched over the alley leaning against the houses from the other, shutting out all light from above. The air hung rank and foul, a steaming brown cloud. Insects swarmed about my head, an army of bloated overfed flies, guarded at their flanks by an assortment of other insects—biting, stinging and cutting. Large black rats sat brazenly in the open, chewing upon the rotten debris that coated the alley floor in a thick layer of slippery slime. I could barely discern the outline of the man we followed. He steadied himself with hands against both walls as he made his way down the slope. Then he vanished into a doorway halfway down.

We waited at the top of the passage to see what transpired. Soon we heard faint chattering and saw two black shadows form amidst the murk. Burke's two guardians trod gingerly up the incline, heads lowered, arms out to their sides, balancing. We dropped back to the corner of Sopar Lane, from where we saw them brush down their fine clothes and smack their hands together afore heading west.

We tarried a while, cautious they might return, afore venturing downwards. I feared I might fall with every step, it was so slippery. We slithered down the hill as if skating on ice.

The house loomed tall and narrow, a decrepit stack of timber leaning forward into the alley as though it would keel over and die. Small rotten windows framed black glass, never cleaned. The front door stood propped open by an ankle-deep pile of shit and filth.

I stepped over the heap of rubbish into the room beyond,

a cramped space five paces square. The stink pervaded my nostrils like soup and lingered on the back of my tongue. I wanted to choke. I heard sounds of rustling, moving, faint squealing in the inky blackness.

There was a staircase in the corner. A sharp screech sounded close to my foot as I trod on something. The boards of the stair appeared bent and twisted. I eased my weight gently down upon the first step. It creaked loud, serving as a trumpet to announce our presence. I cursed and withdrew my foot.

'It is quiet up there,' I whispered.

'Aye, and dark.' Dowling nudged me forwards. 'He must be at the top of the house.'

The second step took my weight without complaint. Yet every other step squeaked or squealed, especially beneath Dowling's ponderous weight. By the time we reached the top of the stairs my skin prickled from head to toe, anticipating an attack at any moment from whoever waited above.

As my eyes accustomed to the gloom, I made out a mattress on the floor, thin and uneven, straw poking out of numerous small holes that peppered it like a long cheese. The smell was foul, wet and putrid.

By my reckoning there was but one set of steps left to climb. I peered up the stairway, discerning light at last. Still no sound, just the noise of my pounding heart and the low hiss of Dowling's laboured breathing. There seemed little to be gained by attempting to walk quiet, so I leapt up the stairs two at a time and jumped out into the space above.

'What in God's name are *you* doing here?' an angry voice barked. Burke glared, his glistening face burning fiery red.

'We followed you,' I replied truthfully.

Shards of light shone through tiny holes in the roof, onto the bent back of an artist sat hunched over a canvas clamped to an easel. He worked quickly, squirrel-hair brushes dancing in swirls of thick paint. 'You should not have come,' the artist said, without turning round.

Burke's two bags lay upon a cot in the corner of the room, beneath his jacket and coat. Next to the cot stood a small table with jug and a plate.

'Is this where you plan to stay the next few weeks?' I asked, incredulous. The air was stale and putrescent, the walls damp. Mould grew upon the rafters, green and grey.

Burke squeezed his knees together and clenched his fists. 'Who are you? How dare you follow me!'

The artist turned. 'They are agents of Lord Arlington. Harry Lytle and David Dowling.' He looked to me with bright intelligent eyes, shining out from a dirty face that had not been shaved for a week or more. 'Is it not so?'

The breath stuck in my lungs. How did he know?

Burke sneered, pebble eyes hid beneath a long dark

brow. 'Spies then?'

'Investigators,' Dowling snarled. 'You are the one skulking about London afraid to show your face.'

Burke straightened his jacket and lifted his chin. 'You said your name was Baker,' he said to me. 'You tried to get me to tell you things at The Mermaid last night.' He strode to where the artist still painted. 'I told him nothing, of course.'

'You told me a lord guaranteed your transaction with Wharton,' I reminded him.

'I did not tell you which lord though, did I?' He watched the artist, eyes wide and fearful. 'Tell him!'

The artist kept on painting. What was happening here? Burke did not present as a man with the wit or resolve to commit the murders we witnessed. He seemed scared of the painter, had seemed intimidated by the two men that fetched him here. 'No,' I agreed. 'You would not tell me that, nor would you tell Lord Arlington.'

'So you persecute me then, hound me. It is your doing I find myself in this poor hovel.' He put a hand to his nose and regarded the walls like they would close in and bury him.

'Hardly our doing,' Dowling snorted. 'Two men are dead. Wharton at the Vintners' Hall, as you clearly know, and another at The Bull Head, pulled from a vat of wine supplied by you.'

Burke blinked. 'Not by me, sir. I can assure you.'

'Aye, sold by you,' Dowling said. 'Delivered two days ago with a dead man inside it, belly full of wine and a cork in his throat.'

Burke opened his mouth and put his hands to his chin. He resembled an outraged washer woman.

'What *have* you been doing, Burke?' the artist murmured. 'I didn't realise what a murderous beast you really are.'

'None of it my doing,' Burke protested. 'Wharton cheated me, but what good is it to me he is dead? It will not get my money back.'

I cleared my throat. 'Revenge? Once he persuaded you your money was gone.'

He held out his hands as if he expected me to tie them. 'I have never killed a man, and if I did, would I kill him in my barrels, with my bottles?'

The artist sighed deeply and leaned back upon his stool. 'Burke did not kill Wharton, gentlemen. Surely that much is clear.' He stretched and yawned. 'You ought not have come here.'

I stepped forward to see what he painted. A large room, taller than ten men. A long gallery half way up the wall and a man hanging by the neck.

'What do you call it?' I asked, mouth dry.

'God's Black Finger,' he replied, cocking his head. 'Do you not recognise it?'

'I do,' I nodded. 'I recognise it very well, though I doubt the deed was God's doing.' I peered closer into the shadows of the gallery. Three men stood talking. 'You were there?'

'Not I.' The artist selected a fine brush and began to colour the fine clothes of the man in the middle. My clothes. Dowling was recognisable besides, and a giant in a black cloak. The perspective was from the far wall, someone well hidden.

'Then who?'

The artist laid down his brush and palette, and turned to me, mouth sad and regretful. 'It matters not, Lytle. You should not have come.'

Dowling leaned and placed his mouth against the artist's ear. 'What is your name?'

'John Tanner,' he answered. 'As I don't mind you knowing.' He tidied his brushes. 'For you will discover nothing else about me.'

His conceited arrogance pricked me hard. I drew back my hand and sent the brushes flying across the room. 'Talk to us,' I commanded. 'Who do you work for?'

He raised his brow and watched a brush roll slowly toward the top of the stair. 'I'll not tell you that,' he replied, calm. 'Nor will he.' He caught Burke's attention for a moment, his slate grey eyes steady and hard. 'Leave now. While you can.'

Fury welled within, which he watched without a trace of fear, only curiosity. As though he planned to paint my portrait. I felt naked and exposed.

'We will come back,' I said through gritted teeth.

Tanner set to gathering his brushes from the floor. 'I doubt it,' he grunted. 'Though should you prove me wrong, then I will be delighted to show you the finished painting.' He stood straight and bowed. 'Farewell, gentlemen.'

Dowling looked as frustrated as I, brow sunk over the bridge of his nose.

Tanner turned to Burke, who stood quaking by the easel. 'You might as well go with them,' he said, afore sitting back upon his stool. 'You cannot stay here now.' He dipped a brush and commenced painting once more, ignoring us all.

Burke watched him, uncertain what to do. He dithered a while, fidgeting, afore walking slowly over to the cot. He let himself fall upon it and lay on his back, head behind his hands.

We left.

'What now?' I exclaimed, as we scrambled back up toward the street.

'All is not simple as it seems,' said Dowling. 'I will try and find out who John Tanner is, and those other two besides. Seems they know more about the murders than Burke does.'

'Aye,' I agreed, miserably. A simple assignment became complex. We emerged back onto Thames Street.

'I have to buy a bell-rope,' Dowling announced grim faced. 'I will meet you at dinnertime.'

'I will go to the Willis house,' I said, unable to think where else to go. I could not face Jane. 'I will come to your house by eleven.'

Dowling gave a brief wave and was gone.

I walked slowly east. A heavy smoke drifted north on a wind off the river. I supposed the soap boilers and brewers still worked as busy as ever.

An arm draped itself about my shoulder. 'Where are you headed, Harry?' A handsome young face looked down upon me, twisted in complacent stone-eyed viciousness. He wore a beaver hat upon his head.

The older man appeared at my other shoulder, smiling broadly, dark eyes shining bright from beneath long lashes. 'I am Forman, and this is Withypoll.'

I tried to look behind for Dowling, but they wouldn't let me turn. The one with the fair hair, Withypoll, squeezed me so I hard I thought my shoulder would crack. 'You followed us yesterday, you followed us today, yet you claim not to be a spy.'

Forman stopped at the door of the Three Cranes. 'We want to talk to you.'

The Three Cranes tavern was a doghole. 'Here?'

'Yes, Harry, here.' Forman shoved me forward. 'We require only a few minutes of your valuable time.'

The folks in here were dirty and malodorous; dockers, sailors and lightermen mostly. We had been at war with the Dutch since March. Now the French and Danes joined against us and rumour was the fleet would be sailing soon. The shipyards were busy and yet the King had not the money to pay. Everyone was in arrears. Men grew anxious and resentful, inclined to fight anyone that moved or spoke.

Forman pushed me ahead, straight into the barrel-chested taverner. A drip hung from the end of his red nose, which, I reflected, must occasionally fall into the drinks he served. He ran his eye over our fine clothes, face chiselled of stone.

'Somewhere private to talk,' Forman demanded.

The taverner nodded, silent, and hurried us through the inn. The noise reminded me of Bedlam.

'You stare at me with that fishy eye and I will slice it for thee,' Withypoll objected to a man who gawped. The taverner jostled the fellow out of our way and steered us toward a quiet room in the back. Withypoll shoved me into a corner and bid me sit. Wall to my right, wall to my back, table in front. Withypoll squeezed in to my left so I couldn't move. Three mugs of cloudy ale arrived quickly upon the table, and we were left alone.

Forman settled himself opposite and showed his teeth. 'Now we might talk.'

I took a sip of ale to relieve the dryness of my lips, afore remembering the drip on the taverner's nose.

'Did you meet John Tanner?' Forman asked.

I knew not what to say.

Withypoll stabbed his blade into the table. 'Forman asked you a question.'

Rage boiled up inside me. How did I allow myself to be so easily trapped? I stared into Forman's fierce eyes. 'Yes, I met John Tanner.'

'Then you know where we planned to hide Burke.'

'Who do you work for?' I blurted out.

Forman blinked, and Withypoll chuckled noisily.

'Lytle.' Withypoll breathed into my ear. 'No one was supposed to know Burke was staying with Tanner. It was a secret. Indeed, no one is supposed to know where Tanner lives.'

I sensed the violence lurking behind the toothy smile. 'I am trying to find out who killed Thomas Wharton. Burke is the main suspect and so we followed him.' I dared catch his eye a moment. 'Not you, not John Tanner.'

Withypoll leaned back, puffed out his chest, then exhaled deeply. 'You need not worry who killed Thomas Wharton, Lytle, for we will discover that for ourselves. All we seek from you is confirmation you work for Lord Arlington.'

And what then? 'Why should I tell you that when you tell me nothing?'

Withypoll pointed to his knife, still stuck upright in the table. 'Because if you don't tell me then I shall cut David Dowling's throat.'

I clenched my fists, holding on to the last crumbs of courage. 'It is no secret.'

'I wonder why he chose you and the butcher,' Withypoll mused, stroking his chin. 'Evidently he thought little of it, assumed Burke was guilty. Unless.'

'Unless what?'

'Unless Arlington arranged for Wharton's death and appointed you two with the expectation you would see no further than the obvious.' Withypoll turned to Forman. 'What do you think?'

Forman stared. 'I don't know.'

'He appointed us because his other agents have all fled London,' I explained. 'This is not the first investigation we have undertaken, and so he would have little reason to suppose we would not apply ourselves. What I don't understand is why you would seek to prevent us. Perhaps you killed Wharton?'

'Perhaps,' Withypoll shrugged. 'It is of little concern to you now, anyway. Finish your ale.'

I looked to my pot, almost full still. 'I am not ready to leave.'

'Aye, well ye had best prepare yourself.' Forman lowered his arm beneath the table and pushed his knife into my thigh. 'We must put you to death, Lytle, because now you know something you shouldn't. It is not your fault, I own, but what has occurred, has occurred. We will walk you to the river since it will save us dragging you there.'

They watched me intently, gauging my reaction. I thought of shouting to the crowd outside but knew my plea would garner no response. The taverner would have warned all to leave us alone. This was ridiculous.

'What is it I know?'

'You know who Tanner is.' Forman pushed the blade deeper.

My skin stretched beneath the knife. 'Move him. Find him another place to live.'

Forman shook his head sadly. 'No, Harry. You saw his face.'

I could think of nothing to respond. 'Well, I am not walking to the river.'

'I prefer to see a man die with dignity, Harry.'

'I care not what you prefer.' Terror and anger came together and threatened to make my eyes water. I determined they would not see it, sensed they watched for it, had seen it before. What would happen if I were to wrap myself about the table so they could not move me? Surely they would not kill me here in the tavern?

Withypoll inspected his fingertips. 'If you don't *walk* out of here, Forman will strike you hard, and we will carry out your prone body like we are friends. To the river.'

My bladder loosened.

Forman settled back. 'Finish your ale quickly, Harry.'

I didn't wish to drink the ale at all. My mind clouded with unholy fear and I could not recall my own name, let alone devise an ingenious plan to escape these villains. I thought to debate it further, but couldn't find the words to start a sentence.

A door slammed. Hope lost. Footsteps. The door flung open.

'Have I not warned ye of the perils of drink?'

I turned with lungs paralysed, unable to breathe. There before me the ugly face of Newgate's noblest butcher. Behind him the taverner and two others.

Dowling stepped forward and cuffed Withypoll about the head, knocking his hat askew. 'Aye, Harry, now let's be going. We have work to do.'

Was he as lunatic as Franklin? It was madness to antagonise Withypoll—they would take their revenge. Yet he committed to it now. Despite my fear, it was all I could do not to laugh at the sight of Withypoll, hat fallen askew over one eye.

'You are Dowling?' he asked, voice almost a whisper.

'David Dowling. Butcher.'

Withypoll nodded, straightening his hat. 'I too am a butcher.'

'I know it.' Dowling pulled the knife from the table. 'Perhaps we might form a guild?'

Withypoll smashed his fist down upon the table. 'We are different categories of butcher, David Dowling.'

'So I believe.' Dowling turned his attention to Forman. 'You might give me your knife too, else have your fingers broke.'

Forman shook his head. 'You think we will not kill you, butcher?'

Dowling kept his left hand low, knife gripped hard. 'Not today, you won't.'

Forman sat still, contemplating the situation, afore standing slowly and smoothing the creases from his beautiful silk jacket. 'I will keep my knife, Mr Dowling.' He bowed his head afore eyeing the small crowd that watched, enthralled. 'It has been a most enjoyable morning, gentlemen.'

Withypoll shuffled his feet, eyeing Forman with stubborn disagreement, contemplating Dowling like he would fight him on the spot.

'Come, Withypoll, we shall renew acquaintance soon enough,' Forman snapped, before walking out the door with purpose and a fury.

Withypoll followed, reluctant.

I felt reborn. A great calm descended upon my soul and I thought to kiss him. 'You saved my life, Dowling.'

'Aye, me and Robert.'

'Robert?'

Dowling turned to the taverner. 'Aye. He buys my meat.'

Still the drip hung from the taverner's nose.

'Thanks to ye, Rob.' Dowling clapped him about the shoulder and looked at me, waiting.

'Aye, thanks, Rob,' I said sincerely.

Robert grunted, wiped his nose with the palm of his right hand and held it out for me to shake. Under the circumstances I could hardly refuse.

CHAPTER 10

What shall be the occasion of hindering the marriage
Consider what evil planet it is who does hinder the reception of the disposition of the man and woman, or who frustrates their aspect, or interjects his rays between them.

We headed east, my heart still brimming over with love and gratitude for the filthy butcher. It was past eight o'clock and people were out on the streets. Plague or no plague, they had to eat.

'How did ye know to return?'

Dowling shook his head. 'I was as slow-headed as you. I hadn't reached halfway up the hill afore I realised they might have waited for us. I ran back and saw them trailing you, watched them take you.'

A great wave of emotion engulfed my chest, threatening to erupt out my eyes and mouth. 'They wanted to take me to the river, cut me up.'

Dowling stepped to one side, avoiding an unsteady looking fellow with moist brow. 'They may be trailing us still.'

Relief washed through my body and my hands trembled. I hadn't realised how frightened I became. All in the service of finding out who killed a man who no one loved, not even his wife. 'What is the sense in all this, Davy?' I asked, hearing my voice shake.

'No sense that I can see,' Dowling puffed, striding ahead. 'Why do ye not take Jane to Cocksmouth as you planned? I will tell Newcourt of those two brutes, tell him to send soldiers after them.'

'Go to Cocksmouth and watch my uncle slaughter pigs? Methinks not.'

'Ye'd rather stay here and be slaughtered yourself?' Dowling stopped on the corner of Bread Street. 'As you said, where is the sense in that?'

Where indeed. Yet where was the sense in fleeing? I'd spent the last several years bemoaning the tedium of my life. Now someone waved a knife in my face I was tempted to run. It was time to prove my worth. I drew myself up to my full height and punched the butcher lightly in the kidneys. 'Thank you, Davy.'

'Thanks for what?' he frowned.

'For helping clarify my thoughts.' I breathed easier. 'And we have two avenues to explore. First, what's happening at Bedlam. Second, find those four dogs Burke told us of, at Winchester Palace. They must know something.'

Dowling raised his brows. 'Which first?'

'Pateson,' I decided. 'For that should be quickest. I want to know why the keeper of Bedlam never visits, and what he knows of Edmund Franklin.'

'Then we'd best find out where he lives,' said Dowling. 'Back to the Guildhall.'

Pateson lived at Bell Alley, just inside the city wall. There was no door to knock upon unless you cared to kneel down, for it was a split door and the top half was open.

Inside smelled like the burrow of a small furry animal. They sat within, a man and a woman, one either end of a small table, eating from bowls in which floated lumps of gristle on a greasy soup. They put the gristle in their mouths, chewed it, then spat it back into the foul oily liquid.

'Mr Pateson,' I called.

Flat yellow teeth protruded from his mouth and short white whiskers covered his face. His body was short and round, back crooked. His wife was of similar build and appearance, though her face was less whiskery and a few brown strands still streaked her hair.

'Who are you?' she squeaked.

'King's agents, come to ask a few questions.'

Pateson huddled over his broth. 'If it is so,' he mumbled.

There was no other chair in the room and they did not invite us to enter. Dowling leaned over the top of the door. 'You are the keepers of Bedlam, are you not?'

'Aye, keepers of Bedlam. A fine job,' the woman spat, glaring at her husband. 'Living among lunatics. No better than animals, most of them, and this one suggesting we live there with them.'

'You would rather live here in this damp hole.' Her husband glared back at her. 'There we had brick walls, room to stretch a leg and a front door besides.'

'If a man says a pile of bricks is a wall, then he might as well live in the open air and call the rain to land upon his face.' She waved a hand dismissively, though I had no idea what she meant. 'And there are more criminals there so as to make a front door a barrier, not an entrance.'

He buried his face in his bowl and peered out like he would happily strangle her. Seemed this was a conversation they enacted regularly. I opened my mouth, but Pateson spoke first. 'It is a job, you flaky hag, and pays well.'

She leaned back and wrinkled her nose. 'Then get you back there.'

He gripped the edge of the table with white knuckles. 'Aye, get me back there to work like a dog twice-over, while you sit here and do nothing and expect your share of the money, I'll be bound.'

'You do as you will. I can earn my own way. You just want someone to cook and clean for you and your lunatics, and know you'll not find another as cheap as me.'

'Aye, that be right,' he sneered. 'There be none as

cheap as you.'

Now it was her turn to change colour. I was pleased to be at safe distance.

'How often do you visit the place?' I asked, taking advantage of the lull in proceedings.

There was no reply, just the sound of deep breathing as they sat staring at each other in furious contemplation.

'You have not been there for a while,' I said.

Pateson's gaze returned to the greasy broth. 'You visited then?'

I sensed his fear. 'We have no interest in your stipend, Mr Pateson. That is no affair of ours.'

'What do you want then?' asked his wife.

'The Earl of St Albans was murdered on Lord's Day. His brother sits inside your asylum and we would know what you can tell us of them.'

Pateson stared blankly. 'The Earl of St Albans?'

'Did he visit Franklin?'

'Franklin? None visit Franklin. He is a dangerous lunatic. He will bite pieces out of you. It is why we keep him on his own.'

My stomach sunk towards my groin as I recalled our own visit. The fear upon Daniel's face. The way he sat with his back to us while we talked with Franklin. 'Morrison allowed us to approach the bars.'

Pateson scrunched up his furry face in perplexed

bewilderment. 'Morrison did?'

Dowling cleared his throat. 'We were told the Earl's brother is an inmate and Morrison directed us at Franklin.'

Pateson stared down at the bottom half of the door. 'Really?' His brows knit together so low and close you could not see his eyes. 'I don't see how Morrison could know.' He looked me in the eye, curious. 'Franklin is the wildest lunatic in the asylum. We have had him locked up twenty years.' He shook his head and smiled cautiously. 'None know where Franklin comes from since he is incapable of telling us, but he is not related to nobility.'

'When were you last there?' I asked.

'A month ago. Morrison and Gallagher are able,' he replied, defensive.

'Gallagher?'

'Hugh Gallagher,' his wife answered. 'Cruel to the lunatics and doesn't mind provoking them to anger.'

'Gallagher was not there when we visited,' I said. 'Morrison said he was sickly. Said he carried the only key to the vestry.'

Pateson frowned. 'Who was there beside Morrison?'

'A young man with ginger hair,' I told him. 'The two of them stood on the doorstep drinking wine. The place stank like a cesspool.'

'It always stinks like a cesspool,' said the wife. 'It is

another reason I will not abide there. Dirty and unclean. You would have to be mad to go close to it with plague about.' This place seemed dirtier to me.

I watched Pateson hide his face in his hands.

'Someone has to tend them,' I said. 'You cannot leave two men alone to tend sixty lunatics, especially if they neglect their duties. Why do you not visit? You don't have to live there to ensure the place is cared for.'

'He cannot,' his wife sneered. 'He is paid coin to keep away.'

'Who pays coin?' Dowling growled.

'Morrison,' she replied.

Pateson raised his head, face scarlet, fists clenched, eyes fixed upon his wife.

'Generous of him,' I observed.

'I don't know why he did it,' Pateson mumbled. 'They didn't tell me, just paid me coin to stay away. Then after we shook hands Morrison threatened me with death should I set foot into the place again.'

'Morrison?' The same short avuncular Morrison we met?

'He may be little to look at, but he is a demon.'

'How long has he worked with you?'

'Three months. Gallagher recommended him. He was sober and confident and well able to deal with the lunatics, at least when I was there. He worked with us a while, then made me the offer.'

'Did he not say then why he made it?'

He shook his head.

'It was a lot of coin,' his wife remarked.

'Aye,' he conceded, 'it was a lot of coin. And he made a generous first payment.'

'What happened then?'

'I returned to see what state the place was in, for I did not desire to lose my tenure in case the inspectors arrived. He calmly assured me he would keep the place in order, but refused me the right to walk around. When I insisted, he took me into my own office and held me down with his arm across my throat. He said it was his facility to run so long as he desired, and he would keep paying me. But if I returned or revealed our arrangement, then he would kill me.' Pateson mopped his brow. 'As if I would reveal it! But later he and Gallagher came here.'

'Aye,' his wife snorted. 'And what did they do?'

He stared at the table, but did not reply. Hate emanated from her eyes. 'Tell them.'

'They made her remove her clothes and threatened her with a knife.'

'They removed my clothes for me and held a knife to my breast and said they would cut it off if ever again he returned,' she jeered.

'I could do nothing,' he said to the table.

'He has always been afraid of Gallagher.'

'I am no more afraid of Gallagher than I am of the lunatics,' Pateson retorted. 'I suspected he might be becoming lunatic himself, the way he behaved. A consequence of working in the place too many years. So I treated him with caution.'

'You are a great coward,' she sneered.

'And you are a bucket head that divorces thyself of all responsibility.'

It made no sense. 'So you say Franklin has no relatives, yet Morrison says otherwise.'

'I have been there longer than Morrison.'

'What else can you tell us of Franklin?' I asked.

'If you saw him for yourselves I can tell you little else I have not told you already.' Pateson curled his lip. 'They say he was driven to madness by the pox, since when he has been lunatic.'

Which did make sense. The deformity of the child we saw at St Albans might well have been caused by pox. But what of Franklin himself? 'If Franklin was poxed I would have expected to see more signs of it.'

'What signs would you seek?' Pateson watched me, wary. 'Did he not look poxed to you?'

Truth was I recalled no sign of the pox whatever. I looked to Dowling, who appeared as mystified as I.

'His face is pitted and scarred,' Pateson said, observing

our mystification.

I shook my head. 'I don't recall it.'

Pateson's wife tapped a finger on the table. 'Gallagher was a mean spirited cur who would slice his mother's throat for a pipe of tobacco.'

'Aye,' Pateson nodded fervently, relieved to be able to agree with her, but I no longer listened.

We should go back to Bedlam, I realised, and put this little mystery to bed. Not today, though. The sun shone too hot to risk a visit north of the wall. Today to the Bishop of Winchester's palace at Southwark. I tapped Dowling upon the shoulder and we left Pateson and his wife to finish their intimate dinner in private.

CHAPTER 11

Of the goodness or the badness of the land or house
If you find in the fourth house the two infortunes, very potent, or peregrine, or of the Lord of the fourth be retrograde or unfortunate, or in his fall or detriment, 'twill never continue long with your posterity.

Carts and wagons jammed the Bridge tight, loaded high with essential possessions. The procession reached as high as the crossroads 'twixt Fish Street Hill and Eastcheap, almost to the door of the Boar's Head. We burrowed through the crowds, shoving when we needed to.

'You think ye are the King?' shouted a man sat upon a stationary cart. He glared at me then spat on the ground.

'I am a King's *man*.' I stabbed a finger at him. 'Spit on me again and I'll smooth your passage to Newgate.'

I prayed we would not get stuck long enough to incite a riot, but the wall of people ahead of us loomed solid and unbreachable, no room to stick out an elbow. Dowling peered over the top.

'Albemarle's men are preventing passage,' he called. 'Hold onto my coat.' He propelled himself the last few yards like a cleaver slicing meat.

A flustered soldier blocked our progress, struggling to keep his feet. He banged his pike upon the cobbles. 'You cannot cross the Bridge this morning,' he shouted above the din.

'We are King's men,' I yelled back. 'On King's errand.'

'No matter.' The sentry clattered his pike into the face of a man who pressed too hard. 'A cart lost its wheel and cannot be moved nor mended. As you can see, there be no room for a carpenter to reach it.'

'Then we will walk past it.' I nudged him.

'Aye, if ye have all day to do it. Then you might reach the Square. Beyond the Square there is no hope for any without a fine pair of wings.' The Square was a wide open space that sucked the traffic in, yet blocked its passage out.

Ahead red faces stretched upwards, searching for breath. Men held children to their chests and tried to shield their women. The sentry spoke truth. I twisted myself about and pushed back the way we came, escaping the frantic congregation.

'To the river then,' I suggested, smoothing the creases in my jacket.

'If you have the funds,' Dowling growled.

'I do,' I owned with sinking heart. It would cost us at least five shillings to cross the river and another five to return.

Boats covered the water, a vast flotilla of wherries, old ferries and naval longboats, all dressed with canvas and waxed cloth to protect from sun and rain. These citizens took to the river to wait out the plague's tempest. Ferrymen were obliged to negotiate a winding path, for if you ventured too close to one of these vessels, you risked attack. Some of these people floated a month or more already, a way of living that invited madness.

Fat drops of rain started to fall before we reached halfway and thick grey clouds swept across the skies, exposing us to a chill sodden breeze. I wished we went to Bedlam instead. The boatman strained hard and got us to St Mary Overy Stairs before the water penetrated to my drawers.

We ran up the stairs, towering brick buildings on either side, across Clink Street, to shelter beneath Stoney Street arch, one entrance to Winchester Palace. The rain poured down in a single sheet, battering the cobbles in relentless assault.

'The Well-house is as good a place as any,' I shouted above the noise.

We pushed through the door next to which we shivered. The Well-house nestled this side of the Great Hall. Wooden pipes carried water from the river to the cellars beneath us. The well had once supplied the kitchens, afore the palace was deserted forty years before and broken up into tenements. Now any man might buy water here.

A short stout woman waited within, next to the well. 'Raining?' she asked, sharp eyes watching the water drip from our sodden clothes.

'Raining,' I confirmed.

'You come in for shelter then?' she asked.

'Aye, we also hoped you might direct us.'

The woman stuck out her jaw and scratched her head. 'Where would ye like me to direct you?'

'We're looking for four men.'

She shrugged. 'I could point you in any direction and you'll find four men eventually.'

'Four particular men,' I clarified. 'We know them only as black dogs. Friends to the Earl of St Albans.'

'Him what is dead.' She nodded. 'I know who you refer to, and if you are wise ye will not call them black dogs.'

'What then should I call them?'

'Call them what ye will, but I should not call them dogs.'

I calmed the impatience within. 'Where might we find them?'

'The Cock and Two Hoops,' she replied.

Stoney Street led us west of the old palace through

Deadman's Place. What was once a great garden now decayed into a straggling mess of unsteady wooden cottages. A channel was cut for a sewer, heading back down toward the river, but the land ran flat, the ditch was clogged and the air stank. The rain drummed a steady beat upon my head, trickling down my neck in cold rivulets. We hurried through the shadows of the stone walls until we reached the tavern.

All conversation stopped when we entered. Five tables spread about the dark and dingy room, each occupied by five or six men. We sat at a space at the end of the table closest to the door. A wench brought two mugs of ale without asking what we wanted. I tried to engage her in conversation, but she ignored me, so I went in search of someone who might tell us more, leaving Dowling at the table.

'Will you talk to me?' I asked a fellow who stood holding a brush, watching from a passageway.

He squinted and showed me his teeth. 'About what?'

'I am looking for the four men who worked close with the Earl of St Albans.'

'What for?' he said with disdain.

'We need to talk with them.'

'I will fetch them if you like.' He placed the brush against the wall and disappeared into the gloom behind.

I followed tentatively. Three small rooms branched

off the corridor, each of them piled high with rubbish. At the end of the corridor a door led out toward the cathedral, stood ajar. The fellow was gone into the downpour. I returned to Dowling and we settled to bide our time. Conversation about us resumed, though quieter than before.

The door opened again, the cacophony of rain against cobbles drowning out all other sounds until the man closed it behind him. He stood dripping, black jacket drenched and heavy, wide brimmed hat sodden and misshapen. A sword protruded behind his legs. He tipped off his hat and threw it to the table, revealing the same bony face we saw before at the Vintners' Hall.

He removed his coat and straddled a chair, adjusting the sword so it swung free to his right. 'Lord Arlington sent you here, did he? How did you know where to come?'

'We were sent in search of four black dogs.' I remembered too late the Well-house woman's advice.

'Dogs, you say?' He spoke with soft tone and stony intent.

'Know ye who these four dogs might be?' Dowling asked in his soft Scots brogue.

The man's blue eyes shone hard as sapphire and the skin of his face gleamed, thick as tanned leather. 'Call me a dog again, cur, and I shall kill you where you sit.'

'I didn't call you dog.' Dowling folded his arms and stuck out his chest. 'Others did.'

'No matter.' The giant smiled broad, revealing an enormous mouth full of big yellow teeth. 'You are here now and we must share with you our hospitality.' He tapped the table with thick forefinger. 'Come! And I will introduce you to the other dogs.' He jumped to his feet and donned his watery clothes once more.

'Is it far?' I asked.

'No,' he beckoned us, impatient. 'Five minutes' walk.'

We followed him back into the deluge, Dowling as anxious as I. He headed back toward Clink Street, rather than toward the slums on St Margaret's Hill, and soon we were back at the Well-house. He waved an arm west down the street toward The James Brewhouse. 'Here we are.'

Two more men stepped out onto the wet cobbles from a doorway to our left. They too wore black cloaks and breeches. The rain fell heavy as slate and I couldn't make out their faces.

'War,' called one.

'Pestilence,' our man shouted back to him, and 'Famine,' to the other.

What code was this?

'Come.' Our man took me by the elbow and directed me to a low archway.

'The Clink?' I thought the Clink was closed up years ago. I tried to jerk my arm from his grasp and dig my heels into the slippery cobbles, succeeding only in falling back into his arms. There was no one to call to, none who might help. The other two took Dowling by the arms, forcing him down the steep stone stairs.

They dragged us down into a dark dank hole, tiny streams flowing from the black walls. They said the river ran through it when the tide was high. I felt more frightened than ever afore in my life, for what motive could there be to haul us down here?

Torches lit the way ahead from holders on the walls, creating black shadows in which lurked all manner of creeping insect. Quiet squeaking somewhere far ahead, a nest of mice or rats. We were the only prisoners.

They jostled us forward, ever deeper. The last torch signalled our destination, a small square cell with low stone bench and chains about the floor, connected to four rings set into the wall. They flung us toward the bench and forced us to sit, then one of them fitted manacles to our ankles. Dowling attempted to resist, but even he was helpless against these great behemoths. They stood before us, admiring their handiwork, afore carrying away the last torch. The last thing I saw before the light died was a large cockroach creeping across the floor toward my feet.

'Will they come back, do you think?' I whispered, barely able to speak.

Dowling reached over to grasp my hand. 'Have faith in God.'

Have faith in God to do what? If he was happy to send us plague, why should he save us from Clink? I sat frozen, listening intent. All I could hear was the air rolling noisily in and out of Dowling's nostrils. None would think to search for us here. If they left us, we would die. Perhaps that was their objective then, to play upon our fears, to destroy our spirit. I took a deep gulping breath and clung to the thought. Dowling started muttering beneath his breath, reciting passages from the Bible. Thank God he was there with me. Every second, every minute, I struggled to maintain my emotions. Refused myself permission to consider we might never leave. So when eventually I heard footsteps it felt like I lived again, joy abounded in my heart and seeped out my eyes. I rubbed a hand against my wet cheeks.

The man with the craggy face appeared, torch in hand, his companions behind. 'You may call me War,' he declared. 'These you may call Famine and Pestilence.'

Horsemen of the Apocalypse? A vain pretension, but where was Death?

'You went to The Bull Head last night,' War said, as if it were a sin.

'We were summoned.'

'You pulled a man out of a barrel,' Famine said, sharp brown eyes belying the fleshiness of his face. 'That was Death.'

Pestilence stared like he would kill us there and then, straight-backed and severe, hairline receded halfway back his skull. A trickle of sweat rolled down my spine and into my breeches.

'We pulled him out,' I protested. 'Not put him in. We came seeking your help in bringing the killer to justice.'

War laughed out loud. 'Arlington's men come here promising justice?' He spat on the floor.

Pestilence fidgeted, as if impatient.

'What did Arlington tell you about Thomas?' War demanded.

'Little,' I replied. 'He met us at the Vintners' Hall and told us to find out who killed him. Not long afore you arrived.'

'Nothing else?' There was a warning edge to his voice.

'Said he was a shirker and a shammer,' said Dowling. 'Said he cheated Henry Burke of a fortune in wine.'

'Burke the wine merchant.' War leaned over and breathed into my face. 'And whoever killed the Earl put a wine bottle down his throat and money in his eyes.

Whoever killed Death packed him into one of Burke's barrels.'

I wasn't sure what he wanted me to say.

War's face reddened. 'But Burke is a coward, so he didn't do it. Whoever killed Wharton would see an innocent die for it. Another coward then.'

I wished he would speak quieter, else further from my face. 'Who do you think killed Wharton?'

'Arlington!' War snarled, saliva bubbling on his lips. 'And now we will see what else you know.'

He clicked his fingers and Pestilence stepped forward to seize Dowling's right arm. Famine took a rope from his jacket and tied it tight about his wrist, looping the rope through one of the huge iron rings. Dowling jerked his arm, frantic, but Famine had done this before. Then they tied his other arm. I waited for them to do the same to me, but instead Pestilence smiled at Dowling and dug a hand into his pocket. He took out a small metal device and held it to Dowling's nose. The device resembled a church window, two arches with a long screw betwixt.

'Do you know what that is?' War asked me.

'Yes,' I replied, mouth dry. 'A thumbscrew, but you don't need it. We will answer your questions without torture.'

'No.' War raised a finger, smiling again. '*You* will answer our questions while we torture him.'

Pestilence held Dowling's nose and thrust a filthy cloth into his mouth. Then he climbed onto the bench and attached the thumbscrew to Dowling's right thumb, screwing the plate down far enough so it would not fall off. He fitted a spanner-shaped key against the bolt, then twisted the screw so it pushed firm against the bone. Dowling's body tensed and his eyes roved the room like he hoped his Lord Jesus would come rescue him.

War crouched down and stared into my eyes as if trying to read them. 'Who killed Death?'

'We don't know who killed Death, nor Wharton, else we would not have come here.' I spoke fast. 'The circumstances of their deaths suggest Henry Burke killed them both, yet if we believed that then why would we have come? We have met Henry Burke.'

War shook his head. 'No.'

I leaned forwards to see Pestilence twist the bolt again. The plate flattened Dowling's thumbnail and the blood bulged from the tip of his thumb. He clenched his teeth together and squeezed his eyes closed.

'What do you want me to say?' I cried out loud. 'That is the truth!'

Pestilence turned the plate another degree and I heard Dowling's nail crack. He jerked his arm backwards and his body twitched in slow spasm.

'I cannot tell you what I don't know!' I screamed.

War stuck out a hand and rubbed a thick finger down my cheek. 'Think of something to tell me,' he advised. 'Else Pestilence will turn that screw another degree.'

'I don't know what else I can tell you,' I pleaded. 'You saw Wharton's body and you told me how Death died.'

'You have found out more than that.'

'Yes,' I declared. 'We have found out more than that and I will tell you all of it. But we don't know who killed Death!'

War stroked Dowling's hair while the butcher stared at the ceiling through red eyes. 'Talk.'

'We went to St Albans.' I struggled to think, tried to slow down my speech. 'A man there told us that the Earl has a brother, who is locked up at Bedlam.'

War frowned.

'No!' I held up a hand. 'It's true! That is what he told us! We went to Bedlam and found a man there called Edmund Franklin who may be that brother. We spoke to Pateson, who is the keeper there. He seemed to think not, but you asked me to tell you what we discovered.'

'What else?' War asked, grim.

'We found Burke. Two men called Forman and Withypoll took him to a house on Three Crane Lane, to stay with another man called John Tanner.'

War's eyes widened. 'Forman and Withypoll?'

'Aye,' I nodded eagerly. 'Brutish fellows who would have killed me if Davy hadn't rescued me.'

'Why would they kill you?' War asked, perplexed.

'Because we followed them to Three Crane Lane,' I said.

War pursed his lips and gazed first at Famine and then at Pestilence. 'You may be as diligent as you portray.'

Pestilence grunted and eyed the thumbscrew longingly.

'You are but a butcher and a clerk.' War shrugged. 'Why should Arlington confide in you?'

Arlington again. Why did he suspect Arlington of killing Wharton? It made no sense.

'What of the ranting cleric?' War asked, eyes fixed on mine. 'What have you discovered of Perkins?'

'Perkins?' I racked my brain, searching for meaning. A faint recollection, but no mention of any such man in the last two days, at least. Yet I feared what he would say if I said I knew nothing. What would Pestilence do?

'No, then.' War read my expression and was satisfied, it seemed.

'I can think of nothing else,' I pleaded. 'It has been but two days and one of those was spent on the journey to St Albans.'

'I believe you,' War said quiet. He gestured at Famine to unlock my chains. 'Yet you must leave here convinced of the need to keep us informed.' He turned to Pestilence. 'And to tell Arlington nothing of this meeting.'

He gestured once more and Pestilence turned the screw another notch. Dowling's eyes rolled in his head and his body slumped back. Blood seeped into every groove of the screw and dripped slowly onto the floor.

'Take care of your friend,' War warned afore leaving the cell. 'You will need him.'

On the way home I urged Dowling hold his thumb up high so the blood would not fall into it. The tip was purple and changed colour as it throbbed. It appeared hot, so swollen and taut there was no way of telling if there was damage to the bone.

I decided to take him back to my house where Jane could tend to the wound. I bid him walk fast past St Peter's, onto Cheapside and alongside The Mermaid, plans forming in my head as I went. I looked back down the street. I fancied I saw a man hanging about under the eaves of a house fifty yards or so away. One figure or two? I strained to see better, but the figure vanished.

I banged on my door with my fist, then banged again. My knuckles were wet. Paint on the door—I could just make it out—gleaming red. I dabbed at the markings with my finger. It was paint all right, red paint, in the form of words. I crouched down to look closer.

'To the pest-house,' I read.

A long cold blade plunged itself into my guts and my skin froze.

Plague.

CHAPTER 12

A dog missing, where?

Living in London where we have few or no small cattle, as sheep, hogs, or the like, as in the country; I cannot give examples of such creatures.

I had spent most of my life trying to avoid Alderman Fuller. He was a thin man, nearly seventy years old. As a child I saw him as a mean spirited misery, beady eyed, with little tolerance for the sound of children's laughter. I retained a loathsome fear of his black spirit. He was voted alderman every year of my life.

Fuller lived round the corner on Bow Lane. The door was open when I arrived and I wandered in. He sat at a large desk covered in paper, head held in one hand, staring at a ledger. Four men stood about talking while he slumped, exhausted. The bags beneath his stern grey eyes sagged deep and round.

He looked up bleary, jowls like a loose skinned dog. The lines softened. 'Harry Lytle.'

I hadn't heard him speak for many years. I was surprised how tender were his words, how tired his voice.

'Sir, my house is shut up with plague this very day.'

He watched me carefully. 'We have been looking for you, Harry.'

'I was home only this morning. Jane was not plagued.'

'Your servant?'

'Aye, Jane.'

'Jane.' Fuller scratched his head. 'She is in there, but it's her aunt that is afflicted.'

'Her aunt?' What aunt?

Fuller looked at me kindly. 'Her aunt took ill while she stopped there. Your servant called for a searcher.'

Probably the only servant in London who would be so honest. 'What did the searcher find?' I asked, blood pounding in my neck.

'The aunt is stricken,' he said simply. 'I am sorry, Harry.'

'I must see Jane,' I said, without thinking.

He shook his head slowly, talking like I was the one afflicted. 'They will be cared for, Harry. A watcher has been appointed and will be sat there soon.'

'Her aunt lived on the Bridge,' I recalled, mind talking aloud. I didn't recall her ever visiting the house before, nor was I aware Jane visited her more than occasionally. She was stern and prim and drove Jane madder than usual.

'Aye,' the man sighed. 'Several houses are locked up on

the Bridge this week.'

'Who is the watcher?'

'Sit down a moment, Harry, and I will tell you.'

Though I was not in the mood, I sat anyway, while he slowly turned the pages of the ledger, squinting at the book and licking his lips as if he nursed some inner pain. It was not the Fuller I remembered from childhood.

'The watcher's name is John Hearsey,' he read from the book. 'Not of this parish. He volunteered. I remember him now.' He scratched at his ear. 'He particularly offered to stand at your house.'

'My house?' I felt my heart shrouded in a heavy dread. 'Why my house?'

He laid a hand on mine. 'He didn't say why, just said he noticed it and would be prepared to guard it. I need as many people as I can get.'

'Where does he live?'

He returned to the ledger. 'Well I don't know,' he said slowly. 'He said he came from Moorfields. It is the only address he gave.'

Moorfields. Where stood Bedlam. What did it signify?

'Harry?'

'Who is he?' I demanded.

Fuller rubbed his eyes. 'It's the money, Harry. He lives on the north side of the wall and has no job. He is not the only one wandering the streets looking for red crosses.'

Which could be true, I supposed. Ours was a safe parish where few were afflicted. In truth I had no idea what to think, my brain was so dull. 'Will she have a medic and a nurse?'

'Yes, Harry, though there are few medics left in London. It may take a few days to arrange.' He paused and saw the anxiety in my eyes. 'I know a woman that wants a job as nurse.'

Misery hung from my heart like lead. 'Can I not talk to her once?'

'Only if you want to stay there with her,' Fuller answered wearily.

'Very well.' I nodded. 'But you will know what news?'

'I will talk to the medic, aye,' Fuller said. 'You may talk to him besides, once we know who he is.'

I muttered some thanks and hurried back to Bread Street. The latch on my front window was still broken, and I could see the jug standing where I had left it by the window in my bedroom. All was as always, except for the thick red cross painted onto my door, crude and bright. I placed my palm against the wood. Jane, my very own foul mouthed tyrant that never let me be. Jane, who did all she could to persuade me to leave, who stayed here angry and frightened because I would not countenance our departure. If there was a God then he had a cruel sense of humour. That mine was one of the first houses afflicted in the whole parish, the house that Jane battled so hard to keep clean despite my efforts to thwart her.

I peered through the downstairs window into my little room, but saw no one. I considered knocking upon the door, insisting Jane admit me afore the watcher arrived. But what good would that do? I was no use locked up in there.

Two people, a man and a woman, paused on the other side of the street to watch what I did. A nosy couple who lived near the Cordwainers' Hall. He was a cobbler like my father, though not a very good one. She spent all her days complaining as to the unfairness of life and wore a permanent crease between her eyes. They stopped still, as if suspecting my intentions. Well meaning busybodies. Else wondering what I did without, whether I had escaped my own house. I turned and glowered. When they didn't move I took a step toward them and shepherded them all the way up Bread Street until they scampered off down Basing Lane.

I returned to my door just as Alderman Fuller appeared, accompanied by a stout man with slow miserable face, the new watcher, I assumed. He seemed familiar, but I struggled to recall his name or the context in which I met him afore.

Time to leave. For now. I turned and bumped into Dowling.

'I took you home,' I exclaimed. 'I thought you were going to lie in bed until tomorrow.'

Dowling's face was white, eyes red. He held his hand to his stomach with the thumb turned upwards. Someone had bandaged it. 'I did,' he said, hoarse. 'Newcourt waited for me.'

Arlington's man. 'What did he say?'

The muscles about Dowling's jaw twitched. 'There is another body.'

'Already?' I answered flat, feeling useless. I watched the pain twitch on his lips, saw the blood spots form upon the white bandage. 'You are in pain.'

'Aye, so I am,' Dowling grumbled. 'Yet sitting on a chair will make it no less painful.'

'Where is this body?' I asked.

'Back where we came from not two hours ago,' he replied. 'We must take a boat.'

'Back to Southwark?'

He nodded. 'Winchester Palace.'

I heard the reluctance in his voice and felt the same dread bid me walk away. Yet what choice did we have? What was left of the moon already shone bright, keen to witness what next transpired.

The river ran thicker at night, black oily surface running slow and mysterious. Candles lit a thousand windows upon the bridge, illuminating our journey from bank to bank as we drew steadily away from the bright lights of the city toward the blackness of Southwark. A long row of tall narrow buildings, six or seven storeys high, perched precariously above the heavy stone arches. Small steepled roofs pointed toward the heavens, each tiny window glowing yellow.

The boatman stared at me as he pulled the oars, face glowering in the light of the lantern, still furious we forced him to make the trip. Only before the King's seal and under threat of imprisonment had he acceded.

The current pulled strong toward the Bridge, gathering pace as the wide river gathered itself into fast narrow streams that shot through the boulderous stone starlings. The boatman worked hard to keep us on an even keel.

As we approached the south bank tiny lights emerged from beneath the thick blanket of darkness, small flickerings from houses set back away from the water. A cluster of brighter lights took shape ahead of us, directly in front. Sometimes the tip of the boat pointed right of them, sometimes left, but always came back. They danced and quivered, moving from side to side, like the flames of torches held by men.

'Go slow, boatman!' I ordered, leaning forwards into the night. If these were Wharton's dogs, we must stay out of their reach.

As we drifted closer, so I saw four men stood at the top of St Mary Overy Stairs. Difficult to see who they were. Even in the light of the torches all I saw were shadows.

'Hail!' I called. 'Who are ye?'

One man stepped out with his torch up. 'Robert Judkins,' he called through the heavy air. 'Parish constable. Who are you?'

'Lytle and Dowling, sent by Lord Arlington.'

'You have come to see the body then?' Judkins called. He was short and thin, clearly not one of those that tortured Dowling. He carried a stick in his left hand. The other three wore simple shirts and shapeless breeches, workmen's clothes. No black cloaks nor sinister hats.

'Land us,' I instructed the boatman, 'and wait a while. We will pay you upon our return to Coldharbour.'

'How long?' he growled between clenched teeth.

'Not so long,' I replied, hopping off the boat as we bumped gently against the wooden posts.

'Lytle and Dowling, you say?' Judkins' face shone out from light of the torch, inquisitive and alert. 'You have credentials?'

He held the stick between his thighs while scrutinising Dowling's papers, holding them at arm's length like he had a problem with his eyes. 'Over here then.' He passed them back to Dowling, then led us the short distance to the corner betwixt bank and stairs where the other three men stood staring down into the water.

I followed their line of sight, but all I saw was a patch of black weed and mine own reflection in the torchlight.

'What are we looking at?'

Judkins poked the patch of weed gently with his stick. It bobbled gently in the water. 'It's a man's head. Something is pulling the body down so it doesn't float.'

'Who found it?'

'Eve Hart,' said Judkins. 'The woman from the Wellhouse.'

Which meant War and his dogs would have likely been informed hours before. 'When did she discover it?'

'Not long ago,' Judkins replied. 'Two hours perhaps.'

Dowling took Judkin's stick and kneeled at the water edge. He lay it flat across the dead man's brow and tilted it back. The face stared upwards, pale and ghostly, dull eyes staring sightlessly at the moon. A hand waved gently in the current; the rest of the body disappeared into a dark void. Hair drifted in the water, spreading from the scalp, tugged gently by the tide. His mouth sat open, a little black hole around which swam small fishes. Thick neck, small round chin and large ears flat against his head.

'Do you know who he is?' I asked Judkins.

'No.' Judkins pursed his lips. 'Doesn't mean he's not from here. People come and go through this parish.'

'Famine.' Dowling prodded the dead man's chest, easing the body backwards. 'No cloak, but same clothes he wore before.' He lifted the stick and watched the corpse swing back. 'Killed soon after we left. The skin on his face is loose and wrinkled.'

Judkins squeezed himself between us, peering sideways at me and up at Dowling. 'Who is Famine?'

'A colleague of the Earl of St Albans,' I answered. 'Him and three others. We don't know his real name but seems he lived here, somewhere close to the Palace. We met him earlier today at the Clink.'

Judkins frowned. 'The Clink's been closed this last ten years.'

'Not today it wasn't.' I glanced once more at Dowling's hand. The stain upon the bandage grew to the size of a guinea. He would need to treat the wound again afore the night was finished. 'The tavern keeper knows of them. He fetched one of them today. Perhaps he can tell us who they are and where they live.'

'Lived,' Dowling corrected me. 'Two of them are dead, Wharton besides. Three dead in three days.'

'All in Southwark?' Judkins exclaimed, voice tight and indignant.

'No,' I assured him. 'This is the first we have found at Southwark.'

'Famine?'

'Famine, War, Pestilence and Death,' I said. 'They call themselves after the four Horses of the Apocalypse. So they might keep their real names a secret, I suppose.'

'I see.' Judkins stared at the body with a new understanding.

'Then we should find someone who can tell us his real name.' He issued instructions to the other three men about us and handed me his torch. 'You hold this and give us light that we might pull him out.'

Judkins' men rolled up their sleeves and stood hesitant, uncertain how to proceed. They could not all grab his head and pull by the neck, else they might leave the body behind.

Dowling knelt once more. 'We must take him by the shoulders, pass a rope beneath his arms and pull on that.'

Everyone looked at everyone else until all looked at the boatman, still sat with his arms folded in his boat, like he had been most grievously offended. All boatmen carried a rope.

'The sooner we are done here, the sooner we may leave,' I persuaded him, and he tossed it up without grace.

Dowling bid two men hold him by the waist while he leaned out with the rope and struggled to pass it beneath the man's armpits. He leaned so close to the water his chin brushed the surface. He worked as if his thumb gave him no pain at all, which I knew was not true. He clenched his teeth firmly together, lips drawn back and eyes closed. I would have done the task for him, but I was too short.

'Ha!' Dowling grunted at last and sat up straight, both ends of the rope pulled taut. 'One more time.' He bent down again and passed another loop of the rope beneath the corpse, this time faster. 'Now you four will have to pull,' he announced, standing. 'For I cannot.' The whole of the bandage about his thumb was now soaked scarlet.

Judkins stepped forward to take the rope ends. He twisted them together and laid the rope out upon the landing so that all four could take weight. They pulled, slow at first, then harder, straining to lift the body even an inch.

'He is tied to something heavy,' complained one.

'Pull harder,' Judkins replied, impatient.

I passed the torch to Dowling and kneeled down to guide the head, for now it started to move. If we were not careful it would catch beneath the jetty. I leaned backwards on the wood and pushed the body off the edge of the jetty with my feet as it rose slowly from the depths. First the chest and then the legs slid onto the boards. Chains tied the body's ankles to some heavy weight.

I stared down into the water as Dowling pored over the drenched body.

'It's a barrel!' I declared, watching it rise slowly from the gloom below. 'A wine barrel.'

It broke the surface of the water with a heavy splash and, with one last effort from Judkins and his friends, rolled sideways upon the landing next to Famine. Someone had wound the chains about the barrel and bolted them in place.

'No surprise.' Dowling appeared at my side. 'No doubt one of Burke's.'

'I reckon I know him,' said one of Judkins' deputies, stood over Famine's long body. 'Don't know his name, but he was a sailor, I reckon.' He screwed up his face and stared at Judkins.

Judkins peered at the body like it was a puzzle. 'Where did he live?'

'Can't tell ye.' The man shook his head. 'Reckon he turned up a few months ago. I seen him maybe twice. He worked over other side of the Bridge.'

'Where?' I asked.

'Couldn't tell ye.' The man shook his head again and grimaced. 'Only saw him walk that way in the morning and walk back in the evening.'

'Every little helps,' Judkins pronounced. 'As the wren said when she pissed in the sea. Now.' He looked toward the palace. 'Let's see what's happening on Clink Street.'

He took back his torch and headed off toward the palace, followed by his deputies. I hesitated a moment, as did Dowling, before considering there were now six of us altogether and only two of them remaining.

Clink Street was black as pitch. The flame of the torch lit up the way only a few strides at a time, but Judkins strode forwards with confidence, leading us quick to the prison door. He held up the torch and pulled at the door handle. 'Locked.' He turned to me, chin jutting.

'Look, though,' I pointed to the torch holder above the

door. A torch sat in the hook, tiny spots of orange still burning. 'This torch is still hot.'

Judkins placed his hand about the burning tip. 'Well, I'll be hanged!'

I stared out into the darkness and imagined what lurked there, watching. I recalled the fury in War's eyes when recounting the killing of Death. He would be doubly furious now, and if still he suspected Arlington, doubly determined to extract from us whate'er he thought we might know. I pricked my ears, but could hear only the gentle splash of the water against the river's edge, voices shouting faint, a long way away.

'Time for us to leave,' I decided, suddenly afraid. 'We might return in the morning and find out what else there is to know.'

'A grand notion.' Judkins scratched his head. 'Meantime we will see if we can't find out who this Famine really was.' He slapped his colleague about the shoulder. 'Need to know where to take the body.'

As we hurried back to the stairs, I considered. Three dead in three days. If we could survive the rest of the week, then at least these Four Horsemen might all be disposed of, and who would mourn them? Yet who was it that picked off these great brutes with such casual assurance? I shivered, though the night was warm, and prayed the boatman hadn't left us behind.

CHAPTER 13

From what cause the sickness is
The significators in signs fiery, and the signs ascending
in the first, and descending in the sixth of the same
nature, show hectic fevers, and that choler is predominant
in this sickness.

If Fuller wouldn't find Jane a medic, then I'd do it myself.
No medics to be found for a few days, Fuller had said.
What use was that? The plague could kill a man in a day.

I was up early next morning, promising Dowling I
would return within the hour. With Forman, Withypoll,
War and Pestilence all against us, it was foolhardy to walk
the streets alone, yet I had an agenda Dowling would
want no part of.

Though hawkers and criers were prohibited, a new form
of trade flourished; the selling of pills, potions and other
concoctions as cure for plague. Whilst I would not consider
lancing a bubo myself, nor did I much believe in bleeding
or purging, I could gather what remedies seemed most

likely from the apothecaries.

Theriac was reckoned to be the most powerful antidote; a mixture of garlic, vinegar, walnuts, onion and the flesh of a poisonous snake. The poison of the snake was supposed to suck out the poison of the plague. Many other drugs were but variations of theriac, such as Venice treacle and London treacle. Unlikely remedies included unicorn horn and phoenix egg yolk. I was not so foolish to suppose they were real, but bought a small bottle of each besides, together with sea holly. I purchased onion and lily root to make a poultice and sweet smelling herbs to spread about the house. By the time I finished I spent nearly three pounds. Now I just needed a medic.

Whilst medics were scarce, the city seemed as good a place to search as any to hunt them, for it was safest. Moreover they were easy to spot, marching the streets in their sinister attire; thick waxed over-jackets, leather masks and glass eyes. They resembled nothing less than giant carrion, stalking the streets in search of weakened prey. The wax upon the jackets stopped the sticky atoms from sticking, and perfumed soaked linen packed into the long beaks of the heavy masks acted as barrier to any atoms that might penetrate nevertheless. An ingenious costume, I mused, and a guarantee of gaining entry to an infected household. I needed to acquire one.

I walked for almost an hour before I spotted my quarry.

He crossed Old Fish Street twenty paces afore me, heading down Dowgate Hill. I hurried to catch him, unworried that he might hear me, his ears hidden beneath leather. He turned left on to Thames Street and stopped afront of Cold Harbour.

Cold Harbour once stood a great mansion, the pride and joy of Lady Margaret Beaufort—mother to Henry VII. That was two centuries ago. It was still the most magnificent building on the river, tall and palatial, towering over all about. But now the splendid exterior was but a shell, the inside a rotten maze of poor tenements piled six storeys high.

The medic paused to scrutinise the facade, neck craned like a great heron contemplating flapping to the roof to build a nest. Then he disappeared inside. A wave of fear washed through me. I hadn't realised Cold Harbour was infected. If one in there was afflicted then the rest would follow, and they would spread it about this whole parish afore it was recognised. And to the next parish, and the next. I cursed myself anew, felt metallic fingers of self-loathing wrap about my throat. How could I have thought we were safe?

I waited on the street, fear of being stalked outweighed by my determination to see Jane. An hour later the medic emerged, hot and bothered, pulling the mask from his head to reveal a wet scarlet face plastered with thick plaits of soaking hair. Lines etched his eyes and pulled down the edges of his mouth. He trudged back to Dowgate, mask hanging from his hand like the head of a dead bird.

I followed him to a large house on Poultry. He pushed open the door and went inside. I waited about the mouth of Grocers' Alley, standing well back in the shadow. I waited there for more than an hour, as if I waited for an acquaintance, before he left again, this time without the costume. As soon as he was out of sight I ran across the street and knocked on the door.

An old face peered out and whispered, eyes bright and questioning. 'What do you want?'

'I am here on an important errand,' I replied, quiet for fear of frightening her.

She squinted at me. 'The master of the house is out. You can return later if you will.'

I pulled a face. 'Madam, it is more urgent.'

She looked me up and down as if afraid I would try and sell her something. The door began to close. 'You can return later if you will.'

I kept my voice calm and body still. 'It is your own safety at stake, madam.'

The door stopped closing.

'You and all who bide here are in great danger, but I can save you.'

The door opened again. She startled, half afraid and

half curious.

'The costume your master wears when he tends to the afflicted.'

She continued to stare.

'It is covered in wax so the sticky atoms do not stick.' I paused for theatrical effect. 'The fellow who waxed your master's costume did not apply enough wax. I am sent to fetch it so I can take it away and apply sufficient quantity.'

She looked as though she would cry. 'You can return later if you will.'

'Madam, you don't understand. Your master has worn the attire this day. It is possible it carries the sticky atoms upon it now, which I must remove, else you and all in the house may suffer the plague afore the day is out. The atoms will fall off if I don't remove them, all over the house.'

She blinked, then disappeared. Within a minute I had the medic's mask and jacket in my possession. She closed the door in my face before I could thank her. I hurried west down Cheapside, searching a quiet place. I stopped on the corner of Watling Street to don the jacket, which was most unpleasant, since it still hung heavy, wet and sodden. The mask was worse.

Fortunately it was not far to Bread Street, for the air I breathed stank, an acrid brew of garlic and grease. Though the glass eyes in the mask were thick and the view distorted, still I recognised the steady figure of John Hearsey sat outside my house, sober and watchful. He stood when he saw me, scratched his head and came walking over. He put his mouth against my ear. 'I didn't know a medic was coming.'

'Talk to Fuller,' I shouted through the mask. 'Now open the door.'

He shrugged, dug in his pocket for my key and did as asked.

The first thing I saw upon entering the house was a strange woman sat in my chair, head flung backwards, snoring loudly. It was not Jane's aunt. I heard stories of nurses neglecting their patients, taking money to tend for the sick yet fearing to go near them. Was this one of those, Fuller's appointment? Was she lazy, or so diligent she exhausted herself? I removed the mask for a moment so I could smell the air. Cheap wine hung in a low cloud about her figure, billowing out of her open mouth each time she exhaled. I poked her in the stomach, but she barely noticed, just slurred something that made little sense. Drunk.

I stared at her miserable form with disgust and contempt. Time to deal with her later. I climbed the stairs, trying to walk quiet for fear of scaring Jane and her aunt. I went first to Jane's room and pushed the door open, unable to free myself of the fear it would suddenly slam closed, for I had been forbidden to enter this room since Jane arrived.

It was simply furnished; a bed, a table and a chest. She lay upon the bed, eyes closed, face flushed and swollen, red hair wet and limp. The sheet beneath her was soiled and stinking. She slowly rolled onto her side and curled into a ball, arms clutching at her stomach. She opened her eyes and looked toward me, but it seemed she saw nothing. I felt tears in my eyes, horrified she succumbed so quick.

I took off the mask so I could see clear and knelt at her side to peer at her pale skin, in search of tokens and buboes. None that I could see, yet it was little satisfaction, for if the aunt visited yesterday and brought the sickness with her, then Jane could only just have been infected. The first signs were fevers, headaches and vomiting; the tokens and the buboes would not appear for at least three days. I saw no sign she had been tended to. Anger trembled all parts of my body. I went immediately to the linen cupboard and took a new sheet.

How to clean her up? For this was not an art I had experience of. However I went about the task I would need to place my hands upon her, which meant risk of contact. I had no wish to carry the disease out of the house, nor indeed contract it myself, so I placed the mask back on my head and endeavoured to do of my best.

First I placed my arms about her sides and persuaded her to step weakly from the bed, whereupon she sank slowly to the floor and lay there instead. No matter. I changed the sheet without difficulty. How then to change her fouled nightdress, for I had no wish to compromise her dignity. If ever she thought I had seen her naked she would gouge out my eyes with burning pokers. Yet what else could I do? I was not about to entrust her to the muddled crone below. Also I would need water and a cloth. I found a new nightdress in the chest and applied myself to the task, relieved to see no sign of swelling about the rest of her body, especially about her groin. Once finished I opened the window so the smell might dissipate and placed herbs about the room. I lay a blanket at her feet and left her uncovered, given the rising heat of the day. I thought to kiss her gently upon the forehead, but forced myself to leave, shaken by the strange thought.

Now to find the aunt. I went to my room first, since it was the only other place with a bed. I opened the door slow and peered in. I heard myself utter a stifled shriek, for she stood in the corner, staring at me with terrible red eyes, glaring out of a grey worn face. Death's wife come a-visiting, ghostly and cadaverous, thin and hungry, salivating at the prospect of tearing me to pieces. I stood paralysed, waiting to see what she would do next. She breathed hard and sagged, and I realised how weak she was.

The bed was a mess, sheets and blankets tossed about the floor, mattress pushed askew and curtains pulled loose from the tester. How quickly the disease took her, I reflected, for if she had visited only yesterday, then she must have seemed well. Surely she would not have come if she knew she carried infection.

I withdrew gently, again with plans to clean the room and restore some order. The moment I moved she lifted her hand and pointed straight at me and laughed, a tight frenzied laughter that racked her body and caused her to grimace in pain. Then she stopped, stared blankly and fell to the floor.

I repaired the bed as I had done before, then stripped the old woman naked upon the floor, preparing to wash her. My heart pounded in my ears and blood pumped in my temples at the sight of her naked flesh. It was all I could do not to run straight down to the river and jump in it, for the disease embraced her completely.

Small round spots covered her chest, hard and red. These were the tokens that condemned her. Worse, cradled in the damp warmth of her armpits and between her legs, nestled evil swellings, risen like flat mountains. Swellings that stretched from beneath her breast round to her back, purple and angry, peaking in dull blackness. These were the buboes, huge sacks of poison to be broken if the victim was to live. Yet these burrowed deep, untouchable in their current state. If she were to have any chance at all of living then she would need constant attention. But the nurse slept.

I descended to the kitchen and poked the grate. Cold and dusty. No one had cooked, no one had eaten and no one had attempted fumigation. Again, all chores for the drunken harridan across the hall. Little wood remained, which task I resolved to nail upon Hearsey's forehead.

I used what fuel there was to start a small fire. I found a knife and board, peeled and chopped six onions and placed them in a dish. Once the fire caught, I placed the dish above it so they would roast. I took the piece of lily root from my bag and pestled it into a fine mash with the cooked onions. I took the mixture upstairs, still warm, and spread it upon the older woman's buboes, in and around her armpits. Then I screwed my courage to the sticking place and did the others besides. I left her naked so the poultice might do its work and watched her breathe a while, shallow, as though her chest was crushed and tender.

I went back to Jane, who appeared to be asleep. Unsettling to watch her in this gentle stillness. I laid a hand upon her shoulder and saw her wince. She grimaced again and whimpered. Sweat trickled from her forehead and down her temples. Someone should be mopping her brow. I pulled the mask back down over my head and marched downstairs, furious.

The nurse had fallen down my chair another degree. Saliva dribbled slowly from the corner of her open mouth, from which continued to rumble a deep bellowing snore. I poked her again, this time in the shoulder, but she slept, oblivious. So I tipped up the chair and she fell in a heap on the floor.

She pushed herself up onto all fours and looked up through narrow slits, eyes struggling to manage the bright sun shining through the window. I offered her a hand and pulled her to her feet. She attempted to right herself by placing her hands upon my shoulders, but I stood back, unwilling. She continued to stagger around the room, senseless and unaware. Poor useless creature that she was, I found my anger redirect itself toward Fuller, he who assured me he knew a woman who wanted a job as nurse.

I opened the front door and directed her by the scruff of the neck out onto the street. She muttered and cursed, and put her hands up to protect her eyes against the daylight.

I turned to Hearsey. 'Did it not occur to you that there is no smoke coming from the chimney, that she asked you for no provisions?'

He held his arms down by his sides and licked his lips.

I pointed at the woman who had slumped now to the ground and sat against my wall with head sunk upon her chest. 'Both the women inside this house are sick and yet she has done nothing. You will acquire tar, pitch and frankincense and ensure the house is fumigated.'

I waited for some acknowledgement. He nodded.

'You will inform Alderman Fuller his nurse is an intoxicated harridan and that she is not worthy of appointment.' I forced myself contain the grief that threatened to overwhelm me, for already he frowned, suspicious. 'A new nurse is to be appointed immediately to tend to the two women within, one of whom is on the point of the death, the other who might yet be saved.'

He peered at me. 'Who shall I say instructed it?'

'The medic, of course.' I roared. 'I will be back before the day is out and you will comply with my instruction if you wish to retain your own poor post.'

I glared at his distorted face through the glass eyepieces, turned on my heel, and marched back to Newgate.

CHAPTER 14

Any man committed to prison, whether he shall be soon delivered?
Behold the moon, if she be swift or slow of course: if she be swift, it shows short tarrying in prison; the contrary if she be slow of course.

I entered Dowling's house quiet and hid the medic's garb inside a basket by the door.

'Where have you been?' Dowling bellowed, stomping into the room just as I straightened. 'You've been away all morning. Did it not occur to you I might think you captured again?'

I eyed the fresh white bandage. 'How is your thumb? I fetched some fleabane.'

'Fleabane?' Dowling exclaimed. His face appeared pale, eyes tired. I reckoned he had been up most of the night. 'Will ye stop agonising over me like an old woman?' Yet his eyes searched for the powder.

'Let me dress it for you,' I offered. 'I have seen Jane do

it many times. I'm late because she's become infected besides. The nurse is a drunkard sow and Jane was not being cared for.'

Dowling grunted, bashful now, which was my intent. I fetched the bandage and unwrapped his thumb. The skin stretched tight and red so you couldn't distinguish where his knuckle began and ended. Where his fingernail should have been was but a thick crust of dried blood. I washed it for him, while he did his best to demonstrate how incidental was the pain, then spread the fleabane thick. If an infection took hold he might lose his hand, his arm, even his life. 'We will get you to an apothecary later,' I said, 'unless you're a bigger fool than even I.'

'Aye, later,' he agreed with strained tone. 'Burke is at Ludgate.'

I looked up and pressed his thumb too hard. He flinched and gasped. 'Ludgate is a debtors' prison.'

'I know not *why* he is at Ludgate, Harry,' Dowling hissed through gritted teeth. 'Only that he *is* at Ludgate and they say he killed Wharton.'

'Aye, then.' I bandaged his thumb quick and allowed him to shuffle me back out onto the street.

Though my legs carried me to Ludgate, my heart and mind still lingered inside my little house. Now they lay there with no nurse at all. Would Hearsey do as I ordered, or would he sit himself back down and go to sleep? What if the nurse begged to be forgiven and asked for her job back? What if she denied her drunkenness and accused me? I needed to get back there soon, make sure Fuller did his job. I pledged to return forthwith and tried to clear my mind for just a short while.

'Remember the poor prisoners!' I heard the sound of the cryer even from the shadow of St Paul's.

It was expensive being a debtor. It cost three shillings to be arrested, two pennies to have your name entered in the register, fourteen pence to be admitted, a penny for lodging, eighteen pence for sheets, four shillings to keep your own clothes, and sixteen pence table money. To get out again cost two shillings, fourteen pence to open the door the other way, and twelve pence for every action taken against you. Debtors being debtors had no such funds, so they had to beg for money from within the jail, so they could give it to the jailers.

Two guards stepped forth at our approach, ready to prevent us passage beneath the great arch, for Ludgate Hill led to St Giles-in-the-Fields, where the plague roamed unrestrained.

We sought no passage out the arch, only into the prison, which was not usually difficult. Today though, the tower was locked tight closed. King Lud frowned down upon us with black and crumbling face.

Dowling rapped on the prison door. Lazy eyes appeared

at the iron grille, atop a long narrow nose and thin-lipped mouth. A spidery moustache crept sideways and down toward a pointed chin.

Dowling held up his seal. 'Open the door.'

'No,' replied the guard.

Dowling pushed the paper up hard against the little grate. 'This is the King's authority.'

The hooded eyes regarded the seal without great interest. 'So it is,' he agreed in muffled tone. 'But our instructions are also royal, and says we can admit no man until the plague is gone.'

Dowling banged his palm against the door. 'We are here at the request of Lord Arlington, in whose name were *writ* the Plague Orders.'

The man pushed his head closer. 'What request?'

I nudged Dowling aside so he could calm himself. 'We have come to talk to one of your prisoners.'

The long nose wrinkled. 'What prisoner?'

'Henry Burke.'

'Methinks not.' He clicked his tongue. 'Though I be only the Assistant, I can tell you Burke cannot be seen by any, even those within the prison. I, for example, may not see Henry Burke.'

'Lord Arlington has not requested you to see Henry Burke,' I pointed out.

'Well I cannot help you,' he declared. Yet the grille

remained open and he remained behind it, staring out.

I hid my frustration behind an iron smile. 'Who can help us?'

'I don't have the key to his cell.' The Assistant shrugged. 'Nor does the Under-steward. Only the Master-of-the-Box has that key. Ye may ask the Under-steward and he may commend ye to the Master-of-the-Box.'

'Then we will talk to the Master-of-the-Box.'

'So ye may,' he replied. 'Once ye have spoken to the Under-steward.'

'Then we will talk to the Under-steward.'

He sniffed and rubbed a finger across his nose. 'To talk to the Under-steward ye must pay me a shilling.'

'A shilling?' I retorted.

'Aye, and then the Under-steward will charge you two shillings to talk to the Master-of-the-Box.'

'No,' I snapped, fed up of leaking coins in service of the King. 'You saw the royal seal. We will talk to whosoever we wish without paying you a shilling, nor so much as a penny.'

The man's lazy brow dropped further in disappointment. 'Then I cannot help you.'

Dowling jabbed a finger in my ribs. 'If we paid you three shillings then might we speak immediately with the Master-of-the-Box?'

The eyes looked doubtful. 'The Under-steward would

not be happy.'

'Four shillings then.'

'Come to the begging gate.' The grille snapped closed.

'You have four shillings?' Dowling growled as we walked around the corner.

'Aye,' I fessed, reluctant. Four more shillings I would never see again.

The Assistant stood waiting for us, long and drawn out, narrow-chested like a boy, trousers hung at half mast down his legs. He pushed a jar out through the bars, full of vinegar. 'Put the money in the jar.' Once I complied he nodded his head and disappeared back to the grille.

The bolt slid open and at last we were permitted entry. The Assistant took one long tentative step out onto the street and craned his neck to inspect the bright sun. 'A good day to be outside, yet you insist on coming inside.'

'Only for a short while,' I replied, impatient. He stared again at the sun like he would spread himself upon the street and soak up its rays, afore retreating slow. He locked the door behind him, and led us up the spiral stone staircase. The stones were big and grey, and cool to the touch.

We heard the low chatter before reaching the long room above. Twenty men dwelt between its walls, all dressed well-to-do, merchants and tradesmen. Seemed they had little opportunity to wash their fine clothes, for the stink of unwashed bodies soaked the humid air. Several gazed out the windows, clutching the bars, faces pressed against the grille, scanning the empty road hopefully for miracle benefactors. Others sat on the floor and stared at the ceiling, resigned to their fate. Some played cards, oblivious. None of them was Burke.

The Assistant led us across bare boards to an open door opposite. 'Up again. Burke is locked up in his own cell.'

Another stone staircase led to a wide corridor, an open office at the end. The cells to our left and right were obviously home to the men downstairs, for the doors stood open. Each cell housed a bed or two and a smattering of other poor possessions. Anything of value would be sold.

'Master-of-the-Box,' the Assistant announced.

An old man sat at a desk in the middle of bare boards. His white head hung over a thin book, forehead touching the table, snoring. He was quite a large gentleman, with broad shoulders and broader belly.

When I knocked on the table next to his ear his snowy head jerked up, bleary red eyes searching for the source of his disturbance. His gaze lighted upon the Assistant and he blinked quizzically.

The Assistant bowed quickly. 'These men say they come from the King. They have paid for the honour of your company.' He hurried out the room.

The Master-of-the-Box stretched his arms out wide in a mighty yawn and rubbed his sleepy face. 'The King?'

'We have come to see Henry Burke,' I said.

He cleared his throat and gathered his jacket about his shoulders. 'No one can visit Henry Burke. By order.'

Dowling showed his credentials. 'By order of the King?'

'By order of Lord Chelwood,' the man replied, standing up.

'The King outranks Chelwood.'

'Aye.' The older man looked down his nose at me. 'But I think Mr Forman and Mr Withypoll outrank you.' He lifted his arm and let his hand drop toward Dowling. 'You look like a boatman.' He turned to me. 'And your clothes are as creased and crumpled as those we keep here. Show me *your* credentials.'

'You would be foolish to deny us.' Dowling scowled. 'For if you do, then we will return with a warrant and soldiers.' The tip of his nose and the crown of his cheeks burned red. 'Come on, Harry.'

'Hold!' The white haired man lifted a finger, clearly shocked. 'We can come to an arrangement.'

Dowling turned. 'How much?'

'Mr Forman and Mr Withypoll paid me a surety of five shillings.'

'Then we will also pay you five shillings,' Dowling said.

The Master-of-the-Box nodded in satisfaction afore reaching in his desk for a small leather bound journal and another jar of vinegar. All tradesmen now used vinegar when receiving money, to clean the coins of sticky atoms. Once we settled his account, he led us out, keys clanking on his belt, down a small dark passage to the left. At the end was a locked door. He fiddled with his keys for what seemed an age, afore admitting us to a small ante-room with three cells lined up behind it. Burke lay upon a wooden bench in the cell to the left, face to the wall. The other two cells were empty.

'Open the cell,' Dowling commanded. 'We will leave Mr Lytle here awhile to talk.'

The Master-of-the-Box stared as though he'd been slapped about the face. 'You don't wish to talk to him besides?'

'I will come with you,' smiled Dowling. 'So you do not seek to earn yourself another five shillings by alerting Forman and Withypoll to our presence.'

The Master opened his mouth and closed it again, then did as he was told. I stared at Burke's rounded back. He remained curled up like a little piglet for several minutes, before peeking over his shoulder. His wig was gone, revealing a loose baggy scalp dotted with peppered bristles. He wore the same black trousers and billowing white shirt he wore last we saw him. His jacket and waistcoat had been taken.

'Burke,' I greeted him in low voice.

His face wrinkled. 'You,' he slurred. 'That asks so many

questions and will not leave me alone.'

I grabbed a rickety chair and sat down. 'They say you confessed to the murder of Thomas Wharton?'

'Murder?' He pulled himself up straight. 'What nonsense is that? I have confessed to no murder.'

'Ah, well,' I settled myself. 'That's not what the news says.'

A single window high up the wall admitted a square of sharp light. It was silent in here, so quiet you might hear the sound of your own heart beating the seconds and minutes away.

Burke wriggled into a sitting position, indignant and afraid. 'I have committed no murder,' he repeated. 'It is *your* fault I am here!'

'How so my fault?'

'They were going to let me stay with Tanner until the real murderer was discovered,' Burke exploded. 'After you turned up they said prison was the safest place.'

'They brought you here because it is *safe*?'

Hatred and fear fought upon his face. 'Aye, so they did. Safe from you, yet here you are again, and I will not talk to you.'

'You will.' I pulled a blade from out beneath my breeches, taken from Dowling's kitchen. 'Else I will stab you.' This was the third time we spoke to him and little had we gained thus far.

He backed against the wall. 'Godamercy!'

I pointed the blade at his chest. '*Did* you kill Wharton?'

His face blazed ruddy scarlet. 'No,' he exclaimed. 'I am a wine merchant.'

'And what of Death and Famine. Who killed them?'

'Who are Death and Famine?' he spluttered.

I did not have the patience to explain fully. 'Wharton's dogs named themselves after horses. Death was found inside one of your barrels at The Bull Head and Famine at the bottom of the river chained to another.'

Burke shook his head, staring at the knife. 'Not me!'

'Who then?'

Burke pushed his face into his palms and glared through his fingers.

I lifted the blade. 'Your friends Forman and Withypoll tried to kill me yesterday.'

He glared. 'You should have stayed away. Why can you not mind your own business?'

'My business is finding out who killed three men,' I answered. 'What is your business with Forman and Withypoll? You were with them at The Mermaid, and then again at the Guildhall.'

Burke closed one eye and muttered to himself.

'What did you talk to them about at The Mermaid?'

'Why would you know that?' he grunted.

'Because I would know who killed Wharton, you great

oaf!' I lost my patience. 'These men, Forman and Withypoll, in whom you place such trust, have locked you in a prison cell and let it be known you killed Wharton! Why will you not talk to me?'

'It is Forman and Withypoll tried to kill you,' he exclaimed. 'Not you that tried to kill them. I am afraid of them, but I am not afraid of you!' He slouched against the wall and folded his arms in a great sulk. 'I have nothing to say to you.'

At which point I leaned over and stabbed him in the thigh.

He yelled, staring at me indignant, then scrabbled at his slashed trouser searching furiously for blood, of which there was but a small round puddle. Then he jabbed a finger at me and made shrill noises.

'Quiet!' I commanded, calmer than I felt.

He panted soundlessly.

'You told me your deal was guaranteed by a nobleman. Who?'

Burke peeled the cloth from his thigh to inspect the damage. 'You will not find that out from me,' he cried, hoarse. 'Stab me again if you must.'

'I will if I have to.' I wiped the blade upon a cloth I brought for the purpose. 'Nor would your friends Forman and Withypoll object, for as I told you, word is you killed Wharton. I think they are the ones spreading that word.'

'That cannot be,' he muttered. Yet his eyes sunk deep into his head and his lips quivered.

'The Master-of-the-Box says Forman and Withypoll act on behalf of Lord Chelwood,' I remembered. 'Who is Lord Chelwood? Are you working for him?'

'I can tell you nothing of Lord Chelwood. I don't know him and never met him. You must ask the Master-of-the-Box.' Blood began to seep from the small round hole in his leg. He eyed my knife. 'Ask me something else!' he urged me, face pale.

'Who was involved in your wine deal?'

'I could not involve others, the contract forbade it,' Burke protested. His eyes said he deceived me.

I tapped the blade upon my chin. 'Yet you didn't have enough money of your own.'

'Aye, then,' he let out a mighty breath. 'So I did invite a few others to invest what I could not afford. But why would you ask me that? None of them invested what I invested, and were I to reveal to you their names then I would not be able to do business in this city again.'

I bent toward him. 'You must tell me their names, Burke, for they are as likely candidates as you. I have no interest in betraying your confidences. I will watch from afar and monitor.'

'I cannot.' He clenched his fists and hissed through his teeth. Then he lay back limp, water in his eyes. 'I

wish I never heard of Thomas Wharton,' he whispered.
'I had no need of that deal. I supplied a quarter of the
city with wine.'

'Tell me who else invested,' I insisted. 'You would protect
their identities when one of them may be the killer? You
would die for one of them?'

'None of them killed Wharton.' He wiped away the
clotting blood from his thigh, gently, so not to cause it to
bleed once more. 'I thought if I impressed the King I
might win new business at court. Instead I lost it all. I owe
more than I will ever be able to repay.'

I began to resent his lachrymose self pity. He lost his
business because he was greedy. 'Tell me who invested with
you else I will stab you in the other leg.'

He rubbed a hand across his forehead, perspiration
dripping in rivulets between the folds of his fleshy face. 'I
have lost my business, now you would have me lose my
dignity?'

'What dignity?' I snorted. 'First you hide yourself away
in a slum by the river. Now you lie here ensconced in a
debtors' prison accused of murder. How dignified will you
feel when the whole of London watches you swing by
the neck with your guts hanging about your knees?'

'I have only your word I am accused of murder!' He
stood up and started shouting. 'I have only your word I
am to be tried for that! They told me this was a safe place!

Somewhere I would not be disturbed!'

'They lied.'

He leaned forward, arms hanging loose, gulping deep breaths.

'Tell me who invested with you.'

'One other invested with me.' A tear rolled down his cheek, so perfectly round I put away my blade, ashamed. 'No others would. He said he could afford it easily, for he contributed less than five per cent, but I think he deceived me. I think he may have lost more than he could afford besides.'

'Who is he?'

He stared from beneath a black bushy brow. 'A local merchant named Willis.' He sat down heavy on the bench. 'Oliver Willis.'

I forgot to breathe. 'Oliver Willis of Seething Lane?'

'The same,' Burke confirmed miserably. 'And now I must trust you to be discreet.'

He looked to me for assurance, moist-eyed and anxious, yet I could see little in my mind beyond Liz's pale face, anguished and sorrowful, a prisoner to her father's desperate plight. I focussed again on Burke's pathetic aspect and saw for a moment Oliver Willis. Just as greedy, just as careless.

'I will be discreet, Burke,' I said, slow. 'But what will you do?'

'Don't taunt me, King's agent. You say you work for the

King. Why do you not release me?'

'I can if you wish it,' I replied.

'And what then?' He pursed his lips and regarded me with fury. 'I have nothing against you, King's man, even though you stuck me in the leg with that short blade of yours. I will trust your intent, for what it is worth. So trust mine. You have already overstepped your mark. If you would avoid same plight as Wharton, then leave London while you can.' He contemplated the grim bare cell. 'Else you will find yourself here with me.'

'Very well, Burke.' I bid my muddled mind be still. 'But when you realise Forman and Withypoll plan to hang you, send for me.'

'Send for you?'

'Aye, Harry Lytle.'

'And what will you do for me, Harry Lytle?' he asked quietly. 'You and your little knife?'

It was a good question. Yet not the one foremost on my mind.

CHAPTER 15

Signs of a long or short sickness

If the sign of the sixth be fixed, expect a long disease; a moveable sign, short continuance, a common sign, a mediocrity, neither too long or short, but for the most part, an alteration of the disease, and return of it again.

I thought of visiting Alderman Fuller first, to see if a new nurse was appointed, but was wary. Too many people looking for me. So I donned the moist medic robes and went direct to my house.

I recalled the look of suspicion upon Hearsey's face the last time I visited, yet it might have been but a distortion of the lens. When I arrived though, he had a companion. No time to hesitate. I strode to the door like the King himself.

Hearsey hopped to his feet and stuck his thumbs in his belt. 'You are the medic?'

'Aye,' I replied pointing at the door. 'And busy besides.'

Hearsey tried to peer through the glass of my eyes, while

his partner hovered, curious. 'There are two of you then?'

'There are a dozen of us,' I snapped. 'Now will you kindly open the door.'

'Very well.' He fetched my key again from his pocket and stood aside while the second man wandered away. I watched, nervous, wondering if he went to alert someone. Once inside the house I heard Hearsey lock the door behind me. He hadn't done that this morning. I considered climbing straight out of the window and making my escape back to Newgate, but not without knowing how Jane fared.

First I checked the front room to make certain the drunkard nurse was not returned. Instead I found Jane, sat upright on my chair, faced toward the door, as though expecting a visitor. She stared full ahead, unblinking, the skin of her face grey, the crescents beneath her eyes almost black. Bedraggled hair tangled about her nose and ears like dead river weed, fiery orange faded to dry brown. Her body was thin and twiggy, bones pushing out through soft de-fleshed skin. The eyes didn't move.

Grief weighed so heavy on my heart I fell to my knees, staring up at her still face. I took one of her hands and held it in my glove, cursing myself my pig-headed stubbornness. This was my work, my fault.

She coughed sharply and a piece of green sputum landed upon the lens of my mask. My heart jumped so high it crashed against the back of my teeth and got stuck in my throat. Queer to think phlegm could make a man so happy. I wiped my sleeve across my eyes that I might see better and took medicine from my bag, babbling to myself in hysteric relief.

I bought a new concoction on the street, a mixture of wormwood, mint and balm. I held little faith in it, but something was better than nothing, though it would be difficult to administer with these thick gloves on.

I hurried to the kitchen to fetch a spoon. A fire burned fierce in the grate. A chafing dish rested on the coal, vitriol or vinegar bubbling into the air. A broth bubbled gently in a pot.

I returned to Jane and fed her the medicine. To my great joy she swallowed. I put the glove back on and left the bottle on the table in full view. The happiness evaporated fast. She was alive, but barely. I poked about her neck and chest, searching for tokens or sign of swelling, praying I would not find them. Though clammy and pale, her skin was clear.

Where was the nurse? Or had Jane done all this herself?

I headed upstairs, progress arrested by a piercing wail sounding from my room, a noise like you'd hear in Bedlam, full of pain and fear. I approached the room with trepidation, cautious of the aunt leaping out, mad-eyed and dangerous.

Another fire blazed in the fireplace, twice the size of the

one in the kitchen. Inside burned like an oven. Jane's aunt lay stiff upon my bed, eyes wide open, staring at the ceiling. She held her arms rigid at her side, body gleaming, soaked in sweat. Her nightdress was pushed up, gathered about her chest. It was not a place I would normally look, but I couldn't help but inspect the things that grew on her groin, enormous black grapes pushing out of her skin.

A nurse perched next to the bed, slight and contained. She watched me, expectant, bowl upon her knee, holding a thin cloth to wipe the patient's brow. The suffocating heat left her as drenched as the lady on the bed.

'What have you been giving her?' I asked, loud so she might hear from beneath the mask.

'The other medic said to keep her hot,' she replied, wary. 'He said he would return this evening to bleed her.'

And lance those buboes too, I wagered. I doubted it would save her. Beneath her arms and all about her chest the flesh was swollen, puffed and tight. Too much poison ran beneath her skin. The old woman let forth another moan, face contorted in agonised grimace, before screaming again.

'She asked if I might kill her,' the nurse said quiet, eyes brimming with hot tears.

'They often do,' I replied. 'It will end soon, one way or the other.'

She nodded.

'What of the one below?' I asked. 'When did she get out of bed?'

'She sat there when I arrived,' the nurse said, timid. 'The other medic said it was all right to leave her there so long as she wished it. I have lit the fire and tend to her regular.'

'Aye, then.' I left her alone, somewhat comfitted.

Downstairs Jane still sat like stone. I knelt, removed my gloves and took her hands in my hands, felt how cold they were. How so cold? I worried anxiously. Did it signify she neared death? As I crouched there holding those frail fingers, her eyes moved and settled upon mine. I thought I saw a question there, afore they closed and she emitted a deep sigh.

I could think of little else to do. The nurse seemed able and she spoke of a medic. My mind turned again to escape.

Who did Hearsey's colleague leave to fetch? I banged upon the door to be released. The key turned in the lock.

'That was quick,' Hearsey remarked, stepping aside to let me out. Then someone seized my elbows and pulled them back and Hearsey punched me hard in the stomach. I was allowed to fall upon the ground where I focussed on breathing.

'You will come with us,' he exclaimed. 'Medic!'

He gripped one arm, while another man took the other,

the same that waited my arrival. They dragged me along the street, laughing and kicking at my ankles to keep me unbalanced. Passers-by stood horrified, hands upon their mouths, that a medic could be treated thus. But Hearsey marched oblivious, while the second man walked with a small man's pride, like a kitten with its first mouse.

Who did they work for? Though Hearsey punched me hard, neither possessed the vicious menace of Forman and Withypoll, nor Wharton's Four Horsemen. They tugged me into Bow Lane and afore I knew it, with great surprise, the front room of Alderman Fuller.

Fuller eased his arthritic frame up from behind the desk. 'The mysterious medic.' He shambled toward me and reached out with bony fingers to lift off the mask. He shook his head, stern. 'I thought it was you.'

He breathed silently through his nose, chest heaving, reminding me at last of the man who terrorised me years before. 'I understand the anxiety for your servant's welfare, but this is not the way to discharge it.'

The old goat would not talk to me as though I was a child again. 'Had I done it any other way I would not have discovered the lazy villain you first appointed as nurse.'

'So say you,' Fuller retorted. 'She says she slept exhausted from having worked all the night.'

'Malicious deceit!' I exclaimed. 'The fire was cold, there

was no food upon the table, and neither Jane nor her aunt had been treated.' I jerked my arm free and pointed a finger at his rickety chest. 'She sat there in my front room, snoring, while the two of them lay dying upstairs. Is that the kind of nurse you have been appointing?' I turned to Hearsey and his friend. 'You might as well appoint one of these great oafs!'

Fuller gathered his coat about his shoulders. 'Did the nurse you met today satisfy your high standards?'

'Aye,' I nodded, 'so she did, and my standards are no higher than yours ought to be.'

Fuller considered my hands and looked me in the eye. 'Did you take off your mask or your gloves while ye were in there?'

'No,' I lied.

'Good,' he said at last. 'Else I would have to lock you up in there with them.' He shook his head again and returned to his desk. 'If you seek further news of them, Harry, please come talk to me and I will oblige.'

I could think of little else to say. Was that it? With a final stare at Hearsey and his ugly friend, I departed, half expecting to be called back.

I hurried on to Newgate, mask back upon my face. I was getting angry.

CHAPTER 16

By what means attain it

When you have sufficiently examined your figure, and perceived that the querent shall have a substance or will come to have riches, it will be demanded, how? By whom? Or what means it may be obtained?

'Mr Willis and Mrs. Willis are dining, sir,' the servant told me at the door.

'Dining alone?'

'No, sir.' She shook her head firmly. 'They have guests.'

'What guests?' I demanded. Odd they would invite guests to dine so soon after Hedges' death.

I heard a rippling laugh, loud like a badly hung bell. Marjory Henslowe.

'I know the Henslowes,' I assured the servant. 'They will not mind if I join them.'

'Sir!' she protested, but I ignored her.

Oliver Willis stood as I entered the room. 'Harry.' He held his arms out, welcoming. I noticed anew how lined was his face, how less certain his demeanour.

Liz sat like Lady Castlemayne herself, dress shining like a silver blue night sea, face white as the moon above it. She greeted me politely, but her eyes were hard, bankrupt of feeling.

'Oliver,' I replied, unsure what to say. 'I felt compelled to visit.'

He saw me stare at Liz. 'Please join us then.'

Edward stood forward, uncertain, fetched a chair and laid a plate afront of me. Phillip Henslowe watched with warm curiosity. I liked Henslowe in an inn or a tavern. Not so in the company of his wife, when he just sat quiet and observed. Marjory greeted me quite perfunctorily, which was not unusual. She did not like me.

'I hear you are appointed to investigate the murder of Thomas Wharton,' Henslowe said, eyeing me with new respect.

'In a manner,' I agreed, watching Oliver.

Marjory Henslowe sat with head cocked to one side, eyes stony as Liz's. 'I heard this afternoon the merchant Henry Burke killed the Earl of St Albans and sits now at Ludgate awaiting trial.'

Willis whipped a napkin to his mouth and bent over in a bout of choked coughing. A piece of chicken shot across the room and landed on the floor. An embarrassed silence ensued. Marjory twitched and fidgeted, her mouth dried up into a thin prim curl, contemplating me like I was an unwelcome nuisance.

'Is it true, Harry?' Henslowe regarded me quizzically. 'Tell us the story.'

'Aye,' I replied, watching Willis dab at his eyes. 'They say he killed Wharton because the Earl cheated him.'

Willis blew his nose and frowned.

'Yet I doubt he was the killer,' I continued. 'I saw him on Tuesday when one man was killed, and again on Wednesday when another was killed. He could not have killed them all.'

'Godamercy!' Henslowe exclaimed. 'How many men have been killed?'

'Three,' I answered. 'All in brutal fashion, all with some reference to wine.'

'Then Burke is the killer,' Marjory Henslowe shrilled. 'For he is a wine merchant. If he were not the killer he would not be at Ludgate waiting trial.' She drew her head back upon her chins and wrinkled her nose at me. 'Perhaps you are not so important as you think.'

Oliver Willis' shoulders slumped like he wished he could go upstairs and go to bed.

'I don't know why they would appoint you,' Marjory Henslowe continued, eyeing her husband as though the appointment was a sleight on him. 'I understand you were here *that* night too, Mr Lytle, that it was your idea to leave

Dr Hedges outside the door?' She eyed her plate with renewed appetite now she found words that satisfied.

'Hardly a reasonable account,' Henslowe admonished his wife nervously.

'Indeed,' Liz snapped. Anger brought new life into her dull eyes. 'I would call it a malicious account.' She stared at Marjory Henslowe so hard, the older woman was compelled to turn away.

'If you would prefer I leave, Elizabeth, then I will leave,' Marjory Henslowe replied in self righteous whine. 'I merely repeated what you said to us. I didn't know it was a secret.' She caught her husband's baleful eye. 'I was just remarking.'

'True enough, Mrs Henslowe, it was my idea,' I ceded. 'Surely his body was best buried quickly, and by his family. Yet we could not have taken the body to his house, for we might have infected the entire household.' I looked around to see how my words landed. All gazed at the table except Marjory. 'Were it not that James died as a consequence, then I would still say now it was the right thing to do.'

Marjory drew her arms to her side in straight-backed indignation. 'The *right* thing to do, you say?' She pursed her lips tight like a little dog's arse. 'Have you not read the Plague Orders?'

'Aye,' I replied. 'The day they were issued. But this is not the abode of Nathaniel Hedges, so it cannot be said the infection stemmed from this house. Surely the sensible course was to remove him from the house as quickly as we could? Every moment the body stayed inside this house was to put at risk the life of each and every person who lives here.'

'The Plague Orders make no such provision,' Marjory said.

'Some decisions a man must make for himself,' I answered. 'Those who have the wit.'

Marjory's cheeks reddened. 'So you oppose the practice of locking up the sick?'

'They have been locking up houses in St Giles these last few weeks yet the sickness is not dissuaded.'

'You would have the sick walk freely?'

'The sick *do* walk freely, is what they say,' I said with studied composure. 'Some men paint their own doors with a cross, so the constables pay no attention and no watcher is appointed. Then they walk in and out without restraint.'

'Yes, Mr Lytle.' Marjory straightened her back. 'And others remove the sick themselves before the examiners arrive.'

It seemed a futile discourse to me. If Marjory Henslowe really felt so passionate then she would not have come here to eat. I looked sideways at Liz, who glared at Marjory Henslowe with an intensity that would have sliced a softer woman's throat.

Henslowe broke the silence, staring across at his wife

with appalled anguish in his eyes. 'Marjory?'

'I'm sorry.' She put her hands to her nose and mouth. She was frightened, and we all saw it.

Oliver Willis attempted to play the role of wise conciliator. 'These are terrible days.'

I sipped a glass of wine and decided to change the subject to something more entertaining. 'A time of great uncertainty,' I agreed. 'Which some men choose to exploit. Let me tell you of Owen Price.' And so I related my conversation with the uncomfortable astrologist, determining to enjoy myself until able to confront Willis alone.

Marjory Henslowe straightened herself once more, and with hands upon her lap, met my eye severely. Too late I saw she blamed me for her earlier embarrassment and would see me suffer for it.

'Mr Lytle,' she began. My heart sank. 'Astrology is a heathen philosophy, William Lilly is a heathen, and the astrologers should be severely punished for taking advantage of the fears of the weak. So.' She paused for effect. 'Why did you invite one of these creatures into your house?' She said it with such sweet lips and steady eyes, I was pinned like a butterfly.

If Marjory Henslowe was a friend then I would have happily described the unusual circumstances of my household, but I didn't feel disposed to subject Jane to the contempt of this preening shrew.

'William Lilly is orthodox Anglican,' I answered at last. 'The Lord is not constrained by astral determinism.' Words so wise I hardly understood them myself.

'That Lilly claims to be orthodox Anglican does not make him so.' She waggled a long finger in my direction. 'Astrology is a magic, employing ritual and graven symbols. So it is ungodly and idolatrical.'

'If God gave us an art, then the use of that art must needs be lawful,' I argued, irritated by the finger in my face.

She lifted her chin and sought support from her husband. '*I* did not say it was an art.'

'My dear, astrology is a science, it is an ancient science.' He realised too late he spoke to her as though to a child.

Marjory Henslowe did not blink, yet the pink upon her ears said Phillip's patronising tone shocked her. My heart sneezed. Little though I liked her, I would have to rescue her if normal conversation were to resume. Yet I could hardly start agreeing with her now, for that would be even more humiliating. Neither could I change the subject for it would be to same effect. She would have to fight her own corner. Unless they both left. Which would be humiliating for Oliver. He watched me from above the rim of his glass. I wished I had stayed away.

'It is true many believe the scientific foundations of astrology to be valid and many use it to diagnose illness,' Willis ventured carefully, eyeing Phillip Henslowe. 'Yet others see it as a dying art, upheld only by the old and credible. Perhaps we are old, Henslowe, not attuned yet to the new philosophy.'

That wouldn't work! I could feel Marjory Henslowe sink deeper into her chair without even having to look. 'Methinks it is a matter of belief, not age,' I declared impulsively.

Henslowe turned his clear eye upon me. 'And what do you believe in?' A mischievous question, for he well suspected the nature of mine own atheist beliefs.

'I believe it is strange there is but one God, yet his intent is interpreted so diversely.'

'Heathen words,' Marjory declared, much to my relief, for I feared she had withdrawn for the evening. 'If sinners entice thee, consent thou not!' she exclaimed. She spoke with such passion I wondered what Henslowe had been telling her.

I was suitably chastised, a state of affairs that suited everyone, including me. The next hour passed cheerfully enough, though Willis appeared tense. I sensed my presence discomfited him, yet I determined not to leave before speaking to him alone.

As the sun descended behind the chimneys, Willis stood abruptly.

'Phillip,' he announced, smiling unconvincingly. 'Would you drink a while with me? For I would discuss something of import.'

Henslowe opened his mouth and looked to his wife, reluctant perhaps to align himself once more agin her.

'What about Harry?' Liz admonished him, embarrassed by his rudeness.

'Next time, Oliver.' Henslowe held up a hand before standing himself. 'I think we should leave afore it gets dark. Thank you for your hospitality.'

I stayed seated. Willis raised his brows, enquiring. I smiled for the benefit of the Henslowes. 'I will drink with you, Oliver.'

He blinked. 'I'll say goodbye to Phillip and Marjory first.'

Henslowe shook my hand firmly, eyes berating me fondly. I pledged to visit him soon. Then I thanked Marjory Henslowe, who by now was warmly disposed toward me, convinced both that she bested me intellectually and that I humbly acknowledged it.

Oliver escorted them out.

'What would you speak to my father about?' Liz whispered.

I scratched my scalp and avoided her eye. 'I cannot tell you.'

She crouched down and placed a delicate hand upon my knee. I stared into her bright green eyes and tried not to peek down at her chest. 'What would you speak to my father about?' she repeated. Her creamy lips curdled in a sour pout. She clenched her jaw and dug her nails into my thigh. I sensed her father kept a great secret, which she believed I might be privy to.

'Ask him after we have spoken,' I answered soft. 'It is his story to tell, not mine.'

'He will not be moved,' she said. 'I would have left weeks ago, but he will not be moved. If you know the reason why, Harry...' She shivered.

I placed my hand on hers and attempted to loosen her fingers. 'Let me talk to him, Liz.'

Oliver Willis entered the room and paused, waiting while Liz stood straight. He frowned, perplexed, while she withdrew, lines etched upon her forehead, eyes wet.

'What would you drink, Harry?' he asked, once she closed the door behind her.

'I spoke to Henry Burke today,' I said, watching his expression closely.

Willis folded his arms. 'You saw him?'

'Aye, at Ludgate,' I watched his twitching lips. 'He doesn't believe he is blamed for Wharton's death, but I think Marjory Henslowe is right, I think Burke was arrested for his murder.'

Willis nodded slowly. 'Would you have another cup of wine?'

'No more wine,' I replied. 'Burke spent a lot of money

on wine, at the behest of Thomas Wharton. Wharton kept the wine but didn't pay for it.'

'I heard,' Willis whispered.

'It was a significant transaction, Oliver. Burke needed others to invest, else he could not have afforded it.'

Willis clutched his arms tighter about his chest. 'So they say.'

'I heard you were the only one who Burke could persuade.'

Willis raised his chin. 'Burke told you?'

'It matters not who told me,' I replied. 'You invested money at Burke's behest, telling him these were funds you could easily afford, when in fact you could not. When Wharton reneged you must have been devastated. This is why you will not leave London. You prayed Burke might get his money back.'

Willis stared, unflinching.

'Is that the truth of it?' I asked.

Willis placed his hands on his hips and breathed slow. 'Listen to me, Lytle,' he said. 'I have treated you as a friend, allowed you to court my daughter. Now you descend upon me uninvited, you are rude to my guests, then pry into my affairs?' His pale face turned puce. 'It is too much to bear.'

'Wharton is hung in the Vintners' Hall. One of his colleagues is discovered in a barrel, and another is weighted to the river bottom by another barrel.' I pointed at his chest. 'I am charged with discovering who killed them. Of course I ask you questions. Be grateful I come alone and not with a King's guard.'

'Grateful?' he said. 'Twice now you have dined here, once uninvited, and both times the evening has ended in disaster.'

Behind the fury I noted desperation and despondency. He was usually a steady fellow, stoic and unflappable. 'You hoped to borrow funds,' I realised. 'That's why you took such a risk in inviting a medic to your house. You had reason to believe he might help you. Henslowe too. You hoped it would be he who stayed behind afterwards to drink wine.'

'Enough,' he hissed, eyes wide, face bright scarlet. 'Begone now, Lytle, and do not come back to my house. If you come within a hundred yards of my daughter again then I shall personally run my sword through your sticky heart!'

'Very well.' I feared his own sticky heart might be about to explode. 'I will leave you, Oliver, but I hope you know what you are doing.'

He exhaled and stared at the floor. I walked out the door into the hall, where Liz waited.

'What is going on?' She stepped forwards to peer into the dining room. 'What did you say to him?'

My little soul tremored afront of her rage. 'You must ask him, Liz.' I ducked my head and headed for the door.

Things were getting out of hand. It was time to call upon Newcourt for help.

CHAPTER 17

Of ambassadors or messengers

For if he be in the tenth, and there dignified essentially, the ambassador will stand too much upon the honour of his own prince, and has an overweening conceit of his own abilities.

It was a strange experience travelling this road I once walked every day. I had not passed through the Lion's Gate for more than year. The familiar surrounds stirred residual feelings of dread, the prospect of another tedious day sorting old records. Whilst I had not actually been a prisoner here, still I thought of the Tower as my jail. I had been a clerk, working for the formidable William Prynne, he of cropped ears and the letters 'S. L.' branded into his face. He still lurked here, I assumed, somewhere within the walls of the Wakefield Tower.

Familiar yet different. In my time the guards and the soldiers were aimless and slovenly, often drunk and never diligent. Today though they presented smart and correct, every item of their dress pristine. Sentries checked our credentials with extraordinary diligence at the Bulwark Gate, the Lion's Gate and the Byward Tower. Sir John Robinson, now Commander of the Tower guard, was reckoned to be a fastidious tyrant with little tolerance for indiscipline or disorder.

'Where is Newcourt?' Dowling asked a guard beneath the Bloody Tower. 'We hear he is come to meet Sir John.'

The guard jerked a thumb in the direction of the White Tower without saying a word nor moving a muscle of his face. I thought I recognised him, though it was difficult to be certain. They all appeared so elegant and clean.

I spotted Newcourt straightaway, lean and lithe, stood bowed with feet together in obsequious pose afront of an older looking gentleman with stern eyes and imposing bulk. Sir John Robinson spoke with great intensity, chopping at the air with his arms and pointing at Newcourt's chest, while the younger man nodded so hard I feared his head might fall off. Robinson finished his performance with a final flurry of barked instruction before marching off in the direction of the Lieutenant's Lodgings.

'Mr Newcourt!' I called.

'What do you want?' he scowled, glaring miserably at the floor.

'Lord Arlington said we should come to you if we

need help or resource,' I reminded him. 'We are in need of both.'

Newcourt rubbed his hand across the surface of his pristine wig. 'I have to go to Hampton Court,' he muttered, hurrying back toward the Byward Tower.

Dowling clamped a giant paw upon his shoulder and pulled him back. 'Will you listen to our request?'

Newcourt made a discreet attempt to free himself afore turning back. A faint tremble of his lips belied his anger and frustration. 'Tell me quick,' he snapped. 'I am busy.'

'We need money, but more important we need protection,' I told him. 'Men are trying to kill us.'

He dug into his jacket. 'How much money do you need?'

'I have spent nearly two pounds already,' I said. 'In less than a week.'

He pulled out some coins. 'Here is a pound, thereabouts. The rest I will reimburse you next time we meet. What else?'

'Two men have tried to kill me, two others tortured him.' I pointed to Dowling's bandaged thumb.

Newcourt shrugged, impatient.

'Can you not borrow some soldiers from Sir John?' I asked. 'We can tell you who to arrest.'

'Listen.' He drew himself up straight. 'Sir John demands

yet more funds to extend the pest-house at Stepney. He wants to buy more land about the Cripplegate Pest-house, and he wants to extend the garrison so to be able to properly monitor the activities of the dissenters.' He blew out his cheeks. 'I am not about to ask him for soldiers to protect you from a few ruffians.'

'I am not talking about ruffians,' I protested. 'I am talking of two men who seem to be working for Lord Chelwood, and two of Wharton's old entourage whose profession includes torment and abuse.'

'Lord Chelwood?' Newcourt blinked. 'What has he to do with Wharton's death?'

'He has some connection with Burke is all we know,' I said. 'And his men tried to kill me after I followed Burke to the house of John Tanner.'

'Who is John Tanner?'

'We don't know.'

Newcourt stared over my shoulder, deep in thought. 'Wharton's entourage. You speak of the four men who call themselves after the Four Horsemen?'

'Yes.'

'You found two dead, I understand,' he said.

'Two dead, aye, and two remain alive. They seem to think Lord Arlington is responsible for the death of Wharton, he or some cleric...' I struggled to recall the name.

'William Perkins,' Dowling helped me.

'You have discovered more than I thought you capable.' Newcourt glanced at me briefly. 'I will see you again when I return. Meantime you must manage alone.' He placed a hand on my shoulder, surprisingly tender. 'For there are ungodly men, turning the grace of our God into lasciviousness, denying the only Lord God, and our Lord Jesus Christ.'

'Amen,' Dowling echoed.

I was trapped between zealots. I preferred Newcourt the mean-minded incompetent.

'A fine fellow,' Dowling pronounced, watching Newcourt disappear.

Fine fellow or not, he reminded me we had yet to pursue the ranting cleric. I looked up at Dowling and wondered why he hadn't thought of it either. 'He told us nothing, promised us nothing and gave me but a pound.'

'If Forman and Withypoll work for Lord Chelwood, then Lord Arlington cannot arrest them,' Dowling said. 'Not without more evidence.'

'Who is this William Perkins?'

Dowling avoided my gaze. 'He works for the Bishop of London, Humphrey Henchman. He is devoted to driving dissenters out of the city.'

'Why do Wharton's dogs think Perkins may have killed Thomas Wharton?'

'They asked what we had discovered of him, they did not say they thought he killed him.'

'You remember the conversation well,' I noted. 'Yet you seem to hold little enthusiasm for seeking Perkins out.'

'Harry, did you not hear me?' Dowling stopped beneath the arch of the Middle Tower. 'Perkins is close associate of the Bishop of London. The Bishop is close to the King, worked hard for his return. He is loyal to the Crown. The Bishop of London would not murder nobility, nor sanction it.'

'Yet Perkins had some relation to the Earl of St Albans,' I pointed out, unmoved. 'Else why would War ask us what we discovered?'

'So what would you do, Harry? Arrest the Bishop?'

'No,' I replied. 'Just ask questions and become a great nuisance. Same as always.'

'And always you end up with your head broken or locked up in a jail somewhere.' Dowling raised his voice, unlike him. 'Which surely will be the case if you embark upon a hare-brained, ill-considered, holy siege!'

'Then you must come with me,' I reasoned. 'And save me from myself, as is your wont.'

'So be it,' Dowling growled. 'We will go and talk to a friend of mine. Better than going straight to the Bishop and ending up charged with heresy.'

'And if my aunt was a man she'd be my uncle,' I

retorted. 'Let's visit this friend of yours now, then. Where does he live?'

'George Boddington is the rector at St James Garlickhythe.' Dowling led us through Petty Wales. 'A serious man who I will thank ye not to offend.'

'I can promise not to offend,' I said. 'Though I cannot promise you he will not be offended.'

Dowling glared as though he would happily break my neck, and so I walked in silence.

St James Garlickhythe was a vintners' church, just across the street from the Vintners' Hall on Thames Street. Inside was dark and silent. Dowling led us down the aisle, footsteps echoing loud.

'Your friend Boddington is still here, or has he fled like all the others?' I whispered.

Dowling stopped in front of a large gravestone, laid into the floor. Engraved upon it was the figure of a man, broad shouldered and tall, curly haired, with a little forked beard.

A short figure strode to meet us. 'I am still here, and I am staying here,' a deep voice boomed. He pointed at the figure upon the ground. 'That is Richard Lions, once Sheriff of London and master to Wat Tyler. Tyler was an evil man who came back to chop off his head and parade it about London on the end of a spear.'

'Lions was a tyrant then?'

'Lions was a great man,' Boddington replied, authoritatively. 'Tyler was insane, an agent of the Devil.'

Since Boddington invited no debate, and Dowling's beady eyes stuck to me like glue, I passed no further comment.

'Woe to the idol shepherd that leaveth the flock,' Boddington announced, looking at me. 'The sword shall be upon his arm, and upon his right eye. His arm shall be clean dried up, and his right eye shall be utterly darkened!' He didn't seem to like me much.

Dowling sighed. He stuck out his hand in greeting, whereupon Boddington seized it and pumped it up and down as if he expected water to gush forth from the butcher's mouth.

'You are well, George?'

'God watches over me.' Boddington waved a hand. 'Come to the vestry and we will talk.' He turned on his heel without waiting for response and led us toward the back of the church into a gloomy little room.

Boddington lowered himself into a large wooden throne, like God Himself, while we sat upon smaller chairs afore him. Upon the arms of the chair, and about the back of it, were carved little scallop shells, like those the pilgrims fetched home from the cathedral at Santiago de Compostela, where St James lay buried.

'This is Harry Lytle.' Dowling held out his palm as if I

were a foreign object to stare at and scrutinise. 'He works at the Guildhall under the eye of Sir Thomas Player.'

'A worthy occupation.' Boddington crossed his legs. 'What can I do for you?'

'We seek your advice, George,' said Dowling.

'Advice?' Boddington sounded wary. 'Many men seek advice these days. I give them all the same answer; Thou shalt worship no other god but the Lord, whose name is Jealous, who is a jealous God.'

'Aye, so,' Dowling nodded. 'The advice we seek is more specific.'

Boddington twitched his nose.

'We are investigating the death of Thomas Wharton.' Dowling spoke low. 'We found him on Lord's Day.'

Boddington's eyes widened. 'How so it was you that found him?'

Dowling shuffled slightly. 'We work for Lord Arlington. He instructed us to investigate.'

'Great is the mystery of godliness.' Boddington clasped his hands together. 'Men have talked of little else since that night. I heard rumour of what they found, a tale so wicked I can scarce believe it. Will you confirm it to me?'

'We found him hanging by his neck,' I replied. 'Whoever killed him pressed coins in his eyes and pushed a wine bottle down his throat.'

Boddington leaned forward. 'He was naked?'

'Naked.' I confirmed.

'And the beast carved out the seventy-fifth psalm upon his back.' Boddington held his fingers to his lips. 'For in the hand of the Lord there is a cup, and the wine is red. It is full of mixture; and he poureth out of the same. But the dregs thereof, all the wicked of the earth shall wring them out, and drink them.'

'It would have taken the murderer half the night to carve that upon a man's back,' I pointed out.

Boddington scowled. 'So it is not true?'

'No, it's not true,' I said. 'What is true is that William Perkins had some business with Thomas Wharton. We would find out what that business was.'

Boddington pushed himself back into his great chair. 'William Perkins?'

'Aye, William Perkins.' Dowling reached out a hand to silence me. 'Wharton had four colleagues, though we are not sure what they all did together. One inferred that Perkins was known to Wharton, had some kind of business with him.'

'William Perkins is a devout fellow and labours long and hard in God's ministry.' Boddington replied, furious. 'He a passionate fellow and would not shirk from confronting evil. What do you imply?'

'We imply nothing, George,' Dowling said, 'nor doubt his purpose, but we don't know what that purpose was. He may be a player in these events, albeit innocent and pure.'

Boddington's arms relaxed. 'As I told you, he is a passionate fellow. His purpose these days is same as all of us. To bolster the courage of those who think of fleeing. Every church deserted is occupied by a dissenter. By our temerity we betray our own faith.'

Dowling bowed his head solemnly. 'Just so.'

'Meantime the Quakers swarm about Westminster, knocking on doors and shutting themselves up with the sick to administer comfort.'

'God will dispose of us as He wishes, according to his plans,' Dowling agreed earnestly.

Which was all too much for me to stomach. What kind of God sought to torture his people so cruelly, that many now died of grief? What kind of God favoured the rich and wealthy above the poor and doughty?

'What then was Perkins' purpose *before* the plague?' I demanded. 'What of his involvement with Wharton then?'

'I cannot tell you for certain.' Boddington spoke slow and hesitant. 'Though Wharton was an evil man, suspected of nefarious deeds.'

'What nefarious deeds?'

'You might talk to Perkins yourself,' said Boddington. 'For I heard only tales. If Wharton's colleagues speak of Perkins, then it can only be that he persecuted them with just cause.'

'What tales did you hear?'

'As I said,' Boddington snapped. 'You might talk to Perkins yourself.'

'Then you don't believe Perkins might have killed Thomas Wharton?' I thought aloud. 'Vengeance is mine, saith the Lord?'

Boddington's head snapped about like an angry chicken. 'Fear God, and keep his commandments: for this is the whole duty of man.' He stared at me as if I was a spirit to be cast out. 'Whoever killed Thomas Wharton is a devil, and William Perkins is no devil. Be sober, be vigilant, because your adversary the Devil, as a roaring lion, walketh about, seeking whom he may devour.'

I did not appreciate being lectured by righteous clerics. 'Someone did it, and there are devils in the clergy as there are in all places.'

'Get ye gone!' Boddington proclaimed, face suffused with scarlet blood. 'And take your devilry with thee!'

Dowling glared at me with similar ruddy cheeks. I feared I had offended him after all and so went to wait outside.

Strange how these godly men so quickly became anxious. Wasn't the Lord supposed to rejoice over them with joy, and joy over them with singing? Where was all the joy gone?

CHAPTER 18

Of a brother that is absent
If they behold him with the aforesaid aspects, and be in reception, the brother is in great distress, but he will with ease evade it, and free himself from his present sad condition.

Since Dowling wasn't talking to me I had plenty of time to think during the walk up to Cheapside. We now had two lords and a bishop involved, as well as a couple of murderous torturers. Everyone we met stayed tight lipped. All had the same tendency to stare off into the distance at critical stages of the conversation, and tell us nothing. We skirted the heart of this black affair, still to win a glimpse of the essence of it. The only intelligence given freely came from the gravedigger at St Albans, he who directed us to Bedlam.

And what of that? What was the significance of Pateson's testimony? We were told two days ago that Morrison paid to keep him away, yet still hadn't followed up. Now was as good a time.

'Bedlam!' I declared, striding north. 'Let's find out what Morrison and Gallagher have to say for themselves.'

Dowling muttered some dark utterance, but followed anyway. Unlikely he would talk to me again this day. A blessed relief.

Crowds thronged at Bishopsgate. Not to get out, but to get in, for the plague worsened in that parish by the day. The happy sun, shining bright in cloudless sky, sustained the sickness with a force that allowed it to multiply. The hotter the earth baked beneath our feet, the greater the poison rose, unseen and merciless. I thought again of Jane, determining to visit her before the day was out.

The spikes above the gate displayed only one rotten head, tattered, torn and peeling. Beyond spread a wasteland of disease and death. Only the watchers roamed with intent, now beholden to guard several houses at a time.

Bedlam was but a few yards up Bishopsgate Street. The air bloomed foul from behind the Bedlam gate. The great cesspit had not been emptied for several years, and on days like today, sun blazing, the smell hung in a steaming fog. Flies settled upon my jacket even as I walked, buzzed about my nose and mouth, occasionally touching the inside of my nose, cold and disgusting. I maintained a steady breath of air outwards as we crossed the courtyard.

The small ante-room was empty. None lingered, none

drank wine. We made our own way down the dark gloomy passage toward the cells, lamentations echoing from beyond the open doorway. We stopped upon the threshold, listening for any sign of attendance, reluctant to call out or step further unaccompanied.

'Oddfish,' I remarked.

Dowling whispered behind me. 'Since there is none here, I might have a look at the office.' He hurried back the way we came. 'I want to see their records.'

The office was bright and square, with one large window looking out onto the bleak landscape out front. Three panes were missing and two were cracked. Stacks of paper covered a large desk, piles flowing onto piles in an unholy mess that would take weeks to sort.

Dowling shuffled a handful of notes. 'They have not been paying their bills.' He continued poking. 'I would find the register. They must have it in case they're inspected.'

He cleared a space on the floor and began shifting paper from desk to floor, excavating for whatever lay beneath. I cleared a chair of debris, sat down and opened the top drawer. There sat a large blue leather-bound book. I pushed a pile of paper onto the floor to make space for it. Dowling was at my shoulder before I could open the front cover. He quickly turned the pages. A neat spidery hand covered each one, filling five columns a page. In the first column a number, in the second column a name, in the third the date of admission, in the fourth the date of discharge and in the fifth were writ comments, usually a description of the inmate and his symptoms.

'The last entry was made two months ago.' Dowling stabbed a finger upon the last written page. He ran his finger fast back up the column of names, surprising me how fast he could read. 'This place is Pateson's life and blood. If men are unaccounted for, then he will be punished.'

'What are you doing in here?' a voice demanded. The ginger man stood at the door, the man we had met before, with hair like a carrot. 'You shouldn't be in here without Morrison.'

'Where is Morrison?' I asked.

'I don't know where he is. I haven't seen him.' He frowned. 'Neither Daniel nor Franklin has been fed neither.' He surveyed the room then pointed to a hook. 'Yet he has left his keys behind, which is peculiar, since he never takes them off his belt.'

'So now you must feed Daniel and Franklin.' Dowling walked over to retrieve the heavy ring.

The ginger man shook his head. 'Not I. I would not go near Franklin if you paid me. He is a savage beast. No man is safe even close to his cell. He grabbed a fellow by the neck last year and near pulled his ear off.'

'Someone must feed them,' I said. 'We will come with you.'

'We cannot go to the vestry without Morrison,' the ginger man protested. 'He ordered it.'

'Yet Morrison is not here,' I pointed out. 'What of Gallagher? Can he not feed them?'

'Gallagher has not been here since Monday,' the ginger man exclaimed. 'I'm on my own it seems.' He scratched at his scabby scalp and clicked his tongue. 'Morrison has been gone three, four hours.' He fidgeted and looked to the front door. 'He never said he was going any place.'

Something was wrong. 'Come.' I grabbed the keys and led the way. I walked the passageway betwixt the cells without looking left nor right, and skipped through the Abraham Ward afore the thin man could tap me on the shoulder. The vestry door was the first one we found locked.

The ginger man leaned over my arm and pointed at a small dark key sat snug amongst its fellows. 'That one.' The lock was well oiled and the key turned easily.

The first thing I saw was Daniel, long body stretched out in calm repose upon his tall-backed chair, wide smile upon his lips, lost in warm reflection, an expression of divine bliss on his big face. His eyes were closed, like he relished a long rest after many nights without sleep. He breathed slow and regular, arms folded upon his chest. Why was he so happy?

Franklin's cell was quiet. 'Hold!' I put up a hand and shuffled backwards. 'Franklin's cell is open.' I could see his head and shoulders. He sat on a chair facing away from us. 'He is still inside.'

'We must close it,' the ginger man whispered. 'Else he will leap upon us. He once bit a man's hand clean off his arm.'

'A good story,' I muttered, though I still recalled with a shudder those animal brown eyes and ravenous mouth. 'He doesn't move.'

There was no key in the lock. It would take no time to run to the cell door and throw it closed, yet to find the key on this great ring might take a minute. A picture formed in my mind of Franklin eating off Dowling's fingers one by one as he attempted to hold the door shut while I fumbled. 'Do you know which key locks Franklin's door?' I whispered to the ginger man, eyes fixed upon Franklin all the while.

'No,' he replied, a drip of sweat trickling down his nose.

'Then, Davy, you will have to hold the door closed with a chair while I find it.' I turned to him. 'Do you have the strength to hold off a deranged lunatic?'

'I am well acquainted with the machinations of deranged lunatics,' Dowling replied, smiling without humour.

I pointed at a chair lain upon its side on the floor in front of us. Had it not been in Franklin's cell last time we were here? 'You run, pick up the chair and hold the cell door closed while I find the key.'

'I will wait here,' the ginger man said, quick.

'If it is him at all.' I peered. 'Franklin had long black hair. That man's hair is cut short.' I glanced sideways at the ginger fellow. 'Has he had his hair cut since Tuesday?'

'He has never had his hair cut at all,' the ginger man replied. 'No sane man would go close to him with scissors.'

'What strange mystery is this?' Dowling growled, stepping forward. The figure did not move at the sound of our shoes upon the stones. His head tilted backwards as though he slept.

'Godamercy!' Dowling exclaimed, stood at the bars. 'His throat is cut!' He marched into the cell and took the dead man's hair in one hand.

This man was big, bigger than Franklin. 'Who is it?'

Dowling peered into the corpse's white face. 'Pestilence.'

'Pestilence?' I felt a small thrill of guilty delight.

Dowling rubbed his fingers across the dead man's face, pulling at his loose flesh to see what spring remained. 'Aye, the same. The flesh is cold, yet still hard.' He pushed the head forward so it sunk upon his chest with a thick squelch. 'He was killed last night.'

I felt suddenly unsafe, for the lunatic might be anywhere. If he had ne'er left this cell in ten years, likely he would be reluctant to venture too far away. 'Where is he?'

'Not in here.' Dowling ran his finger along the edge of the man's jagged flesh.

'Yet the door was locked.' I strode back to Daniel's cell. 'What happened?' I shouted at Daniel through the bars, trying to awaken him.

Daniel opened his eyes slowly, still smiling like he was gone to Heaven.

'He used a boning knife.' Dowling called.

'Daniel!' I cried.

Daniel sighed deeply.

'Who killed him, Daniel?'

A low rumble emanated from Daniel's mouth. 'He discovereth deep things out of darkness, and bringeth out to light the shadow of death.'

Bible talk. I nodded to Dowling. 'You speak to him.'

'Who killed him, Daniel?' Dowling called.

Daniel turned slowly, eyes distant. 'He is the wolf that dwelleth with the lambs.'

Dowling walked toward the bars of his cell rubbing his palms upon his shirt. 'What is the wolf's name?'

'His name is Abimelech,' Daniel declared. 'He that toucheth this man or his wife shall surely be put to death.'

Dowling pushed his nose through the bars. 'Was it Franklin?'

'Franklin,' Daniel repeated, shaking his head like the word was sinful. Then he leaned backwards and closed his eyes once more.

Dowling shrugged. 'I don't know what he means.'

'Methinks it clear enough,' I considered. 'I told War that Franklin was here when they tortured you at the Clink. Pestilence came to do to Franklin what they did to you and suffered the consequence.'

Dowling looked down, perplexed. 'Then Franklin took the key from Pestilence and locked the vestry door on his way out? A strange thing for a lunatic to do.'

My own brain started tip-toeing in circles besides. 'And where is Morrison?'

'There is another door.' Dowling pointed. Sat snug in the corner, at the back of the room, was a squat low door I hadn't noticed before.

'The key should be on the ring,' called our escort, still reluctant to come forth.

Dowling took the keys from me and searched on the ring as he walked. He dropped to his knees, for the door was short, and tried the keys one by one, until finally he succeeded in unlocking it.

The door led out to the back of the priory, a place we had not ventured before. We kicked our way through knee-length yellow weeds, grown sickly from the filth. Ahead of us grew the garden, overgrown with long grasses; cyperus and rush-grass among them.

The uneasy peace was broken by the squawking of a

crow above our heads, flapping noisily to the centre of the tiny meadow, descending into an area where the grass lay flatter. Then a second, launching itself from atop the asylum, disappearing into the hollow. What did they seek? I pushed into the grass, surprised to find the ground wet and spongy beneath my feet.

The ginger man followed us, a pace behind. 'Where the cesspit leaks,' he explained.

I steeled my flagging will as moisture seeped into my shoes and surrounded my feet. The crows scrabbled and hopped heavy-footed ahead of us.

The second corpse lay prone, arms and legs sprawled, naked gut spilled over the top of his trousers. His shirt hung in tatters about his torso. The crows pecked at the hole in his stomach that someone had fashioned with a large serrated blade. His face scrunched up into a ball of intense concentration like he was breaking wind. A fly walked light footed across his pursed blue lips.

'Who is he?' I wondered aloud, for it was not War.

'Gallagher,' whispered the ginger man, shaking.

Dowling waved an arm at the indignant birds. 'The other jailer.' The belly bloated, skin mottled purple and red. Fat maggots squirmed within the body cavity, well fed and ripe.

'He has been here about a week I would say.' Dowling opened one eye with his thumb. The eyeball returned his stare, glassy, clouded and dull. He turned to the ginger man. 'You last saw him on Monday?'

'Or the day before.' The ginger man held the back of his hand to his mouth and screwed his eyes up tight.

'Stabbed in the gut and left to rot.' Dowling stood. 'What is your name?' he asked the ginger man.

'Smith,' he replied, afore emptying his guts into the grass. The crows watched hungrily.

Dowling laid a long arm about his narrow shoulders and regarded him kindly. 'What has been going on here the last few weeks, Smith?'

'Nothing,' Smith exclaimed. 'Nothing I can think of. Pateson has not been here for several weeks, but Morrison and Gallagher said it was because his wife couldn't abide living here, and I seen him anyway, he's not dead.' He looked up into Dowling's eyes. 'Leastways he wasn't.'

'We saw him day afore yesterday,' Dowling assured him. 'He wasn't dead then. What of Morrison?'

'As I told you.' Smith's voice sounded shrill. 'He was here this morning, then disappeared.'

'Did he say anything of Gallagher's absence?' I asked.

'Yes!' Smith held up a long white finger. 'Now you say it, so he did. He said Gallagher was sickly and would be coming back next week.' He shook his head as if to clear it. 'And when he said it, he seemed sad. I thought Gallagher might be plagued.'

Dowling turned. 'He has family?'

'Aye,' Smith nodded eagerly. 'They live behind the wall, off St Mary Ax.'

'Morrison and Gallagher knew each other well, it seems.'

'It was Gallagher recommended Morrison to Pateson.' Smith frowned. 'Said they worked together before, but I don't remember more.'

'I heard Gallagher was a hard man.'

'Aye, hard, but you has to be hard working here. They are strong, some of them, and if you don't keep them in their place then they take liberties. That's what he taught me.'

'How did he treat you?'

'Treated me fine,' Smith squared his shoulders. 'Both of them did.' Yet his eyes betrayed him.

'Did you ever see the Earl of St Albans come visiting?' I asked.

'An earl?' Smith wiped an arm across his nose. 'Never saw no earl.'

Dowling puffed out his cheeks. 'We had best move this body,' he sighed. 'Though we'll be lucky to find a box.'

The crows descended once more, their fear of us given way to their hunger for maggots.

CHAPTER 19

Judgement of sickness by ASTROLOGY
Let the physician take the time of his own first speaking with, or access to the patient, or when the urine was first brought to him.

Gallagher lay so long in the grass, his body had assumed a strange shape, his back and sides having settled flat on the ground. He rested snug against the boards of the cart and didn't seem to bounce as much as Wharton did on the way to St Albans.

The guards at Bishopsgate flocked to us like hungry sheep, for Dowling's wagon resembled a death-cart. It took us almost half the hour to persuade them we transported the body on Arlington's behalf and to demonstrate Gallagher was not plague afflicted. Dowling was obliged to cut away his clothes and reveal the dead man in all his naked glory, pierced through the guts but otherwise healthy.

We were granted wide berth as we trundled sedately down Camomile Street and St Mary Ax searching for the alley that would lead us to the small courtyard where Gallagher lived. This was a poor area, houses towering high above us, chattering hives of anxiety and despondency, so many now without jobs nor trade. Men, women and children came to their windows to watch us attempt to steer the cart through the narrow labyrinth, shouting at us in indignant consternation upon seeing the covered corpse. Every body was a plague victim these days. Finally we were forced to unhitch the wagon from the horse and retreat to St Mary Ax, defeated by the narrow passage.

Dowling tied the horse and gave a penny to a young fellow with surly expression. For another penny he led us quickly through the maze to the small door that was Mary Gallagher's. Outside the door sat a watcher, and upon the door was painted a broad red cross.

'This is the house of Mary Gallagher?' I asked the old man.

He sat with arms folded above his tight round belly, blue eyes catching us for a moment. 'Aye, so it is, and you will not be going in there.' He remained seated.

As we stood in shocked silence, so the little door opened and a frightened face peered out. In the woman's arms I saw an infant, tiny and unmoving.

'Get ye back in there!' The watcher flew from his chair and pulled on the door handle to close it. 'The lock is broken,' he explained, wiping his brow with the back of his sleeve. 'Her baby died, and she has been waiting two days for someone to collect it.'

'Godamercy!' Dowling exclaimed in horrified disgust. 'And why do you not fetch the bearer?'

'I am not permitted to leave this seat.' The watcher planted himself firmly back upon his stool. 'Only when relieved. I have sent message to the church twice. What more can I do?' He folded his arms once more and stuck out his lip.

'Let us take the infant to the church,' I volunteered.

'The baby is plagued,' he replied. 'Only a bearer may take the child.'

Dowling stood above him and glowered at his head. 'Let us talk to the mother.'

The watcher regarded the butcher sternly from beneath a lined, white-haired brow. 'You go near that door then I shall see you arrested and thrown in there with her.' He wriggled sharply, settling his bulk comfortable. 'See how you like that.'

'You cannot leave a dead body in that house for two days!' Dowling shouted so loud the whole courtyard heard it.

'It is not I that has left the body in there two days!' The watcher shouted back. 'It is the church that does not send someone to collect him.'

So the infant was a boy. I tugged at Dowling's sleeve

and hauled him away before he shoved the watcher's stool down his throat. 'I have a plan,' I whispered loud in his angry ear. 'One I have executed well before.'

I succeeded eventually in dragging Dowling away, though it had been easier to persuade the horse. I returned half an hour later in the medic's garb, now dry, long beak filled with fresh herbs.

The watcher jumped to attention, blue eyes wide. Since the lock was broken I needed nothing from him, and proceeded direct into the low house.

I removed the mask immediately, since I needed to talk to her and could not hold a conversation with someone who stared at me like I was a beast from the depths of Hell. For the first time in my life I thanked God I was so short, for the ceiling hung just a few inches above my head. The whole house creaked as though the stack of rooms above would crash down upon us at any moment.

'Mrs Gallagher?' I said, quiet, attention drawn to the little cot by the window.

'Yes,' she whimpered, body strung tight upon itself.

I stepped to the cot and lifted the sheet. 'Your baby is dead?'

She nodded, tears streaking her dirty face, nose red and swollen.

I saw his sex clearly, since he wasn't bound. 'Shall I take

him with me?'

'What will you do with him?' she pleaded, kneading red hands upon themselves.

I contemplated the scene about me, the poor house, broken chair, holes in the wall. Likely they would throw the baby in the pit at Cripplegate.

'I will see him buried. Either at St Helen's or All Hallows.'

'All Hallows?' she asked, anxious.

'If St Helen's is full, then I know the rector at All Hallows, and I know he would not turn your child away.' Though I would have to pay him.

'That is kind of you,' she said, like she could not understand why I should wish to help. 'My husband is away and I don't know when he will come back.'

'Where has he gone?'

'I don't know.' New tears welled. 'He hasn't come home since Monday. I am afraid.' She began tearing at the front of her dress. 'He works at St Mary Bethlehem, but he hasn't come home this week and I cannot go out to find him.' She sat down and clutched her arms about her belly. The sadness scored deep into her mouth said she feared he had deserted.

I sat opposite her. 'I am not really a medic.'

Her eyes fixed upon mine while the rest of her face slowly contorted in new anxiety.

'It was the only device I could think of to gain entrance,' I explained. 'For I have news of your husband, bad news.'

She twisted the apron upon her lap round and about her wrists.

I tried to hold her hands, but they continued to wind the apron into a long helix. 'He died.'

'Oh,' she replied, looking about the room as if for the first time, already contemplating life from the perspective of one alone. Tears streamed down her face, mucus leaked from her nose, and she opened her mouth wide, showing all her teeth. She stretched her arms out toward me. I hesitated a moment, for this was a house of plague. Yet my fate was risked long ago. Offering solace to a widow could make no difference, so I took her in my arms and allowed her all the time she needed.

At last she disentangled herself and sat back upon the stool, eyes puffy as her nose, red marks against her pale face where she rubbed against the rough leather of my cloak. Hair long and lifeless. I wondered what she had looked like a year ago, pregnant and hopeful.

'How did he die?' she asked, fetching a cloth to wipe at her face.

'He was murdered,' I said gently. 'At Bedlam.'

She held the cloth to her nose, new tears spilling from her eyes. 'What?'

'He was killed, we think last Lord's Day. We found him

this morning, in the meadow at the back.'

'How could that happen?' she demanded, anger inflating her shoulders, straightening her back.

'I don't know, but I will find out. I am hoping you can tell me something that might help.'

'Me?' She perched once more upon the stool, cloth held to her nose and mouth.

'Did he talk to you of Morrison, the man who started there a few months ago? I have heard it was your husband offered him the job.'

She stared toward the window, concentrating hard on my words so she could hold other thoughts at bay. 'Robert Morrison. He came to see Hugh back in March, I think it was. Paid Hugh to commend him to John Pateson.'

'Paid him?'

'He insisted,' she sniffled. 'They knew each other before. They were soldiers together. Hugh didn't seek to take advantage of him, but Morrison insisted. Said he needed Hugh's cooperation. I'm not sure what it was all about.'

'They were soldiers together?'

'Twenty years ago. We lived at Bury St Edmunds. Thomas Wharton raised an army in support of the King.'

'The Earl of St Albans?'

She nodded. 'Though he wasn't an earl then. He was a member of the parliament and was loyal to the King.'

'Did your husband know Thomas Wharton?'

'No,' she replied. 'He was just a soldier, and I don't think Thomas Wharton took arms himself. Morrison said he knew him. That was something they spoke about when he came in March.'

'What else did they talk about?'

Tears rushed now in a flood and she buried her face in her lap. 'Who will bury Hugh?' she cried, muffled.

'I will see to it,' I offered softly.

'You?' she looked up. 'Why would you bury my husband?'

'I work for Lord Arlington,' I replied, flustered. 'I know he would help you.'

'Really?' Her face crumpled again, and she lost herself in another deluge of loud weeping.

I leaned over and placed my hand upon her back. 'I will help you all I can. Does the watcher bring you food and water?'

'Every morning.'

'Can you tell me what your husband spoke to Morrison about?'

'Why can you not ask him?' she pleaded.

'He is missing since early this morning,' I replied, gentle, fearing further tears might exhaust her completely. 'And Pateson has not visited in several weeks.'

'What is going on?' she frowned, spirit surging again.

'That is what I would know.'

'Well.' She wiped her cheek. 'Robert Morrison paid Hugh to commend him to John Pateson. Said the Earl put him up to it, that's all I remember. I thought the Earl sought to secure him a job, look after him perhaps.'

'I see,' I replied, though I didn't. 'What else has being going on this last three months?'

'I don't know.' She shook her head. 'Hugh told me nothing.'

'Thank you, Mrs Gallagher.' I reached beneath the cloak and into my pocket. 'You have been helpful.' I gave her the pound Newcourt had given to me and headed for the cot.

She tugged at my shoulder. 'Sir, though you are not a proper medic, would you see my other child?' She pointed at the low doorway at the back of the room. 'I think he is ill besides.'

Logic tugged me back out into the courtyard, away from where she would direct me. Ne'ertheless my legs carried me after her.

The small room contained nothing but two beds. Upon the smaller lay a child, no more than three years old. Long swellings, like sausages, nestled upon his thighs and one on his hand. The tops of them had already started to blacken.

She stared down at the little boy, his black hair swept back upon his head, wet and matted. 'It is plague, isn't it?'

As she leaned over to stroke his forehead, the sleeve of her dress rode up to her elbow revealing a ripe bubo of her own. My heart tensed tight and started beating twice as fast. My legs and arms froze in paralysed fear. I was standing next to Death, had embraced him in my arms. Godamercy!

I marched out the room and grabbed for the mask, pulling it down upon my head. 'Aye, it looks like plague,' I called out so she could hear. 'Do you have a medic visit you?'

She shook her head.

'Then I will arrange it!'

I turned and went to take the baby.

'No!' she cried, pushing me away. 'I will wait!' She took the tiny corpse into her arms and held it to her chest. Already it had started to bloat.

I took off the mask again. 'Let me.'

She wept, tears dripping onto the body of the child. 'Will you wait then?'

'Wait for what?' I asked.

'If I cannot be at their funeral, then I would have you place a keepsake in their coffin.'

She placed the child back in its cot and went to fetch a small piece of embroidery from the table behind us, which she handed to me. It wasn't very good, but I could discern it was a design of four people, two adults, a small child and a baby, flowers stitched about the edges. All I could look at was her neck, for now it seemed swollen too.

'I will,' I promised. 'Now I must go.'

I put the mask on again, took the dead baby in my arms and pushed open the door.

She waved as I left and I waved back, though I could barely lift my arm. The watcher stood away, waiting for me to leave.

'Don't come near, Davy,' I warned, back on St Mary Ax.

He stepped toward me anyway, puzzlement writ upon his great lined face.

'They all have plague in there, Davy, every one of them, including her, and I took my mask off, God save me.' I held the corpse out afore me. 'This baby is dead two days. God knows what poison breeds within it.'

'You are a good man, Harry.' Dowling came up close and put an arm about my shoulder. 'You hide it well.' A strange comment. 'Do not fear the plague, for if we are not saved from the Destroying Angel, then there is good reason for our dying.' He squeezed me hard. 'And I think God sees you doing much good in his service and would keep you alive.'

Which thought was no comfort at all. I thought to ask if Dowling would carry the little corpse if he was so assured, but decided that would be to take advantage of his wide-eyed credulity. I prayed I had not killed him already and carried the baby myself in the direction of our cart, for now we needed to take these bodies to St Helen's.

A new thought entered my head which required some digestion.

CHAPTER 20

Who shall be the cause of their strife
If the moon aspect Saturn or Mars in angles, notes a probability of separation or long disagreements.

The fright of seeing plague upon Mary Gallagher's arms still accompanied me, creeping beneath my skin. Still I felt the weight of the tiny grey baby pressing gently into my arms. My heart weighed so heavy it was all I could do to place one foot in front of the other.

The Rector of St Helen's was a sombre fellow, yet a good man I supposed. For he had accepted responsibility for the two corpses we fetched without complaint, and waved away my offer of money. His eyes were sad, yet his manner betrayed none of the self-piteous fury I saw in other clergy.

Dowling walked silent beside me. The fear that seized my soul in the presence of Mary Gallagher, and the despair I felt for her and her family, provoked within me fresh anxiety for Jane. I had to see how she fared. So distracted were we both, that neither of us noticed the red coach following us until we passed St Peter's.

It stalked us at exact same pace we walked, one man flanking either side of it, brutish looking fellows with swords at their belts.

It stopped when we stopped. The man closest to us drew his long sword with a flourish, then opened the door to the coach and stepped aside. Eyes nestled like small currants. His lips lay tight and drawn against his burnt skin, yet his brow was dry, his gait loose and relaxed. This was not a fellow about to stab someone.

Dowling tugged at my sleeve. 'Come. I know whose coach this is.'

Though it was quite a large coach there was little room left inside, barely space for Dowling and I to squeeze in next to each other. Opposite sat a large man with vast stomach and short rounded legs, watching us wriggle and squirm as we attempted to position ourselves. He smiled with his mouth, though not with his eyes, hands folded neatly upon his lap. Up close I saw thin purple veins bulging prominent about his cheeks and nose. Various lumps clung like little boils to his chin, brow and the back of his hands. He was dressed in the conservative attire of a well fed cleric.

'I am William Perkins,' he announced with a lisp. 'Aide to the Bishop of London.' He nodded slightly, as if he expected us to bow.

Dowling did his best, leaning so far forward that Perkins had to push himself backwards against the wall of the coach to avoid receiving a mouthful of heavily stained bristle. I didn't bother.

The coach set off again, heading east. Perkins pursed fleshy lips and arched his heavy eyebrows. He turned his eyes toward me. 'I am informed by those I trust that you hath accused me of murder?'

It was like being stung by a hornet. 'I have not!'

Perkins waggled a finger in front of my nose. 'That is a lie. You told George Boddington you suspected me of the murder of Thomas Wharton.'

'I did not.' I held up my palms, warding him off. 'I asked him if he was sure you did *not* murder Thomas Wharton, which is not the same thing at all.'

'I think it is the same thing.' He dug his nails into his hands. 'And you told him the clergy are all devils, sent by Satan to conquer the earth.'

'I said no such thing,' I protested. 'I know several clergy who I believe to be good men. I met one today.'

Dowling jabbed his elbow violently into my gut. 'It was not Harry who accused you, sir. It was one of Thomas Wharton's brood.'

Perkins clasped his hands in a steeple afront of his chest. 'I know of you, David Dowling, and I know you are a good man.' He nodded his big head in my direction. 'This man though is a vile sinner that hath offended God. It was clear to Boddington as it is clear to me, that he hath the spirit of an unclean devil and is tempted by it.'

The old anger welled up within. Why did I feel compelled to defend myself afront this nincompoop? 'This is all absurd nonsense,' I exclaimed, unwise. 'You are a man with two legs and two arms that farts as loud as any other. It is a man with two legs and two arms that killed Wharton, and we must look in every corner if we are to discover where he hides.'

'Ye shall make you no idols nor graven image,' said Perkins, struggling to control his breathing. 'You commit thy horrid deeds in the service of Lord Arlington, do ye not? He who preaches liberty of conscience.'

I opened my mouth to speak afore Dowling elbowed me again, shunting me hard against the edge of the seat with his hip. 'We do work for Lord Arlington, sir, indeed.' He spoke quiet. 'Though we know nothing of liberty of conscience and assume his lordship is as faithful to God as he is loyal to his king.'

Truth was, many suspected both the King and Lord Arlington nurtured latent tendencies toward Catholicism. Which was all of little interest to me. Perkins sat silent, eyeing me like he would pile rocks upon my chest, while Dowling sat frozen, barely breathing. It would have been a good strategy to remain quiet.

I looked out of the window and thought to climb out before I suffocated. 'The point is that Lord Arlington works direct for the King,' I said.

'As did Wharton,' Perkins smiled again, bright-eyed. 'Wharton was a King's agent and performed evil deeds in the King's name, he and his accomplices.'

'You accuse the King? Is that not treason?' Not that I minded particularly. I spoke more out of astonishment.

'I did not say the King knew of it.' Perkins shook his finger. 'Upon that I will not comment. I say they performed evil on his behalf. Now they lie dead, four of the five, so I hear, four dead in four days and you discovered all the bodies. Tell me you did not kill them on Arlington's behalf. Tell me you do not plan to usurp them, Harry Lytle.'

'I have never killed anyone in my life,' I protested, which was not quite true. 'Nor did we discover all the bodies. The only body we discovered was the one at Bedlam.'

Dowling wrung his hands and tried to catch Perkins' eye. 'That is true, sir,' he whispered.

A vein popped up on Perkins' nose and he stabbed the air with his finger. 'If ye act not in league with the agents of God, then ye act in league with the agents of Satan.' He bared his teeth and pointed at me. 'And you are a deceiver! Wharton and his beasts tortured men, good men some of them. I have spent many hours with the families

275

of those that were taken and ne'er returned. John Ricketts, Matthew Horne, Roger Cline, all good men whose sons are lost.'

I snorted. 'And you think I am a torturer besides?' It was a ridiculous notion, an idiot notion indeed.

He sat back to gloat, an ugly delectation smeared across his bulbous countenance. 'Thy association with the dark spirits hath resulted in the shrouding of your weak soul in their black shadow.'

'My weak soul remains unshrouded,' I assured him, 'and your dramatic pontifications serve only to vex.'

He glared, the hate abiding in his soul revealing itself in all ugliness. 'Thou shalt not be afraid for the terror by night, nor for the pestilence that walketh in darkness, nor for the destruction that wasteth at noonday. A thousand shall fall at thy side, and ten thousand at thy right hand, but it shall not come nigh thee. Only with thine eyes shalt thou behold and see the reward of the *wicked*.'

I shoved back hard against Dowling, creating space for myself, meeting Perkins' poisonous stare. His eyes protruded from their sockets, so hateful were they. How did he dare, this loathsome beast, how did he dare associate me with the pestilence? I thought again of Mary Gallagher and her children, of Jane lain dying, and clenched my fists. I felt Dowling's hand upon my thigh.

'You are a *little* man,' Perkins hissed, mistaking my stillness for helplessness.

'And you are a fat man,' I replied.

His eyes widened in surprise. 'How dare you?'

'Indeed you are fatter than a great pig.'

His jaw clenched and his face turned puce.

'You are fatter than a great cow. A great cow that is due to give birth to a calf.'

I felt a tug at my elbow. Dowling's face was white. 'You cannot talk to him like that.'

'You are a liar.' Perkins rolled the words about his fleshy lips like greasy knobs of fat. 'The wicked are estranged from the womb: they go astray as soon as they be born, speaking lies.'

Enough. I smashed my fist into his nose. At which point was unleashed the apocalypse. The cleric grabbed his face and howled while I felt myself thrown through the coach door and out onto the street where I landed on my face and wrist. I rolled about into a sitting position, clasping my hand to my chest. Dowling reached down to grab me by the scruff of the neck and jerked me onto my feet. The men with swords dashed to the coach to see what happened, and Dowling hauled me toward Gracechurch Street.

'You cannot strike a clergyman,' Dowling roared as we ran.

The two swordsmen stood aghast, peering into the coach while Perkins still screamed. We turned the corner and were gone.

'Did you not hear what he said?' I shouted back.

Dowling led me through a labyrinth of tiny alleyways and out onto Dowgate. 'He is clergy, Harry. He can say whatever he pleases. Now he has every excuse to seek your neck.' He slapped his palm against my forehead. 'Your hand at least!'

I held up my swelling wrist. 'He can have this one.'

For a moment I thought he was going to cuff me again. Instead he muttered beneath his breath words I could barely make out.

I watched him march down the street with his hands dug deep into his pockets and thanked the Lord he was on my side. Whatever the consequences for me, the consequences for him bode just as dire. For he was a devout man, a devout man that had just helped me escape.

'Dowling.' I stopped him. He turned to face me, old eyes worn and tired. 'We must go east.'

He scowled, perplexed.

'I know where Roger Cline lives.'

Of the three names Perkins mentioned, two I forgot already, but Roger Cline worked at the Navy Offices. He lived in the parish of St Olaves', not far from Oliver Willis. I knew nothing of his family.

I knocked upon his door while Dowling waited outside.

It had been a long day already, and Dowling stank like an old man. He tore his stained shirt upon launching me out of Perkins' coach, and now resembled Death triumphant, a grim executioner. Neither of us would get past Cline's front door with him in tow.

My own clothes were creased and crumpled, but without my jacket I appeared almost presentable. Sufficient to pass muster at the door anyhow, for the servant admitted me with but a cursory glance at the King's seal.

I was shown into a small square room hung with printed calicoes coloured a deep blue, almost black. Thick curtains covered the window, bestowing a funereal mood upon the room's bare contents. My attention was drawn to a large mirror hanging upon the opposite wall, its ornate golden frame chipped and cracked, the glass broken or removed. Strange to leave it hanging.

'Sit down,' a voice commanded.

I stepped back, startled, for I hadn't realised I had company. Sunk deep into a large armchair sat an old man, smaller than me. There was but one other chair in which to sit, from where I could barely make out the features of his face in the gloom.

'You carry the credentials of a King's man. Who are you?' His voice tremored, yet bore traces of hatred and resentment.

'I am Harry Lytle, a King's man, investigating the death

of Thomas Wharton.'

He snorted loudly like he sought to clear his head of mucus.

'William Perkins told me that you knew him.'

'Aye, I knew him. But I have no desire to talk with you, King's man.'

'Why not?'

'For it is the day of the *Lord*'s vengeance, Mr Lytle, not the day of *man*'s vengeance,' the old man laboured. 'God will exercise judgement upon the man who killed Wharton, for in truth that man has rid us all of a foul and evil beast, so I cannot be certain it was not God's will.'

'King Charles is God's agent on earth, and it is his will we discover what happened.' I felt a pain in my side. 'If God wishes it otherwise, then we shall fail, no matter what you disclose.'

As I grew accustomed to the dark, so I became aware of his beady eyes staring intently above the tips of his fingers. 'What sort of King's man are you?' he asked.

'You said Wharton was evil.'

'Aye, so he was, as evil as any man ye could hope not to meet.'

'Tell me about his evil.'

'Tell you what?' I saw his hands stiffen clench and heard the tension in his voice. 'You say you are a King's man and still I don't know what that means.'

'I am not seeking to entrap you, Cline.' I edged closer. 'I need to know more about Wharton. There is no more to it.'

He rubbed his forefingers against the tip of his nose. 'My son disappeared a year ago, King's man. I suspect Wharton took him. It is no secret, for I told my story to William Perkins.'

'Why would Wharton take your son?'

His eyes seemed to sparkle and I suspected he shed tears. 'I don't know,' he replied.

I waited for him to say more, but he clasped his fingers to his mouth like they feared his words.

'You suspect some conspiracy?'

He grunted and rolled his eyes, like I was simple and foolish.

'Cline, if you ask me not to relate your story for fear it will betray you, then will I not relate it.' I spoke quick and quiet. 'I was not Wharton's colleague.'

Cline wrinkled his nose 'Wharton was a fiend, surrounded by fiends, and he worked for the King. He was appointed Earl of St Albans soon after the King was restored.'

'That I know.'

He nodded. 'My son was not the only one to disappear.'

'What did your son do?' I asked.

Cline shook his white head. 'He worked for the Protectorate for a while. He administered Jamaican land rights and organised passage. He was a clerk, nothing more. But I was here when Wharton's men took him from this house, and I was there when they fetched him back to Southwark.' His lip quivered. 'They took him to Winchester Palace, and when I went there to protest, one of them told me if I did not desist then he would stick his blade through my poor wife's neck!'

'What then?'

'What then—nothing!' he cried, leaning forwards. 'Since then I have not seen my son.'

He sat tight a few moments longer, staring at me like *I* killed his son, afore slumping back. He closed his eyes and waved a bony hand. 'I have told you all I know. If you would know more, go back and talk to William Perkins, since he has knowledge of others.'

'Thank you,' I mumbled, standing.

I looked upon the mirror one more time, wondering of its history, wondering where Cline's wife was these days, if she remained alive. But that was all none of my business.

I had to see Jane.

CHAPTER 21

When, or about what time the querent may die?
The ancients have ever observed, that the Lord of the
ascendant is more in this judgement to be considered than
the moon, and therefore his affiliation or conjunction with
the Lord of the eighth, or combustion with the sun is
especially worth consideration, and most to be feared.

Arms folded, Hearsey leaned against the wall of my house
like he owned it. A small knot of hatred pulled tight in
my gut.

'Forgive men their trespasses, and your heavenly Father
will also forgive you.' Dowling warned. 'He will tell you
nothing if you threaten him.'

Which advice was unnecessary, for I had plans for Hearsey
I would discharge another day. He pushed himself off the
wall when he saw us coming and squared his shoulders,
unnerved by Dowling's imposing bulk.

'Has the medic been?' I demanded.

'The other medic, you mean?' Hearsey leered. 'Aye, so

he has.' He folded his arms again, shrugged and pursed his lips. 'The old woman will likely die. Your maidservant is sick, but he said he lanced her buboes. The nurse may also be sick, for she has a fever.'

'Will they send another nurse?' I asked, fearful.

'The medic said he would come again tomorrow.' Hearsey spoke clear beneath Dowling's imposing stare. 'I think he would wait and see how she fares.'

'You are providing them with food and water?'

'So I am,' he pouted. 'And wood besides, and whatever provisions they request.'

I sighed and peered through my front window. Would that I could enter mine own house again.

Hearsey smirked. 'I have one key, Alderman Fuller has the other, so don't you be thinking about trying to enter. If it were me then you'd be locked up in there now.'

'And if it were me,' I replied, jabbing a finger at his chest, 'I would wait for you to fall asleep and lower a rope about your neck.' Which is what happened to several watchers already, so they said.

Hearsey's ugly grin disappeared. I contemplated breathing hard in his face in case I did have plague, but felt guilty straightaways, then depressed.

'I must visit Alderman Fuller a minute, Davy,' I muttered low. 'Wait here and I'll return soon.'

Dowling retired to his wagon while I walked the short

journey to Bow Lane. Fuller's house was not so busy as it had been the last times I visited. The alderman himself sat scratching at the same vast ledger while another man counted coins. Upon the wall hung a panel of wood with hooks. Upon each hook was a key.

Fuller looked up, eyes curious. 'Harry.' The man counting coins looked up.

'I wish to lodge a complaint.' I clenched my jaw. 'About that man Hearsey.' I pointed to his ledger. 'Write it down.'

Fuller leaned back in his chair and rubbed his eyes wearily. 'What is this complaint?'

'Yesterday, when he brought me here, he struck me forcibly and kicked my legs as I tried to walk, he and his friend.' I leaned down and tapped my finger upon his desk. 'Also I heard he was a watcher before in Bishopsgate-Without. I heard he entered houses during the night and stole things.'

Fuller sighed. 'Who told you that?'

I moved to lean against the wall, key hooks to my right. 'Write it down and I will tell you.' I met the eye of the curious man who placed coins into piles and stared with withering ferocity until he looked away.

Fuller fetched in his drawer for a smaller journal, opened it to the first page and dipped his quill in the inkpot.

'The fellow's name is John James Meredith,' I recited slowly. Fuller scratched out the name with due diligence, squinting with old eyes at his own writing.

'Hounsditch,' I continued, watching his slow scratching. 'At Bishopsgate-Without.'

It took him a minute or more to write the address. He raised his brows. 'What would you have me do now?'

'Investigate it.' I marched toward the door and returned to Bread Street with mine own key tucked safely in my pocket.

Dowling sat already in the cart. 'Are you ready?' he called, impatient.

'Aye,' I hopped up beside him. 'Why the hurry?'

'That great oaf tells me there is plague at Ludgate.' Dowling tossed his head in the direction of Hearsey. 'If we would save Henry Burke we must get there before they close it up.'

Two wooden boxes lay outside Ludgate Gaol, each the size of a man's body, one stacked untidily atop the other. A rank odour lurched sluggishly upon a slight breeze from the direction of the bars above, a stench of necrosis and contagion.

I jumped down onto the cobbles just as the jail door burst open. A man strode out, a tall strong fellow wearing the clothes of a workman. He carried his hat in his hand and marched up the hill toward St Paul's, head down. I called after him, but he took no notice, so I hurried after, urging him to wait. He was reluctant to stop, reluctant to slow even.

'Wait now.' I struggled to breathe. His legs stretched longer than mine. 'I am a King's agent and I demand you stop a brief moment.'

At that he stayed. His long face was drawn and dried hard, like it might never smile again. 'King's agent?'

'Aye,' I panted. 'What business do you have in Ludgate?'

'They imprisoned my father, accused him of not paying a debt.' The acid in his voice spoke of grave injustice, real or imagined.

'He is no longer imprisoned?'

'He is dead!' the man snapped, cheeks flushed.

As I feared.

'What's it like in there now?' I asked.

'Go in and see for yourself.'

Which was my plan. 'The smell of the pest is strong.'

He nodded. 'And many times stronger inside. If you would truly know, then go inside yourself. It is difficult to describe Hell.'

'I am sorry,' I said, inadequate. He turned away and strode off.

It would be sensible to follow him up the hill, away from the prison, I reflected. Instead I returned to where Dowling waited.

I poked my head inside the door to the tower and listened to the shouting, loud and frantic, coming from the top of the stairs.

I returned to the cart. 'I will go in by myself.' I grabbed the hated cloak and mask. 'Then I will be able to go as I please, find Burke and perhaps bring him out.'

Dowling stood awkward, grunting to himself as though he would object. Yet the medic's clothes were too small for him, and if he were to accompany me then the Assistant would realise who I was.

I marched toward the open door and climbed the stairs, wondering what lunacy awaited. As I emerged into the quadrant I found all the prisoners sat huddled together against one wall, while three guards, the Assistant and Master-of-the-Box besides, staggered about the room shouting slurred protests at each other.

'What is happening?' I shouted at the Assistant, his long body waving like a sapling in the wind as he lurched from foot to foot.

He waved a hand at my beak as though he thought to catch it. 'The plague is happening.' He staggered. 'Have ye been asleep this month?'

'How many dead?'

'Five so far,' he slurred, before tripping over his feet and cracking his head against the stone floor.

Against the wall to my right slumped a man by himself,

avoided by all others, grey faced and foggy eyed. His legs lay straight afore him, his arms limp in his lap. He didn't blink.

The Assistant climbed to his feet and rubbed a finger gingerly against his forehead. 'We have them locked in the cells upstairs.' He pointed to the corpse. 'That one is dead, so we fetched him down.'

'You touched the body?'

'Ha!' he spluttered. 'You cannot leave dead men with living men, and you cannot leave plague in the middle of a prison, else men will break out of their cells with their heads. We have a box downstairs and will move him soon.'

'Are you not afraid of contracting the sickness yourself?'

He shook his head, pulled a bottle from the pocket of his coat and offered it to me. 'I have had the pox already and we drink sack to kill any poison that would try to infect us.'

'You know the door stands open downstairs?'

'Aye, as I said.' He pointed again at the dead man. 'We must take him out.'

'I will help you then.' I walked toward the corpse and knelt, probing with my fingers to check he was truly dead.

The Assistant drew close and I bid him take the feet while I took the shoulders. I looked into his face and saw James, smiling and excited. 'Lift!' I cried, and we carried the corpse easily, for it was light.

I walked backwards down the stairs, afraid the Assistant would fall over. As it was he tripped over his feet twice and almost stumbled.

Out on the street Dowling's cart was gone.

I laid the body on the ground and scanned both directions while the Assistant removed the lid from a box. I thought to ask the guards where Dowling went, but then I saw Withypoll stood with Forman up in the shadow of the cathedral. Dowling must have ridden away when he saw them.

'Hurry,' I urged the Assistant. 'I have others to visit as well.'

We placed the dead man inside the coffin and replaced the lid. Then I climbed the stairs two at a time, praying Forman and Withypoll didn't know I had the medic's uniform. I wondered if there was another door out. There must be.

The Master-of-the-Box stood with eyes closed in the middle of the room. I grabbed him by the lapels of his jacket and shook. 'How long has the pest been here?'

'It came sudden.' He gazed upon my chest. 'Six men were brought here late yesterday and taken to the cells. By this morning five were dead. Now more are infected.' He puffed out his cheeks and took a swig at his bottle. 'I can't remember how many.'

'Who brought them in?'

'Floor-man and Lily-pole,' he stuttered. 'King's men, so they say. Insisted.' He shrugged. 'I told 'em they was sick. Told 'em, I did.'

'One wore a beaver hat, the other a fine suit?'

He rocked back on his heels. 'That's them. Knew they were sick, I reckon. Wouldn't touch 'em.' He sunk to the floor where he squatted, looking as though he would vomit. 'Just poked them with a stick.' He put a finger in his ear and spoke louder. 'That stick.' He pointed at a long rod about the height of a man, leaning against the wall.

'Am I the first medic to visit?'

'No.' His eyes wandered. 'Other fellow told us to put the infected all together in the same cell. Keep them away from the rest.' He pursed his lips. 'King's men said they were debtors, see. Told us we has to keep them here until they dead.'

'So now they are isolated?'

'Nope!' He shook his head so hard his hair flew about. 'King's men came in after and told us we couldn't put five men in one cell. Said it was inhospitable.'

'I see.' Which meant they might be back soon to check. 'I will go and look upstairs.'

The Master-of-the-Box pulled his head back into his neck and stared at my costume. 'Are you a medic too?'

'Aye, a medic too.' I put out my hand. 'Give me the keys.'

He obliged, eventually, and I climbed the stairs. All was quiet. I approached the passageway leading to Burke's cell and unlocked the door.

I walked straight into a wall of foul sickness, sweet and cloying, penetrating even the ball of herbs in my mask. Each small cell was full, three men in each. In the first cell to the left nothing moved. Two bodies lay prone on the floor and another sat with its back to the wall, all clothed, none moving. Flies scuttled unmolested over all three, wandering in all directions as though they searched for something, fat blue flies scavenging off grey dying skin. I assumed all three were dead until one moved. Another groaned.

In the second cell were three more men. One stood on a florin in one corner and two sat shivering on the floor. The one standing was Burke, eyes dull, face swollen, head pouring with sweat. He clutched himself about the chest, legs close together as if he stood on top of a tall building, terrified to move. The three men in the cell to the right lay motionless.

I tried talking to Burke, but he showed no signs of hearing. I lifted the hood high enough to speak. Another wave of fetid air engulfed my moist head. 'What are you doing in there, Burke?' I called.

He held his hands to his head and stared at the men afore him. 'I don't know.'

'Yesterday you had a cell to yourself.'

'I did, aye. Then they brought six men in here, all of them diseased, and Forman and Withypoll ordered the Master-of-the-Box to lock them up with me.' Burke clenched his fists and held them to his temples. 'They wouldn't let me out.'

So that was it. Dispose of Burke discreetly. Lock him up in a small prison with plague victims.

'This is murder,' I reflected. 'Forman and Withypoll brought the plague here to kill you. Kill you so none might know you have been killed.'

'In truth?' he said, eyes filling with tears.

'Aye.' My own heart filled with misery. 'No need for a trial, no need for a hanging.'

Tears rolled down his cheeks.

I tried unlocking his cell, but no key would fit.

'Withypoll took the key from the Master-of-the-Box and kept it for himself,' Burke sobbed. 'I don't feel well.' He held a hand to his chest.

I pulled at the bars, but the door was locked. I watched him weep, saw the terror in his eyes, the trembling of his legs. 'I don't know how to help you, Burke.'

He watched one of the men dying at his feet, lain prone now, eyes closing. 'I am already infected, I know it.' I saw in his eyes the certainty of his own suffering, the death of all prospect and hope. Then the man dying on the floor let forth a weary sigh, followed by a great sneeze, and then was still.

Burke shook his head. 'You should not be here, not without that hood upon your head.'

He spoke wise, I reflected. I had to be out of this place afore I got shivery myself.

'Is there anything I might fetch you?' I asked.

He didn't reply, just raised his face, eyes so wet they might swim out of his head.

'Tell me who Forman and Withypoll work for.'

He nodded, all hope of salvation extinguished. 'Lord Chelwood,' he said.

'Say it again,' I wanted to be sure I heard well.

'Lord Chelwood!' he called out clear.

'Why did they take you to John Tanner's house?' I asked.

He laughed, a broken sound. 'All I wanted was some recompense.' He looked to me like I might make his life whole again.

'I'm sorry, Burke.'

He lifted his chin. 'I will declare mine iniquity and be sorry for my sins.'

'Why did they take you to John Tanner's house?' I repeated.

'Lord Chelwood guaranteed Wharton's wine deal. He sent Forman and Withypoll to talk to me after Wharton was killed, said he would hide me away until the real killer was found.' He looked to me with the flicker of a flame in his dull eyes. 'Then when you followed me, they put me in here.'

'Who is Lord Chelwood to you?' I asked.

'No one.' He sat upon the bench, oblivious to the body afore him. 'Just the man who guaranteed I would be paid, so it said on the document Wharton gave me.'

'Forman and Withypoll work for him?'

'And they will kill you as well.' He waved a hand at the bodies about him. 'You and the butcher.'

'God bless you, Burke,' I said quiet.

Burke bowed his head.

I pulled the mask back down over my head and hurried out the cells, leaving the door open behind me.

The Assistant would need more boxes.

CHAPTER 22

If rumours be true or false, according to the ANCIENTS
You may then judge the rumours are true and very good;
but if you find the Lord of the ascendant afflicted by the
infortunes, or cadent in house, you must judge the contrary
though he strong in the sign wherein he is.

I returned to Newgate up the Old Bailey, outside the wall,
for though I saw no sign of Forman nor Withypoll, I feared
they might lie in waiting for me in the shadows of St
Paul's.

Dowling's house sat quiet and empty, no sign of his cart
neither, so I dropped off the medic's clothes and waited a
while. If Forman and Withypoll pursued us, then this was
no safe place. Where would Dowling go? If Forman and
Withypoll had taken him, they would not have been
chatting idly on Ave Maria Street.

I saw no one out the window. Orange streaks slashed
the purple sky and candles flickered in the first dusk. The
only place I could fathom he would hide was the Guildhall.

The Guildhall indeed, for it was a public place where none could molest a man undeterred.

I left the house and hurried down Newgate Market toward Cheapside, keeping to the shadows of the eaves. Still I didn't see my assailant before he stepped out of the alley mouth and smashed a wooden club across my stomach.

A heavy hand descended upon my head and pulled my chin up into the air. 'Lytle,' hissed a familiar voice.

War's blue eyes shone bright and alert. Creases and stains adorned his black cloak. The hand on my shoulder squeezed so tight, my arm went numb. The last of Wharton's dogs running wild.

'Time to talk,' he whispered hoarsely. He grabbed the scruff of my jacket and pulled me to my feet. I bent back over double, the muscles of my stomach crying out in agony.

The tip of a sword pressed against the small of my back. 'We don't have time, Lytle. Forman and Withypoll followed you earlier. They may still. Move.' He pressed the blade deeper into my flesh and steered me south.

'I am not going to the river.' I stood my ground. 'It's a long way and I can shout very loud.'

He smiled thinly. 'I could slice off your head where you stand.'

'So you could, but you have come to talk, have you not?'

My heart beat so hard my voice trembled. 'Else you would have sliced off my head already. St Paul's is closer.'

He snorted. 'You take me for a fool? We are not going to Paul's, nor anywhere else public.'

'Then let's go to the graveyard of St Vedast,' I thought fast. 'The lock to the gate is broken and we will be the only ones there.'

He sneered. 'What is at St Vedast?'

I attempted to stand straight. 'Nothing is at St Vedast. I used to play there as a child, and I know we can talk undisturbed.'

'St Vedast then,' he ceded, eyeing the quiet houses about us. 'Betray me and I will cut your throat back to your spine.'

I led him across Cheapside and up Foster Lane to the small churchyard with high walls. The lock to the gate broke more than twenty years ago. It creaked loudly as I swung it open, hinges rusted and arthritic. Not much better than the river, I reflected, as I led him onto the gravel path, for he could do as he willed to me here without fear of being disturbed.

It was as well I knew this place, for the moon showed us little. The headstones stood white, grey and green, those I could make out in the darkness. I felt naked and exposed as we walked away from the gate.

I followed the wide arc of the path to the left, feet

crunching loud upon the stones, until we reached the familiar stone seat tucked beneath the giant oak. Crooked branches cast crazed black shadows behind which War might feel secure. A great wave of ivy tumbled down upon the seat, falling from the wall behind.

War sat cautiously and peered out into the night. 'What did Burke tell you?'

'You have been following me,' I realised.

War turned his craggy face toward mine. He resembled a chopping block, a multitude of scars incised upon his face. 'Answer me.'

'He told me it was Lord Chelwood who guaranteed your wine deal,' I replied.

'It took you five days to discover it,' War snorted.

'Had you confided in us instead of torturing us, perhaps your friends would still be alive,' I answered, irked.

War held his sword out afront of him, catching the light of the dying moon upon the blade. 'You work for Lord Arlington.'

'What of it?' I hissed. 'You tortured Dowling because we work for Arlington, yet wouldn't tell us why.'

'Arlington or Perkins. One of them killed Wharton, and the others besides.'

'Why so?' I demanded. 'What of Forman and Withypoll?'

'Forman and Withypoll want to kill you, Lytle. They

don't want to kill me, nor Wharton.'

'Why?'

'You first,' War growled. 'What have you found out since last we met?'

'I do have a thought,' I replied. 'But I will not share it with you until you tell me what you know.'

War held the tip of his sword to my thigh, but I pushed it aside. He stared at me, teeth bared and eyes narrowed, but did nothing. He seemed smaller tonight. 'Very well,' he said at last. 'We have as long as we need, after all.' He cleared his throat. 'Chelwood was Wharton's master. He directed foreign affairs in the King's name and pledged to manage those that fought against the King at home. Charles had need to appear magnanimous when restored and only those that signed his father's execution warrant were officially put to death.'

I felt disgusted. 'You and Wharton were the King's secret executioners?'

'Not the King.' War lowered his voice. 'The King makes sure he knows only what he needs to. He trusted Chelwood to ensure his transition was peaceful and that the guilty were punished.'

'You murdered men at Chelwood's behest. You killed Roger Cline's son.'

'We seized the guilty and did what was needed to discover the truth.'

'The King was restored five years ago,' I said. 'What have you been doing all this time?'

'Ask your master that. He plotted against the Earl of St Albans e'er since he discovered what services he provided, just because he would see Chelwood disgraced.'

I didn't understand. 'You think Lord Arlington killed the Earl to disgrace Lord Chelwood?'

'No, I think he killed Wharton because he *could*, once he persuaded the King to send Chelwood to Ireland, leaving us exposed.'

It made no sense. 'Why should Arlington hang Wharton by the neck at the Vintners' Hall? Why should he drown one of your friends in a barrel of wine and weight another to the bottom of the Thames?'

'To implicate Henry Burke,' War answered, though with less certainty than before. 'Burke complained to him about the way we cheated him and so presented himself as an easy scapegoat.'

'I don't think so.' I shook my head. 'Arlington left London on Lord's Day leaving only Newcourt behind, and Newcourt is not capable of such barbarity.'

'Arlington has access to whosoever he chooses.'

'Who do you say he chose then?'

'We thought it might be you.' He laughed, unkindly. 'Then we looked for another, but...' He tapped the sword upon the floor.

'You are not sure,' I realised. 'You asked us what we discovered of Perkins, the ranting cleric. You suspect he may be the killer.'

'It is possible,' War conceded. 'The Bishop of London has the King's ear these days. Some of the families of those we killed made discreet protest to the church. Perkins played the role of advocate. He sent Wharton letters, threatening retribution.'

'What did Wharton think of that?'

War's head jerked like he saw something, eyes staring out into the dark. 'He laughed at him,' he whispered. 'So long as he had Chelwood's support, he feared no one.'

He knew less than we did, I realised with heavy heart. 'I cannot see Perkins setting men's heads on fire and stuffing them into barrels.'

'Wine is wicked, the king is wicked, women are wicked, all the children of men are wicked, and such are all their wicked works; and there is no truth in them; in their unrighteousness also they shall perish,' War recited. 'If you researched Perkins well you would know it is one of his favourite proclamations.'

'The clergy are well-practised at the art of inquisition,' I said. 'Methods they may stand behind and justify. What cleric would go to the extraordinary lengths that we have seen, actions that would see him condemned if discovered?' It was nonsense. 'And there is little that is godly in implicating an innocent man.'

'Then tell me what else you know,' War's voice grated. 'Afore I slice open your chest.'

'The killer sought to implicate poor Henry Burke.' I edged away, ready to run if he lost his temper. 'It was Forman and Withypoll who locked him up at Ludgate with plague victims.'

'Forman and Withypoll work for Lord Chelwood,' War answered, confident. 'They would see Burke die only because you interfered with their plan to hide him away.'

My throat constricted as I imagined what Burke was doing at that moment. 'How do you know Chelwood didn't kill Wharton?' I asked. 'The King sent Chelwood away. So he could no longer control events. Seems to me he is as likely a candidate as Arlington.'

'That is the thought you spoke of?' War jeered.

A light breeze blew across the graveyard, rustling the leaves of the oak above our heads.

'No,' I admitted. 'I told you we found Wharton's brother at Bedlam.'

'So you did,' he grunted. 'Pestilence went yesterday. He will tell me if it be true.'

'No he won't,' I retorted. 'We found him dead this morning. You didn't follow us to Bedlam, evidently.'

War grabbed my neck with one huge hand. 'Dead?'

I said nothing, determined to stay quiet until he released

me. He stared into my eyes like he searched for something, afore pushing me away.

'Someone cut his throat,' I said, rubbing mine. 'We found him in Franklin's cell.'

'Who is Franklin?'

'The brother,' I said. 'As I told you before.'

War stared into the darkness.

'Except I don't think it was his brother.'

War's head jerked toward me. 'What do you say?'

'I wonder if Wharton is truly dead.' I spoke the thought aloud for the first time. 'Or has he been hiding at Bedlam in the place of his brother?'

'Madness!' War stuttered, white faced.

The gate swung open again, thirty paces back the way we came, too purposeful to be wind.

War pushed his sword deep between my ribs, breaking the skin. 'Friends of yours?'

Shadows emerged into the faint moonlight, two of them. 'Not mine,' I whispered. 'Yours neither, I'll wager. Methinks Forman and Withypoll.'

War inspected the wall behind us, twelve feet high, too smooth to scale. 'Good fortune, Lytle.' He patted me upon the arm and ran off deeper into the churchyard. I thought to call after him, but feared attracting attention. There was no other gate out, nor wall to climb.

He ran without care, feet crunching across gravel and

through undergrowth like a loose horse. I heard voices to my right, sharp and urgent, then another set of feet running, but only one. That meant one remained, guarding the only passage out. I sat still and listened hard. More voices, a low voice and a higher voice, then the sound of a man groaning.

I stood up and trod carefully toward the trunk of the giant oak. The gnarled bark offered a multitude of handholds amongst its pits and ridges, easy climbing as I remembered from childhood. I pulled myself up to the lowest branch without problem. The next branch above me stretched out from tree to the wall, then out and over Foster Lane. Twelve feet was a high drop to the street below, but if I managed it twenty years ago I could manage it now. I hoisted myself up to the thicker bough and straddled it, then shuffled along, holding tight with my thighs. Halfway across, the branch jerked and cracked. I had put on weight this last twenty years. My trousers caught and tore.

'Harry Lytle,' a low voice called out from below. 'Climbing a tree.'

I almost toppled off. Withypoll stared up from below. He jumped and tapped his sword against the sole of my foot.

'Will you come down or shall I come up?'

Something snapped and again I nearly toppled, but the end of the branch fell to rest against the top of the wall. I scraped along, yanking my leg forward and tearing the cloth further. The gap between me and the wall stretched no thicker than a man's upper arm. I leaned forward quickly, reaching for the brick, just clinging to it. I pushed onto my lower arms in an attempt to take my weight off the branch and pulled myself forwards. A short sharp piece of wood cut through the trouser into my thigh.

Withypoll disappeared. I heard him run back toward the gate. The wall was six inches thick, enough to balance on while I swung my legs down the other side. I turned and lowered myself, face to stone, sliding down, shirt riding up about the top of my naked stomach, grinding against the rough brick. I swung back and dropped the last three feet, twisting my knee on hitting the ground. I hobbled towards Cheapside, knee throbbing, stomach and leg bleeding, and flung myself behind the cross at St Nicholas Le Quern.

Withypoll burst forth, looking left and right in frantic search. I pushed deep into the shadows, blood pounding in my temples. He did a little jig, feet uncertain which way they wished to carry him, then kicked the cobbles in furious temper. Forman emerged beside him, laid a hand upon his shoulder and stared out with him into the night. For a terrifying second I thought he saw me, but neither moved. Forman said something, and they disappeared back into the churchyard.

I breathed a sigh of relief and contemplated running for home, but I wanted to know what happened to War. Soon

Forman came out again, this time on his own. He stood as if waiting.

A cart rattled into view at the far end of Foster Lane, from direction of Cripplegate. Forman whistled between his fingers and beckoned with one hand. The cart trundled up the street, a plague cart it looked like. Forman signalled toward the gate and Withypoll emerged, pulling War by the armpits. Then the two of them picked him up and threw him onto the cart.

Forman spoke to the driver and money exchanged hands. Then the cart continued on toward me. A pair of legs dangled from the back of the wagon, short and thin, swinging freely as the cart bumped over the cobbles, a child's legs. As the cart turned east onto Cheapside I saw the pile of bodies, War lain spread-eagled on top. Then the cart turned left up Greatwood Street, on its way back to Cripplegate and the pit beyond.

It could have been me, I realised. I took off my shoes and walked as quiet as I could west toward Newgate.

CHAPTER 23

Of the crisis, or days critical

For discovering whether the crisis will be good or ill, you must note what planet she is in aspect withal at those times, whether with a friendly planet or an infortune.

I needed to rest somewhere Forman and Withypoll would never find me. I walked fast, unnerved by the emptiness and silence. Pitch and tar slowly sizzled in the burning braziers that lined the streets, and scented smoke drifted about the jetties of the houses. I thought I might be followed, yet each time I stopped to peer into the gloom all I saw were flickering shifting shapes, dancing in the light of the candles that lit the windows. I could think of only one place I would be safe that night.

There was a second house afflicted on my street now. Henry Hilton was a young fellow who took over his father's business a year before. He had a wife and two young children, six and four years old, I guessed. He left home early and arrived late, wild black hair always set in some untamed shape. Soon as he saw you he would smile, eyes telling you how happy he felt. Now he had a red cross upon his door.

I didn't recognise the man that watched my house and had never thought to ask Fuller who they appointed as nightwatch. I wondered where Hearsey slept, whether he still returned to his home outside the wall. This new fellow seemed less diligent, for he sat slumped, chin resting on his chest, legs splayed forward to stop him toppling over. I approached quiet and placed the key in the lock. Still he didn't move, just snored, arms held tight about his chest. With but a quick glance up and down the street, I turned the handle and slipped inside.

A slight figure leapt to her feet, thin shawl clasped about her shoulders. She walked toward me, candle held high. 'Who are you?'

'Harry Lytle.' I held up my hands. 'I live here.'

'You can't come in!' she whispered, shrill. 'There is plague in the house.'

'I know there is plague in the house,' I assured her. 'It's my house.'

She bustled closer, shooing me back toward the door. 'You must go. Lest they make you stay here.' She held her pale face forward, peering at me like I was a ghost, black locks hanging beside her cheeks.

'They told me you have fever.' I stepped toward her,

looking for signs.

She jumped back, trembling now with indignant agitation. 'You would have a fever too if you stayed here hour after hour.'

It was hot as an oven. A fire burned so bright in the kitchen it lit up the staircase.

'You are not afflicted?' I saw no swelling about her face. 'Why do you hold that shawl to your shoulders?'

'I have come from upstairs,' she replied, 'where it is much warmer. Your maidservant is still very sick.'

I looked to the stairs. 'I must see her.'

The nurse pulled at my sleeve as I climbed the staircase. 'You mustn't go to her, else you too might become infected!'

'The plague doesn't enjoy my taste.' I shrugged her gently aside. 'It has had every opportunity.'

Jane lay upon her bed, still and grey, naked beneath a thin sheet, lips dry and brow dripping. The fire raged so bright I had to stand back for a moment, my face burning. I held an arm up to protect myself. 'Surely this is too hot.'

'Hearsey says you came before posturing as a medic,' the nurse scolded. 'It was you that came last afternoon dressed in the costume. I would like to know where you acquired that costume and how many people may not have received physic because of it.'

'There are few enough medics left about the city,' I replied, scrutinising the buboes about Jane's chest. They had all been lanced and poultices applied. 'I doubt there is a shortage. Are there any new swellings since the medic attended her?'

'No,' the nurse snapped. 'Which doesn't mean there isn't poison deeper within. The medic said to make sure she sweated, to be rid of the poison through her skin.'

'Does she speak lucid?'

The nurse pushed me backwards. 'She hasn't spoken at all since I have been here. She is sick and needs rest.'

At least Jane seemed peaceful. Though pale and thinner than e'er before, her face rested in calm repose. 'Does the medic say she shall live?'

'The medic says she will probably die, for there is so much poison within her. Yet I do all I can to make her comfortable and pray for her every hour.'

For a moment Jane seemed not to breathe, then gasped sudden, a long deep breath. I turned and left her alone, much to the relief of the nurse.

'What is your name?' I asked.

'Ruth,' she replied. 'And rest assured I know what I am doing. Now leave this house afore I wake up the great dog upon the street. Should he smell you he will take you in his jaws and not let go. He is not an intelligent man.'

'How is the aunt?' I asked.

'She is dead,' Ruth replied. 'As should come as no surprise to you.' She spoke matter-of-fact, yet she bowed her head and her mouth twisted like she wanted to cry.

I pushed the door open. A sheet covered her from tip to toe. 'I didn't know her.'

'Just as well.'

'How long has she lain here?'

'She died late this afternoon,' Ruth answered. 'The medic came after she died and confirmed it. The bearer will take her tonight.'

'Take her where?' I asked. The churchyards had been full afore the plague. Now there was little assistance for those without monies. The poor were buried in shrouds in the plague pits.

'Back to her parish, I suppose,' Ruth shook her head. 'I understand she lived on the Bridge.'

'Aye, she lived on the Bridge, but she had little money and no husband.'

Ruth shrugged.

I scratched my face and tried not to think of money. 'Tell the bearer to take her to All Hallows. I will see her buried there.'

'Very well,' Ruth nodded. 'Now you must leave.'

'I will stay until morning, I have no choice.' I looked to the night sky through the window. 'What time does Hearsey arrive?'

'Six of the morning,' Ruth replied. 'But you must leave now.'

'I cannot leave now, Ruth.' I walked slowly downstairs. 'Else I will likely end up in the pit myself afore dawn.' I thought of War, pictured his body being tipped upon the vast pile of corpses at the Cripplegate pit.

She noticed for the first time my limp, my torn clothes. 'You are hurt?'

'Cuts and blemishes.' I waved a hand. 'I can clean myself up. You should get some rest. I will sleep in my chair in the front room.'

'Nonsense,' she replied, then set about fussing worse than Jane until my scratches were washed and my body besides.

My clothes were torn beyond repair. I fetched new ones from my room, watching Jane's aunt out the corner of my eye in case she moved. I settled myself to sleep a few hours in the front room downstairs, behind the open door, where none might see me from the street. I fell asleep afore my eyes finished closing.

I was awoken by a loud banging. I crept to the window and took a swift peek to see who sought entrance to a plagued house in the middle of the night, head full of ill-formed escape plans should it be Forman and Withypoll standing there. But it was a short man with thick arms and a cart. The bearer, of course.

I watched from the crack in the door as Ruth bid him enter. 'Good evening and God bless you,' I heard him say. He entered with a board beneath his arm. 'If you'd be so kind as to show me where she lies. Are there any menfolk here?'

Ruth shook her head emphatically. 'No.'

'Aye, then.' The bearer turned back to the street. 'You, fellow. You will have to help me carry the body to the wagon.'

'It's not my job,' a faint voice protested. 'I am paid to wait outside and prevent others from going inside.'

'Aye,' the bearer grunted. 'And prevent those from inside going outside. In this case the lady must come outside to be carried away and buried earthside, and I cannot carry her on my own.'

'It's not my job,' the voice complained again.

The bearer cursed quiet, then cleared his throat. 'Plague Orders state that said watchmen are to do such further offices as the sick house shall need and require, and in this instance the sick house requires that you take one end of this board and help me carry the dead lady.' I saw him step angry toward the open door and jab a finger. 'And if you choose not to fulfil that duty then I shall go away and leave the lady here and hold that conversation with Alderman Fuller in the morning.'

'Very well,' the watcher exclaimed, crestfallen. He poked

his head through the doorway and looked left and right, like he expected to be leapt upon. The bearer watched him tread cautiously across the threshold, shaking his head. The stairs creaked as they made their way upstairs.

'Where we taking her?' the bearer called as they carried the corpse out.

'To All Hallows church,' Ruth replied.

'All Hallows?' the watcher demanded, curious. 'Why so, All Hallows?'

'The man that owns this house said All Hallows,' Ruth replied. 'Said he is paying her costs.'

'When did you talk to the man that owns this house?' The watcher stood still while the bearer struggled to hold the weight.

Ruth raised her chin. 'Alderman Fuller told me yesterday, when I was appointed.'

The watcher's eyes narrowed.

'Kindly move your feet,' the bearer urged him. 'Afore I drop this lady upon the floor.'

The watcher did as he was bid, expression betraying his live suspicion. Ruth closed the door as soon as they stepped out onto the street and emitted a curse I had not heard from a woman before.

She glared at me as though she would slap my face. 'What now do I tell Alderman Fuller?'

'Should he ask, tell him I knocked upon the window

while the watcher was asleep. Tell him you did not wish to get the watcher into trouble.' I contemplated. 'Indeed you might tell the watcher that yourself afore he leaves so he doesn't raise the affair with Alderman Fuller at all.'

'Yes,' she relaxed. 'A good lie.' She scowled again. 'How now will you get out? The watcher is wide awake.'

I looked to the sky. No sign of dawn. 'At five o'clock you call to the watcher, tell him your tale, tell him you would not see him lose his job. Then tell him you need cold water immediately.'

The nurse stared. 'You are a devious fellow.'

Which I took as commendation.

I returned to my chair and took what more sleep I could afore the sun crept up again.

CHAPTER 24

Of a captive or slave
Behold the hour at what time the captive is taken in, and
if the Lord of the hour be an infortune, it signifies long
imprisonment; but if he be a fortune, it signifies short
imprisonment or captivity.

Dowling had not been home since yesterday afternoon.
The mask and cloak lay where I discarded them, the house
was closed and musty. I made my way east toward the
Guildhall, though it would not yet be open.

Wharton and his four accomplices were all now dead.
Could it be that the killing now was over? Perhaps Forman
and Withypoll would leave now, back to wherever they
came. My gut told me I was optimistic.

I shivered and looked over my shoulder in time to see
a dark shape slither into the shadow of St Mary-le-Bow.
I increased my pace and glanced again. Sure enough,
black and lithe, sliding down the side of the street like a
snake. I started to run. A figure stepped out into plain

view. Long flowing cloak and legs like twigs. It was the lunatic, Franklin.

I screamed like a woman and ran as fast as I could down Cheapside, swollen knee forgotten. He pursued, cloak flowing behind, fast, like an animal.

I passed the turn to the Guildhall. No purpose in being ripped to pieces in front of a locked gate. The Tower! The Tower was full of soldiers. I veered right down Walbrook, almost slipping in a pile of something slimy and wet. I punched my arms in the air as hard as I could, straining each short leg as far as it would stretch. I felt a stabbing pain in my side, but paid it no heed. I glanced again over my shoulder to see the lunatic not twenty steps behind.

I pivoted left into Cannon Street. By the time I reached the crossroads with Fish Street Hill he closed again. I thought of diving left or right into an alley, in search of some dark cranny where he would never find me, yet good sense told me it would be a mistake. I raced past Mincing Lane. I heard his steps as loud as my own. On to Great Tower Street, fifty yards to go. He screamed, furious. He realised my intentions! Past Barking Church and out onto Tower Hill, the Bulwark Gate in sight. Two sentries stood staring at the sky, watching the sunrise. I cried out and they raised their pikes slow.

'Wait!' one called, jumping into a crouch.

I peeked over my shoulder again. No one there.

'Godamercy!' I panted, slowing down, guts threatening to spill out of my throat. I bent over, hands on knees, lungs searing. I peered back into the red light. No one. He must have stopped at the end of Tower Street.

The guard aimed the pike at my shoulder. 'Who are you?'

'Harry Lytle,' I gasped. 'I was being chased by an escaped lunatic.'

I managed to stand straight, felt the sweat beneath my armpits, upon my chest, groin and the insides of my legs. My bowel churned and threatened to erupt.

The guard took a step closer, pike still raised. 'An escaped lunatic?'

'Aye,' I crouched again, nursing a sharp pain in my stomach.

I heard footsteps.

'Good morning,' said a low voice, one I hadn't heard before. I gazed up into the face of the lunatic.

Gone was the vacant stare, the naked hunger. The hair about his eyes was growing back, and his brown eyes gazed at me from within a calm face, studied and composed.

'This is him.' I stepped back, falling over my feet. 'This is the man who chased me. He is escaped from Bedlam.'

Franklin's lip curled into an amused smile. He shrugged and spread his palms wide, laughing as if sharing a joke with the two bemused sentries. He had changed his clothes and trimmed his hair. 'My name is Edmund Franklin. I am a physician and this is my patient. I have come to take him back to Bedlam.'

'They know you lie, Franklin.' I scrambled to my feet. 'I used to work here, they recognise me.'

Franklin put his hands behind his back. 'I think not.'

The sentries watched, faces creased in bewilderment. Then one turned to point his pike at my chest. As soon as he moved, Franklin drew a blade from behind his back, long and thin, and with three quick motions stabbed the first sentry through the neck, parried the lunge of the second, and stabbed him through the throat. One lay still, blood gushing from his neck in a short arc, while the other twitched his legs, before he too sprawled motionless.

Franklin stared a moment, then clicked his tongue. He turned to me, unblinking. 'I just wanted to talk to you, Harry.'

'Edmund Franklin is a lunatic who hasn't spoke a word in fifteen years,' I managed to speak. 'Who are you?'

'I think you guessed that already.' He bowed. 'Thomas Wharton, first Earl of St Albans.'

The two dead men lay upon their sides as if listening to our conversation. He hadn't needed to kill them. 'Lately of Bedlam,' I said.

'Safe refuge, I thought,' he replied. 'For the short time I required it. You found me though, and Chelwood shows more interest than I predicted. So now I have more work to do.'

I peered at his bare chest, visible beneath his unbuttoned shirt. Were those freckles? 'Chelwood left you exposed.'

'Indeed.' Wharton rolled up his sleeves. Though it was warm, his skin seemed to burn, fiery red, covered in a sheet of sweat. A familiar sense of dread declared itself at the base of my stomach.

'Arlington would have moved quicker were it not for the plague.' He spoke as if in pain. 'I counted on his distraction. I did not count on Chelwood's diligence. He betrayed me.'

'You used the hiatus to vanish,' I said, watching him return the sword to his belt. 'You staged your death, then set about killing your colleagues while they wondered from where the blows were struck.'

Wharton winced, breathing hard. 'Had I left them to live they would have pursued me.' He coughed. 'They know me too well.' The brown eyes spoke of an iron will, a terrifying ruthlessness.

'They thought they were your friends.'

Franklin stared blankly. 'Friends?'

I recognised those freckles for what they were. 'You have the plague.'

'Aye, so I do,' he acknowledged. 'Which is none of your business. As I said, I have more work to do and so do you.

You will meet me at Leadenhall at midnight.' Pain scored creases about the corners of his mouth. 'You and Dowling. Not before, not after. You will tell none other.'

He was going to let me go? A surge of hope and fear coursed through me. 'Very well.'

He laughed, as though he read my mind. 'Let me tell you my new secret, Harry Lytle. You will not like it.' The pain disappeared from his eyes and he smiled. 'I have seized Liz Willis.'

'No!' I groaned.

Franklin grinned. 'Oliver's daughter, of whom you are most fond.' He watched me carefully, savouring the pain he saw in my ravaged soul. 'Though no harm need come to her. Just meet me tonight. Else I shall introduce her to *my* daughter.'

A picture of his deformed child came to mind. 'You don't have a daughter.'

'Yes I do, for I am a scavenger, and my daughter is the scavenger's daughter. You have heard of the scavenger's daughter?' I heard the laughter in his tone.

Indeed. A simple apparatus. A collar for the neck, loops for wrists and ankles. When a man turned the screws, the ankles were drawn closer and closer to the head, squeezing the victim's knees tighter and tighter to his chest. Once the muscles of his leg were stretched to their limit then they tore, ligaments and tendons pulled tight until they snapped. They say the blood was forced from a man's fingertips. The chest cavity would be squeezed so hard it became impossible to breathe and the victim died.

'Why so worried, Lytle?' he asked. 'Do you not trust me?' Then he laughed again, a manic cackle to signal the dawning of the new day. 'Leadenhall at twelve,' he said, then turned and strode back toward the city.

The dawn sky burned red as a devil returned to Hell. I left the two bodies where they lay and hurried after him.

Though it was not yet six o'clock, Willis' door stood ajar. I pushed it open and entered the house. Willis himself strode the hallway, fully clothed.

'Lytle,' he exclaimed. He blinked, unfocussed, as if he had been up all night. 'What are you doing here?'

'Where is Liz?' I demanded.

'She is missing.' He marched toward me and seized my shirt in his fists. 'What do you know of it?' His hands shook.

Edward appeared from the kitchen, wide eyed. A maidservant stood upon the stairs, waiting for me to speak.

'I would prefer we talk alone.'

He pulled back his hands and nodded sharply. 'Come with me, if you please.' He turned on one well-built heel and led me to his study, where last we met he banished me. 'May I give you something to eat or drink?' he asked, to my surprise.

I shook my head. 'What happened?'

'She went out last night to visit a friend and didn't come back.' Willis perched on the end of a low leather bound chair. 'When she didn't return I sent Edward to fetch her back, but they said she left hours before. They live on Mark Lane. It is two minutes away.'

I saw the lines on his forehead, sensed the turmoil inside his head. He blamed himself. Had he left London when he could, Liz would not have been taken. I knew the feeling. Jane, Liz, Burke, the two guards, all would still be alive and well had I not insisted on assuming this idiot assignment.

His head jerked up. 'You know who took her.'

'I think so.' I nodded. 'But I will not tell you.'

He leapt to his feet and went for my throat, but I pushed him away. 'I want to find her as much as you do,' I assured him. 'But if I tell you who has her, you will endanger her life. You will have to trust me.'

'Trust you?' he choked.

'Aye, trust me. I will have her back before tomorrow morning.'

He levelled a finger at my nose. 'Tell me who has her.'

'No.'

He shook his fists in the air and hissed at me through clenched jaws, trembling. 'It is not your decision to make.'

I headed to the door. 'Yes, it is.'

'Sit down,' he bellowed.

'My house is affected by plague, Mr Willis, so you will not find me there. You may leave message for me at the Guildhall.'

With that I left him to his misery, having an abundance of mine own.

The only places I could think to search for her were Bedlam and the Clink. Wharton could hardly hide her at Bedlam, and Judkins would be watching the Clink with gimlet eye.

I needed Dowling.

My heart bid me run through the streets without stopping, check if he returned home, interrogate the rector at Christ Church and the other churchwardens. Yet my head stopped me. Wherever Dowling was, he knew Forman and Withypoll were searching. The only place I could think he would go was the Guildhall. Yet was that not an obvious destination besides? If Forman and Withypoll wanted to catch me, that is where they might go, and whatever happened, I couldn't miss my appointment with Wharton at the Leadenhall. I had been careless so far. Now I had to employ self restraint. It was only six of the morning—I had time to prepare.

St Lawrence Jewry was a fair parish church, once a

favourite haunt of Sir Thomas More. Within its walls stood thirty-six monuments to various individuals, including two of Anne Boleyn's ancestors. All very interesting, but not today. Today it would serve as my watchpost. I reached the church through empty streets, confident none could follow without my spotting them. At the church I waited for the bell-ringer, who allowed me to climb the tower upon close inspection of the King's seal. I told him I watched for Catholic agitators.

From the tower I had clear view of the approach to the Guildhall, New King Street down to Cheapside. The ringing of bells vibrated inside my ears, but wasn't painful. I perched high enough that none would think to look up, yet close enough to the ground I could make out clothes and discern base features. I settled myself comfortably to watch.

The beaver hat and swaggering gaits betrayed them. Forman and Withypoll arrived before eight o'clock, along Catte Street, from the direction of Newgate. They strode purposefully toward the south gate, and through it. My heart beat as hard as the clappers in the bells as I awaited their return. Or would they leave through the north gate, so I would miss them?

Thirty minutes later they emerged again, alone and walking fast. At that moment I was sure they had him. Dowling wasn't the sort to hide himself away in hidey-holes. He went about his business with an unshakeable trust in God. At the moment *I* played that role, watching down from my little heaven. Forman and Withypoll turned west again, back down Catte Street, and I ran downstairs, determined to follow.

By the time I reached the street they were gone, but I hurried down Ladd Lane in time to see them disappear into Maiden Lane, toward St John Zachary. Sure enough they headed directly towards Dowling's house, which meant I could follow from afar. Ne'ertheless it was all I could do to stop the trembling in my arms and legs, for they chose a path through narrow streets, where curious eyes watched me pick my way across the damp morning cobbles, dancing to avoid the splashes of yet another chamberpot. I couldn't be sure that none spied on Forman and Withypoll's behalf, prepared to dash forwards to advise them of my pursuit.

They pushed open Dowling's door as if they knew he wasn't home, and stayed inside. Waiting for me, I assumed. I lingered upon the street a short time, conspicuous in my silks, afore slipping into the shop of a fellow I recognised, a butcher friend of Dowling. There I sat, staring at Dowling's house, not daring to take my eyes off the door.

Three hours later they had still not re-emerged. The sun climbed to its loftiest vantage point, drenching us all in a bath of sticky wetness. In the shop at least we enjoyed a light breeze through the open windows. Dowling's house baked like an oven with door closed. I wondered how long they would last.

On the stroke of midday they appeared, wiping their faces and picking their clothes from their skin. Withypoll carried his beaver hat in one hand, the first time I saw his naked head. He stood with hands on hips afore kicking angrily at the ground. Forman carried his jacket on his arm and appeared no less ill-tempered. They headed south and I followed.

St Paul's was quieter these days, the printing presses silent and shops closed. I cursed as they entered the churchyard, for here I was exposed. If they were to stop and turn they would recognise me. I maintained enough distance to allow for escape, yet I feared losing my chance to find Dowling. They walked fast though, with no sign of stopping.

They led me onto Creed Lane, toward the King's Wardrobe, where they pushed through the front door, barely acknowledging the guards.

'Boggins!' I cursed and stamped my foot. The King no longer kept his robes at the Wardrobe, for he had room sufficient at Whitehall and Hampton Court. Now it was home to the King's secret service, so it was rumoured, housing confidential documents and other covert objects. It was guarded day and night, and not by the drunks that protected most state buildings.

It took me nearly ten minutes to devise a scheme for entering.

The short walk along Thames Street took me past warehouses and store sheds, through the fumes emanating from the scores of little factories, soap boilers and brewers.

'Boddington!' I called out, throwing open the door to St James Garlickhythe. 'Where are you, you pompous windbag?'

Loud footsteps tapped a rapid beat from deep within the church, heralding the appearance of the astonished cleric. He thrust his arms out straight at his side and bellowed at me. 'How dare you!'

'How dare *you*, I say.' I stepped forward and tapped my finger upon his ample stomach. 'Here cometh I, in all good faith, in service of the King, and you spread malicious inventions as to the content of our conversation to William Perkins.'

Boddington thrust his considerable bulk forwards, legs apart, fists dug into his waist. 'I do not spread "malicious inventions". I told Perkins truth, that you cast aspersions upon the good name of our church, and therefore upon the sensibilities of the Lord our God.'

'Tut!' I exclaimed. 'I came here to protect the good name of the Lord our God, and you behaved in a manner that doth signify your own infirmity. I told Perkins what really happened and suggested to him your behaviour might indicate a propensity to flee.'

'Flee?' Boddington roared.

'Aye, flee,' I said again. 'He was most displeased and hath summoned you to appear before him. Good luck to you.'

'Summoned me where?'

'I suggest you use your own intelligence,' I replied, for I had no idea. 'I, meantime, shall retire to the King's Wardrobe, where I currently reside. Fare-thee-well.'

The bells rang for one of the clock.

Perkins' red coach appeared at the junction of Ave Maria Lane and Paternoster Row. I watched it turn from my hiding place in the shadow of a tall fir tree in St Paul's churchyard. It travelled faster than it had the day before, the four guards accompanying it having to run long-legged to keep up. I heaved a sigh of relief and followed at safe distance.

Another hour and a half was gone. Forman and Withypoll had left again, almost an hour before, while I prayed Perkins would arrive before they returned. The coach pulled up to the front door, both horses snorting and flicking their tails, as if resentful. Perkins clambered out with all the dignity he could muster and marched up to the two guards, purple nose raw and swollen. I felt the tiniest pang of guilt nibble at the edge of my conscience.

Perkins drew his garrison about him and remonstrated with the two unfortunates, waving his arms and shouting at the top of his voice. I crept closer, approaching from behind. The two guards scratched their heads and sought guidance of each other, until Perkins could stand it no more, pushing between them to open the front door. His four attendants followed. Two of them exchanged blows with the guards, fighting for control of the pikes they carried. One fell back, and the mêlée tumbled into the building. I ran forwards and into the grand hall, where Perkins stood arguing with another officious fellow, spitting my name like it was the name of the Devil.

I headed left into the mouth of the nearest corridor, treading carefully, wary of more guards. The passage was six feet wide, lined with chipped wood panelling and naked plaster. Some rooms had doors, others didn't, but none appeared to be in use, for dust lay thick over tables, chairs, books and shelves full of papers. The passage turned sharp right. It seemed it would carry me a full circuit of the building. Voices sounded, Perkins among them. I walked faster. At the end of the second passage an archway led into a great kitchen, and at the back of the kitchen a door led into a pantry. In the pantry I found Davy Dowling.

He sat unmoving, leaning backwards against the wall, legs bound at the ankles, arms at the wrists. His right eye shone purple and swollen, coated with dry blood. His mouth gaped, lips dry and flaking.

'Davy,' I poked him in the stomach. 'Wake up.'

He groaned, and I scanned the kitchen for water, but found none. I took my little knife from inside my coat and set to cutting at the rope. I stopped when I heard Perkins' voice louder and pulled the pantry door closed. Sitting next to Dowling I continued sawing at the bindings, praying he wouldn't moan. I cut at his ankles first, so at least he could run, if ever he woke up. Finally I freed his hands and kneaded at his wrists to restore circulation. A large bruise covered the left side of his face. He'd been struck close to the temple.

'We have to go, Davy,' I whispered. 'Forman and Withypoll will be back soon.'

He stirred, blinking, then raised a hand to his head. He moved his neck and grimaced. I offered him my hand. He took it, then staggered to his feet, wobbling like he might topple.

I eased open the pantry door and stepped into the kitchen. Perkins must have proceeded on and round. By now he likely searched upstairs. Without knowledge of other ways in or out, I decided to return the way we came, relying on being able to surprise the guards at the door and run off into the city.

Dowling plodded like an arthritic bear, leaning too

heavily upon my shoulder. I relieved myself of his weight and poked him in the arse. Wounds or no wounds, he had to recover his wits now. He stood unsteady, arms out to his side, balancing.

'Come on, Davy,' I urged him. 'I need you to run.'

He put a hand to his eye. 'I can't see.'

I tugged him by the arm and waved a hand in front of his good eye. He blinked and shook himself free.

At the threshold to the hall all seemed quiet. The main doors were closed. Just as I was about to prod Dowling forwards, the doors flew open, crashing against the wall. Withypoll cursed, throwing his hat across the hallway, striding straight toward the kitchen, the most direct route I assumed. Forman followed in his tracks, dropping his fine jacket in a heap.

'We must go now,' I whispered to Dowling.

Dowling lumbered in a strange crouching shuffle like a giant baboon, but made good speed. I ran past him and opened the door, stepping out into the sunshine.

'Lytle!' Perkins rubbed his hands together and laughed with delight. 'I was just about to leave.'

His men descended upon me and all went black.

The Compter stood on Poultry. A man might mistake it for a house were it not for the barred gate covering the door, but inside was as dank as every other squalid hole I visited this last week. Had I sought to infect myself and paint a red cross upon my own forehead, I could not have devised a better schedule.

I sat by myself in a tiny cell at the end of a shadowy passageway. Across skulked a young fellow with wet blue eyes and lank greasy hair falling limp about either side of his face. He spoke incessantly about his deep and personal journey from abject sinner to clean soul and glorious redemption. To my left, a poor fellow with bald head and loose lower lip said less, muttering from time to time about ravens plucking out his eyes. To my right lay a man on the floor, sweat pouring from his forehead, jaws clenched tight and body shaking. Familiar symptoms.

My heart pounded with rage and fear. I could not dwell here long. I wrung my hands, chewed at my lip and wondered what to do. Where was Dowling? Had they arrested him too? I reckoned I had been here half an hour, which would make it about five o'clock. Seven hours to our appointment at Leadenhall. I had to get out.

I called for the gaoler, a small fellow with thick dark brows stuck upon a round white face. Short cropped black hair covered his head in a layer of fine bristle and he shuffled with a stoop, carrying his round belly like a pregnant woman. He looked as if he woke up here one day and couldn't find his way out, a giant mole. He appeared afore me, shambling and unhappy.

'Release me,' I urged him, 'and I will pay you five pounds.'

He rolled his eyes as though he regretted the long walk. I imagined I was not the first to make such an offer.

'I work for Lord Arlington.'

'So say you,' moaned the Mole. 'I release you and never see you again, nor your five pounds, and William Perkins comes and asks me where you've gone. When I confess to him I know not where you went, nor how you escaped, what do you think he does?'

'Then don't release me.' I gripped the bars in my fists. 'Send word to a man called Newcourt at the Guildhall. That is all I ask. For that you will still be paid five pounds. And if the money is not forthcoming then you may make my life a misery.'

'Why should I wish to make your life a misery?' the Mole grumbled. 'It is miserable enough in here, do ye not think?'

'I beseech you,' I pleaded. 'I am a King's agent.'

The Mole grunted to himself and stood motionless. 'Where should I deliver this message?' he asked at last.

'The office of Sir Thomas Player,' I replied, quick. 'Or else to one of the guards. It matters not.'

'I shall think on it,' he pronounced finally. 'I shall go out to eat my dinner and shall think on it then.'

'Thank you,' I leaned back on the hard bench, some

shred of hope restored.

An age later, I still sat alone. I called out for the Mole, but no one came. I called out until my throat was sore. The Mole heard, he could not help but hear, yet he chose to ignore me. I banged my fist against the stone wall and succeeded only in skinning my knuckles and causing my fingers to swell.

The man next to me was plagued. The closer he journeyed to death, moaning piteously, the louder the young fellow opposite chattered. My mood oscillated between rage and despair. Would that the man died and put us all out of our misery. Why did they not take him to a pest-house? His symptoms were clear enough, for I saw tokens upon his neck even from where I sat, small raised brown marks.

Hours later the Mole appeared again, long nose reaching out afore him as though he walked by smell and not by sight.

I flung myself at the bars. 'What time is it?' I whispered, hoarse.

'Ten o'clock,' he muttered.

Godamercy. Two hours to midnight. 'Have you had dinner?'

'I have,' he answered, avoiding my eye.

Newcourt emerged in the Mole's tracks. 'Harry?' He stooped to avoid catching his wig upon the ceiling. He held a mouchoir to his nose and walked gingerly, as though afraid of stepping in something indescribable.

'Thanks be to God! You must ensure my release!'

Newcourt watched the sick man. 'Who ensured your imprisonment?'

'William Perkins,' I said. 'The cleric. He is convinced Wharton tortured men at the King's behest and that Lord Arlington knew of it besides.'

'He is a passionate man.' Newcourt shuffled uneasily. 'You should have left him alone.'

'Wharton's dogs said he pursued Wharton like he was a dog himself. All I did was ask George Boddington some questions.'

Newcourt edged further away from the afflicted man. 'I cannot stay here.'

'Neither can I,' I replied. I pointed at the Mole. 'You must tell him to let me go.'

Newcourt shook his head and stepped back the way he had come. 'I will talk to his lordship.'

'But he is still at Hampton Court?'

'Yes,' Newcourt affirmed. 'I saw him yesterday. He is busy. I will go there again on Monday.'

'I cannot stay here until Monday,' I exclaimed. 'You must release me now.'

Newcourt pointed a finger at me. 'Lord Arlington is not pleased, Lytle,' he grumbled. 'He did not expect to hear his own name mentioned in connection with the Earl's death. It would have been as well you proclaimed Burke to be guilty.'

'That was Chelwood's agenda,' I protested.

Newcourt pushed his face close to mine. 'The same agenda. Chelwood determined to proceed discreetly in discovering who killed Wharton. It was best for all our sakes that Burke was kept quiet.' He stepped backwards. 'Now you are the one attracting too much attention.'

I felt my jaw drop.

'I will send message once I have spoken to his lordship again,' Newcourt snapped. He clicked his fingers at the Mole and pointed at the shivering fellow. 'That man is dying of plague. You cannot leave him here.'

The Mole bowed his head and shuffled away, embarrassed. With one last peek at the dying man, Newcourt was gone besides.

Two hours to go, and I remained stuck here. I seized the bars and shook them, to no avail. Then, unbidden and unanticipated, I experienced a sudden urge to scream at the top of my voice, a giant roar of unrequited fury. When it was done my heart pounded so hard my chest shivered. The blood pumped in my ears, and I heard the sound of my own panting, like a terrified dog. I rested silent again, amazed by what I did. I felt much better, as though I regurgitated all my tensions back out into the fog of body smell, where they lingered in like company. Then the tension began to brew again, driven by the sense of impotence I felt locked up in this wet burrow. When the medic arrived I approached my second scream.

The medic loomed vast, waxed cloak barely reaching his knees. The Mole unlocked the cell next door, hands shaking. Then the medic pushed him aside and dropped to one knee next to the figure on the floor. He touched him upon the neck, undid his shirt, and poked about.

A muffled voice mumbled through the heavy mask. 'I need a man to help me carry him. That man is the right height.' He pointed at me. 'Unless you will carry him yourself.'

The Mole reached for his keys and unlocked my cell door. The medic crooked his finger. I shook my head as hard as I could shake it. I had no intention of approaching the infected man, but the medic insisted and stamped his foot hard, which is when I noticed he wore Davy Dowling's boots.

We carried the unconscious victim of plague with bare hands, out through the passage and up towards the sun, the Mole close behind. As we lay the man down on the cobbles our heads came together, and I heard a muffled sound coming from Dowling's beak that sounded like 'saltpetre'. Once we stood straight the Mole bore down upon me with little steps.

Dowling removed his mask and stared down at the Mole through swollen eyes. The whole right side of his face was now purple and yellow, and the bristles on his head stood up in fierce indignation. The Mole shrank before him.

'Run, Harry,' Dowling whispered.

I turned and ran, and as I did so my head cleared, and I realised that 'saltpetre' was 'St Peter'. The Mole and Davy Dowling pursued, though the Mole lasted but twenty yards before he stopped, hands on knees, gasping like he would explode.

'In the cart, Harry,' Dowling panted when we reached the church. 'We must hide.'

Aye, but only 'til midnight.

CHAPTER 25

If one be afraid of a thing, whether he shall be in danger of the same or not

Behold the ascendant and his Lord, and the moon; if you find the moon unfortunate, or if the Lord of the ascendant be unfortunate, and falling from an angle; or especially in the twelfth and moon with him; it signifies the same fear is true, and certain that there is cause for it.

Leadenhall was two centuries old, built as a granary and market hall at a time of famine. It resembled a great fortress, with high stone walls and octagonal turrets on each corner. The ground floor consisted of a series of large arched windows, all traceried and barred with iron. The entrance was of simple design, two enormous oaken doors behind huge iron gates, locked and chained.

Dowling peered through a ground floor window. 'Did he tell you to meet him inside or outside?'

'He didn't say.' I struggled to be sure. 'He just said for you and I to meet him at midnight, no earlier, no later.'

It was midnight, and Wharton was nowhere to be seen. I wanted to run around the building calling his name, terrified he waited somewhere else. I recalled Oliver Willis' face, furious and petrified. I prayed he hadn't followed from a distance; Wharton would smell him, for sure.

Cornhill was empty to the west and Leadenhall Street to the east, no one within a couple of minutes' walk. I banged my fist against the thick stone wall. 'He is late!'

'He is a torturer, Harry.' Dowling laid a hand upon my shoulder. 'Now he tortures you. Let's walk about the building and see what we can find.'

I sighed, ready to eat my own arm. 'What if he comes here while we are away?'

'Leave your jacket at the grille,' Dowling suggested. 'If he comes then he will guess we are searching for him.'

I wriggled out my jacket, pushed it through the iron lattice and tied it in a loose knot. 'Let's be quick then.'

We hurried east, along Leadenhall Street. A passage led down the side of the building, lit blue by the sickly moon. Halfway down we found another door, again locked. Just before reaching the end we came across a narrow alleyway, rustling and whispering, pitch black. We walked the alley blind, each feeling our way down one wall until we met at passage end. No door, no way in.

Houses nestled up close to the south wall, leaving but a small corridor, a dirt floor covered in rubbish and debris.

Halfway down we found a third door, again thick, yet older and less well cared for, the wood beginning to twist and gnarl. I tried the handle without much hope, but it opened. Behind lay a naked yard, unkempt and sparse, shadowed about the edges.

We walked the perimeter, aware of the multitude of black windows staring down upon the small quadrangle. A dark porch beckoned at the far side, drawing us in, another open door enticing us further. We stepped into a long narrow room, wooden partitions within stone walls creating hiding spaces.

I nudged up close to Dowling. 'You think he means to kill us?'

'Methinks it likely,' he whispered.

We stood in silence, listening as hard as we could. A faint dripping sounded in the distance.

'We need light,' Dowling muttered.

We proceeded one step at a time, senses strained. Halfway down the market stood a tall archway, barely visible in the gloom, and beyond it a glimmer of light, tiny and distant. We scuttled toward the beacon like mice. It stayed small, dancing in the weak draught, the work of just a single candle. As we drew closer, so we saw the light shine from beyond a doorway, inside a small room. Then I heard a moan, a tight sound, someone in great pain, exhausted. It didn't sound like Liz Willis.

Dowling craned his neck and peered inside. I watched his face light up in the weak orange glow. Then he exhaled as if punched in the belly and clasped a hand to his gaping mouth. This was the butcher, the man who ran his hands over dead bodies like sides of meat. I knew I didn't want to share his vision, knew also that I must.

Even now, in the middle of the night, I still see those milky blue eyes staring forward. Sightless or no, I couldn't tell, but they didn't move when I moved, nor did they seem focussed on anything. Then I saw his entrails fallen in a steaming pile, glistening and pink. Foulest of all, two black rats sat upon their haunches, gripping with tiny claws and gnawing with sharp yellow incisors. Morrison, the vanished gaoler, innards upon the floor, his organs revealed for all to see.

He hung by his hands, tied to thick iron rings fastened into the walls, staring and alive. Someone pulled his hat hard down upon his head so it sat just above his eyes, making him look ridiculous. His guts spilled over the top of his thick black belt and short legged trousers. His shirt hung in tatters about his torso. The smell of blood and fouling meat ripened the air, stinking like a dog trapped beneath the wheel of a heavy cart, left to die upon the road. The candle burned halfway down which said he had been here for two hours, open mouthed and gutted.

The hide of his stomach flapped open like a cow. Pearly

white skin on the outside, peppered with fine black hairs. Thick red meat on the inside, so rich in blood it seeped and slowly dripped. His stomach sat snugly inside his body cavity, surrounded by sheets of glistening fat.

'How long will he live?' I asked, appalled.

Dowling wrung his hands, unable to bear the man's misery. 'He should be dead already.'

I walked as close to the body as I dared and placed my mouth quite close to his ear. 'Can you hear me, Morrison?'

A short gurgle rumbled from the back of his throat.

I turned to Dowling. 'Can you deliver him from his pain?'

'It is not my place to kill a man,' Dowling whispered hoarsely. 'If it's God's will he lives, then live he will, until God decrees otherwise.'

'If you kill him then it will have been God's will that you do it,' I replied. 'You are the kind of fellow God would choose as his instrument.'

Dowling held his hands together and looked to the wooden beamed ceiling. 'If it were so then I would feel compelled to do it, which I do not.'

Then I felt compelled. I picked up Morrison's jacket from the floor and thrust it over his mouth and nose. He hardly attempted to draw breath, but stilled quickly, faint trembling subsiding into calm.

'Now you should lower his eyelids,' Dowling said quietly.

I shivered at the sight of his eyes, bulging like they would escape their sockets. 'I don't feel compelled to do that.'

The two rats watched from the safety of the wall, waiting patiently for us to leave.

Dowling stepped up to the corpse, happier now it was dead, and closed the eyes himself. 'Only a devil could provoke such unholy mutilation.'

I agreed. 'Yet Morrison guarded Wharton at Bedlam. Why would he kill him in such hideous manner?'

'Because he is a devil,' Dowling declared. 'Be sober, be vigilant; because your adversary the Devil walketh about, seeking whom he may devour.'

I shook my head, baffled. 'He is plagued. Why does he continue to kill?'

Dowling held his hand to his forehead. 'An ungodly man diggeth up evil and in his lips there is as a burning fire.'

I stared at Morrison, big round head, hat atop of it. The hat was curiously deformed. I held the peak of it with finger and thumb and gently tugged, which was not enough, so I pulled harder, seizing it with my whole hand to work it loose. There on top of Morrison's head rested a stone, and beneath the stone a yellow letter.

'God save us,' Dowling exclaimed, taking the hat in his hand and rubbing his palm upon the dead man's hair.

I held the letter to the candle. Liz's death warrant perhaps.

> *For the next journey thyselves prepare*
> *To battle with a Nordic king*
> *To a place of worship go ye now*
> *To hear the Bishop's man vent his spleen.*

I handed the letter to Dowling. 'The Bishop's man is Boddington or Perkins.'

Dowling scanned the words quickly, horror pulling his face out from all sides. 'We must go.' He looked to Morrison. 'Yet we cannot leave him here.'

I thought of Liz. 'The bearers will pick him up. We will tell them he has plague, but we must go.'

We stepped away, taking the candle with us. The last thing I saw was the two black rats trotting back to resume their feast.

'St Olaves', methinks.' Dowling wiped an arm across his forehead as we ran. 'It was once Lucy's parish church. St Olaves' on Old Jewry, just a few minutes away.'

We ran west toward Poultry, then north up Old Jewry. St Olaves' was a modest church, with small graveyard, big door at front and little door at back. It did not take us long to discover both were locked. We walked about the building two more times yet could find no other entrance.

'What test has he set us this time?' I exclaimed, frustrated.

'God in Heaven!' Dowling kicked at the wall, savage. He punched himself on the chest. 'There are three St Olaves' in London!'

'Of course,' I realised, feeling foolish.

'Lord save us,' he muttered. 'The others are at Silver Street and Hart Street.'

'Silver Street is closer,' I calculated. Which it was, but the two churches could not have been further apart. Silver Street was west, close to Cripplegate, while Hart Street was east, not far from Aldgate. 'It makes sense to go to the closest first,' I thought aloud. 'Yet my instinct tells me Hart Street.'

'Why so?' Dowling asked.

'The church at Silver Street is as small as this one, and Wharton has a preference for the grander stage,' I replied. 'Hart Street is at the end of Seething Lane, where Willis lives.'

Dowling set off brisk. I followed him, silent, attempting to cast from my mind a picture of Liz in same predicament as Morrison. We arrived in ten minutes, immediately heartened by the sight of the door stood ajar.

'More candles,' Dowling remarked as we entered. We were surrounded by light, hundreds of dancing flames. We proceeded slowly down the centre aisle, footsteps loud against the flagstones.

'Stop!' a strangulated voice screeched. There at the pulpit stood William Perkins.

I took another step forward at which Perkins began to behave in an extraordinary manner. He began to recite Ecclesiastes and did so most extremely loud and fast.

'All things have I seen in the days of my vanity: there is a just man that perisheth in his righteousness, and there is a wicked man that prolongeth his life in his wickedness.'

He read the words almost in a scream, beseeching us with his eyes, though beseeching us to do what? Then I saw he was naked, at least the bit of him that we could see. His skin was white, like uncooked pastry, with irregular blotches of red. He continued reading from the Bible afront of him, calmer now, but reluctant to take his eye off us for more than a second or two.

'Everyone we meet appears to be insane,' I whispered.

Dowling squinted into the gloom. 'He is anxious about something.'

I took another step forward, evoking the same passionate reaction from Perkins. He recited the text with such animated ferocity it was clear he would use other words if he could. When I took a step back his intensity diminished.

'He does not move his hands,' Dowling observed. His hands were placed either side of the lectern upon which he stood, but were just hidden from sight. At some point he would need to turn a page.

'He does not wish us to approach him.' I stepped to one side, determining to rest my body, parts of which were gone to sleep; but again he began to squeak and screech with eyes that begged.

'So he would not have us approach him, nor be seated,' I concluded. 'Let us see if we are free to move back the way we came.' When I stepped backwards his face shone a deep shade of crimson.

'Look ye.' Dowling pointed to the floor. 'We are in a circle.' It was not a circle, but a star, marked in red paint, the same colour that these days signified pestilence and sin.

I sidled toward the boundary of it, while trying to make it look as if I stood still. 'How can he see from there whether we be in it or no?'

'He is focussed on a marker,' Dowling replied impatiently. 'These three pews, for example, and on ensuring we do not stray from the aisle.'

Was someone about to drop some great weight upon us, or pour boiling oil over our heads? There was nothing above us other than the ceiling.

'Perkins,' I shouted.

He just kept reading. 'I applied mine heart to know, and to search, and to seek out wisdom, and the reason of things, and to know the wickedness of folly, even of foolishness and madness.'

'If you do not talk to us, then I will turn around and

leave you here!' I shouted again. It made no difference, though I thought I detected an extra note of despondency in his voice.

'This is absurd,' I complained, exasperated. 'We have to find Liz.'

'Ah!' Dowling raised a finger many minutes later. 'He recites Chapter Eight, Verse Fifteen again.'

We stood quiet a while listening to the cleric read. I squinted into the shadows, where someone might lurk with gun or bow. 'Whatever he is scared of, where could it be?'

'He would duck and bend his knees if it was from afar.'

I turned to the jabbering cleric once again. 'Then there must be someone up there with him.' I peered forward, searching for any sign of movement. 'Perhaps we should run forward and attempt to reach him afore any might harm him. If someone is there, they will have to leave by one door or other, and the vestry door is shut.'

'Though it is but a short distance from lectern to vestry and the killer may have unlocked the door.' Dowling sounded doubtful.

'Then one of us should run to the vestry and one to Perkins,' I suggested.

'Or we wait until morning.'

It was a grim prospect. 'In which case the killer might strike at any time while we be asleep and Liz might die.'

'If we rush forward, which I know is your preference,

we must rush quick,' Dowling whispered.

'Then I will rush toward Perkins and you run to the vestry door.'

'Nay,' Dowling shook his head. 'I will go to Perkins.'

Perkins watched us keenly. 'Lo, this only I have found, that God hath made man upright.'

It was thirty long paces from where we stood to the lectern afore us. Candles had been placed further from this side of the church and closer to the main entrance so the door to the vestry was barely visible.

'Ready?' Dowling growled.

'Aye.'

Perkins watched us with darting eyes. He stumbled on his words then concentrated on reading faster.

Dowling and I counted to three together, quietly, then dashed forwards. As soon as we moved Perkins screamed at the top of his voice, a shattering shriek. His body jerked taut, back arched, and this before we took barely two steps. It was difficult to tear my eyes from him, and when I did, the vestry door was open. I flung myself into the black room. I dimly made out the shape of the door to the street, and launched myself forward, catching my knee upon the edge of a solid table. The door was locked and the key was in the lock.

I returned to the lectern, where awaited a horrible sight. Perkins' head was flung back, eyes tight shut, teeth clamped hard together in bare grimace. Though his groin was thrust forward against the lectern, his fleshy white buttocks hung down in four rippling waves. It was like the rump of a great bullock and from that rump protruded a black iron stake, about which poured a river of rose red blood.

Dowling turned toward me and held out a short heavy hammer. His grey bagged eyes were wet and tearful. 'He is still alive.'

'Not for long,' I assured him. There was too much blood creeping steadily towards my feet. 'Did you see who did it?'

'No,' Dowling looked aghast. 'Was he not in the vestry?'

'No.' I shook my head angrily. 'You sure you saw nothing?'

'Nothing.'

Damn fish teeth. Our killer was cleverer than us and more confident. He had known what we would do, known that we would leave the main door free, known that the sight of his handiwork would render us incapable.

'What next?' I turned wearily to the lectern, unable to resist another glance at the spike. In front of his falling thighs was empty space, beneath his feet nothing. Betwixt the pages of the Bible? I reached forward, avoiding the touch of the dead man's skin, turned the page and found another yellow letter. Stepping close to a candle, I read aloud.

Now King David was old and stricken in years,
And they covered him with clothes from the king's wardrobe,
but he gat no heat.
Wherefore his servants said unto him,
Let there be sought for my lord the king a young virgin,
And let her stand before the king, and let her cherish him,
And let her lie in thy bosom, that my lord
the king may get heat.

'What direction is this?' I felt like screwing it into a ball and throwing it. 'Why can he not simply tell us where to go?'

'He does.' Dowling took the letter from me. 'This is from the first book of Kings with four words inserted; "from the King's Wardrobe".'

We exchanged sombre stare. I recalled Wharton's mocking laugh when he talked of trust. 'This is why he abducted Liz Willis,' I realised. 'So we have no choice but to follow his instruction.'

Dowling's eye leaked a thin yellow pus. 'No choice then.' He turned on his heel and headed for the door.

'What of the rest of the letter?' I hurried after him. 'What does it signify?'

'I don't know, Harry,' Dowling replied. 'Unless we are about to discover an old lord being cherished by a virgin.'

'Lord Arlington perhaps?' I wondered aloud, much to Dowling's disgust.

It was a long walk. Candles burned low in the windows, and the streets were silent, save for the sound of our own footsteps. With all our recent exposure to the dead and dying, it was a sobering thought that still the plague had yet to truly infiltrate the city. I saw enough these last few days to imagine what life would soon be like for those who remained. How right Jane had been. I wondered if she lived still, then felt fresh pangs of guilt and fear that I had not managed to see her that day.

At last we reached the Wardrobe. Two new sentries guarded the front door, awake and alert. Were Forman and Withypoll sleeping?

'Look at the door,' Dowling whispered, hoarse. 'It is marked with the cross.'

A big red cross, indeed, bright and fresh. Perhaps God was more discerning than I gave Him credit for.

Dowling puffed out his chest and spoke to the sky. 'Be not afraid, neither be thou dismayed: for the Lord thy God is with thee whithersoever thou goest...' He stepped out in full view of the sentries and marched toward them. I followed.

The sentries pretended not to notice us until we approached close. They glared, stony-faced.

'May we enter?' I asked, half expecting some unknown

magic to open the door and transport us across the threshold.

'Why would ye want to enter?' asked one. 'Have ye not seen the cross?'

'Methinks we have been summoned,' I explained.

'By who?' the guard snorted.

'By they that are in there.'

'And who is that?'

'Forman and Withypoll.'

The guard shoved me backwards, angry. 'Forman and Withypoll are gone. There is but one man behind these doors and he is not receiving visitors. Be on your way.'

Dowling fetched his credentials. 'We are King's men.'

'There is no credential says I should allow you to enter the Wardrobe when it be cursed with plague. The only one that may enter here is the medic.'

At which point the clouds parted and the light shone through. Wharton knew I had the medic's robes.

An hour later I trudged back down the Old Change, Dowling at my side. My head floated light and porous while my stomach weighed heavy and sick. It was not far away, the hour of waking, yet we were still living the day already gone.

It was clear I must enter alone, but we decided Dowling would wait as close as he might without attracting the sentries' attentions. I walked the last fifty yards with as purposeful a step as I could muster. The sentries had their own torches by which light I saw their suspicious faces once I approached close. I could read the mouth of one that wanted to know why I did not arrive by coach as usual, but I pretended not to understand and tapped a finger against my ear. Another made a sign that I take off my hood, but I waggled my finger and shook my head. While they dawdled I stepped forward and opened the door.

Soft moonlight shone through high windows, bathing the wood panelled walls. A fiery torch blazed in a holder upon the wall, creating sinister shadows. Was it for me, I wondered? I removed my mask, dropping it upon a small yellow table with thin carved legs. I took the torch and approached the double doors opposite. Beyond was an ornate dining room, with long oak table and sturdy upholstered chairs. Drapes hung about the walls, long and golden, all very French. I watched myself walk past a mirror spanning floor to ceiling, encased in gilded frame. I felt lonely and exposed, heard my footsteps echo too loud, reverberating about the whole house. I imagined Withypoll's ears pricking, saw him scuttle silently toward me, to pounce, to subject me to the same barbarity he inflicted on others. I hurried back the way I came.

Back in the hallway something slipped beneath my feet. I looked down to find a flower petal, several in fact, scattered about the floor. Red rose petals, fresh and recently dispersed. I held up the torch to see they marked a trail, leading across the hall and out toward the wide staircase.

I trod graceful as a blind bear. No matter how soft I placed my feet, my footsteps tapped loud against the tiled floor. All else I could hear was the noise of my own laboured breathing.

The staircase wound upwards in a long square spiral, red petals upon ancient wooden treads that creaked as I climbed. I followed the way down a corridor leading long and straight. The doors to either side were closed, the door direct ahead stood ajar. The petals led all the way to the end.

I stood by the opening with my ear to the gap. As I accustomed to the quiet, so I heard faint noises; an occasional moan, the soft clearing of a throat, the creak of a bed-board. Someone lay asleep. And the petals led forwards. What if this was nothing to do with Wharton, after all? Perhaps I interrupted a romantic assignment. But in a sick house?

I eased the door open and held the torch forwards. Two pairs of eyes sought mine, two men wriggling and struggling to be free. I scanned the rest of the room to check no one else lurked, ready to assault me, then returned my attentions to the two naked men. Each was bound to a naked woman, yet the women lay inert and flaccid.

Two big candles stood upon a console. I lit them with the torch, bestowing full light upon the bizarre scene. The two men wriggled and kicked, eyes wide like they saw for the first time who they were tied to. Each man's arms were wrapped about the waist of the naked woman to whom he was attached, tied at the wrists. Each man's legs were wound about the woman's waist in erotic embrace, bound at the ankles. One couple lay entwined upon a bed, the other bounced and rolled upon the floor. I held my torch to one man's face. Blue eyes darted about the room in terror, not an expression I had seen in them before, yet even without the fur hat I recognised Withypoll. The other then was Forman. He writhed as hard as Withypoll. The dead woman's face fell against his, eyes closed, lips slightly apart. He strained to push his head away from hers, but her hair kept falling into his mouth. I pulled out his gag.

'Lytle!' he gasped, lips dry. 'Cut me loose!'

He stared at the woman afore him to whom he clung in intimate embrace. She was young and pretty, a fair maiden indeed, except she was dead. Withypoll made a loud grunting noise, so I removed his gag as well.

'Cut us loose, Lytle,' Forman gasped again.

'I cannot,' I replied. 'For though I don't relish your sordid predicaments, yet you both threatened to kill me. What logic says I should free you?'

PAUL LAWRENCE

'The logic that says if you don't, then I will slice your throat in a minute once I am released,' cried Withypoll. 'This woman is a dead woman! Cut me loose!'

I stepped away, listening for any noise outside the door. 'Shout again and I will gag you. Who tied you?'

Withypoll twisted his head sideways. 'We were eating, downstairs, then I don't remember. Forman?'

Forman attempted to lift his arms above the woman's neck, but his arms were bound too close to her back. 'I don't know who this woman is, nor how I came to be tied to her.' He kicked his legs and roared out in frustration. 'For God's sake, she is dead, Lytle! Cut me free!'

I waved the cloth in front of his eyes. 'You both fell asleep?'

'No,' Withypoll snapped. 'It was witchcraft, devilry of some descript. One moment I was wide awake, the next I am lying in the dark upon this bed, strapped to this wench.' He tried to blow the dead woman's long black hair away from his face. 'Lytle, in God's name, I beseech you. Cut me free, and as God's my witness I will not harm a hair of your head. I will get down upon my knees and pledge you my eternal loyalty!'

'I don't doubt your sincerity,' I assured him. 'Nor my own dispensability.'

I knelt down next to Withypoll's partner. She was curved and shapely, an attractive woman, yet the knowledge she was dead turned her to something rotten and decaying, an extinguished spirit. I felt sorry for Withypoll, the heat of his own warm flesh seeping into her cold corpse. Yet if I were to cut him free then he would kill me. What if I left him bound though? He would not rest until inflicting upon me a similar fate. I wished I had not come at all, yet Wharton arranged it. To what end? Then I noticed the swelling upon her neck.

I stepped backwards, tripped over my own feet and landed flat on my back. Withypoll strained his neck to watch me, curious and pleading. I realised he could see nothing but his partner's face, Forman besides. I jumped up and retreated to the corner, as far from each of them as I could be. The dead woman stuck to Forman's chest had her arms tied about his neck too. I peered beneath her armpit, stepping closer to see better. No mistaking the black shape tucked hidden away.

'What are you doing?' Forman growled, face red.

Following Wharton's trail of death, I reflected, as I had been this past week. Each one an elaborate tableau of pain and misery, this one the worst, the moment they realised what Wharton had done to them. Now I was the torturer, exploiting their belief that truth might lead to redemption. The knowledge I deceived them revolted me.

'Why did you kill War?' I asked. 'The man you killed at St Vedast's. He thought you would be pleased to see him.'

Forman snorted, wriggling his body in an attempt to become more comfortable. 'He was one of Wharton's dogs.'

'Why did you kill him?'

Forman sighed, clearly uncomfortable divulging further detail of his relationship with Chelwood. Yet what choice did he have? He attempted to catch Withypoll's eye, but Withypoll couldn't move.

'The Earl of St Albans performed an important role for this country after the Restoration,' Withypoll replied, impatient. 'More recently he has been acting in service of his own needs. When he used Lord Chelwood's name to defraud Henry Burke, Chelwood decided to act. By declaring his intent to remove himself to Ireland, he knew Arlington would move quickly to remove Wharton. Wharton overestimated his importance.'

'Once Wharton was found dead, then was not Chelwood's objective achieved?'

Forman spat the dead woman's hair from his mouth. 'Yet the nature of the death was curious. Arlington would not have killed Wharton in such circumstances, he would have killed him quiet and discreet. Chelwood asked us to find out who killed Wharton, and it was not Henry Burke.'

'Who was it then?' I asked.

'We have not yet discovered it,' Withypoll replied, surly. 'Arlington, after all? Some say William Perkins, yet that too seems unlikely.'

What next, I wondered? I searched the room for another letter, some sign as to what Wharton would have me do next. I picked up the torch and inspected every corner. 'Have you seen a letter lain about here?' I asked.

'Untie us, Lytle!' Withypoll roared. 'We have told you all you asked. You untie us now! Then it is in the service of Lord Chelwood and he will see you amply rewarded.'

'I cannot release you,' I answered, heavy hearted. 'It is too late for that.'

'Too late?' Forman hissed.

'I will come back,' I promised. 'First I need to find a letter, or other sign.'

Withypoll rolled about his partner so he could continue to watch me as I walked outside his field of view. 'Untie us now and we will help you search.'

I mumbled in response afore leaving the room, for I saw no letter there. I followed the path back along the creaking passage and to the top of the stairs. Another passage led off in the opposite direction, unlit and silent. I stepped downstairs back into the hallway. Picture frames and panels. Nothing. Then I saw it tucked beneath my hood on the small yellow table with carved legs. I stopped still and surveyed again the quiet space about me. Was he here with me? If so then I would likely not find him, not if he walked in the dark. I thought to release Forman and

Withypoll, set dogs upon the dog, but dismissed the notion, quick. This message was simple.

Come ye alone to 7 Broad Street

The night was old, the new day close. The last visit perhaps? A journey I would have to make alone. Was that the purpose of leaving the letter upon my hood—to tell me I was watched?

Then I heard the scream, an anguished wail of terror and dismay. A short silence, then a second scream. Forman and Withypoll discovered their mortality.

I removed the medic's jacket and left it with the mask.

Fearful of Wharton's presence, I turned the opposite direction to where Dowling waited. Broad Street was north of the Exchange, a long walk via Thames Street, fifteen minutes or more.

Number seven was tall and thin, the house not much wider than the front door. It was as if someone had decided to live in an alley between two big houses and filled it in. A mean looking abode with glass missing from many of the small square panes that filled the three protruding bay windows, frames rotting, eaten away. Upon the uneven door was painted another red cross, yet no watcher sat upon the street. The paint was old and faded. Were all within already dead, carted away and rotting at Moorfields?

In the tiny front room was space only for a small square table, upon which rested a child size coffin, a rudimentary object. Inside, the fragile body of another dead infant covered with thin white cloth. What was it doing here? Where were the parents?

Three planks of wood leaned against a wall in the back room. A man crouched in the corner, legs tucked up beneath his chin. He had the same grey skin as Burke and stank like a dead animal. His head was bowed and his ribs were still. Were all here dead?

I climbed the narrow staircase to a small square room and scanned the space quick, expecting to see nothing in the gloomy silence. I almost died there and then when I recognised Wharton sat motionless in a chair in the corner.

'Welcome.' He held a long bladed knife down at his leg. 'Sit down.'

I obeyed, feeling naked and helpless, eyes on the weapon. He sat back, stiff. 'Have you enjoyed your evening?'

'I don't understand why you killed all those people,' I said, low. The tokens upon his chest seemed larger now. 'You will die soon yourself. Did you do it for amusement?'

'No,' he smiled, eyes gleaming black. 'Curiosity.' He raised his knife, leaned across and touched my throat. I stayed as still as I could and averted my eyes. 'When my men broke

Dowling's thumb, what did you learn about yourself?'

I allowed myself to meet his gaze again. His eyes were so dark you could not tell exactly where he looked. 'I learned how brave I am.'

'How brave are you?'

'Not very.'

He lowered the knife and tilted his head. 'Few of us are, Lytle. It is a remarkable thing.' He held his hand out flat and eased the tip of the blade beneath the fingernail of his own left forefinger. 'People are terrified at the prospect of having a nail torn from their finger.' He pushed the tip harder so the nail lifted slightly. 'Yet it is only a nail. It serves no crucial purpose and it is easy to remove. The pain caused is sharp, but not intolerable, far from it. Yet the fear can drive a man mad. It is not logical.' Mercifully he lowered his sword and his finger. 'Pain is not a thing inflicted. Pain comes from within ourselves, yet we cannot control it. Does that not interest you?'

'I think it is part of the design.'

'God's design you mean?' Wharton wrinkled his nose. 'Then why cannot all men control it, since some men can? What use is it, this inability to withstand pain? Some men scream in response to the pain you inflict without fear of it. They anticipate its end at the same time they anticipate its arrival.'

I prayed this was not to become a test of my own

poor resolve. If it was, then I would have to attack him even though he held that sharp sword. 'I am not one of those men.'

'I know,' Wharton assured me. 'I have discovered that. You have no need to be ashamed of it either. It doesn't mean you are a coward. If you were a coward you would not be here now.'

'What is the fascination in torturing men?'

Wharton rubbed a hand about the top of his head and yawned. 'Partly the search for that rare man who travels with you to the end of the journey. But more what people will say and not say in an attempt to dissuade you. It speaks instantly to what they hold important in life. I have tortured men of God that have sworn to slit the throats of babies, if it will ease them of the distress I cause them. It is the quickest way I know to discover a man's soul.'

Did it not occur to him that he was himself a source of this fear, that through his actions he caused men to live in fear for the rest of their lives? That every man he tortured was forced to face a new reality: that a man could inflict this thing upon another man? I myself would never forget the sights I had seen this week. 'What you have done is a grievous sin.'

'Aye,' Wharton agreed softly. 'I regret what I became.'

I looked to see if he mocked me, but he appeared to speak in earnest. 'If you regret your life it seems strange you have spent the last week killing people in such savage fashion.'

He smirked. 'Think who I have killed, Lytle. Is it not obvious?'

'No,' I replied. 'If you would kill them at all, why not kill them simply? All you did was attract attention to yourself.'

He held out his sword so it caught the faint light of moon shining through the window. 'What we did was sinful. I came to recognise it, but I knew the others would not. So it became my destiny to kill them all in the same manner they killed others. It was a service conducted on behalf of all men that I completed tonight.'

'You killed Death and Famine to suggest Burke was the murderer. What was noble about that?'

'I didn't say I was noble,' Wharton murmured. 'It was my intention to escape England and see Burke hang for it. I sought no redemption, not until I realised that I am soon to die.'

'Redemption?' I said, incredulous. 'You killed a man of God tonight.'

'William Perkins was an evil man that brought misery to many people's lives.' Wharton shrugged. 'Did you not say yourself there are devils in the clergy?'

I blinked. 'You were there when we talked to Perkins?'

Wharton held up his hands. 'Not I.'

'I think it unlikely that God desires for you to wander London murdering and maiming his people.'

He stared at me in obvious arrogance. 'I have rid the city of six men that were as evil as I was, yet would not repent; Morrison and Gallagher, that conspired with me to release poor Bedlamites who we might torture, a cleric whose only message was of hatred, and three murderers besides. I think that makes me a good man.'

'All these murders then were penance?'

He narrowed his eyes as if he was thinking about being penitent one more time.

'Why did you abduct Liz?' I blustered. 'What do I have to do with your atonement?'

He leaned forward, serious. 'It is necessary when seeking the forgiveness of the Lord that it is *understood* to be an act of penance and not self-interested brutality. I chose you as witness. You are diligent and steadfast. You discovered me at Bedlam and attended your maidservant in your own house, even though it be plagued. You escaped the wrath of Forman and Withypoll, though with some good fortune.' He regarded me quizzically. 'I think you are a lucky man.'

A lucky man at the end of a lunatic's sword. The thought struck me as odd. 'Why not seek a priest to make your penance? I am not a religious fellow.'

'You are the witness, Lytle. I said nothing of seeking your forgiveness.' He turned away. 'I want all to know what happened and why.'

'You think they will understand? You are the royal torturer who has just killed ten men in the most bloody brutal fashion, including your own brother. You think they will see that as an act of repentance?'

'Nine,' he waved a hand. 'I did not kill War.'

I breathed deep, head spinning. 'How did you manipulate all these people you killed, alone?'

'A man will always choose to have his wrists bound rather than be run through the guts.' He read the doubt on my face. 'I know how to manipulate a man's fear, Lytle. What would you do now if I demanded that you bind your own wrists to the chair you sit upon?'

'I don't know,' I replied.

He held up the blade in front of my eyes. 'It will occur to you to attack me. You may seriously contemplate it. But then you will find yourself focussed upon this knife and how it will feel slipping between your ribs. Then it will occur to you that if I want to tie you to the chair then perhaps it means I don't want to kill you.'

'Is that how it works?'

'Shall we try it?'

I shook my head.

'Only Morrison resisted, so I cut his stomach open first, then tied him up.'

I saw Morrison's agonised stare once more in my mind's

eye. Wharton had left me with a library of legacies that I would never forget. I didn't want to ask about Liz; I wanted him to tell me she was still alive.

'Who died at the Vintners' Hall?' I asked quietly.

'My brother,' he said simply.

I put my hands to my mouth. 'You killed your own brother?'

He leaned forwards and hissed in my ear, a low whisper. 'I hated it. It was born an aberration, a curse on our family. When it was born my mother stopped smiling and my father left to wander. Neither could fathom what they had done to deserve the birth of one so strange. God touched him on the forehead with his finger. When the child was born the Devil took him. It had to be killed.'

'But you put him in Bedlam.'

'Where he belonged. I didn't expect it to live long. I gained some satisfaction from its suffering and now it is dead.'

'The child?'

'It was poxed, so the child was born cursed. It was born at Bedlam and is touched by the finger, so it will die too.' He shook his head. 'Though not by my hand.'

He stared silent; the trace of a smile still hung upon his wretched lips. He knew what I wanted to know and would make me ask.

'Where is Liz Willis?' I asked, dry mouthed.

'The first question on your mind, yet the last question you ask,' he mused. 'So you fear I killed her already.'

I breathed slow, watched his eyes.

'I turned the screw until her knees pushed back against her chin.' He licked his lips. 'Turned the screw until the blood dripped from the ends of her fingers.'

This was a repentant man? His mouth hung open, tongue stroking his top lip. His black eyes gleamed, excited. He coughed, pain in his eyes, then stood, unsteady. 'Her name is Alice,' he spluttered. 'You may find her at the Tower.'

'Alice?' It made no sense.

His face reddened, but he grinned anyway. 'You had better hurry, Lytle,' he gasped. 'Else she shall die soon.' Then he sneezed, an almighty spray of poison, fine droplets flying through the air and landing across my neck and chest, a few upon my lips. I leapt to my feet wiping at my face with my sleeve as he fell forwards.

He lay prone. I stood motionless, unable to believe he might be dead. I turned his body with my foot. His eyes stared at me, unblinking, a slow line of spittle trickling down his chin. The death mask of a man possessed. Perhaps he and his brother were not so different.

I ran down the stairs, past the corpse in the corner and out into the street. Curséd night.

A bell rang five times as I ran across Gracechurch Street, telling all that the sun would rise within the hour. The

Bulwark Gate was locked, but it was in poor condition. I pushed hard and saw the gatehouse lit behind. I flung myself against it backwards, not with hope of breaking through, but in an attempt to wake the guards that no doubt slept soundly within. Upon the third or fourth assault I heard the crunch of splintering wood. So encouraged, I slammed my shoulder against it with renewed rigour, each time the doors pushing forward a little further. Then I stumbled and caught my arm in the chains that held it. I clambered up and checked myself for damage. The hook about which the chain was wound, on the door to the right, broke away from the wood, the metal eaten away by years of rain.

At the gatehouse one man slept, legs splayed, chest heaving in slow rhythm. The other stood wide awake.

'Halt!' he ran out with pike aimed at my chest.

I stopped and raised my arms into the air.

'How did you get in?' he demanded.

'The door is broken,' I walked slowly forwards. 'I am sent by Lord Arlington. You have a prisoner here called Alice?'

'Aye.' He regarded me curiously. 'Fetched here yesterday. She is in the Salt Tower.'

I ran east 'twixt the Hall Tower and Traitors' Gate, past the Lanthorn Tower. The Salt Tower was locked, though lights burned at the upper windows. I banged my fist upon the door until the lock turned.

'It's early,' the guard complained, shirt unfastened and trousers unbuttoned. His hair sat flat on the right side of his head and stuck up in tufts on the left.

I showed him my credentials. 'The prisoner, Alice. Where is she?'

He blew out a mouthful of green air and scratched at himself, stretching. I pushed past toward the stairwell.

'You need the key,' he grumbled, staggering after.

At the top of the stairs the door was locked. Behind was silent.

'Better knock first.' The guard pushed me to one side. 'She is a lady, you know, and might not be wearing all her clothes, for it is very hot.'

He knocked, then waited with officious look upon his wrinkled face. He knocked once more, then took his keys and inserted them with great show. 'She doesn't answer, but prepares herself quickly.' He tapped his finger against his nose.

I held the candle forward and prayed it was indeed Elizabeth. The door opened into a round room with stone walls and wooden floor, dominated by an empty fireplace. A slight figure sat upon a bed beneath a slatted window.

'Hello, Harry,' she said quietly.

I turned to the guard. 'Give me the keys and wait downstairs.'

'I cannot do that.' He seemed most offended. 'The prisoner is entrusted to my care.'

'You may safely leave us. He is a friend,' Liz said, soft.

'A friend, you say?'

'And in the King's name I ask you to leave us.' I waved the seal afront of him.

'Aye then,' he ceded unhappily, 'but you are not having my keys.'

I sat down next to Liz and considered her small pale face. She looked down at my hands. In her eyes I saw pain and fear.

She lifted her chin. 'Why am I here?'

'So that I would do as I was bid by Thomas Wharton. Was it he who brought you here?'

She nodded. 'I thought he was dead.'

'So did we all.' I took her hand in mine. She slowly took it back again. 'He killed four men last night and for some reason was determined I witness each and every one. He imprisoned you here to ensure I pursued him.'

'Where is he now?'

'Dead.' I felt tears well. 'He was plagued.' I took a deep breath to control my mood. 'I thought you might be too. He told me...' I stopped. It would do no good to share with her the image he painted for me.

She gazed into my face and touched my cheek with one long finger. 'You look tired.'

'As do you.'

She smiled tightly. 'I have just been sitting here.'

Again I fought unmanly tears. 'How did he succeed in bringing you here?' I asked.

She brushed her dress straight with palms of her hands... 'He simply came up to me in the street. He told me he wanted to bring me here as Alice Matthews. He said if I consented then it would only be for a few days. If I refused, he would cut out my father's eyes.'

'Godamercy.'

The tears now leaked from her eyes instead. 'He said it so easily, and I got the feeling that he would be just as happy if I refused him.'

I put my hand upon hers again without really thinking of it. 'I think we can leave now.'

The tears stopped, as if I reminded her I was there, and that it was wrong to cry in front of me. Her hand slipped away again.

CHAPTER 26

If the querent shall obtain the office desired or not
If the Lord of the tenth be joined to Venus or Saturn, and they or either of them in the ascendant, and themselves as oriental and direct, and not one opposite to another, this does argue obtaining the preferment, though with much importunity.

I sat in the middle of the Banqueting Hall, Dowling to my right and Newcourt to my left, no one close to us, in a great open space upon the fine polished floorboards. Sun blazed into the room from the windows to our right, illuminating the beautiful paintings above our heads.

'The King would see you himself, Lytle,' Lord Arlington called from his chair on the raised dais at the end of the hall. 'But none are allowed to visit him while there is still plague, while everything remains so...so *infected*.' He rolled his eyes. 'He sends me instead.'

Behind him sat two other fine dressed fellows, each at a table with journal and quill to the ready.

Arlington leaned forwards. 'I must take a full report with me, Lytle,' he shouted. 'Since you seem to be the one at the centre of all, you must tell me precisely what has happened this last week.'

Newcourt sat with arms crossed tight, brow furrowed and jaw clamped. Upon first arriving he had strolled toward Arlington and friends, only to be shooed back in most undignified fashion. A petulant display from one who was happy to leave me rotting in the bowels of the Compter.

'You have been busy, I hear!' Arlington cried.

Really he did not need shout so loud. The Banqueting Hall was tall and wide and empty. A man might whisper at one end and be heard at the other. I assumed the vast emptiness was why he chose to meet us here, us poor afflicted.

'Yes, your lordship,' I said in normal voice.

He held his head with one ear pointing at me. He nodded to acknowledge he heard. 'Tell me about it!'

'It is a long story, your lordship.'

'You've both done well, Lytle, and I have time to spare until dinnertime.' He looked over his shoulder to check his scribes were ready to begin. 'Come on.' He snapped his fingers impatiently.

I stood and walked behind my chair. It was easier to speak loud standing. 'Well, your lordship, it began when you summoned us to the Vintners' Hall, a week ago today.'

'Aye, so it did.' Arlington turned to the men behind. 'At

380

a time when there were none sick in the parish and the bearers and searchers had not yet assumed residence in the churchyard. Please make that clear.'

'Indeed, your lordship,' I agreed. 'We found a man dead, a man we assumed to be Thomas Wharton, Earl of St Albans.'

'So,' Arlington rubbed his hands together. 'Why did you assume that?'

'You told us it was he,' I replied, lost for a moment. 'And we found his clothes in the hall, piled neatly in one corner.'

'So, Lytle.' Arlington tapped his cheek with one finger, seeming thoughtful. 'I don't recall telling you it *was* the Earl of St Albans. I may have mentioned the *possibility* it was he. So I propose the record shows that you assumed it was the Earl of St Albans because you found his clothes.' He arched his fingers and cocked his head. 'Is that your recollection?'

I nodded, for it made no difference. 'When we took the body to St Albans, the man Conroy helped us carry it to the church and he said nothing to contradict it.'

'Odd,' Arlington exclaimed.

'The dead man's face was burned,' I explained. 'To hide his identity as it turns out.'

'Yes.' Arlington waggled a finger. 'But I meant odd the widow would not wish to keep the body in the house.'

'She said she could not bear to sleep under the same roof,' I told him. 'Which I did not think was so odd, since he was

381

an awful sight and there were few servants still employed.'

'Odd also that there are few servants.' Arlington rocked forwards with hand on lap. 'For Wharton is a wealthy man.'

I recalled the empty rooms and overgrown gardens. 'We thought he must be in debt.'

'Perhaps you might have asked me.' Arlington spread his palms wide. 'I should have been able to advise you.' He looked behind his shoulder again. 'Make a note of that please.'

Newcourt glanced at me with bright laughing eyes, happy to bear witness to another's noble injustice.

I held my anger tight inside a giant fist. 'Odd, then. Yet wheresoever the oddity lies, the family accepted the body as Wharton.'

'Do proceed,' Arlington leaned back. 'And please don't consider my enquiry a slight upon your services. I think you have both done an outstanding job, and will say as much to the King.'

'Aye, sir,' I bowed. I believed not a word.

'So you discovered a body you *believed* to be Thomas Wharton.'

I watched the scribes. 'Aye, sir, and took it to St Albans where Lady Wharton accepted it as that of her husband. Also, we learned Wharton had a brother, a lunatic locked up at Bedlam.'

'How did you discover that?' Arlington asked, intrigued.

'The gravedigger told us,' I replied. 'The brother of a

gardener at the estate.'

'A gravedigger and a gardener?'

'Aye, sir.' The patronising smirk upon his face made me want to slap him. 'Whose advice proved most useful, since that is where we found Wharton.'

'What good fortune.'

I breathed deep and sought to clear my mind. 'We found the man we supposed to be the brother, at Bedlam, living there under the name Edmund Franklin. He indeed appeared to be a lunatic, yet when we visited John Pateson, the warden, he described a different man. When we visited Bedlam again, two days later, we found Franklin missing and another of Wharton's dogs killed.'

'Two days?' Arlington clicked his tongue and shook his head. 'What were you doing in the meantime?'

'We were discovering bodies, pursuing Henry Burke and avoiding being killed by Lord Chelwood's men,' I exclaimed, anger leaking. 'And seeking assistance from your man Newcourt, who told us he was too busy to help.'

Arlington sat motionless a moment, as did everyone else in the great hall. 'Don't write any of that down,' he said at last, finger in the air. 'For Mr Lytle gets ahead of himself.' He raised his chin and looked down his nose, as if to remind me of his status. 'Do proceed, Mr Lytle.'

'Henry Burke wouldn't talk to us. Each time we saw him he was accompanied by Forman and Withypoll, two attendants of Lord Chelwood who were among those killed last night, or likely killed, I should say.'

'*Likely* killed?'

'I found them at the King's Wardrobe, each bound to the body of a dead woman infected by plague.'

'Are you sure?' Arlington demanded. 'The King will not be pleased. How did you get into the King's Wardrobe? There are confidential documents stored within.'

'It was not difficult,' I replied. 'And I ought tell you they are both still there, unless others have rescued them.'

'You left two men tied to infected bodies?' Arlington held up a finger again. 'Don't write that down either.'

'They tried to kill me at Three Crane Lane,' I growled. 'They worked for Lord Chelwood and were under instruction from him to find out who killed Wharton. They suspected *you*, so they said, until they considered the manner of the killings. I discovered Burke hidden at the house of a man called John Tanner. For that they would have killed me. And they killed the last of Wharton's men.'

'They suspected me?' Arlington's cheeks turned a shade of puce. 'Stop writing,' he ordered his assistants. 'On what basis did they suspect me?'

'Lord Chelwood suspected you,' I answered happily. 'Chelwood was unhappy Wharton exceeded his authority and so he went to Ireland in the expectation you would have him killed. It was only the manner of the deaths that led him to doubt it.'

'Devious dog!' Arlington exclaimed, squaring his shoulders and pulling at his jacket. 'How dare he.'

The two scribes waited patiently.

Arlington mopped his brow and leaned back, plucking his lip. 'Proceed, Lytle,' he snapped. 'Why do you keep stopping?'

'Yes, your lordship.' I collected my thoughts. 'Then we discovered Robert Morrison and Hugh Gallagher, wardens at Bedlam, were once soldiers under Wharton's command. They paid Pateson to stay away from Bedlam. We began to think then that Wharton might have been the lunatic we first saw there.'

'Very astute,' Arlington jeered. 'By which time he was gone.'

'He left only because he knew we'd found him,' I protested.

'You should have asked for help before,' Arlington sulked.

'We did.' I pointed at Newcourt. 'We went to see *him* at the Tower before we went back to Bedlam. He told us we should manage alone.'

'I told you I would inform his lordship.' Newcourt wriggled. 'I had just finished speaking to Robinson,' he pleaded with Arlington. 'You told me to return forthwith once I had his response.'

'Don't write any of this down either,' Arlington directed, bestowing a look of pure disdain upon poor Newcourt. 'What next?'

'William Perkins told us he also thought you killed Wharton, that you sought to blame another for his death, and that I must be the one that killed him, because you sought to install me in his place.' I blew out my cheeks, exasperated. 'Then Wharton murders two more men at the Tower and tells me he will torture Liz Willis unless I meet him at Leadenhall at midnight.'

Arlington pursed his lips, guilt sculpting his face.

'You might say I should have asked for help, and so I did.' I pointed at Newcourt. 'He arrives and tells me I should never have spoke to Perkins at all, and that you were displeased with me.'

'So you were!' declared Newcourt, staring at Arlington.

'Newcourt,' Arlington winced. 'If you do not keep quiet, then I shall ask you to leave. Do you understand?'

Newcourt lowered his head back to the floor.

'Dowling rescued me from the Compter and we followed Wharton all about London. Meantime he killed Perkins, Robert Morrison and Forman and Withypoll besides, assuming they do so die of plague. I caught up with Wharton on Broad Street, where he then died of plague himself.'

'So I understand,' Arlington gathered his green jacket about his chest and resumed a noble pose. 'So why did he kill all these other people first if he knew he would die soon himself?'

'At first he wasn't infected. He saw Chelwood left him exposed, and so he staged his death in such a way Henry Burke was bound to be tried and condemned. By staging his death he rendered himself invisible, able to kill off his own men without them suspecting.'

'Why did he kill them?' Arlington frowned, perplexed. 'Why not leave them to live their own lives?'

'Because they were dogs, I think,' I replied. 'They knew him better than any and would have sniffed out the truth of it eventually. One of them was there the day we inspected Wharton's body at the Vintners' Hall. If they suspected he deserted them, then they owned all the information they required to see him condemned.'

Arlington leaned forwards with his elbow on his knee. 'But if he was going to die anyway?'

'I don't think he knew,' I answered. 'There was no sign of plague about him when we saw him at Bedlam. At that time I think his mind was set only upon escape.'

'So he was infected sometime this week,' Arlington drummed his fingers upon his teeth. 'How unfortunate.'

'When he realised he would die he sought redemption,' I explained. 'So he said. Morrison was complicit in finding poor souls upon whom Wharton practised his dark arts. Perkins was an evil fellow, so he said, and Forman and

Withypoll were two murderers. By killing them he hoped to gain redemption for his own black deeds.'

'Why did he not simply confess all and pray hard?' Arlington waved an arm, perplexed. 'That's what I do.'

'He described it as his penance, your lordship, that he rid the world of men as sinful as he.'

Arlington snorted. 'Penance? You think he seeks God's forgiveness for all he has done?'

'That's what he said, your lordship.'

Arlington cast a wandering eye upon the magnificent frescoes painted upon the ceiling and formed a bridge with his fingers. 'In essence then,' he considered, 'you discovered little. The gravedigger and the gardener told you he might be locked away at Bedlam, which you naturally investigated. Then he came to see you at the Compter and laid a trail that you might find all the people he slaughtered last night?' He regarded me in mock puzzlement.

I had not the energy to debate it. 'Yes, your lordship.'

'All this so God would forgive him his trespasses?'

'Yes, your lordship.'

Arlington stood up and walked behind his two busy scribes, checking what they wrote. Once they finished he placed his arms behind his back, ready to address us. 'Well, Mr Lytle, let me avail you of a few facts I should like you to remember.' He cleared his throat. 'First, you and Dowling have investigated this affair on my behalf and have done so successfully. You made some mistakes along the way, errors you might have avoided had you chosen to seek my guidance. But you are not experienced, and taking into account your inexperience, you have done remarkably well. Are we agreed so far?'

'Yes, your lordship.'

'You too, Dowling,' Arlington waved his hand royally. 'You have done well too.'

Dowling bowed his head obediently. 'Thank you, your lordship.'

'Second, gentlemen, the Earl of St Albans was not the King's torturer. If torturer he was, he conducted such activities solely on his own behalf, else in league with Lord Chelwood. Is that clear?'

'Yes, your lordship,' we answered together.

'Third, Perkins' death is fortunate, for I don't know where he got the idea that I had anything to do with Wharton's death, nor that I had any involvement with torture. I had nothing to do with his death, nor was I a friend of Wharton's.'

We nodded.

'Fourth, I do not understand this sudden and dramatic desire for penance.'

'No, your lordship,' I answered in truth, for nor did I.

'Fifth, I am concerned that you left in your wake a trail of bodies, some alive and some dead. I am still not sure how to explain to the King how you came to leave those two poor souls in his Wardrobe. And you left the Earl's body behind while you went running off to the Tower to rescue someone who was in no danger whatsoever.' He wagged his finger like he scolded an urchin upon the street. 'It is as well Lady Wharton was in London and able to send her own man to collect him.'

'Write that in your report and you will make a great fool of yourself,' I heard myself say.

The two scribes opened their eyes wide and turned pink. Newcourt's head snapped up like a puppet. A quiet whining noise came from somewhere close to Dowling's mouth.

Arlington, in the meantime, raised his arms out wide. He shook them as if seeking to straighten his sleeves, folded his arms meaningfully, then made great play of crossing and uncrossing his legs. All the time he smiled gently as if I had suddenly made his day interesting. Like the cat that ponders whether to bite off the mouse's head or else shake it by the tail.

The men behind his shoulder stared at me as though they strained to remember every detail of my face in the expectation of never seeing it again.

Time for me to explain whilst I had a tongue to waggle. 'Wharton is not dead.'

Arlington blinked and looked only marginally less inclined to recommend my execution. 'Mr Lytle,' he leaned forwards. 'He died twice. The second time in front of your eyes. Is that not what you just told me a moment ago?'

'It is what I thought at the time, your lordship.'

He frowned quizzically. 'Either he had the plague or he didn't, Mr. Lytle. You said you saw him dead.'

The sky outside shone blue and cloudless. 'So I thought. Now I see the ruse, your lordship.'

'Another ruse, Mr Lytle?'

'I have just realised. Strange.'

Arlington sighed and let his arm fall limp about the arm of his chair. 'Because it did not seem strange before? If you choose to suggest to his face that a lord is a great fool, then you had better have a good story to tell.' He waved a hand. 'Please cast from your mind the need to soothe my soul with platitudes and save your efforts for the sake of enchanting me with your wisdom and unanswerable logic.'

My career wilted fast and needed quick watering. 'Yes, your lordship.' I managed to speak, finding it difficult to think beyond fear of the consequences of not successfully negotiating the next few minutes.

'Your lordship.' Dowling at last found his voice, though I fervently hoped he was not about to join me in the predicament I fashioned for myself.

Arlington levelled his calm gaze upon the butcher. 'Yes?'

'Your lordship, I agree with Harry that the circumstances are strange enough to warrant further consideration.'

'I am sure Harry will thank you for giving him some

time to contemplate, but I assure you that I do not.'

'Yes, your lordship.' Dowling bowed his head again, but Arlington's eyes were already back to me.

'Your lordship,' I began. 'It is only through relating this tale I realise how it does not sit snug. Some of your own observations go toward the construction of a new theory.'

He watched me with feline grace. 'Perhaps you ought concentrate on the detail of these observations, since I doubt you have formed a theory yet, but do it quickly.'

'Well, your lordship, the first odd circumstance is the state of the Earl's finances.'

'How so?' Arlington purred. 'He is well off, as I told you. Odd that he is not a pauper?'

'Aye, odd indeed. For the estate is run down and half the house closed. There are few servants and the last remaining gardener is soon to leave. If the Earl was so well off, then where did he keep his money?'

'Odd perhaps,' Arlington conceded, 'but of little relevance to Wharton's death.' He raised his brows and avoided my eye. 'Perhaps I am misinformed as to the strength of his finances.'

'Perhaps you are,' I agreed. 'But another possibility is that he and Lady Wharton are planning to leave England and have already been directing their funds accordingly.'

'Not a compelling argument,' Arlington said, blunt.

'The tokens,' I said. 'He appeared at the Compter with

brown spots upon his chest, raised brown spots. I immediately assumed he was plagued and he was quick to confirm it.'

'He died in front of you, Lytle,' Arlington exclaimed, impatient.

'No,' I remembered exactly. 'He made me wonder if he had already tortured Liz Willis to death. Then he told me I should hurry to the Tower if I wished to save her. Then finally he sneezed and fell over. I spent no more than a few seconds checking he was dead, and that without touching him, for who in their right mind would lay a finger on a plague victim?'

'It would be the same story if he did die of plague,' Arlington pointed out. 'Why do you assume he feigned death?'

'Because the tokens appeared so quick,' I said. 'Yet what other signs were there? I saw no swellings. He seemed feverish, but no more so than if he had run down the street.' I shook my head. 'As you reflected, the timing was remarkable. He kills five men he would be rid of, then contracts the plague in time to kill four more men in some peculiar act of redemption.'

'My point exactly.' Arlington seemed willing to be persuaded.

'Once discovered at Bedlam then his plan was in tatters,' I realised. 'Chelwood would know, you would know, the whole world would know. Where then his plan to withdraw discreetly?'

'Then he should have fled.'

'Aye, the natural response, yet Wharton is not a natural man,' I gripped Dowling's shoulders and squeezed. 'He feels no fear,' I recalled. 'He told me himself. The experience of seeing a man in pain served to rid him of his own fears. His plan failed the first time, so he merely repeated it.'

Arlington rubbed his hands. 'Go on.'

'He said I was there as witness and so I was. That is why I am alive. He needed someone to watch him die. In the meantime he killed four more men that might scrutinise his death too closely.'

'Now I am listening, Lytle,' Arlington said. 'Though not yet persuaded.'

'Lady Wharton.' I removed myself from Dowling, given his fondness for the lady. 'She has behaved very strange this whole week.'

'I have met Lady Wharton,' Arlington mused. 'She did not strike me as an odd woman. A little shy perhaps. Anxious, perhaps. Any woman would be anxious married to Thomas Wharton.'

'We had not met her before, your lordship, and if our experience of her is different to yours, then that may be further evidence of my argument. At St Albans she was very strange indeed. She did not grieve, nor shed a tear. She told us nothing about him and told us to take the coffin to the church.' I gave a short bow. 'Which you yourself said was odd.'

'I didn't think she behaved strange,' Dowling muttered.

'No,' I agreed. 'But then you behaved strange yourself that day. I think she entranced you.'

Dowling blushed red about the tops of his cheeks and the tips of his ears.

'When we visited her she implied with ferocious gravity that her husband rarely came home, that he was barely an acquaintance, that she could not be expected to know much of his daily life.'

Arlington raised an eyebrow. 'I will leave aside the fact I have no idea what 'ferocious gravity' is and ask you instead why this should strike you as odd. Wharton by all accounts was a murderous vagabond. Lady Wharton, as I recall, is quite a splendid woman.' A wistful look shimmered across his eyes.

'Your lordship, the last piece of evidence you just told us yourself.'

'What evidence is that?' he asked, doubtful.

'You said Lady Wharton was here in London and had already collected his body.'

'What of it?' Arlington demanded. 'Is it not natural for the widow to collect her husband's corpse?'

'For some,' I agreed. 'But why then did she not come running the first time he was killed? The day after his death and she was still at home, supposedly unaware he died. When we told her the news she showed few signs of distress, claimed to know nothing of his life and sent the body to the church. It all makes more sense if it was not his death, nor his corpse.' Even Dowling looked up now, interested. 'But this time she is already in London? Why did she come to London at all? For she did not have time to receive the news at St Albans and travel here. If she has already collected the body, then she was already in London.'

Arlington nodded sagely. 'Indeed.'

'Even if she was in London for some reason, how did she find out of his death? He died in some sickhouse on Broad Street before the day had dawned. Who told her he was there?'

'That is odd,' Arlington agreed.

'And the reason she *had* to collect the body so quick is that if we were to inspect it, we would find the tokens to be false and the man alive,' I concluded. 'I wager she is already on the way back to St Albans.'

Arlington clasped his hands behind his back, then turned to his scribes once more. 'I hope you have written this all down,' he barked. 'I would have it on the record how Mr Lytle here helped me formulate my thoughts clear and lucid.' He caught my eye. 'For I believe it was I that mentioned the odd timing of Wharton's affliction. It was I mentioned how odd she sent her husband's corpse to the church. I who raised the issue of her sudden arrival in London. And I who remarked on the topic of his finances.'

He looked to Newcourt. 'Not so?'

'Of course, your lordship.'

'Indeed,' I ceded happily, eager to proceed.

He snapped his fingers again. 'Then that is how it shall be written. So what now will you do to apprehend him?'

'First, your lordship, we must find his body before it is disposed of. If I am right then there is no body, and even now Wharton sits alongside his wife on the road back north. We must ride to St Albans and demand to see a body. Unless we see Wharton himself laid out cold, with tokens upon his chest that cannot be washed off nor prised off with a knife, then we cannot assume he is dead. If I am right, then they must return to St Albans, so there are witnesses to the Earl's new burial. As soon as they have done what needs to be done, then they must flee the country, which in itself will be difficult now the plague is upon us. He has only three options, I think. Hide himself away in the house at St Albans, hide by himself somewhere outside London, else travel north and find a ship at a port where the plague is not yet arrived.'

Arlington snapped his fingers decisively. 'Very well. How may I presume to help?'

'Your lordship, if you might provide us with six capable soldiers.'

'Soldiers.' Arlington stood and stretched. 'Newcourt.' He pointed. 'You will accompany Mr Lytle and Mr Dowling to the Tower and request six good men of Sir John.' He seemed pleased with himself. 'I meantime will look forward to soon learning as to your progress.' He looked to me and Dowling. 'Well done again, good fellows.'

We watched Arlington's scribes pack up their journals and their quills and follow him out the door. Arlington walked with a swagger, confident and pleased.

'That went well,' I murmured.

Dowling looked at me with a white face, otherwise devoid of expression.

I turned to Newcourt. 'When can we pick up our soldiers?'

Newcourt put his hands on his hips and cocked his head. 'Since Sir John is no longer talking to Lord Arlington, since Arlington has denied him everything he requested, I cannot tell you.'

'Arlington pledged us six soldiers.'

'No,' Newcourt shook his head. 'He told me to accompany you to the Tower to *request* six soldiers. If the request is denied then he will write it in his report.'

'Can we not inform Sir John of that?'

Newcourt smiled, a thin smile of anger and resentment. 'You mention Arlington's name, and you will find yourself staring from Traitors' Gate watching your body float past you in the river.'

I turned to Dowling. 'Let's begone then.'

CHAPTER 27

To find a thing hid or mislaid
Be careful to take your ascendant exactly, and consider the nature of the question.

A sprawling pile of mattresses, sheets and assorted linen lay about the front of the house at Broad Street, awaiting burning, guarded from those that would sell it as clean. A second man washed the red paint from the door with a stiff brush and a bucket of water.

The coffin was gone from the front room and the corpse from the back room. Up the stairs Wharton's chair stood empty. No body, no thing to find. Someone had swept the floor clean. I had hoped to find one of those 'tokens'. I returned to the street, disappointed.

'Were you here when the bodies were taken?' I asked the two men.

The man scrubbing the floor shook his head. The man guarding the bedding materials grunted and nodded.

'Who fetched them?' I asked.

'Bearers,' he replied. 'One carried the coffin. They took the corpse out on a board.'

'Just one corpse?'

'Aye, one coffin, one corpse.'

'What of the other body?'

He pursed his lips. 'Weren't no other bodies that I know of.'

'Others had been here afore you arrived?' I asked.

'I suppose.' He looked away, uninterested.

Something niggled 'twixt my ears, but I had little time for long rumination. I returned to Newgate where Dowling prepared for our departure. It was almost ten o'clock already. We would need to leave soon to be sure of returning to London by nightfall.

I arrived to find the wagon prepared and hitched to three enormous horses, huge beasts with hooves like dish plates. Dowling stood talking to three men, two of whom I recognised as fellow butchers. He hurried over on spotting my approach.

'I have found three men to ride with us, Harry, though I want you to promise me to behave with good sense.' He laid a hand on my shoulder. 'I would not see them come to harm.'

Each wore a knife at his belt. Two carried boning knives and the third a large square cleaver.

Dowling introduced me to two lean young fellows, one

with hooded eyes and short cropped hair, the other shaggier with trace of a smile upon his lips. 'Luke and Isaak are brothers.' The third man was short and rotund, shaven headed and quiet spoken. 'Gyles owns the wagon we have used afore.'

'They will need certificates of health,' I realised, anxious to leave.

'I procured them this morning,' said Dowling. 'While you slept.'

We didn't leave the city until almost eleven. I climbed upon the wagon next to Dowling. The butcher's horses were strong but slow, each step an exhibition of rippling muscle. I sat tense and silent, unable to still my anxiety that we would arrive too late, find the house empty and Wharton gone. What if they decided to forgo any pretence of burial and left forthwith? What if they decided not to return to St Albans at all?

At Whetstone we asked after the day's traffic. Yes— three riders passed that way earlier in the morning—one woman and two men. Same story at each turnpike, each description painting clearer in my mind a picture of Wharton, his wife and the man Conroy. Though we rode slow, the distance between us remained constant, no more than two hours. We passed through St Albans in early afternoon. The town baked under the towering sun, flagging in the midst of gathering miasmas. Red crosses adorned the doors like roses in bloom.

No one came out to greet us at the Old Palace, and the stableman was gone. Three horses chewed happily on grass and drank from buckets of water, their hides warm and wet. A ball of twine lay in the long grass next to a twisted tree. Curtainless windows gazed down upon us like blind eyes. Then I saw movement, a head withdrawn.

'Up there.' I pointed. 'Someone's watching.'

Four butchers stared at the small square frame.

I strode through the weeds toward the kitchen door. A thick metal bolt barred our way, secured with a padlock.

'Over here,' Dowling called. I followed his voice across the terrace to an enclosed courtyard. He rapped a fist against two thinner glass doors, also locked.

'Thou shalt not be afraid of destruction when it cometh,' he sighed regretfully before crashing his boot through the glass. A few more hefty kicks and the door shattered completely, admitting us entry to a large square room with yellow painted wallpaper.

Sheets covered the floor and furniture. Dust swirled about chairs and table legs in little eddies, as a light breeze swept through from outside.

Gyles tugged the corner of a sheet and more dust billowed into the air. 'No one livin' here,' he said.

Footsteps sounded from behind the door as if to

contradict him, heavy and fast. The door flew open and Conroy appeared, wearing the same tailored costume he had worn afore, though today it was crumpled, his shirt soiled.

'What in God's name have you done?' he demanded, staring at the broken glass upon the floor.

I stepped toward him. 'Where is Lady Wharton?'

'She is not here,' he said, scanning us all, paying particular attention to the assortment of knives. 'I'll thank you to leave afore I have you punished.'

'We know they are here,' Dowling growled, pushing past and into the passage beyond, discovering Lady Wharton listening at the door.

'You,' she hissed, tight-jawed. She wore a simple woollen skirt and linen jacket, appropriate for riding.

'Yes, madam.' I bowed. 'Come to look around your house.'

She regarded me like I was mad.

'Where is your son?' I asked.

'Resting,' she snapped. 'Now will you kindly begone. You have no authority.'

'We have Lord Arlington's authority,' I replied.

'Nonsense!' she exclaimed, eyes wide. 'You have no such thing. Now I insist you leave.'

I spoke low and soft. 'As I said, madam, we will look round your house.'

She shook her head, perplexed and distracted. 'Why should you want to search my house? My husband is dead. Would you not leave a widow to grieve? This is abominable.' She glared at Dowling, appealing to his soft belly.

'Your husband is not dead,' said Dowling.

She paled, as though pricked. 'I have just come back from London with my husband's body and you tell me he is not dead?' She stumbled on her words like an actress struggling to remember her lines.

'We passed every turnpike this morning and no one has passed with a coffin,' I said. 'Show us the box.'

Conroy stared into my eyes as if he would tear them out. 'He lies at rest in the church.'

I watched Lady Wharton put her head in her hands. 'I think not,' I said. 'I think it is a ruse. If two of us were to leave for the church that would leave three of us against you and Wharton, and Wharton is a murderous beast.'

Lady Wharton gasped, apparently outraged.

'Dead or not, Lady Wharton, he is a murderous beast,' I reasoned. 'I spoke to him last night and he happily confessed to all the blood he spilled.'

I wondered how near Wharton was, whether he too stood close, listening. I led the butchers down the passage out toward the main hall, a wondrous space, with huge panelled walls and painted ceiling. Yet the walls were bare and all furniture had been removed. Lady Wharton emerged from behind Conroy and positioned herself at the bottom of the staircase, hands clasped at her waist, haughtiness regained.

Isaak, Luke and Gyles stared up at the frescoes as though they had never been inside a big house before. I breathed hard to quell the frustration within, contemplating the impossibility of our task. The house was huge and the grounds vast. Wharton could happily flit from place to place leading us a dance for as long as he chose. Conroy's mouth curled in a great sneer.

I could think of little else to do other than lead us on a long meander about the ground floor, room to room, each one bare and bereft of hiding places, Conroy and Lady Wharton following us each step. I sensed their silent mockery, their desire for us to give up and leave.

Twenty minutes later we arrived where we started. I tapped my knuckles against the wood panelled wall to see if it sounded hollow or solid, uncomfortable beneath her withering gaze. 'These old houses often have hidden panels and the like,' I whispered to Dowling.

'Aye,' Dowling raised his brows, resigned, 'and we stand little chance of finding them.'

'We will go upstairs now,' I declared.

Lady Wharton barely nodded, then stepped aside inviting us to climb the wide staircase. Long dark corridors stretched left and right.

'Where will you go first?' she asked.

'Your bedroom,' I replied, frustrated.

The room was bare as the others we had seen. The bed itself was dismantled, curtains gone, sheets and mattresses stowed away. All that remained was the naked tester and a truckle.

'You are leaving today?' I asked.

'The tenancy expires,' Lady Wharton replied, eyes darting to Conroy.

I recalled my conversation with the gardener six days before. 'You have almost two years left on the lease.'

'It is none of your business,' said Conroy, hardly breathing. 'Finish your inspection and begone.'

I walked the walls, tapping with my knuckle again, feeling foolish.

Dowling sidled up to me and spoke low. 'He could be anywhere, Harry. You'd have to chart the outside of the house against the dimensions of each and every room to map all the cavities and spaces that might exist. He'll be hidden well, if he be here at all. He might be hiding in the forest.'

'Aye,' I muttered, 'so tell me what we should do.'

He shrugged. 'We could watch the house, wait for them to leave.' His miserable face belied the futility of his suggestion. 'We need an army of soldiers to search this place.'

Lady Wharton stood taller as we emerged back into the corridor, cheeks pink and eyes aflame. I suspected she eavesdropped our whispered exchange. The corridor also was wood panelled. If there were secret doors then we would never find them. It would be an elementary precaution for Wharton to hold a thick panel behind a thinner panel so it sounded solid. I poked my head into the rooms we passed, wandered into a few, wandered out again. Then we came to a small staircase, three steps up leading to a closed door.

I turned to Lady Wharton. 'What's up there?'

She lifted her chin and nose. 'The Earl's private chambers.'

I sensed renewed discomfort. 'Will you unlock it, please?'

She raised her brow. 'The Earl had the only key.'

Dowling's right eye twitched as it did when suspicion beset him. 'And now he is dead, you will never open it?'

'I am in no hurry to open it.' She lifted her chin and folded her arms. 'When I do decide to open it, I will fetch someone to change the lock.'

I felt like putting her over my knee and spanking her. 'You had better fetch them now, else I will break it open.'

Her lip trembled and her cheeks fired. 'Preposterous,' she stuttered, again looking to Conroy. There was a long pause while both of them fidgeted, indignant.

'Perhaps there is another key,' she said finally, voice quavering. She nodded at Conroy, who disappeared. Disappeared where, I wondered. To fetch the Earl?

We waited in silence, me on the top step, determined to get into that room, Dowling on the other side of the corridor, silent and patient, humming to himself in thoughtful repose. At last Conroy appeared with a key.

'My servants have a copy,' Lady Wharton explained. 'They are instructed to keep it clean while Lord Wharton is away.'

'I see,' I replied, without bothering to ask why she had not said so before. I put out my hand and Conroy gave the key to me, eyes burning.

Sun shone bright into the room that was eight paces square, lit by two windows looking out onto the woods. A serene environment, peaceful and reflective.

I ran my finger down the back of one of the leather bound books that covered one wall. *Christian Astrology* by William Lilly and *The Resolution of All Manner of Questions and Demands*. Next to it, *Anima Astrologaie*.

'The Earl believed in astrology?' I asked.

'Have you seen enough?' Lady Wharton sounded, shrill.

Why did she seek to hurry us? I took my time, pulled out a few books, leafed through the pages looking for anything unusual; hidden notes, handwritten text, but there was nothing of interest and I had not the appetite to inspect each and every volume. I turned and faced the enormous oak desk, the most promising vassal left until last.

I lowered myself into Wharton's great chair, with its heavy rounded arms, and made myself comfortable. Upon the desk stood an empty snuff box, a set of scales in a flat wooden box and a long metal pointed instrument, similar to that owned by Owen Price, Jane's astrologer. On either side were three deep drawers and at the top, one small shallow drawer. In the top right hand drawer I found a ribbon, red and faded. I held it up in front of Lady Wharton. 'What is this?'

Lady Wharton turned crimson about her ears and neck but said nothing.

'A red ribbon.' I rubbed it gently between my fingers. 'Thin and very old.' I looked to her for understanding, but she turned away.

'I might guess,' Dowling stepped forward. He took the ribbon and inspected it close. 'Indeed very old,' he reflected. 'I am reminded of Genesis: "And it came to pass in the time of her travail, that behold, twins were in her womb: and one put out his hand: and the midwife took and bound upon his hand a scarlet thread, saying, *This came out first*".' He looked to Lady Wharton for confirmation. 'His brother was a twin?'

I thought I saw a tear, yet no words escaped her mouth. Conroy's lips twitched like he would say something.

'You know he killed his brother?' I said to her, returning the ribbon to the drawer. 'He keeps the ribbon that is memorial to his brother's birth as well as his own. Yet he burns his face off his head and hangs him by the neck.'

She turned and walked quickly from the room. Her footsteps stopped halfway down the passage and I thought I heard weeping.

'Where is he, Conroy?' I asked.

He followed her out into the corridor without replying.

I followed after. 'Where is the Earl, Lady Wharton?'

She walked away from us down the corridor, toward the staircase, waving a hand in the air. 'He is not here,' she called before disappearing.

'Would you have us tear down your house brick by brick?' I shouted, hurrying after, butchers in tow.

She reached the hall before rounding on us, legs astride like a cat that has its tail pulled too often. 'Get out of my house, now!' she spat. 'Else I will get the village to tear you to pieces, King's men or not!'

Dowling cleared his throat. 'The villagers we spoke to bear no love of your husband.'

'You will not find him!' She held her arms out wide. 'Search all day and all night if you will.'

'But neither can you leave while we still linger,' Dowling pointed out. 'And we will not leave this house until we have found him.'

'Sooner or later the King will send soldiers,' I assured her.

As if waiting for summons, a fist crashed against the door in furious knocking. Conroy hesitated a moment before striding across the tiled floor to unbolt it.

'Good afternoon!' Lord Arlington walked across the threshold. He surveyed the scene afore him, hands on hips and chest protruding. Despite the heat he wore a flowing periwig. A trickle of sweat dripped down his red cheek and the black plaster upon his nose was sodden. 'Lady Wharton.' He smiled broadly.

She sighed, body relaxing as though glad to see him. I was so amazed I could think of nothing to say.

'Lytle.' Arlington shook his head regretfully, approaching me close, fears of plague apparently allayed. Up close I saw for the first time how grey his eyes appeared, how dead. He regarded the butchers with amusement. 'You fetched your own little garrison.'

'I thought you were returning to Hampton Court,' I said.

His gaze lingered on the knives the butchers wore at their belts. 'I decided you might need some assistance.'

He called out in French. Four great brutes appeared in

the doorway, tall and wide. They wore strange thin tunics with peculiar cut about the neck, belted at the waist. All were dark, swarthy and large lipped. They appeared foreign. Between them they carried an ugly assortment of weapons; two muskets, three broad swords and a heavy axe. They stood silent, casual and callous.

'Did you find Wharton?' Arlington asked me.

'No,' I replied. 'He is well hidden.'

Lady Wharton stared at Arlington, hard blue eyes staring out against the chalk white of her painted face, holes in the ice. She nodded her head at the five of us. 'What will you do now?'

'I don't want to kill them.' Arlington regarded me sadly, like I was some prodigal son. 'I need men such as these.'

Lady Wharton's body stiffened. Only her mouth moved, a doll's mouth, with stiff wooden lips. 'They know you collaborated with Thomas.'

Arlington blinked as if astonished. 'Lytle. Are you under the impression I collaborated with Thomas Wharton?'

I shook my head, watching the four beasts frown and lick their lips. 'I don't know what is going on.'

'Indeed.' Arlington looked back over his shoulder, pleased, as though he searched for one of his scribes. 'I will write that in my report.'

Lady Wharton stared at Arlington as if she feared a terrible deception.

He slapped me upon the shoulder. 'I urged you to fly here, did I not?'

I nodded.

He stretched out his arms in magnanimous gesture. 'And now I come to ensure your success.'

Lady Wharton drew back her crimson lips and snarled. 'You promised us safe passage.'

Arlington placed a hand upon his chest. 'Promised whom? You imply that I, Lord Arlington, hath entered into some unholy alliance with a murderer? A beast who hath killed a man of God and two trusted confidants of Lord Chelwood?'

Lady Wharton breathed heavily through her nose. Fear thawed the ice in her eyes.

Arlington turned to me. 'Did you witness such a pact, Lytle?'

'No, your lordship,' I assured him.

'Yet I see you doubt me.' He turned to Dowling, upon whose face disgust was clearly writ. 'The lady hath persuaded you, has she not?'

'What did you do?' I blurted out.

His head jerked forward and I felt warm breath upon my neck.

'Did you promise them safe passage?' I asked, dry mouthed.

PAUL LAWRENCE

'It seemed like a good idea,' Arlington grimaced. 'He guaranteed to rid me of his little band and indicated an interest in working overseas.' He shrugged. 'He can be of great service to his country overseas.'

'All in the name of the King,' Dowling growled.

'In his *name*, indeed,' Arlington affirmed. 'Though he would not want knowledge of it. I will finish my report of your excellent endeavours. It will be a grand tale, ending with your deaths upon the Wharton's sword.' He bowed to Lady Arlington. 'Then his death upon my sword.'

I looked into the faces of the monsters behind, giants with arms thick as tree trunks. The butchers could not hope to hold them off. They would slaughter us all.

'What of your warriors, Arlington?' I said. 'Will you not kill them besides? Now they know your secret.'

Arlington tutted. 'They don't speak English, Lytle. They are French.'

He turned back to Lady Wharton. 'Come with me, your ladyship.' He raised his voice. 'I shall escort you to the garden, where I shall slice your throat, should your cowardly husband not emerge from his hiding place.' He raised a finger and one of his mercenaries descended upon her with sword drawn.

Conroy jumped in front of Lady Wharton, his own thin blade aimed at the monster's chin.

The Frenchman turned a puzzled face to Arlington afore

plunging his sword straight into Conroy's belly. Conroy collapsed upon his knees, hands clutched to his stomach. A thick red circle of blood spread across his shirt. He panted twice, then was silent, still kneeling, the top of his head rested against the wet floor.

The Frenchman wiped his blade against his trouser while Lady Wharton stared at her dead servant, mouth open, aghast. Arlington turned back to us.

'Tuez-les!' he demanded, crooking a finger.

'Run!' I roared, headed for the stairs.

Over my shoulder I saw the biggest of them pursue me, axe hanging from his right hand. Fortunately the axe was heavy and he ran slow. I reached the landing afore him and darted left, back the way we came. He appeared at the top of the stairs, barely breathing, while I panted like a fat puppy. I still had the key, I realised, the key to the Earl's study. I dashed down the corridor and up the three stairs, flung open the door, stepped through quick, and slammed it behind me, locking it. I succeeded only just in time, for the Frenchman smashed his fist against the door, screaming out in his own tongue some obscenity I didn't understand. Then all was quiet.

I trod silently to the window and looked out upon the fields and forest. Arlington and one other of his guard dragged Lady Wharton away from the house. That meant Dowling and the other three butchers must be fighting against just the two Frenchmen. They might stand a chance.

Something crashed against the door, shaking it upon its hinges. Then another blow, slamming against the thick oak like a hammer. It would take him a while to cut through, but only a while.

I opened the window and stuck out my head. It was a drop of thirty feet onto the stones below, I reckoned, the fall guaranteed to break a man's leg. There was no ledge on which to climb, no escape. The axe thudded against the door again, this time leaving a deep crack from top to bottom. I looked down again and imagined the fall. Could I somehow roll upon landing and cushion the impact? Too high.

The axe crashed against the door, splintering it. Light shone through the gap. I whisked off my jacket and lay it upon the ledge of the window, as if it tore from my back, and stepped back against the near wall where I could not be seen. The mercenary hoisted his axe two more times, then was through, running to the window. I tip-toed fast behind him and waited for him to turn. He leaned out as far as he could, scanning the ground beneath, muttering to himself. Then he turned, and I plunged the astrologer's stick straight into his right eye.

He screamed so loud I feared his fury, but I aimed well. He fell against the wall, mouth open wide and hands splayed.

I turned away, horrified at what I did. I clenched my fists, then put my hands to my face, unable to rid myself the feeling of the metal stick crunching into his skull. I stumbled out of the little room and closed the door behind me, locking it, just in case.

The noise of men shouting sounded from deep within the palace. I hurried down the dark corridor into the brighter space at the top of the stairs. The voices were louder now, interspersed with the sound of metal upon metal. Dowling and the butchers resisted. I bounded down the staircase, two steps at a time, and followed the noise, back through dust filled passage, past panelled walls and ancient portraits, into the banqueting hall.

Dowling stood toe to toe with one of the mercenaries. They danced ponderously, shoulders heaving, gasping for air, shirts wet. The Frenchman lifted his heavy sword and swung it sideways in the direction of Dowling's ribs. Dowling lifted his sword vertically and parried. The second Frenchman lay sprawled across the long table, unmoving.

Luke and Isaak stood either side of Dowling, Luke with a cleaver and Isaak a boning knife. They shuffled from foot to foot, looking to Dowling for guidance. The Frenchman's sword was long, offering no opportunity for them to engage.

Dowling glanced at me. The Frenchman followed his

eye and shifted sideways, back to the wall where he could see us all. He shouted something in French, and beckoned with his hand as if bidding us attack him all at once.

Dowling crouched, white faced. Spittle bubbled upon his blue lips and he stared at the Frenchman like he hated him. What stirred the butcher to such frenzy, I wondered, for he preached love for all men, including the Dutch and the French. A raging fury indeed, to enable him to combat a man half his age. He crept forwards, sword arm outstretched, left arm held out for balance. The mercenary scuttled to his right and brought his sword hard down at Dowling's head. Dowling leaned away, too slow, for the blade sliced into his left arm. He shrieked in pain, but maintained his footing. He was exhausted, and the younger man saw it.

I hurried to the table where the dead man lay. An ugly gash cut deep into the side of his throat. His eyes gazed sightlessly at a musket on the floor. I picked it up and strode toward the battle, muzzle raised. I had little idea how to fire it, but I aimed it at the mercenary's head anyway. He muttered and shambled to one side, but I followed him with the musket barrel. I lifted it high and pretended to take aim. He kicked aside a chair, shouted at me, then turned and ran, back into the house.

Dowling dropped the sword to the ground and clutched his left arm. Luke rushed to his side and pulled the shirt from the wound. The cut was eight inches long but not deep. Dowling grunted, pushed him away, and turned his back on us. He shuffled away toward the far corner, where lay two chairs, smashed into pieces. I followed his gaze and saw Gyles.

Dowling dropped to one knee, rolled Gyles over, then released a deep sigh of misery and despair. A huge splash of bubbling scarlet covered Gyles' guts and his eyes stared dull out of his shaven head. I placed a hand on Dowling's shoulder but he knocked it away. His eyes filled with tears and he clutched the dead man's head with both hands, one on either cheek. Luke and Isaak fell to their knees, grief writ thick upon their young faces.

I tip-toed away and fetched the sword that Dowling dropped. Much as I resented the notion, someone had to attend to Lady Wharton's interests. Quite what Harry Lytle would accomplish against two monstrous troglodytes, I could not imagine. I only prayed Dowling's God would watch over me. I trod silent through the corridor, wary of ambush, until I reached the hall and Conroy's still corpse.

Outside was quiet. I stood still beneath the yellow sun and listened. All I heard was the melody of birds singing from the tops of the trees. I turned toward the arch leading to the gardens and made my way cautiously about the side of the red-bricked palace, feet crunching on the stones. I scanned the gardens from beneath the archway, a wide view of overgrown bushes and tangled weed. All was still save the trees swaying in the breeze. My attention was drawn to the ornamental pond beyond the lawn. In the middle of the green pool protruded something white and flaccid, streaked with black.

I made my way cautiously to the bank, anticipating an attack from any direction. From the edge of the pond I recognised a man's arse, poking out the middle of the water like a strange island. I waded out into the green filth, up to my knees, and leaned down in search of the man's legs. The pond floor was slippery and dragging him out was almost beyond my strength. I slipped and slided, and with much effort, succeeded.

I pulled him out onto the grass and rolled him over. The corpse was white all over, flecked with black mould and sheeted with vegetation. His forehead flapped open where someone sliced across the top of his head. Bone gleamed white beneath, and a thick flap of skin fell over his eyes. The first of the mercenaries.

Only Wharton could have killed him. I proceeded down the path, low bushes to either side, higher bushes beyond. A statue peeked out from atop a white column, a half naked woman holding a harp in one hand and pointing yonder with the other. I followed the line of her finger.

Ahead, the path opened into a wide circle, the ground

worn and level. A vast oak tree stood at the back of the clearing, branches reaching out to cover the earth below in a cavern of gloom. Roots, thick as a man's leg, rippled through the earth, and between those roots lay slumped the body of Lord Arlington, curled up in a little ball, his back to me, motionless.

'Are you on your own?' a familiar voice sung in my right ear.

I twisted fast, almost losing my balance. 'Aye,' I replied, without thinking if it was the right response.

Wharton stood at my shoulder, the tip of a blade visible behind his foot. He smiled ruefully. 'You are clever, Lytle, clever and persistent.' He sighed gently and gazed up through the dense canopy to the tiny glimpses of blue sky. 'I should have been more careful.' Then his eyes fixed upon mine. My heart felt cold and wet inside my ribs. 'How did you know I was still alive?'

I cleared my throat and tried to think how to answer the question wisely, but my thoughts were ragged. 'A few things, mostly the haste with which your wife collected your body.'

'Aye,' he nodded, thoughtful. 'Arlington should not have told you so soon.' He strolled across the glade and kicked Arlington in the back, who groaned. 'An arrogant man.'

'Now what will you do?' I asked, terrified.

He shrugged. 'Leave. As I agreed with Arlington afore he betrayed me.' He leaned forward, deep brown eyes speckled with tiny green flecks. 'Now what will you do, Harry Lytle? Will you try and stop me?'

My bowels loosened, my bladder besides, and I strained to stop myself soiling my breeches. The thought of pursuing this vile creature was unfathomable. To meet his gaze was to stare into the eyes of Satan, an immortal evil that might kill you in unimaginable pain with but a movement of its finger. I dropped the sword at his feet. 'No,' I answered truthfully.

'I see,' he replied, odourless breath warm against my face, nose almost touching mine. 'I should kill you,' he mused.

He reached down and ran a finger through Lord Arlington's white hair. 'Will you mourn for him after I run my sword through his throat?'

I held my breath.

He kicked Arlington again, lazily. 'I spoke truth when I told you I regret what I became. Death is easy, holds no further fascination. I yearn for a world where I might seek to become something different.'

I wondered if he believed his own words, this foul beast who killed without remorse or feeling.

'If I kill you, then I must kill the butchers too,' he sighed. 'But to what end? Even the good King Poodle will be able to deduct the truth of it once he finds the treacherous

Arlington here. It has all gone too far, and now I must leave.'

I breathed a little easier. Would that he didn't change his mind.

He drew his sword. As he stood over Arlington, back to me, so my fear eased. I saw his dead brother, face burnt, jaws ripped from their sockets. I saw Death, the look of agony upon his red-soaked face. Morrison, staring at the world in disbelief as rats chewed upon his guts. The pool of blood washing about Perkins' naked feet. The dead women at the King's wardrobe—who were they? Where were their families?

I saw Wharton's back clear, every thread of the jacket that hung upon his narrow shoulders, each hair upon his head. Without thinking, I drew the cleaver from within my jacket and swung it into the back of his skull. He toppled forwards, slow, and fell over Arlington.

A bird started to sing somewhere deep within the branches above my head. A light breeze swept across the ground blowing about my ankles. I knelt, part of my being terrified he would blink, stand, and remove the blade from his head. Blood trickled down the back of his neck and into the dusty ground, a steady stream, allaying my fears. Yet as I stood, I felt a grief so intense it pulled me back down onto my knees and forced the breath from my body in great choking gasps. I rid the world of a savage lunatic, yet felt unutterably bereft. Even in death he violated me, took something from me I yielded innocently and without regard. Now I was a killer again, like him. I contemplated the butcher's knife sat embedded in his head and drew a deep breath. No. Not like him.

I rolled the body away and off Arlington, whose eyes were closed. Blood seeped from a thin wound upon his forehead, yet his chest moved up and down.

It occurred to me I knew too many of Arlington's secrets, that his life might necessitate my death. I held his head in my right hand and contemplated his cold pale skin. I thought to peel the black plaster off his nose, wondered if it might ease his laboured breathing. Perhaps if we were to leave him here he might die without our assistance. Just the thought of it froze my heart. Right or wrong? What meaning did that hold for me now?

'What have you done?' a voice shrieked from behind.

I turned to see Lady Wharton, gazing appalled at the back of her husband's head. The alabaster on her face slipped down in flat layers. The foundation upon which it was plastered melted into a liquid paste and dribbled down her neck in thin streams. Her eyes darted wild. She saw the discarded sword and leapt to pick it up before I could stop her. She raised it afore her with two hands and hissed at me like a deranged cat.

I stepped backwards and she followed, kicking away her

shoes. 'If you run, King's man, then I will cut off Arlington's head,' she growled. 'You will stay here and fight me.'

I circled about the clearing, away from her husband's body. The only other weapons here were the swords in their belts and the cleaver in Wharton's head. I continued to circle her, praying she would move away from the bodies, but she was too aware. She crept toward me, keeping her body between me and her husband. Then she sprung, catching me off guard.

I stepped back and tripped over one of the gnarled roots, banging the back of my head against the hard earth. She grinned like a demon and lifted the sword high above her head. I held up my hands in front of my face and closed my eyes. Then a musket shot rang out and she toppled toward me, sword aimed at my chest. I rolled aside just in time. She landed next to me, bullet in her head.

'Get up, Harry,' Dowling called, holding out his hand.

I allowed him to lift me.

'A strong spirit,' Dowling mused, contemplating her dead body.

Strong, perhaps, but not compassionate.

Arlington stirred, then raised himself on one elbow. Purple welts streaked his forehead, raised and bleeding. The black plaster hung from his nose, sticking to his top lip. His shirt gaped open revealing a hard white belly. He rubbed his eyes and blinked as if he couldn't focus. Dowling regarded him with cool disdain and headed back to the palace.

'I am sorry for Gyles,' I said, quiet, walking alongside. He did not reply.

Black windows peppered the wall of the palace, testament to the emptiness within, bleak and lifeless. I stopped, troubled by a thought unformed, niggling at the fringes of my awareness.

'The child,' I realised. 'Dowling. The child, where is it?' I struggled to recall Wharton's words. 'He said it would die, but not at his hands. She said it was resting. It must be in the house somewhere.'

'*He* must be in the house somewhere.' Dowling's voice trembled, indignant.

We strode toward the broken glass doors and into the house. If the boy had been hiding with Wharton then he hid where we had been unable to find him before.

'We don't even know his name,' I said. 'We cannot call for him.'

'Then we must search the house again,' Dowling roared. 'Luke, Isaack where are you?'

The brothers came running from direction of the banqueting hall, open-faced and expectant.

'We will stay the night,' Dowling bellowed. 'Indeed we will stay the week if we must. There is a child in this house somewhere and we cannot leave until he is found.'

'I will fetch the axe,' I said, sombre.

'We will fetch it together,' Dowling replied. 'Luke, Isaak, search downstairs. Harry and I will search upstairs.'

I listened outside Wharton's door a moment before unlocking it. I held my breath and pushed it open. The mercenary lay where last I saw him, the stick still stuck in his head.

Dowling paused a moment before picking up the axe. 'God help us, Harry.' He clicked his tongue. 'How did you reach so high?'

'Very funny,' I replied. 'Let's be starting.'

I locked the door again behind us.

We followed the same trail we did before, knocking on panels, calling out for the boy, though not by name. As we ploughed our fruitless trail I realised we had ne'er heard him speak even, had no idea of his sensibility. Would he come to our calls or shrink from them? All I recalled from afore was indifference.

The light soon faded and so we lit candles and carried on regardless, but the task seemed hopeless. We took the axe to one panelled wall and chopped through it with ease, but all we found was crumbled plaster. We decided to sleep through what night remained and start again at dawn.

I slept upon a soft couch in one of the long rooms downstairs. I dragged it next to the tall window and lay staring at the blue-black sky, the thick blanket of twinkling stars, fiery and magnificent. Such sights inspired man to create a god, I reckoned. Yet the one he created seemed small and mean in such a context. I sighed and rolled upon my side.

I supposed we had performed a worthy service. Put an end to further misery, death and corruption. Yet I felt no joy, no achievement in it. Just dark despair.

I tried putting names to all that died, an onerous task, for the list was long. Of those I knew, none I liked. Some would mourn for Perkins, I guessed, though more for fear of God than love for the man, I reckoned. Gyles was a good man, but I barely knew him. Worthy men died of plague every day. And the child. Would God stand by and let him perish alone?

And me, Harry Lytle, investigator to the King, reporting to a lord no less. A king I never spoke to once, and a lord that condemned me to die. I did my best to prove my worth, demonstrate what a fine clever fellow I was, secure for myself a position of status. Yet in whose eyes? The eyes of a lord who would slice my throat and a king with better things to do.

I sighed and wallowed in misery and self pity, unable to sleep. I wondered where Arlington went, though with little concern. He revealed himself to be a cowardly fellow. He wouldn't dare venture in the house. No doubt he slept in a ditch somewhere, and would commandeer transport to London next day.

Another hour and I could lie no more. I wandered out into the hallway and fetched a candle. I decided to walk the house once more and listen for shuffling, any noise of crying. I left my shoes by the couch and walked quiet.

A large house is never silent, and wood creaked in all places as it cooled, a haunting sound. Something scratched at the wall ahead of me, low and rapid, a mouse or rat. I proceeded to the banqueting hall, where the last remains of a dying moon shed weak illumination, then out to the broken windows once more, to listen to the night.

Back in the hallway I hesitated to climb the stairs, still mindful of the dead Frenchman in Wharton's office. What if the boy hid in some hole in that room, the room Lady Wharton had been keen to avoid? I climbed the steps, boards creaking beneath my feet.

Then I heard it, a slow patter of footsteps coming toward me. I ran down the stairs and round into a black shadow, praying the groaning stairs wouldn't scare whoever it was. I pinched out the flame of my candle. The footsteps were light and quick, not those of an adult. I held my breath and waited. Then saw something flit across the polished tiles, diagonal, and disappear. I pursued him fast, desperate not to lose him.

'Harry,' a voice called hoarse. 'What's going on?'

'Shhh!' I hissed. 'Follow and be quiet, Dowling.'

A candle lit the passage ahead, from a turning to the right. The kitchen.

There we found him, sat upon a stool, chewing on an old chicken leg.

CHAPTER 28

If good to remove from one house or place to another?
If I found an infortune in the ascendant, peregrine or
retrograde, or if a peregrine or unfortunate planet was in
the fourth, or if the Lord of the second was weak or ill
placed, I advised the querent to remove his habitation.

By the time we reached the city I made up my mind, the
silence of our mournful passage providing ample time for
reflection. Seven bodies in the back of our wagon, two
killed by me and two by Dowling, a sickly affair.

I left Dowling at the Guildhall after seeking from him
a favour that caused his sad face to erupt forth into a state
of appalled horror.

'If you do not grant me it, Davy, then likely I will
attempt it anyway,' I said.

He didn't reply, just readied himself to remonstrate, for
which I had neither time nor appetite.

I held up a hand. 'I will come and find you.'

With that I headed east back toward Seething Lane.

Oliver Willis was out. Liz sat in their library, a thin volume rested upon her lap. *Anima Astrologaie*. I saw Wharton's private room again in my mind. The view out onto the forest. The mercenary lain against the wall with the astrologer's stick protruding from his eye.

'I didn't know you took an interest in astrology,' I said.

'It has played a great part in my life recently.'

'You did not say so to Marjory Henslowe.'

Liz bowed her head and bestowed upon me a faint smile. 'She was not of a mood for civil discourse once you arrived. You upset a few people that evening.'

'Aye,' I conceded. 'So I did.' I waited for her to speak, yet she said nothing. 'Your father is out?'

'Yes.' She held her lips together tight and looked to the floor. 'I think we will go to St Albans.'

'St Albans?' I exclaimed. 'I would go further north. The plague is already at St Albans.'

'We are not leaving to escape the plague, Harry.' She squared her shoulders. 'St Albans is where we come from, where Father built his wealth afore we came here. Now that wealth is gone we must go back to St Albans where he will begin again.' She scanned the room, the hundred or more books that sat upon the shelves. 'One day we hope to return.'

I caught her eye, pained and afraid. 'I had hoped to...'

She folded her hands upon her lap. 'Hoped to what, Harry?'

Hoped to what, indeed.

'Did he hurt you?' I asked at last.

'No, Harry.' She clenched her small fists and screwed up her mouth. 'He terrified me.'

I could think of little else to say. I wanted to ask if we might spend time together before she left, walk or dine, but now did not seem to be a good time.

She leaned over and placed five delicate fingers upon my green silk sleeve. 'Harry, I am a merchant's daughter from St Albans, not much of a match for a King's man.' I opened my mouth to protest, but she squeezed my arm and dug in her fingers. 'Which matters not, Harry, for I see you as an unlikely courtier.'

A short blade in my hairy belly.

'My father was fond of you for a while, but I fear you lost that affection. For my part I find you rather short, Harry, and I hope you don't mind me mentioning it, you are also a little stout.'

I opened my mouth, but no words emerged. It was like being slapped across the face with an old fish. I closed my mouth and breathed deeply. 'I think I am a worthy man,' I replied. Sometimes.

She turned to me and smiled sadly. 'Worthy perhaps, Harry, but I have no desire to spend another night at the Tower in the name of worthiness.'

'No matter then.' I swallowed my disappointment. 'I shall

433

keep my eyes open for a short, stout, woman with a taste for pies and ale and nights abroad.'

She laughed out loud, bright and trilling, before stopping herself and turning upon me a solemn eye. 'I like you well enough, Harry. May God watch over you.'

I stood. 'And you, too.'

My heart was sore, but not broken. The meeting had proceeded much as I anticipated and I had other duties to perform. The day would have to wait for when I might allow myself to feel this pain, allow it to soak through.

'Goodbye, Liz.' I bowed to kiss her hand.

'Goodbye, Harry.'

I found Dowling still at the Guildhall, tight and anxious as always.

'Did you get it?' I asked.

He handed me the document without a word.

'If we are called to see Arlington, you know where I will be.'

'God be with you, Harry,' was all he said. 'I will see you soon.'

I gazed a moment into his old brown eyes and resisted the temptation to hug him to my chest. 'Thank you, Davy.'

He shook his head and handed me the reins to his horse and cart.

'I will return them within the week,' I promised.

He waved like he heard enough, and turned to walk wearily back toward Newgate.

Hearsey sat afront my house still. I took the long sword from the wagon, marched toward him, and pushed the blade against his chest.

'Stand!' I commanded, which he did. I took the key to my door and pushed him toward it.

'How is Jane?' I asked.

'She is well!' he protested. 'The medic says she recovers.'

I opened the door. 'As I always believed. Then you shall have no qualms spending a few minutes inside my house.'

He looked for help, but I positioned the cart so few might see us. The street was quiet anyway.

Jane emerged from the kitchen, pale and thin, with but a few marks only about her face to show for the pox. 'Harry.'

I never was happier in all my life. Joy surged from my belly, up my throat and all over my face. I stopped the smile before it escaped, allowing myself but a small awkward grin. 'Good morning, Jane.'

I prodded Hearsey into my front room, bid him sit, and whispered into his ear. 'You sit here, John Hearsey. If you try to break out through my window then I shall chase you down the street and run you through the guts. I haven't forgotten what you did to me.'

He leaned back, big head pale.

'Harry, what are you doing?' Jane poked me in the ribs from behind. 'I am supposed to stay here alone another thirty-five days.'

'We're leaving now.'

'I can't leave now. I have no certificate of health.'

I pulled the document Dowling obtained for me from my jacket. 'Now you do.'

She clutched at her hair and screamed. 'Harry, I wanted to leave London *before* I was infected with plague, not after. Why should I wish to leave now?' She stamped about the floor in a small circle. 'I am alone in the house, with Hearsey bringing me food and provisions. I am as safe as any person might be. Why now, when I would stay, do you insist that we leave?'

I felt deflated, my heroic endeavour unrecognised. 'There are many at St Giles who rejoiced their recovery from the sickness, thinking they were spared. They were struck again and died.' I spoke low so Hearsey couldn't hear. 'While you have been lain here, insensible, so many more have died this week. More people are infected every new day and the plague is now rampant within the city walls.'

Jane's eyes welled with tears. 'My aunt died.'

436

'I know,' I said, soft. 'I was in here on Thursday and on Friday. It was I chased out the first nurse they left here that sat and snored.'

'It was not!' she replied, indignant.

'Aye, so it was,' Hearsey called from the room behind us. 'And I punched him in the belly for his troubles, for he wore a medic's costume.'

'Ow!' she howled. 'Then you are the one who looked under my nightdress!'

'I did not look under your nightdress,' I exclaimed. 'I changed your nightdress because you had fallen onto the floor and lay in your own mess.'

'You are not a medic!'

'There was no medic, nor no nurse,' I protested, indignant.

'There was not,' agreed Hearsey from the other room.

Jane wrung her hands and hung her head. She wavered, body blowing from side to side as though she would fall over.

'Hearsey!' I called.

'Aye!'

'Will you help me load provisions onto the wagon?'

'You are not allowed to leave this house,' he declared. 'You nor I. Now we all must stay here forty days.'

'I am not staying here forty days,' I assured him. 'If it please you I will be happy to strike you upon the eye and witness that you never stepped over the threshold.'

'Very well.' He emerged into the hall.

We left the house after lunch, after I punched Hearsey in the face.

'Where are we going?' Jane demanded, sullen, bouncing up and down upon the wagon.

'Cocksmouth,' I answered.

'Where your mother lives.'

'Aye.'

'Where it is dirty and the people are lewd and men keep pigs in their house living with them?'

'Aye,' I conceded.

'Could you not have found somewhere better?' she demanded. The sun beamed down upon her red hair, and it shone for the first time in a week. 'I am recovering from plague, and you would have me live in a pig-sty?' She shook her head and clicked her tongue. 'I don't know why I stay with you.'

'You are not staying with me,' I answered, indignant. 'I am going to a boarding house at Ewell. My mother has room only for one.'

At which the ungrateful woman poked me in the eye so hard I couldn't open it again for a week.

Acknowledgements

With love and thanks again to Ruth, Charlotte, Callum, Cameron and Ashleigh, for putting up with a sometimes self-obsessed author in their midst. I'd like to thank everyone who bought and enjoyed *The Sweet Smell of Decay*. To Tara Wynne, my agent. To the folks at Beautiful Books, especially Simon and Louisa. I'd also like to acknowledge the folks at the Well, especially Hope, Sharon, Mike, Sid, Gary, Missye, Donna and Benjamin. And to William Lilly, author of *Christian Anthology*, quotations from which I have used at the heading of every chapter.

**Beautiful
Books**